To Coral

CW01597373

Enjoy (probably over with a stiff drink).

Paul Sarah.

x

Paul Sorak has been interested in Science Fiction for most of his life and began writing novels at the age of 16, although *Space School* is the first of his manuscripts that he has submitted for publication.

He has worked in the entertainment industry for many years and regularly writes radio commercials and newspaper/journal articles.

He is married and lives in England with his wife and three children.

For my mother and father for bringing me into the world and without whose guidance and encouragement I might never have put pen to paper.

For my wife and children whose patience and support have kept me focussed.

Paul Sorak

Space School

Austin Macauley
Publishers Ltd.

A CIP catalogue record for this title is available from the British Library.

ISBN 9781786291356 (Paperback)
ISBN 9781786291363 (Hardback)
ISBN 9781786291370 (E-Book)
www.austinmacauley.com

First Published (2017)
Austin Macauley Publishers Ltd.
25 Canada Square
Canary Wharf
London
E14 5LQ

Acknowledgements

The complexities of actually getting a manuscript published were a complete mystery to me as a first-time author and I am indebted to the staff at Austin Macauley for their dedication, helpfulness and, perhaps most importantly, their friendliness and approachability.

To begin with I'd like to thank Hayley Knight (Senior Editor) and Walter Stephenson (Editor) for their faith in this book and the rest of the editorial team including Sasha Carey, Kirsten Jolly and Luke Marshman who helped in the initial stages.

I am sure that there must be many hard-working people behind the scenes that have made this publication a reality and I am as grateful to them as to those with whom I have been in contact. These include Production Co-ordinators Tom Haynes for getting the process underway, Larch Gallagher and Jessica Norman who happily took on-board my comments and suggestions whilst keeping me fully updated with progress; and Lynne Teasdale whose helpful and informative proof-reading and feedback were gratefully received.

Writing has always been something that I have enjoyed and I should like to record here my indebtedness to my High School English teachers Elsie Kemp and Dominick Fanning whose encouragement so many years ago started me on the road to publication.

Finally, it's always good to road-test a vehicle before you buy it, or indeed, attempt to sell it, and I am grateful to my daughter Megan for test-reading the occasional chapter and the feedback that resulted from it.

Chapter 1

The ice field and its endless expanse of white, frozen landscape made it virtually impossible for anything to exist here in the Antarctic. Yet certain hardy species had, of course, evolved to specialise in these bleak and unforgiving conditions. Human beings, however, were not one of them! Which made the fact that two representatives of that species were currently the only obviously living things to be seen for miles around even more incongruous.

James Rock and Luke Richards from the United States Antarctic Survey Team were currently speeding over the snow and ice on their snowmobiles heading for the distant mountain ranges. Cruising at about 60 miles an hour they had covered quite some distance from their base camp already and were fast approaching their target. Not soon enough for either of them, however. The freezing wind and constant buffeting as the agile and speedy machines tore across the uneven terrain meant that they had already endured over an hour's discomfort. As the machines bounced and reacted to every little dip or ridge with gazelle-like leaps, Luke couldn't help but think of the similarities with being on a speedboat in choppy water, except that the sun was normally shining over a warm sea whenever he was on a speedboat.

They entered an icy pass as the mountains began to loom up on either side of them, and they started to throttle back. Ahead of them the pass appeared to meander through the mountains, but then suddenly and unexpectedly narrowed to a virtual close. Their way was blocked by a wall of ice broken only by a narrow crevasse no more than two feet wide. Certainly far too narrow for the snowmobiles. Despite the discomfort that they had endured, both men were reluctant to leave their transport. The alternative of walking through deep snow and across ice was even less appealing. With no other choice they both brought their snowmobiles to a halt at the entrance to the crevasse and dismounted.

Stretching their tense and aching legs, they collected a few necessary tools and slung their rucksacks across their shoulders. "Well, according to the satellite co-ordinates we ought to be about there by now," suggested James Rock. A mountain of a man, he not only stood at 6' 4" but also weighed-in at about 260lbs. He was surprising agile for such a large person and possessed a stamina that someone half his 34 years would be proud of.

"I sure hope so," replied his companion, "it would have been a hell of a lot easier by helicopter." Luke was almost as tall as James but there the similarity ended. His tall and slender physique suggested an athlete or gymnast rather than James' line-backer.

"Yeah, but the storm warning meant that we had to come out the old-fashioned way," James reminded him as he finished stowing his gear.

"Hmmm. The weather's too risky for machinery, so let's send humans! Makes sense, I suppose?!" suggested Luke, his usual world-weary and cynical outlook coming to the fore.

James was used to it and, having worked with him for the past two years, understood that most of the time it was only meant in good humour. It was Luke's way of coping with the conditions down here at the South Pole, conditions that don't forgive mistakes and rarely take prisoners. "Hey, we're cheaper to replace!" he retorted, as they started to make their way through the crevasse.

The going was fairly easy even though they did have to walk sideways in one or two places. At least being in such a narrow space meant that they were out of the biting wind. "Don't I know it," Luke continued protesting before adding, "So what's the hurry anyway? Why all the secrecy?"

Breathing heavily from the exertion of struggling through the snow and clambering over the ice, James replied matter-of-factly, "Whatever it is needed immediate investigation."

"So what is *it*?" pressed Luke as they squeezed out of the other end of the crevasse to gaze upon a vast plain surrounded by the mountain range.

They both stopped dead in their tracks as they took in the view. If they hadn't been wearing their snow masks and goggles they would have seen the dumbfounded looks of disbelief on each other's faces.

"I guess *this* is it!" exclaimed James. Ahead of him stretched an enormous, relatively flat landscape that must have been at least two miles across. Surrounded on all sides by the precipitously steep jagged mountain range, it gave the impression of the interior of a long-extinct volcano. But since these were often full of vegetation and life, perhaps a more accurate comparison with be a crater on the moon. There were certainly no obvious signs of any type of life here and, like the moon, it was very cold. But the most startling aspect of the entire thing was the complete absence of snow! The entire bowl seemed to be completely devoid of any ice or snow as far as they could see into the distance, yet the cliffs and mountains surrounding it were covered in many feet of the stuff!

Pulling his face mask down and lifting his goggles, Luke summed up what both of them were thinking, "Wow. This is certainly unexpected!"

But James was too busy to reply. He was rummaging in his rucksack and pulled out a computer tablet, upon which he immediately activated a Skype programme.

Not waiting for anyone to respond to his call he immediately began speaking, "Snow Leopard to Base Camp. Snow Leopard to Base Camp. Gerry, are you there?" After what to him seemed like minutes, but in actual fact was no more than about ten seconds, the screen flickered into life and he was looking at the slightly dishevelled face of Gerry Stone. The middle-aged scientist always looked as though he had just woken up and his somewhat shambolic mannerisms did nothing to remove this impression.

"Receiving you, Snow Leopard," he yawned, rubbing a hand over his face. "Have you reached the co-ordinates yet?"

"Yes, we've reached the co-ordinates," came James' rushed reply, "and you won't believe what we've found." He lifted the tablet and panned it around, the view transmitting the baffling scene back to Base Camp. He spun the tablet back around to face himself and asked eagerly, "Did you get that?"

The look on Gerry's face confirmed that he had certainly received it. He was sitting up in his chair and peering at his screen. For once he actually seemed to be wide awake. "Yeah. But where the hell is all the ice?" he asked.

"Search me. It certainly isn't here," replied James, not intending to be either humorous or facetious.

"What's the temperature out there?" was Gerry's next question, a sense of urgency betraying his excitement.

James checked the thermometer on his wrist. "The mercury's reading one degree Celsius – just above freezing."

Luke, who had been standing idly by while the conversation unfolded, began flailing his arms around to keep warm and muttered, not without a hint of sarcasm, "Pretty warm for these parts."

Ignoring Luke, Gerry responded direct to James, "Still, that doesn't explain the complete disappearance of over 4,000 feet of snow and ice. This has to be global warming gone berserk."

James nodded, "I can't think of a better explanation, Base Camp, but it just doesn't seem possible that it could have all melted this quickly. We're gonna go and take a closer look."

"OK, Snow Leopard, but keep an eye on the weather. Remember we're expecting some pretty unfriendly activity in the next few hours," Gerry warned. He was legitimately concerned for his colleagues' well-being, but his professional curiosity was urging them on.

"Understood," James reassured him. "We've got a storm shelter with us, but we've had to leave the snowmobiles on the other side of the entrance crevasse. Not that they'd be much good on this terrain anyway! We'll contact you every hour. Snow Leopard out." James terminated the Skype conversation and returned the tablet to his rucksack.

"Well there's nothing like a gentle stroll in the Antarctic to raise the spirits. Let's go," he urged Luke.

His companion was only too keen to get moving again, even if only to return the circulation to his legs, "After you. I guess we won't be needing the snow shoes!"

Chapter 2

The early morning haze had now completely disappeared and the spectacular views of the hot, dry Sonoran Desert almost 7,000 feet below could once again be enjoyed from Kitt Peak National Observatory. The assortment of white buildings housing the twenty-four telescopes and various facilities that made up the complex were dazzling in the sunlight and radiated an atmosphere of quiet calm. A calm that was, to some of the junior scientists who worked here, almost akin to tedium.

Inside the control room of the eighteen-storey high building housing the giant four-meter Mayall telescope two of these particular scientists were reviewing the results of the previous evening's observations. The room was jammed full of computers and other hi-tech equipment, all being pored over by various operators, seemingly deep in thought. Jacob Astor and Callum West, however, weren't! Their task, as it had been for the last six months, was to study and compare the readouts and images every morning – fairly routine stuff that was often the first responsibility given to the newer astronomers.

With a weary sigh, 24-year old Jacob, exclaimed in the hushed tones ubiquitous to places of research, "This is so boring! Day in, day out. Does nothing ever change?"

Callum, his slightly older colleague, responded in the same quiet tones, "Oh, we do get to see the odd supernova or something occasionally."

"Yeah, but someday, sometime I'd just like to see something that makes me say *Oh!* or *Wow!*"

With a shrug Callum warned with mock admonition, "You know what they say. Be careful what you wish for!" and grinned.

As if on cue Jacob suddenly sat bolt upright and stared at his computer screen with an intensity that Callum hadn't seen on his colleague's face for some considerable time. "Uh oh. Or I guess I should be saying *Wow!* What's going on here? I've never seen anything like that before." He indicated a clear anomaly in the number sequences currently scrolling across his screen. To the untrained eye that's precisely what they were, a random bunch of number sequences. But to the highly-trained scientists they represented factual data – a comprehensive streaming of coordinates, distances, densities, chemical compositions and a myriad other bits of useful data.

Jacob shook his head slightly, causing his unkempt, loose brown curls to flail about like an octopus crawling over a reef, before shrugging, "Huh! It must be a malfunction!"

Callum eagerly concurred, "Undoubtedly! But what malfunction?"

Pleased that at least he had something to distract him from the daily drudgery, Jacob suggested, "Let's have a look, shall we?" and commenced running a diagnostic program.

Five minutes later when the program revealed nothing unusual, Jacob, with the bit now firmly between his teeth and determined not to be beaten, said, "Nothing on here. Check the scans."

Callum, also keen to use the diversion to maximum effect complied and reported, "They all seem to be OK."

This seemed to deflate Jacob's fledgling enthusiasm and his frustration began to show. "Then the diagnostic results must be wrong."

At that very moment their supervisor, Samantha Mitchell, who happened to be walking past on her way to her office strolled into earshot. She stopped at Jacob's terminal and casually enquired with a wry grin on her face, "You gentlemen having problems?" Her tone was one of a teacher gently chiding unruly students, although since she was only in her early thirties she was, perhaps, more like a school prefect to her younger charges.

Tall, slim and blonde, Samantha had spent the last four years of her career at Kitts Peak slowly, but determinedly, working her way up the promotional ladder. Not only was she incredibly gifted as an astronomer, but she was also incredibly beautiful. In a profession whose image was often one of intelligent nerds who didn't think too hard about style and fashion, she certainly bucked the trend. This meant that, in the early days of her career, she had to constantly be on her toes to ensure that she was taken seriously. Unmarried and rarely in a long-term relationship, she remained completely devoted to her career.

Jacob and Callum represented a long line of newly-qualified astronomers to have passed through her care as she taught and mentored them in the real world of astronomy outside the university. Like many before them they secretly nursed a slight crush on her, both occasionally flirting with the idea that they might be the one to finally ignite her passions.

Of course she was well aware of this and tolerated the resulting banter as a means of developing the team and building loyalty. She also saw no harm in having a few laughs at work. After all, you're there for a large part of your life, she reasoned, and in her case she was most definitely right. In any case she could more than handle herself and secretly enjoyed their attempts to lighten up the day, even if they were both still very green in so many ways compared to herself.

Startled by her sudden arrival, Jacob responded instinctively with, "No. No more than usual."

Samantha decided that a little sarcasm would soon burst his bubble, "That much, huh?"

Realising that he had to find a way out of this without losing face, Jacob tried, "I dunno. A little malfunction, if that helps."

Samantha respected his change of tack and responded in kind, "What do you mean?"

Not wanting to be left out, Callum indicated Jacob's computer screen display, "You ever seen anything like that?"

Samantha had to admit that she hadn't. "No," she said matter-of-factly.

"So the machine must be wrong," concluded Jacob.

Callum felt it incumbent upon him to explain. "We've only just started running the diagnostics, but so far they've come up blank."

"What do mean, so far?" asked Samantha enjoying the cross-examination.

"Well, so far they're showing everything functioning normally. Which can't be," volunteered Jacob.

To which Callum added enthusiastically, "So we're re-checking just in case diagnostics is wrong."

"Or ..." Samantha began.

Jacob looked blank. "What?"

With a slight shrug Samantha blithely continued, "However daft it may be, it could be a genuine readout. Has it occurred to you that, maybe, there is no malfunction?"

Jacob was stunned, "What, and get a reading like that? But that would mean -"

"Yes, that would mean -" Samantha interrupted.

Callum objected, “But -”

Samantha tried to allay the young men’s concerns, “Let’s put it this way. It would at least give us the opportunity to tell the government that all the money they’ve given us over the years has finally proven to be worth something.” She smiled at their bewildered faces. “Look, just run the diagnostics again. If there’s nothing wrong with the machinery I want you to start analysing the data you’re seeing,” then, with a slight steeliness creepy into her tone, added, “and I want a report pretty pronto! OK?”

“We’re on it,” confirmed Jacob smartly, as Samantha continued on her way through to her office.

Once more reverting to the semi-hushed tones of academia Callum chastised his colleague, “I told you to be careful with your wishing!”

Chapter 3

With the familiar chug, chug of its diesel engine once more breaking the early peace after an absence of over one hundred days, the yellow school bus pulled up outside Littrow High School. The warning lights flashed, the traffic stopped and the vehicle began disgorging its complement of children. Students of all ages from 14 to 18 began to make their way to the school gates. Some were laughing, most were in small groups, one or two looked serious or even apprehensive in the warm autumn sunshine. Most of these were the younger students, the newcomers to Littrow who were desperately seeking out their friends from their last school and slowly coalescing into small clusters of relief, like meteors colliding to form planets.

Josh Travis wasn't one of these newbies. At 16 years old Josh was an old hand and just about to enter 11th grade. At six feet tall he was of average height and build for his age and had a mop of unruly mousey hair that flopped about as he walked. Intelligent, but not nerdy, Josh somehow managed to stay just the right side of cool. His apparent amble belied a sense of purpose as he walked towards the school grounds. His head was bowed down as he concentrated on the ever-present computer game that he was playing on a small tablet that he held in his hands. Despite the appearance of being totally immersed in the action he was deftly avoiding groups of other children and associated objects as if using a sixth sense.

The first day of the new school year was always like this, he thought to himself, as he side-stepped a ball. Controlled pandemonium!

As he moved deeper into the grounds a voice familiar to him penetrated the surrounding cacophony and gained access. "Josh! How you doing?"

He looked up without breaking concentration and replied "Not bad. Not bad. I'm at 10,300 with three lives left."

His friend Chris was momentarily confused. "Huh? No, dummy, I meant how are you doing?"

Josh continued with the game, "Oh - Great, thanks. What about you?"

Chris ruefully shook his head and replied long-sufferingly "Fine. Just fine."

As the metaphorical gravitational pull of friendship clusters continued to exert its influence they were joined by John, a mutual friend. "Hi, Guys. What's up?"

"Not much," replied Chris blithely. "Josh is still alive and at over 10,000 points."

Completely missing Chris' attempt at irony, John exclaimed, "Really? Wow! How many lives you got left?"

Shrugging his shoulders at his friend's indifference, Chris replied for Josh, "Three!"

As if on cue the tablet bleeped and Josh looked up momentarily, "Two! I just got shot. Give me a couple of minutes, guys, and I'll be with you. Just got to reach the next level."

"Sure. Don't mind us!" replied Chris with the air of someone who had been here many times before. He sat his muscular frame down on a bench, stretched out his brown arms and, like a reptile charging its batteries for the day ahead, tilted his head to face the morning sun.

"You're just jealous because you couldn't get past 7,000," said John, as he too took advantage of the bench's proximity to park himself while they waited for their occupied friend to spare them some precious minutes of his time. Unlike Chris, whose dark brown skin made him almost immune to the sun's rays, John didn't angle his fair features or ginger head to the sun.

"Maybe. But I'm guessing you're out now since you're not playing," Chris responded to the taunt.

"OK, OK. So I got pulverised last night at 10,175," came the begrudging reply.

Chris chose to change the subject. "See the new kids? All bright and shiny," and nodded his head in the general direction of the hordes of younger students now occupying the grounds. "I wouldn't want to be them again."

"Yeah. I wonder what the new *teachers* are like?" mused John reflecting the curiosity of all returning students.

Josh startled his friends by suddenly joining in. "Saw a really weird looking one when I came in. Looked a bit of a stiff. A bit serious."

Chris indicated a teacher, "Uh oh. Smiler's still here. On patrol already. Some things never change, do they?"

The teacher in question approached the three friends and spoke to them disparagingly, "Good morning gentlemen. I see you've picked up just where you left off in the summer, Travis. I trust you managed to find time to study during the vacation in between your computer 'fixes'?"

Josh replied without breaking concentration, "Yes, sir. All up-to-date."

The teacher's bald head and pointy face bristled slightly. "Hmm, well let's just hope so, shall we?

Computer games are not going to provide you with a future, you know," and turned to walk away, his brown corduroy jacket flapping in the breeze.

"Yes!" Josh exclaimed excitedly. Smiler stopped and looked back suspecting insolence, but Josh saw his reaction in time. "Oh, sorry sir. I mean, 'No'. Of course not sir. A computer game won't provide my future." He continued, looking at his friends, "But I've just got to the next level on 11,420 points with 2 lives left!" Smiler paused for a moment, then huffed and walked off.

As the teacher departed, Chris could barely disguise his excitement and envy, "11,420? How do you do that?"

Turning off his tablet Josh nonchalantly replied, "It's all in the concentration."

To which John responded, "Yeah. Or all luck!"

Chapter 4

The inside of the nondescript van was dull, but comfortably furnished for its purpose. Dull because there was precious little colour apart from blacks and greys and only one tiny blacked-out window. Comfortable simply because there were enough seats for the three occupants. Outside it was simply another black van – the type they use in movies for government surveillance.

Brad McCoy, the 35-year-old male in charge, looked carefully at the two members of his team. They'd been together for a while now and everyone knew their particular responsibilities. Nevertheless he found himself giving the familiar briefing. "Everything set?" he asked.

The older, more studious-looking male sitting at the bank of electronic and computer equipment replied, "Yes sir, everything's set!"

Brad smiled inwardly at Fredericks' reply. He knew that the other agent was probably thinking, "The same as it was the last time you asked, and the time before that," but just didn't see the need to make the point. That was why people like Fredericks did what they did. Analysts analyse, they don't get distracted. Needless arguments would just get in the way.

"Right. Now remember – discretion, tact. There's something going on here and we've got to find out what it is," Brad continued.

"It would make it a lot easier sir if we knew what it is that we're looking for," came the response from the only female in the van. Kimberley Walsh had been on Brad's team for two years now. In her late twenties, she was slim and not unattractive in a smart, businesswomen kind of way. She wore her hair shoulder length and coiffed in something resembling a 1960s look. But pity the person who let her well-manicured appearance fool them. She was more than willing to wade into the fray whenever there was tough, physical work to be done, as Brad had witnessed on many occasions.

"That's precisely the problem! We don't know what it is. We haven't got a clue! For all we know we've been sent down here on some cockamamie goose-chase. Just look for anything out of the ordinary," the team leader found himself replying.

Chapter 5

Despite the absence of snow it was still incredibly cold, thought Luke Richards as the wind, which had been steadily gaining in strength, bit into his face despite the mask and goggles he was wearing. The three layers of gloves certainly helped keep his hands warm, but even they were failing against the bitter onslaught of the driving wind. Despite the discomfort both men continued to explore the rocky plain they had discovered.

The rock was completely bare as far as the eye could see. Wet in most places with occasional icy puddles where deep grooves caused by glacial erosion allowed the melt water to pool. Nothing seemed to be growing here, but then why would it, Luke thought, when it had been covered by thousands of feet of ice and snow until very recently?

The sides of the crater-like bowl were steep, and even sheer in places. Rubbed smooth by millennia of abrasion by glaciers in some areas, or cracked and vertically grooved in others that had escaped the erosion but not the wicked temperatures cold enough to explode solid rock as water ingress froze. Everywhere they looked were scattered rocks and boulders randomly distributed as if some giant hand had scattered a collection of breadcrumbs from a great height.

Picking his way over the loose and extremely hazardous footing about six feet up the side wall, James was still marvelling at their discovery, "This just doesn't seem possible. At our last survey a month ago this area was still frozen under 4,000 feet of ice."

"Yep. Just like it's always been," agreed Luke.

"Well, for the last few million years at least!" James retorted.

"So how come it's now melted? Just wait until the 'global warming' conspiracy nuts get a hold of this. It'll be like Christmas, birthdays, Thanksgiving and Independence Day all rolled into one! They won't stop celebrating for weeks," suggested Luke slightly breathlessly as he continued clambering unsteadily across the rocks.

"Hmm. Probably. But I'd like to be a bit more certain about what caused this first, before we go informing the rest of the world," suggested James, urging his usual caution.

But Luke was having none of it, "What's to know? The planet's warming up and we're looking at the evidence right here," he stated categorically.

"Yeah, but why this particular valley when all around is still frozen?" countered James.

Luke didn't really have an answer yet. "As they say in the real estate business, location, location, location. That ridge of mountains that we just trekked through protects it from the cold Antarctic winds that are keeping the shore areas colder. And, of course, we're more directly beneath the ozone hole," he said trying to sound plausible.

He did have some points worthy of consideration, but James was wary, "All the same, I'd expect this phenomenon to be a bit more widespread."

As he said this, James paused to get his breath and noticed something reflect the brief ray of sunshine that momentarily broke through the scudding cloud cover. "What was that?" he pounced, startled by such an unexpected occurrence in this barren rock field.

"What? I didn't see anything," Luke replied dismissively.

"Over there. Something reflected the sunlight," insisted James, adding, "Like metal."

"Well that can't be possible can it now?" reasoned Luke, his interest slightly aroused by the possibility. "Must be a deposit of mica or something in the rocks," he suggested.

But James wasn't to be deterred, "All the same, I'm going to investigate."

Both men trudged over to where James had seen the reflection and as they neared the location the sun broke through the clouds once more, creating another reflection that both men saw this time. By now the wind was getting quite severe and the sun was fast going down. They struggled through the gusting onslaught until they reached their goal and looked down in bewilderment.

"Well as you said," shouted James above the howl of the wind, "That can't be possible, can it?" They were looking at a flat, obviously metallic, man-made object about 8 inches across, partially buried in the rocky wall.

Chapter 6

As Josh approached the school library the door swung open and Ryan Samuels walked out. "Ryan! Hi. You OK?" asked Josh, smiling at his newly-acquired friend.

But his smile froze and quickly faded when the older student gave a curt, "Hi," and just walked on past. The surprise of this unexpected reaction showed on Josh's face as, deep in thought, he continued into the library and headed for his friends. He found them in their usual place, a cluster of tables half-hidden by the tall shelves of books over in the corner. It was an area of the library that suited them well; just far enough away from the more studious occupants of the room for their chatter not to draw attention, yet close enough to avoid giving the impression of shirking.

Chris and John were, of course, busily occupied on their tablets. Chris looked up as Josh approached. "4,500 and doing well." Puzzled by his friend's thoughtful demeanour he attempted humour, "You look lost. Already? Surely you haven't forgotten where everything is over the summer vacation?"

Josh, realising his face must be reflecting his experience at the door, replied, "No, no. It's nothing. It's just," he thought for a moment, "You can never really be sure about some people can you? They change so quickly."

Intrigued, John asked, "What do you mean?"

"Well, Ryan Samuels," Josh began to explain.

Before he could get any further Chris interrupted, "Samuels?"

"Yeah. The guy in 12th grade," continued Josh.

"What about him?" asked John nonchalantly, with only the flicker of interest as he continued his game.

"He always seemed a bit stand-offish. Aloof. But towards the end of the last semester we started chatting and joking. Well, as I was coming in here I just walked straight into him and asked how he was, but he looked as though he'd never set eyes on me. He just said 'Hi' and walked on," explained Josh, still obviously a little bothered.

Chris suggested cheerfully, "I wouldn't worry about that."

John seemed to agree "That's 12th graders for you. He's at the top of the tree. Perhaps he's changed his mind about having anything to do with anyone younger than him. You know it happens."

Resigned to the fact Josh agreed, "Yeah I know, but I guess I'm just a bit disappointed that's all. It just seemed odd. As if he really didn't recognise me."

"You haven't changed that much, despite three months' vacation. Perhaps he just thought that was the best way of getting over the fact that he didn't want anything to do with you. And who can blame him? Anyway, let's go to our first ever science lesson with Mr Jacks," suggested Chris as he started shutting down his tablet.

"Who's he?" asked John stirring from his distraction as he also turned off his tablet.

"I don't know. One of the new teachers," shrugged Chris.

"OK. Lead on," Josh concurred, seemingly happy that his friends had explained and resolved his recent social humbling.

Chapter 7

The office was large and pleasantly furnished in a very modern and comfortable style. A couple of easy chairs were grouped around a low table in the corner and it was a fair bet that at least one of the light oak sideboards contained a selection of quality spirits for sharing with important visitors. Something that was certainly not a rarity in this particular room. A deep-pile cream carpet added to the sense of importance, as did the variety of expensive modern art on the walls, vying for position with superb large format photographs of spectacular astronomical phenomena.

Situated on the third floor of the ultra-modern office building that is NASA's Washington DC Headquarters, the windows offered a pleasing, and strangely reassuring, view of the Capitol itself, creating a visual pathway between the agency and the government that funded it. A fact not lost on the man who was seated at the large, light oak and aluminium desk that dominated the interior of the office.

Herbert Kennedy, NASA's head of space exploration, officially known as the associate administrator of the science directorate, exuded a patrician authority. His thick grey hair and heavy-rimmed spectacles served to emphasise the seriousness of his position and his neatly-trimmed grey moustache added a vaguely military air to his countenance. This was a man used to making major decisions on a regular basis. A man of resolve, whose clinical, analytical mind had served NASA for more than 30 years and continued to keep a tight grasp on not only his own departmental brief to explore space, but also on the all-important aspect of keeping the politicians happy. He knew all the right people and could schmooze with the best of them, but he wasn't averse to ducking and diving when necessary. He was comfortable with his reputation as a safe and steady pair of hands. Someone who could be relied upon to get things done with the minimum of fuss.

To his team he was a firm and knowledgeable leader who managed to extract the best from the best. Somehow they all wanted to please him, rather as they might a well-respected uncle who showed great interest in their potential. But there was always that authoritative demeanour. The trick, the more experienced staff had learned, was to be straight with him. Never try to sugar-coat anything and never offer vague possibilities. Just relax and keep to the facts.

How much those precepts were at the forefront of Samantha Mitchell's thinking would remain to be seen as Kennedy continued the Skype conversation that she had instigated a few minutes earlier.

"I see, Miss Mitchell. So how long have you been detecting these anomalies?" Kennedy asked matter-of-factly, looking at the pretty blonde on his computer screen.

Trying hard to remain coolly factual, she responded, "A couple of hours, sir."

"And you've tested all the equipment?"

"Tested, double-tested and triple-tested, sir," she assured him.

Whether he'd noticed her attempt to inject a little levity into the conversation she couldn't be sure. "Then unless there's something strangely wrong with those machines -" he mused.

"There is nothing wrong with them," she shot back, unsuccessfully disguising her indignation.

Okay, thought Kennedy, she's clearly done her homework, and he decided to give her some leeway to run with it. "So what do you make of it then?" he asked, sitting back slightly in his large, leather chair.

Realising this was her chance to prove she was in control of the situation and not ashamed of their current lack of knowledge, Samantha decided to tell it like it was. "I don't know. We've analysed it. We're still analysing it. All I can say is that it shouldn't be there. It's not a planetary mass. It's not a distortion caused by solar activity or anything. Yet there is definitely something there. Gravity is being affected somehow."

Kennedy's response startled her a little. "Well, I can't just go to the President and say '*Gravity is being affected somehow'.*"

She pondered his tone and body language for a micro-second. Had he just slapped her down, or was he displaying his famed dry humour? She decided to go with the humour option and continued with her previous approach. "I'm aware of that, sir, but I thought you should know at this stage. It's kind of like -" she hesitated, searching for the right words, "I don't know, well, something's pulling on the star stuff out there. It's too close for it to be the possibility of a planet, or planetoid, or something like that. We'd have spotted it decades ago." She ventured a possible explanation, "It could be some sort of asteroid activity, but it shouldn't be. Not there. It could be an uncharted comet, but if it is it's following a very strange orbit."

Kennedy had heard enough. There clearly wasn't going to be anything else to be had from continuing the conversation at this point. He sat forward and leaned towards his computer slightly, "OK. Well, keep me posted."

Understanding her cue, Samantha ended with a nod of her head, "Yes, sir," and terminated the link.

Kennedy turned off his own connection and slowly rotated in his chair to stare ponderingly at a large, framed picture of a nebula on the wall. One that his own department had photographed about five years ago. Quite what he was thinking was almost impossible to gauge.

Chapter 8

As the three friends rounded the corner approaching the science labs Josh's cell phone cut through the general corridor hubbub and he frantically began searching in his jacket pockets for the offending device. As always in such situations, the ringtone might as well have been a battery of searchlights accompanied by a marching band all serving to identify and embarrass the owner who had forgotten to turn off their cell phone. While the school had long since given up trying to stop students from bringing their cell phones in to school, they did insist that they remained either turned off or in silent mode during lesson times.

Chris and John laughed at their friend's predicament and strode on towards the classroom leaving Josh to locate the source of his torment before a teacher arrived. After what seemed like an eternity he finally found the cell phone in the back pocket of his jeans and, with a sigh of relief, turned it off. He was so keen to project an aura of normality that he didn't even bother to identify the caller, let alone actually answer it.

As he gathered his composure he noticed one of the new teachers come out of a science lab carrying a few small items of equipment. Clearly preoccupied, he walked straight into Ryan Samuels who happened to be passing. The metal tools he was carrying scratched Ryan's hand, drawing blood.

"Oh, I do beg your pardon. I hope I haven't hurt you," exclaimed the somewhat shocked and embarrassed teacher.

"No, no, it's alright, sir," replied Ryan, nursing his hand and examining the small injury.

Clearly concerned, the teacher continued, "Here, let me help," and grabbed Ryan's hand to inspect the damage. Josh watched the exchange with casual detachment, but noticed that Ryan seemed to be trying hard to keep his hand hidden from the teacher, as if he was concealing something.

Eventually, the teacher managed to expose Ryan's hand and, using a tissue from his pocket, wiped the cut. "Oh well. It's not too bad. You'll live. I do apologise, I didn't see you coming," he explained, rather relieved that it was nothing more serious on his first day.

Ryan seemed eager to forget the whole thing and replied, "No, sir, don't worry. I'm sure it must have been my fault," before hurrying away.

Josh continued to observe the whole thing with detached interest, but this quickly morphed into intrigued curiosity as he watched the teacher place the bloody tissue into his jacket pocket and, at the same time push what looked like an electronic car key fob, before heading straight for the school exit.

Chapter 9

The black van had been parked in the same place since early morning and, to the casual observer, was no different to any of the other vehicles parked near the school. Empty, whilst its owner was off about their business.

The casual observer might, however, have had their interest spiked had they witnessed the side door of the apparently empty vehicle suddenly open and a young woman with a slightly 1960s hairdo step briskly out into the sunshine.

She quickly pulled the door closed behind her and hurried across the road to meet a teacher coming out of a school.

He handed her a tissue without exchanging a word and briskly returned to the school building. The woman retraced her steps just as briskly and smartly re-entered the van.

No sooner had the door closed than Brad enquired, "Did you get it?"

"Yes," was Agent Walsh's simple reply. She looked at the small bloodstain on the tissue that she held, "It's not much, but it might be enough to go on."

Addressing the other agent, Brad said, “OK. Do your magic, Fredericks,” and watched with intense interest as the other male agent began analysing the blood sample using the mass of hi-tech equipment in front of him.

Chapter 10

Gerry Stone hunched closer to his computer monitor, trying hard to make out the face of James Rock at the other end of the Skype connection. Outside the wind howled menacingly, supplying the audible explanation for the poor connection. Gerry's balding pate furrowed and he concentrated hard, "What? Are you sure?"

James nodded vigorously on the screen and his delayed speech reached Gerry a split second after his mouth had formed it, "Absolutely, Base Camp. A metallic object."

The computer display became even more shaky as James turned his camera to display the object in question. He attempted to zoom in for a close-up. "But how did it get there?" Gerry almost shouted back, attempting to cut through both the wind outside and the increasing static on the link.

"Search me," shrugged James.

Scrabbling about for explanations, Gerry asked, "Could it be part of our survey equipment, fallen through the melted ice?"

James shook his head, "I doubt it. It's nothing I recognise," he paused before continuing, "and if it is, how did it get half buried in the rock?"

Gerry was forced to accept the reality of James' reasoning, "Okay, Snow Leopard. Keep searching the area for anything else strange." His tone became very deliberate and serious. "But watch out for the weather, it looks like that storm front will hit soon. We'll check this out and get back to you."

"Understood, Base Camp, but don't take too long," responded James, adding a little ruefully, "It's gonna get a bit rough out here. Snow Leopard out."

The screen froze with the image of the metallic object as Gerry turned in his chair to face the head of the US expedition, who had been standing at his shoulder throughout the conversation. Alex Roughedge was a tall, powerfully-built African American who had been a line-backer in his college days whilst majoring in geology. His knowledge of his subject coupled with the care and concern he displayed for his team commanded a great deal of respect from his subordinates. He frowned as Gerry asked him, "What do you think? This is getting stranger and stranger."

Alex studied the picture frozen on their monitor before replying, "Goodness knows. As far as we can work out Antarctica froze over completely about 34 million years ago. That's at least 33 million and 990,000 years before the bronze age, let alone the shiny, highly-polished stainless steel age!"

Gerry nodded, "Then it must be something from one of our surface probes that ended up there when the ice melted."

Alex shook his head, "I'd like to agree with you, but as James said, how did it get embedded in the rock?"

Gerry shrugged hopelessly, "Search me. Some sort of glacier movement?" he feebly suggested.

Alex mocked him humorously, "Hmm, too convenient, I'm afraid, professor. You'll have to try harder than that."

Gerry winced. “You’re right,” then indicating the computer, “Let’s just hope that James and Luke find something else to help us identify it.”

Chapter 11

Samantha Mitchell entered the main control room at Kitts Peak Observatory and walked purposefully towards Jacob and Callum. "I've just had a follow-up call from Mr Kennedy wanting to know what we've discovered about the anomaly," she informed them.

Without any hint of facetiousness Jacob responded, "Well, did you tell him 'Absolutely nothing'?"

"Yeah," Callum added, "How did he react to our ineptitude?"

Samantha's tone was long-suffering, but with a brittle undercurrent, "No, I stalled him, of course, to give me time to justify my total faith in you guys." Then with business-like efficiency she continued, "Let's go through what we know at the moment."

Jacob began to recount the various aspects of their discovery, "Okay, we know that there's an unexplainable anomaly in Sector 30 that's exerting a gravitational influence on light and matter in that sector."

"However," continued Callum, adding a huge dollop of reality, "What we can't explain about this unexplainable anomaly is where it came from, how long it's been there, how long it's going to stay there and how fast it's moving – or even where it's moving to!"

“Wrong!” countered Samantha, “We do know how long it’s been there. The computers registered it on our sweeps of this sector at 09:50 yesterday morning. Now we scan each sector routinely once every two weeks. Which means, of course, that it appeared some time in the two weeks since the last sweep.”

Callum wasn’t sure whether he wanted to scream at her for being so right or kiss the smug look that she was now wearing all over her pretty face. “OK. That leaves us with only two possible origins. Moving across from another sector or originating from beyond our range within the same sector.”

“Well all of our checks on the other scans don’t show anything out of the ordinary,” contributed Jacob, warming to the premise, “Which would seem to indicate that either the anomaly has only just come into existence or was previously out of range.”

Folding her arms with satisfaction Samantha concluded, “So, if it was previously out of range then that means that it is moving towards us.”

Wanting to appear eager to adopt the new theory, Jacob suggested, “How about we bring the rest of the array to bear on this sector? It should allow us to triangulate a more accurate position and maybe calculate its trajectory.”

“Yep,” Samantha nodded. “Good idea. Get on it immediately. I don’t want to keep the boss waiting any longer than I have to.” As she turned away from them she couldn’t resist the sense of satisfaction that she felt now that they seemed to at least have something to focus on. It certainly helped on occasions, she mused, to have two assistants who both harboured a slight crush on her. At times like this they could be as willing to please as a couple of new puppies!

Chapter 12

When the new science teacher eventually entered the room, Josh immediately understood the reasons both for his lateness and his slight breathlessness. He introduced himself as Mr Jacks before proceeding to commence a lesson about gravity. Having briefly covered the history of its discovery by British physicist and mathematician Sir Isaac Newton in 1687, he had now moved on to discussing examples of his three laws of motion. Whether because they were unsure of their new teacher's tolerance of indifference or because he actually managed to hold their attention for longer than the world-wide student standard of ten minutes, the lesson seemed to be moving along at quite a pace when there was a knock at the door.

The door opened admitting a young female student from the same grade as Josh and his friends. Kelly Malcolm was a pretty, slim brunette of average height with a particularly lively smile and a mischievous twinkle in her eye. As she crossed to Mr Jacks' desk she stole a quick glance in the direction of Chris and they exchanged a brief, meaningful, flirtatious eye-contact that went unnoticed by Chris' friends.

She handed a note to Mr Jacks, "Excuse me sir. Message from the principal."

The teacher took the note with a perfunctory "Thank you." After a quick scan of the message he looked up, "Is there a Josh Travis in here?"

"It's me sir," Josh volunteered.

"Well I don't know if it's good news or bad news, but here we are two hours into the new school year and the principal has requested your presence at recess," continued Mr Jacks.

"Thank you sir," Josh replied, wondering what it could be about. There was a general muttering and murmuring from the class and Chris winked at Josh knowingly. "Don't be stupid. I'm sure he's forgotten about that," whispered Josh, hoping that he was right.

The lesson resumed, but somehow Josh found it harder to be interested in 300-year old physics discoveries. He was more concerned with discovering what the principal had in store for him in the very near future.

Chapter 13

As she opened the door for the visitor, Principal McGregor's secretary sensed the young student behind her tense up slightly and almost heard him swallow hard. The muffled noise of recess permeated into her office as hundreds of students filed past her own office door, but it wouldn't make it through to the inner sanctum that was the principal's office.

The door opened into a large, fairly spacious room that was comfortably furnished to match the authority of the occupant. Seated behind a large modern desk at right angles to a picture window that overlooked the school grounds, was Principal McGregor.

In his early fifties, his full head of thick white hair added to his personal gravitas yet gave him a mature handsomeness that had disarmed many a mother hell-bent on defending their errant child. His six foot frame exuded authority, yet he carried it with casual ease and despite his serious countenance he smiled quickly, another tactic that he employed to smooth over difficult parental encounters. His reputation was one of discipline and he certainly wasn't afraid of admonishing students when necessary, yet he was highly respected by almost everyone connected to the school, many of whom had also seen examples of his charm and caring personality. Nevertheless, to be summoned to his office was not something that a student ever took lightly.

The middle-aged secretary announced, "Josh Travis to see you, principal," before stepping to one side to allow Josh past. Once he was in she left, shutting the door behind her, and Josh felt his apprehension intensify as he heard the door close behind him. Surely the principal can't be wanting to discuss that incident at the end of the last school year?

Deciding he might as well get things under way, Josh began, "You wanted to see me, sir?"

Looking up from the document he was working on, the principal removed his glasses before saying, "Ah, Mr Travis. Yes, come in. Glad to be back?"

Josh's reply was standard, "Yes, sir."

A bubble that the principal was quick to prick with, "Don't lie to me. No school student worth their salt is going to be glad to be back at school."

Wrong-footed, Josh felt that agreement was probably the best course, "Oh, OK, sir."

The principal sat back in his chair and indicated for Josh to sit in one of the guest chairs across the desk from him. "So, you got your new subjects and things sorted out?" he enquired by way of breaking the ice.

Josh again responded with "Yes, sir."

"Good," acknowledged the principal before moving straight on to business. "Are you aware that this school has a program of nurturing what might be called *gifted and talented* students?"

Again Josh replied, "Yes, sir."

"And we identify students who fall into this category in the 11th grade – the grade you've just started," continued the Principal.

“Yes, sir” Josh heard himself saying yet again and ruefully imagined what a one-dimensional impression he must be making.

The principal, however, didn’t seemed concerned and got to the point, “OK. Well, there’s a chance, based on your previous record, that you may well be *gifted and talented* and I’d like to investigate the possibility of you joining the program.”

Josh was completely surprised. This certainly hadn’t been on his list of possible reasons for the summons. “Thank you, sir,” he managed to respond by way of variety, grateful for the opportunity to say something different.

Clearly terminating the meeting, the principal concluded, “Anyway, I don’t want to take up all your recess time now. Come back and see me at lunch and I’ll explain what it will involve.”

“OK. Thank you, sir,” was Josh’s reply as he realised he was meant to leave. He got up, crossed the office to the secretary’s door, and with immense relief exited to the less rarefied atmosphere of her room. Smiling briefly at her as he walked to her outer door, Josh escaped into the safety of the corridor.

Waiting for him were Chris and John, seated in the waiting area whiling away the time by increasing their scores on their tablets. “So what’s the problem? How much trouble are you in this time?” asked Chris, only half-concentrating on whatever the answer might be.

“Apparently I might be *gifted and talented*!” Josh informed them with mock superiority. His two friends sneered in fun, prompting Josh to defend himself. “That’s what he said.”

Giving the conversation his total attention now, Chris asked, “So what’s he gonna do? Load you up with a ton of work? I’m glad I’m not *gifted and talented*.”

Josh shrugged, "I don't know yet. I've got to see him again at lunchtime."

Abruptly changing the subject, John seemed both relieved and oblivious to what they had been discussing, "Come on then. We've got 10 minutes left," and handed Josh his tablet as the three all made their way outside into the sunshine.

Chapter 14

Brad was disappointed. "You're sure?" he asked.

Fredericks looked matter-of-fact and replied, "Yes sir. No doubt about it. Nothing unusual at all!"

"Nothing?" Brad persisted, leaning forward in his chair, as if his determination might just change the reply.

"Just regular blood group O, positive. Blood!" responded Fredericks.

Drawing a long breath and reflecting on the news for a moment, Brad suddenly seemed to accept the results. "OK. We've drawn a blank," he sighed.

But his hopes were suddenly buoyed when Fredericks suggested, "There is one thing."

"What?" Brad pounced.

His more analytical and less emotional subordinate continued, "I can't quite put my finger on it. The haemoglobin levels aren't quite what I'd expect."

Kimberley Walsh was now intrigued, "What do you mean?"

Fredericks continued, "I don't quite know. It's almost as if his blood is too new."

"Has he had a transfusion recently then?" Walsh wondered.

Brad responded with not a small amount of incredulity, "A 17-year old kid? There's nothing on his records to show any type of health problems."

The question became academic when Fredericks squashed this particular avenue of thinking, "A transfusion wouldn't account for it, since that's someone else's old blood anyway."

Trying to get things back on track Brad's exasperation was beginning to show through. "Look, what we need to know is, *does he check out?*"

After a pause to mentally review all of the evidence Fredericks replied with a shrug, "Yes, sir. He checks out."

Moving on with the resolve for which he was renowned Brad clarified their thinking. "OK, then we need to find someone else to stick a needle into."

Chapter 15

Samantha Mitchell rubbed her forehead and ran her fingers through her fringe, absent-mindedly tousling it as she and Callum tried to make sense of the data in front of them. Despite the urgency of the situation Callum allowed himself a momentary distraction as he watched his boss mess up her hair. She had a habit of doing so when she was thinking and Callum found it most attractive. It made her somehow appear slightly less in command and even, perhaps, a little vulnerable. A vulnerability that Callum would be only too happy to protect if she ever allowed him to. He was jerked back into reality with a start as Jacob crashed through the door of Samantha's office without knocking.

He had a computer tablet in his hands and was pointing at the screen, "You are gonna want to hold on to your hats when I tell you what those recent tests revealed," he declared triumphantly.

"Don't tell me. It's moving towards us?" asked Samantha wearily, her question almost as much a statement of fact as it was a query.

"Yeah, but it's not only that it is moving towards us that's exciting," replied Jacob completely ignoring the fact that she had guessed correctly. "It's the speed at which it's travelling that's really mind-blowing!"

"Okay, don't get all melodramatic on us," said Samantha, sitting up in her chair and taking control of the situation once more. "What's your estimate of its speed?"

"Well, as suggested we brought the other radio telescopes in the array to bear on the anomaly, which allowed us to triangulate its position. This put it at 500 million miles away, but yesterday morning's first sighting seemed to suggest it was 700 million miles away," Jacob was speaking so fast that it took a moment for the facts to sink in.

"What?" exclaimed Callum. "200 million miles in one day? Are you sure?"

The look on Jacob's face said that he wasn't about to get caught out again, "Triple-checked it."

Samantha exhaled through her teeth, "Well, that kind of focusses the mind, doesn't it?"

"That's way too fast to be an asteroid," Callum asserted.

Samantha nodded, "Agreed. But what the hell is it?"

This time Jacob didn't have anything startling to say. "There's no way to be certain at that distance."

"One thing's for certain, it's gonna make a mighty dent in anything it hits at that speed," Callum volunteered.

Samantha agreed. "That's what I'm worried about," she said, suddenly very serious. "Keep tracking and let me know the moment anything changes."

Chapter 16

The rest of the morning had dragged along, yet now it seemed to Josh like only a few minutes since he was last in the principal's office. He'd probably only ever been in here about half a dozen times in the whole of his time at the school, yet here he was visiting twice in one day! The maturely attractive secretary once more announced him and then stood to one side to allow him past.

"Ah, Mr Travis. Come in. Sit down," said the principal in a somewhat disarmingly jovial fashion. Josh followed the instruction and sat opposite him across the desk.

Continuing to sign some paperwork that he was evidently determined to finish, the principal continued to speak to Josh without looking up, "Now, I understand from one or two of your teachers that you are particularly interested in computer games, PlayStation, that sort of thing. Is this true?" As if to emphasise that he expected an answer, the principal put down his pen and looked straight at Josh with his penetrating gaze.

Josh swallowed. So this was what this was all about after all. "Yes, sir, I do enjoy them. But I try never to play them in class," Josh admitted, trying to sound a little spirited.

“Or at least never to get caught playing them in class!” the principal bounced straight back at him.

Ouch, thought Josh, that one came back like a tennis champion’s return of service. “I understand they even have championships for such things nowadays?” the principal continued half-questioningly.

“Yes, sir, they do,” confirmed Josh, beginning to wonder where this was actually going.

“How many have you entered?” This was definitely a question.

“About 20 so far, sir,” Josh volunteered.

“And how many have you won?” This time the principal was even managing to sound interested in what the response might be.

“18, sir,” Josh admitted, not without some pride.

Then came the bombshell, “And how old were you when you developed this obsession?”

So that was it! Lull him into a false sense of security and then close the trap. But Josh wasn’t going to go down without a fight, “I wouldn’t call it an obsession, sir. But I was about nine years old.”

The principal leaned forward intently and frowned at Josh’s answer, “Hmm. What would you call something that you spend almost every waking moment doing, even to the detriment of your school work?”

“I don’t really know, sir. But I do try and keep up with my studies.”

Josh was trying to sound earnest, but the principal sat back in his chair and sounded doubtful, “Yes, I’m sure you do. Try, that is! I notice that you certainly managed to find the time to join the school computer gaming club.”

Now Josh was defensive, “Yes, sir, but that’s after lessons finish.”

Seemingly ignoring Josh’s rebuttal, the principal ploughed on, “I believe that you have to qualify somehow for membership. How did you do?”

Once again, Josh's pride at his accomplishment was evident, "I got 95% on the entrance game, played over four days."

"Yes, so I hear. And it's for that reason that I wanted to speak to you," said the principal, suddenly getting more serious and leaning forward again.

Josh mentally braced himself as, with a degree of surprise in his voice, he asked, "Really?"

The principal pushed a button on his desk and got up. "Hmm," he muttered, as if thinking something through and reaching a conclusion. The blinds at the windows began to close and some panels opened in the opposite wall revealing a large screen. The principal crossed the room to the screen and entered some details on a keyboard. The entire area around the screen was suddenly bathed in a green glow. He turned and casually motioned for Josh to follow him over, indicating a seat inside the green zone.

Josh moved over and sat down. "Don't be alarmed, Josh," reassured the principal. "What I have to tell you, all I have to offer you, may be very difficult for you to understand, for you to grasp. So the only way I can present it to you is to actually show you." He handed Josh a small device featuring a red button.

"I need you to hold this device," explained the principal. "If you press the red button the demonstration that I'm about to show you will stop, the lights will come on and my secretary will immediately enter the room. OK? I need you to understand that you are perfectly safe. We are also sitting within a memory field and if you push the button the field will break down and you won't remember anything of the presentation. Are you OK with that?"

Thinking that it all sounded a bit surreal, and maybe even a bit far-fetched, Josh absently replied, "Yes, sir."

"Good. Then let's begin."

The principal sat himself down in another chair from where he could both see the screen and watch Josh. He pushed a button on the arm of the chair and the screen flickered to life, showing a three-dimensional image of deep space. Glancing at Josh, he explained, "Space, Josh. We've been exploring it for about 50 years. But in that 50 years we've discovered a lot. An awful lot. We've sent men to the moon and back. We've been building a space station for some considerable time. We've operated a space shuttle program for more than 20 years. When I say 'we' I am, of course, talking predominantly about the Americans, the Russians and, occasionally, the Europeans. And only a few, a very tiny few people, have ever actually ventured into space." He paused for effect before adding, "At least, that's what the public think!"

The images on the screen were constantly changing, like a well-made documentary, to display various aspects of space exploration, both past and present. The principal continued with his voice-over, "About 20 years into our exploration of space, we discovered that we weren't the first people to explore our solar system!" He looked at Josh for a reaction, but the student didn't seem to realise the enormity of what he'd just heard.

The principal continued and elaborated, "We discovered in the first moon rocks brought back evidence that a previous civilisation had been there. Nothing tangible, you understand. No buildings, no body parts, nothing like that. Just something. Trace elements, gases and things, that shouldn't have been there. When we pushed out beyond the moon to explore Mars we then discovered hard evidence. Abandoned equipment and technology. It's meant that as far as space exploration is concerned there are two sides to it: The public side – the Apollo missions, the space shuttle, the international space station and so on. And a highly secret side that the public are very much unaware of!"

This time Josh did seem to register what he'd just heard. He looked at the principal enquiringly.

"The fact is that we have a much, much more advanced space capability than anyone has ever dared to imagine," the principal explained, pleased that he had now got Josh's undivided attention. "The technology that we've unlocked has allowed us to build an alternative space station at a much higher orbit, undetectable from Earth, that houses a large team of astronauts and scientists researching the applications. We also possess space vehicles that are, perhaps, hundreds of years more advanced than anything that the public think we've got."

The screen was now showing film of a variety of small spacecraft flying near a fairly large three-dimensional rhombus-shaped structure. The structure was rotating on a central vertical axis, giving the impression of a diamond slowly spinning in space. As the camera moved closer it became possible to detect a number of gantries and fixtures protruding from the sides at various points and pieces of superstructure forming a lattice-like veil over parts of the surface. Against the backdrop of this structure the spacecraft looked tiny, buzzing about like bees around a hive.

The principal, having made his point most successfully now asked, "Why am I telling you all this?" and went on to answer his rhetorical question. "Well, you see, Josh, the minds that are most able to operate the technology are younger, more fertile minds. Especially minds that are adept at playing computer games!"

Josh reacted to this revelation with a combination of surprise, disbelief and curiosity. Where exactly was this leading? The principal, seeing all of these emotions and a fair few others crossing Josh's face, elaborated. "Highly intelligent scientists are good at slowly unravelling the secrets of the technology, but getting the most from it once we've unlocked it seems to be the preserve of younger, agile minds. And that's where you come in!"

Josh was both stunned and uncertain. Had the principal just said 'we'? "But how sir?" he asked cautiously.

"As you will appreciate, there are only a tiny handful of people who know anything about any of this," came a slightly conspiratorial response. "It was decided a good few years ago to create a worldwide network of special schools from which certain highly-gifted students could be selected to join this space corp. The students are specially trained in the space station to use the technology and to further investigate what exactly it is that we have." Then came the real bombshell, "We are one of those schools!" followed by the coup de grace, "And you have been selected for the opportunity. The opportunity of a lifetime!"

Josh sat up straight in his chair and listened very carefully. Clearly the principal must have gone completely crazy. Either that or he was participating in an incredibly elaborate practical joke. Either way, Josh wanted to hear more. "It won't be easy," the principal was saying. "It involves a lot of hard work and dedication. And the most difficult thing of all is that you can never tell anyone what you are doing. Not your friends, not your family. No-one must know."

Josh decided that humouring the principal was probably the best course of action. "But how do we even get there without anyone knowing?" he asked innocently.

Without missing a beat the principal explained, "The technology is so far advanced that, believe it or not, we are actually able to teleport people to and from the station."

As if to underline the apparently perfect normality of such a procedure he continued, "And while you're there you won't be missed, because we're able to produce replicas who take your place here on Earth. We're not talking long periods of time. A few days here, a few days there, but secrecy is vital. Most of the government don't even know about any of this!

Trying to clear up a few loose ends Josh asked, "But why me, sir?"

"Your skill with computer games. It's that simple!" came the reply with that same quick-fire assurance. "So are you interested?"

Josh hesitated. He so very much wanted to believe the principal, but it was also so obviously ridiculous. But what if it was true? Would he really want to turn it down before he'd seen it all? He decided to call the principal's bluff. "I guess so," he replied, trying very hard to sound nonchalant. After all, this sort of thing happened every day!

The principal pressed another button on the arm of his chair and a closet door opened revealing a corridor. Well, that was certainly unexpected, thought Josh. Where could that possibly go? He tried to calculate the school geography in his head.

"OK then. Let's take your first steps into a new world!" suggested the principal as he got up and gestured for Josh to walk with him into the corridor.

Josh hesitated. It was all too weird. Sensing his indecision, the principal tried to reassure Josh by indicating the device that the student was still holding. "Don't forget, Josh, if this is all too much, just push the red button and it'll all be forgotten." That seemed to spur Josh on. If it was all going to be forgotten he'd rather see everything first.

The two of them entered the corridor and the door closed automatically behind them. The corridor was suddenly filled with bright white light and Josh squinted hard to protect his eyes. He tried to see beyond the dazzling luminescence, but couldn't see anything. The light was all round them as they continued to walk on. After a matter of a mere few seconds he could make out the shape of another door at the end of the corridor. The lighting slowly dimmed to something akin to normality and they opened the door. As they passed through the doorway, Josh noticed that it certainly didn't seem like the doors in the school. It may even have been metallic.

They had entered a modern corridor, perhaps the type found in the most futuristic skyscrapers. Glass and metal was everywhere. Concealed lighting had the effect of making it look as though the actual walls and ceiling were glowing attractively with a pleasant white light. The floor was metal and there was a faint hum in the air. Perhaps an air conditioning unit?

Principal McGregor interrupted his thoughts, "I know what you're thinking. We're just outside my office in the corridor at school. But look out of the windows." Josh did as he was instructed and felt his stomach churn slightly.

The windows were enormous floor to ceiling panels every so often along the corridor and they were just approaching one. Outside, it was dark. Strange, it's only lunchtime, thought Josh, but he then realised why as they actually reached the window. Far below them he could see Earth. Not dirt or mud, but the entire planet Earth! Neither was this the relatively close-up view he had seen on countless TV newsreels taken from the space shuttle or International Space Station. No, this was a view from much further away. The planet looked to be about the size of a giant beach ball way below them, but it was undeniably Earth!

Feeling that he should at least acknowledge that the evidence so far seemed to be supporting the principal's claims, Josh asked what he hoped sounded a reasonably well-conceived question, "Shouldn't we be floating about, sir?"

The principal grinned, “Well yes, you’d think so. But it turns out that it is possible to create artificial gravity, after all.”

They continued to walk towards a large silver door at the end of the corridor and Josh stared unashamedly out of every window that they passed. He could see all sorts of features of the space station, although quite what any of them were, he wasn’t too sure. Docking ports and docks, possibly? Observation platforms perhaps? Launch tubes maybe? And were those things spacecraft?

They reached the door and the principal pushed some buttons on the wall. The door slid open and Josh could see people on the other side. Quite a few of them were about his age. “Come on,” encouraged the principal. “This way to the simulator.”

Chapter 17

The bitter wind had really picked up now, making it difficult for James Rock and Luke Richards to keep upright as they continued to examine the metallic object embedded in the rock face.

"OK, well this thing's not gonna budge at all," sighed James as he gave up trying to dislodge it. "That kind of wraps up any theories that it fell through the glacier."

Luke nodded, "It sure does look like it was put here before anything froze. But that would be impossible."

"Yep, I'd agree," said James. He looked up at the forbidding sky and then ran his gaze over the nearby rocks. "Let's see if we can find anything else."

Luke shrugged ruefully. Part of him wanted to carry on - his curiosity was as much aroused as James'. But he was also inwardly questioning the safety of being exposed in this hauntingly barren landscape in these conditions. Nevertheless, he moved off, battling the wind.

He stopped suddenly, "Over here," he yelled across to James. "I think there's another one!"

James clambered across to where Luke had knelt to examine the object. "Sure looks like the same kind of thing," he agreed. "Well I reckon that confirms they were put here first. Two of the same type of instrument, both lost by our survey teams in the same place, is just too much of a coincidence."

"I guess we'd better tell Base Camp," suggested Luke, before looking up once more at the sky and spotting the ominous storm clouds now crossing the mountains towards them. "But we'd better hurry before that lot hits us," he urged.

James had already taken the Skype device out of his pack and was attempting to make contact. "Shit! That doesn't look good," he agreed with Luke before speaking with an unusual sense of urgency to the computer device, "Come in, Base Camp, this is Snow Leopard, are you receiving. Base Camp, this is Snow Leopard, can you hear me?"

The screen flickered, but stubbornly refused to do anything else. The two friends looked at each other in silent recognition that their situation was not good. Gradually, however, they began to make out voices coming through the static as they faintly heard Gerry saying, "Base Camp to Snow Leopard, we're receiving a voice link, but can't see you."

James spoke again, loudly and quickly, not knowing how long the link would last, "Snow Leopard to Base Camp, we've found another one of those objects, maybe ten yards or so from the first one. It's also firmly embedded in the rock. Over."

They waited pensively for some sort of acknowledgement. Again Gerry's voice, weak and crackling came back to them, "Snow Leopard, we can barely hear you. Did you say you found a second object? Over."

The static was getting worse with every passing second and the howling wind was increasing in intensity as, finally, the snow they had been fearing began to flutter around them. Gently at first, but increasing in intensity as the blizzard hit.

“Say again, Base Camp, say again. Over.” pleaded James, but the signal was lost. “The weather must be interfering with the reception,” he suggested rather obviously to Luke.

“We’re gonna have to get some shelter fast!” Luke shouted back, “This is going to be quite a storm.”

The two of them began frantically scanning for somewhere that might offer some respite from the onslaught. “Can we make it back to the crevasse in time?” asked James, already knowing the answer was probably no.

“I don’t know,” Luke answered not wanting to be the one to verbalise what they both knew. But then he squinted hard in the opposite direction and pointed to some rocks, “Look over there. Is that a cave? Under those boulders.”

The two men struggled as fast as they could over the rough, and now quite slippery, surface clambering over boulders and rocks towards what looked like a hole in the rock face.

They reached their goal and found a gap measuring perhaps twelve inches across. It was dark inside, suggesting that it might, indeed, be some sort of cave rather than just another crevasse. Battling against the wind and driving snow, they struggled with numb fingers to shift the loose rocks that were almost covering the entrance.

Suddenly, without any warning the rocks gave way and both men tumbled through the resulting chasm crashing onto the floor of a large cave about ten feet below. They lay motionless on the rocky floor, stunned onto unconsciousness by the severity and suddenness of their fall. The noise of the wind was muffled and the snow passed harmlessly by the cave opening. But it was still bitingly cold in the dark recess. Then gradually an eerie glow began emanating from the cave roof and walls, bathing the two prostrate forms in a faint green wash.

Chapter 18

As they continued their journey through the corridors of the Space Corps space station, Principal McGregor occasionally paused to introduce Josh to certain senior personnel that they met. But, Josh felt, they had clearly had not yet reached the destination that the principal intended for them. "Well, Josh, I know this is all a huge shock to you and probably somewhat traumatic, but you'll get used to it fairly quickly," the teacher was saying. "Most of our students do."

But Josh wondered, "What happens to those who don't, sir?"

The principal stopped and looked at Josh very seriously, yet with benign intent, "You remember the red button I gave you earlier?"

"Uh, huh," came the reply.

"Well," the principal continued, "We use a similar technology to remove their memories of Space Corps and they resume their previous lives back at whatever school they came from."

"So how long does it take to 'fit in'?" asked Josh.

The principal resumed walking, "It's usually pretty obvious who's going to make the grade by the end of the second week." They had reached another door and the principal once again assumed a more serious demeanour. “Now let me introduce you to some very important people.”

They entered another room with various banks of consoles being tended by adults. A few people were wandering around absorbed in their tasks. One of them, an Asian man in his thirties, looked up. “Jonathan, hi! Good to see you. Is this young Mr Travis?” he enquired.

“Hi, Freddie. How you doing?” the principal replied. “Yep, this is Josh.” Turning to the student he introduced the stranger, “Josh, I want you to meet Mr Han. He’s in charge of the recruitment program here.”

Josh shook the proffered hand as the other man enthused, “Hi Josh. Good to meet you. Principal McGregor has told me quite a bit about you. Apparently you’re quite the whizz-kid when it comes to computer games,” then added with a wink of his eye, “And, I understand, not too unskilled when it comes to reprogramming school timetables as well!”

Josh could feel his face going a little red at the mention of his previous misdemeanor. “Ah, thank you sir, I think,” he replied looking nervously towards the principal who, he was relieved to see, was smiling.

“We’re not so stupid that we didn’t know it was you. But the flip side was that it helped confirm our suspicions about your abilities,” he admitted.

“Well Principal McGregor will have explained what this is all about and, no doubt you’re still a little in shock. What we need to do now is to show you why you’re here,” Freddie was continuing in a more business-like tone. He moved towards the door and invited Josh to follow him. They walked along yet another corridor, passing one or two other adults as they did so. Some of these were dressed in regular office-style attire of suits or ties and jackets, which contrasted noticeably with the light blue or red jumpsuits that most of the Space Corps personnel seemed to be wearing.

Josh assumed that these other people must also be visitors from Earth, since neither he nor Principal McGregor had been invited to change out of their original clothes either. Suddenly the principal stopped to greet one of them in a way that suggested to Josh that they were old friends. A tall, rather striking Indian man with a full head of neatly trimmed grey hair and a grey goatee to match. "Rashid!" he exclaimed reaching forward to clasp the other man's hand. "How are you? I haven't seen you for ages."

The Indian man laughed enthusiastically and warmly shook the principal's hand. "Jonathan! It's been a long time, but I've just been introducing two new students. The first for quite a while," he admitted humorously, before shrugging his shoulders, "but at least it goes to show that Delhi's still contributing."

"I bet it is," Principal McGregor replied. "I saw Chin Lo up here a few weeks ago. He was asking after you," he informed his friend.

Rashid smiled, "Yes, we keep in touch by e-mail, but it seems so 'old school' when we can be in the same place so quickly when the need arises. He seems to be doing well in Shanghai." He looked at Freddie and Josh and, realising that the three of them were in the middle of something, politely changed the subject, "Anyway, I'd better not detain you. After all, I've got a school to run you know!" They shook hands again and, still laughing, Rashid walked away.

The three of them continued down the corridor before entering a large circular room equipped with computers all around the outer walls and reclining gaming chairs in front of them. In the centre was a raised platform surmounted by a desk and numerous monitors, manned by an adult. Two other adults were wandering around the circular walkway behind the chairs monitoring the young people who were seated at most of the consoles. Josh noticed that these fellow students, as he assumed them to be, represented a variety of 'developed' nations and were mainly male.

One of the adult attendants, a male in his mid-forties, approached the new arrivals, "Mr Han, sir. And Principal McGregor, nice to see you again," he politely greeted them.

"Afternoon, George. This is new recruit Josh Travis," Freddie responded, "I'd like him to undergo familiarisation and initial grading please. Usual training scenarios."

"Yes sir," the attendant responded matter-of-factly, before addressing Josh rather formally, "If you'll come with me please, Mr Travis."

He led Josh over to one of the unoccupied consoles, "Please make yourself comfortable," he invited, indicating the chair. "It's been designed to replicate a gaming chair and console as much as possible. Familiarise yourself with the controls and, when you're ready, activate the training game. Just relax and 'play' it like the sort of games you usually play on your computer." He tapped a key on the control console and the screen came to life with an image of spaceships in deep space. After a few trial manoeuvres, Josh soon had one of the ships flying exactly how he wanted and the game began to unfold.

Chapter 19

The wind continued to howl across the cave opening and darkness had now set in outside as James Rock began to slowly come to. He raised his upper torso up on his forearms and peered through the gloom. Further across the cave floor Luke Richards rolled on to his back and began rubbing his eyes. Both men started to gently check themselves for signs of injury and were both relieved to discover nothing apart from bruises and superficial cuts.

"Luke? Luke? Are you there?" rasped James, still feeling somewhat groggy.

"Yeah, I'm over here," came the slightly breathless reply, "Can you see me?"

James focussed on the sound of Luke's voice and peered across the cave floor, "I can now. Wow, that was close. Thank God for this cave."

He took the usual scepticism in Luke's voice to be confirmation that he was alright, "Hmm. Thank God. Imagine - what are the chances of two guys just about to freeze to death in an Antarctic blizzard when they just happen to fall into an illuminated cave? It must be divine intervention."

James had already filtered out the sarcasm and was busy surveying their surroundings, "What? Yeah. So the thing is, how the hell is this cave lit and how long has it been here?"

"And who put the lighting in here?" wondered Luke, straight to the point as usual, "Look, the Ross ice sheet has been covering this part of Antarctica for millions of years. So whoever put the lighting in here had to do so a very long time ago!"

"Unless they drilled down through the ice recently to install it?" offered James, somewhat forlornly.

"And what would be the point in that?" argued Luke. "I mean, to make all that effort to tunnel down through thousands of feet of solid ice to install discrete lighting in a cave and then bury it again to await its possible discovery if the ice sheet ever melts at some point in the future."

By now both men had stumbled to their feet and were in the process of stretching aching and cramped limbs, all the time looking over the interior of the cave. "I agree it does sound somewhat far-fetched," conceded James, "but it's a vague possibility that shouldn't be ignored."

But Luke was having none of it, "And anyway, why would you want to light a cave that couldn't be reached?"

James decided to try another tack. "OK, so the alternative that you're suggesting proposes that the lighting was installed millions of years before the technology to make it existed?"

"Not only to make it, but to make it survive underneath the ice for so long," Luke agreed, starting to wander around the cave as his eyes adjusted to the dim lighting.

"Which, of course, raises even more questions," trumped James. "Not just who, but how and why?"

Luke shrugged and raised his hands in a gesture of surrender. "Well, there must be a reason for it being here. I think my eyes are adjusting, but I still can't make out anything other than rock."

Both men were proceeding around the cave wall in opposite directions, peering and feeling their way over the rocky surface. Suddenly James called across to Luke, "Over here. I think I've found something!"

Luke walked over the rock-strewn cave floor, with a brief glance up at the inclement weather through the cave entrance, and was just as surprised as James had been to discover a metallic door set into the rock. "OK, so this is getting even weirder."

James indicated a smaller panel next to it, "It's got some sort of lock, but how do we pick it?"

Deciding that it was probably their only means of both escape from the cave and further shelter from the storm, Luke took a flare pistol out of his pack and motioned for James to stand back, before firing it at the small panel. The result was as expected. The panel exploded in a fiery display of phosphorous and what appeared to be electrical sparks as the door begrudgingly slid halfway open. "It may not be subtle, but at least it solved the problem!" offered a somewhat smug Luke.

Both men started to push the door open further. Clearly the mechanism hadn't been used for many years. When the gap was big enough to climb through Luke stood back chivalrously, "After you."

James peered into the darkness beyond before reluctantly accepting the invitation, "How kind." He carefully and deliberately stepped through the doorway into an inner cave. As he gingerly stepped forward into the darkness Luke followed him through.

Suddenly the cave was flooded with brilliant white light, making the two men instinctively shield their eyes. As their vision slowly acclimatised to the new clinical illumination they realised that they were both standing frozen to the spot in shock and bewilderment, gazing into a vast cave.

James was the first to speak and break the spell, “Well I guess we now know ‘why’,” he whistled.

Luke was still in shock, “Yeah, but the ‘who’ and ‘when’ just got a lot tougher to answer.”

Chapter 20

Josh was rubbing his eyes and stretching when Principal McGregor and Freddie Han entered the training room. He'd just finished a thirty minute training program and was feeling the effects. His eyes were dry and, despite the reclining position of the chair, he felt tense and slightly hunched up, the result no doubt of concentrating so intensely. He hadn't tried that hard at a computer game for ages, but he didn't want to mess up at all. Although his mind was still reeling from all the information that had been pouring into it in the few hours that had passed since he'd innocently entered the principal's office back at school, he was determined to see where this whole surreal experience would lead.

He was still unsure whether to consider it all some sort of dream or at least an elaborate hoax, or whether to go along with the pretext that it was all real. His rational mind kept telling him that it couldn't be real – space stations, secret space organisations, spaceships and, most far-fetched of all, teenagers at the controls – but his emotional mind kept hoping that it was. Just imagine, he kept telling himself, if it is how cool will it be: like starring in his very own computer game.

The principal caught sight of Josh yawning as they approached him. "Well, Josh, how did you find it?" Seemingly ignorant of any impression that he might be tired, Josh enthusiastically replied, "It's a lot like the computer games that we play, but much more responsive and with a few added features that I've never seen before."

"Hmm," Freddie pondered, almost to himself: then, addressing Franklin, "How'd he do, George?" The attendant was impressed. "Not bad at all, sir. One of the highest scores I've seen from a rookie in quite some time. A natural, I'd say." His clipped English tones somehow underscoring and emphasising his approval.

Freddie nodded and, with the downturned corners of his mouth emphasising the rarity of such a report, replied, "Praise indeed!" Smiling, he continued to Josh, "Well, Josh, I'm impressed. Mr Franklin isn't given to praising unnecessarily. You must certainly have an aptitude for this." Not wishing to rain on the parade, the principal suggested, "The next session will tell us for sure, but in the meantime there's something else you need to see." He beckoned for Josh to walk with him and Freddie into an adjoining room.

The room they entered was about the same size as the training room but, because it was almost empty, seemed much bigger. "What now?" wondered Josh as he prepared himself for yet more introductions and tests. Another adult attendant who had been seated behind a desk stood as they entered, "Afternoon, Mr Han, Principal McGregor," he said politely.

Freddie nodded to him, "Phillips. Are you ready for Mr Travis here?" The large red-haired man nodded enthusiastically, "Oh yes sir, all ready. We just need the memory patterns and we're done."

The slightly concerned look that descended over Josh's face didn't go unnoticed by Principal McGregor.

His deep, resonant voice assumed an uncharacteristic note of concern, "Now Josh, I need you to sit down for a moment. This next stage can often be the most," he searched for the right adjective, "Delicate - for a new student trainee."

Josh sat in the indicated chair, suddenly concerned at this unexpected change of tempo. The principal continued, "You remember I told you that Space Corps uses replicas on Earth while students are on duty up here to help cover their absence?"

Josh nodded apprehensively, "Yes, sir."

Trying hard not to sound too melodramatic, the principal explained, "Well, it's now time to introduce you to your duplicate, or synthetic human as we prefer to call them. This can often be a bit of a shock at first." He smiled and attempted a little humour to lighten the mood, "To the human, that is. It's not often that we get to see a walking, talking, fully operational replica modelled on ourselves is it?"

Josh remained monosyllabic, "No, sir," as he wondered exactly what they had in store for him. Had this all been a huge mistake? Should he have pressed the red button after all? He suddenly remembered, deep from his subconscious, the warnings drummed into him by his parents many years ago about not going anywhere with strangers. Had he just fallen into such a trap? What was it the principal was now saying?

"So in a moment when, Mr Phillips opens the door your duplicate will walk in." Josh forced himself to focus while Principal McGregor explained, "Now, it's important to realise that at this stage in his manufacture he is without any memory. He can talk and think, but he has no memory of anything. All the duplicates are made this way, until they receive the memories of their human counterpart. Once this is done, then they will also start storing their own memories. Do you understand?"

Josh concentrated on steadying his breathing, "I think so, sir."

Freddie Han now joined in. "Once you have met your duplicate, a copy of your own memories will be made and implanted into the duplicate so that he can legitimately impersonate you. The process is painless and harmless and doesn't take very long either. Are you willing to proceed?"

Unfortunately, that contribution did nothing to calm Josh's rampaging imagination. He looked to his principal for reassurance. "Nobody's going to force you, Josh. Remember, there's always the red button option."

Finally, someone had said something that helped to soothe his growing fears. Perhaps it was just a reaction to everything that he had been trying to assimilate in the last few hours. A quite natural panic attack in the circumstances, he told himself. He considered the principal's last words for a moment longer, then swallowed hard. "It's OK, sir. I'll go through with it."

He stole a quick furtive glance at both the principal then Freddie for any sign that they had won. He saw nothing that betrayed any ill-intent, he told himself. But then again, what did he expect? That they would suddenly sprout horns and develop maniacal laughs?

In fact the conversation continued in the same vein and tone as before. "Fine," smiled Freddie. "Then we'll bring in the duplicate." He indicated to Phillips who pushed a button and yet another door slid open. After a moment that couldn't have been more than a couple of seconds, but that to Josh seemed to last a full five minutes, a figure walked into their room.

Josh's jaw dropped and he stared in a mixture of disbelief and wonder. It was just like looking in the mirror, except that this reflection was three dimensional. Not only was it three dimensional but it moved independently of its owner. Clearly this was no reflection, but a living, breathing duplicate. At least Josh assumed it was breathing. But it couldn't be breathing, could it? Hadn't the principal said that it was synthetic? Didn't that mean it wasn't real?

The duplicate Josh stood, facing its human counterpart. "Wow! It's exactly like me," blurted out Josh.

"Of course," grinned the principal. "They're designed to be indistinguishable from the original thing," he explained and then, with mock formality, he invited, "Mr Travis, meet Mr Travis."

Josh stood uncertainly, and in truth a little shakily, said, "Hi." He did his best to sound nonchalant.

"Hi. How are you?" was the response from the duplicate.

All attempts at nonchalance evaporated as the real Josh marvelled, "It even sounds like me."

Freddie nodded and smiled, "Ever since you arrived here we've been monitoring your speech patterns to allow us to reproduce them accurately in your duplicate." His soothing tones were designed to calm Josh, but almost had the effect of re-awakening his fears.

Fortunately the attendant intervened., "If you'll just sit here, please, then we can begin." He indicated a pair of comfortable-looking armchairs.

Josh shot a glance at the principal, who did manage to convey the right degree of reassurance. "Remember, Josh, the red button."

Josh steeled himself mentally and steadied himself physically before settling himself in the recliner chair. Phillips gently placed various pressure pads on Josh's head and temples, then addressed the duplicate: "Please sit down."

Somehow his courteousness to the synthetic Josh reassured the real one. It sat in the vacant chair and the attendant repeated the process with the pressure pads, before returning to his desk and without any further preliminaries, pressed a sequence of buttons.

Immediately the computer monitors on his desk sprang into life, with frantic readouts cascading down and across the screens. Josh felt a brief period of dizziness before the room suddenly went black as he lost consciousness.

Chapter 21

The conversation in Sarah Mitchell's office was excited and animated. Rarely, in fact, had the astronomers at Kitts Peak Observatory been so excited in the last twenty or so years, not since the Shoemaker-Levy comet crashed into Jupiter. Although, of course, their relative newness meant that neither Jacob or Callum realised the rarity of the emotions in the room. Even Sarah herself was still in high school during that last euphoria.

"So when the anomaly got to 400 million miles from Earth it split into four signals," Jacob was explaining. "Now that it's 300 million miles away it seems to have split again."

Callum joined in enthusiastically, "The obvious explanation is that the signal is a cluster of signals so close together that at those great distances, they originally registered as a single entity. As they get closer they are becoming easier to identify as individual signals."

Trying hard to remain calm, Samantha asked, "So how many signals do we think are actually involved?"

Jacob had already prepared his answer knowing that this would be the next logical step, "Based upon the multiplication rate so far and the distances involved, I wouldn't be surprised to see that the original signal is actually made up of about 20 or more objects."

Samantha responded in a matter-of-fact tone that belied her underlying sense of excitement, "I see. But do we have any further information about what the objects actually are?"

This time it was Callum's turn to provide a previously-prepared answer. "Well, we're looking into the obvious natural phenomena – comets, asteroids, meteors, etc., and the dissipation as it gets closer does fit this theory slightly." We're not doing too badly at this, he thought.

But his confidence was shaken when Samantha asked caustically, "Slightly?"

Jacob came to the rescue to get this test of knowledge back on an even keel. "Yes," he began slowly, before continuing with authority, "The problem with it, of course, is that for that many objects to be that close to each other there would have to be something massive at the centre exerting the necessary gravitational pull to keep them all close."

"What about the alternatives?" Samantha asked.

Callum had regained his composure, but decided to tread cautiously. He always found it slightly demoralising when he thought Samantha didn't agree with him. "Well, the obvious one is, of course, even more far-fetched and can't seriously be suggested until a lot more data can be gathered."

Samantha decided to tease it out of him, "You mean something that is not natural in origin?"

Jacob also began to err on the side of caution. "Yes, but it's far too early to begin suggesting 'little green men'. We need it to get much closer before we can determine whether it is acting independently of the laws of nature."

Callum decided it was safe to venture further, "For instance, does it defy the expected effects of gravity?"

“Well, gentlemen, we can’t wait too long.” Samantha decided it was time to wrap up this session, “I need to report to the agency and they’re gonna want facts not guesses. I can stall for another couple of hours but then I’ve got to have something!”

The look on her face told the boys that it was time to leave. But it also gave them hope that she was buying in to their secret hope and suspicions about the true nature of these objects. All they had to do now was get some sort of proof. With this thought planted firmly in both of their minds they returned to their computers for more analysis.

Chapter 22

Josh wasn't too sure whether he was actually surprised to be waking up. It seemed to take much longer than usual, but then he had been in an incredibly deep sleep. Deep enough for him to momentarily wonder whether all his recent experiences had been nothing but a dream. But when he heard Principal McGregor's voice his vague surprise was redirected at the fact that he was still alive and seemed to be unharmed.

"How do you feel? OK?" the principal was asking Josh through the fog that was clouding his senses.

As things became clearer and his alertness returned, Josh was relieved to think that he had made the right decision after all. Relieved and, perhaps, just a bit sheepish for having doubted the principal. "Yes, sir. Nothing strange as far as I can tell," he reassured his teacher.

Freddie's smile was one of relief, "That's good, because the process is something you'll need to get used to."

Before Josh could even think of querying that remark, the principal began explaining, "Every time you or your duplicate spend time on Earth, you must exchange your recent memories, otherwise we can get a 'memory lapse' where one or other of you isn't up to speed with the latest developments in your life on Earth."

Freddie nodded ruefully, as if from bitter experience, "This can lead to apparent lack of memories as far as other people outside this organisation are concerned."

Josh began to sit up straighter as Phillips started removing the various sensors from his head and pondered a sudden idea. "Tell me, sir," he asked respectfully, "Is Ryan Samuels in 12th grade a member of Space Corps?"

The principal sat back in one of the few chairs opposite Josh and replied as naturally as if he was being asked whether he took sugar in his coffee, "Yes. Why do you ask?"

Josh was inwardly pleased at both his intuition and the fact that he was now obviously considered to be enough of a part of this crazy operation for such secrets to be divulged to him. "Well I tried talking to him this morning and he didn't seem to remember our friendship."

Freddie looked slightly concerned. "Ryan was on duty up here this morning. You must have spoken to his duplicate. We'd better look into this." He looked over to the attendant who was now busying himself disconnecting Josh's duplicate from the various wires. "Phillips, make a note to have Ryan Samuels' duplicate memory-scanned to check the last update."

Josh's duplicate had now also sat up and was looking passively at the real Josh. "This is a bit weird, sir," Josh admitted to the principal. "Does he know he's my duplicate?"

"Oh, yes," came the emphatic reply, "'Josh 2' knows that he's a stand-in for you. He's programmed to know that his job is to prevent your absence from Earth being noticed."

Josh's curiosity was now aroused, "What's he made of? Some kind of mechanical skeleton covered in skin?"

Freddie responded gently, "You mean like in the movies? Hmm," he mused. "It's a bit more complicated and advanced than that. They're actually made of living tissue and skeletal structure, but with mechanical organs so that they pump blood, eat and digest food, and breathe air. And perhaps the biggest difference with the movies is that they can be hurt – they are not indestructible machines from the future!"

The principal was quick to endorse Freddie's point. "No, they certainly aren't indestructible. And in fact they are, of course, from the past anyway!"

Josh was enjoying receiving all this information and the evident trust that went with it. "How long ago, sir?"

The principal shrugged, "We're still not sure when these aliens were here, but it's got to be at least a few thousand years ago." He looked at his watch and decided that enough time had been spent up here for now. "Right, now it's time we were getting you back to school." He noticed the brief look of disappointment that momentarily crossed Josh's face and was impressed with the speed with which he removed it. "Don't forget," he reminded Josh, "there hasn't been a duplicate or the real you down there for the last few hours."

Josh thanked Phillips for his help and the two men said goodbye to Freddie. As they left the room Josh couldn't help but look back at his duplicate one last time. It was almost like leaving a newly-acquired pet for the first time, but Josh had a feeling that their paths would, quite literally, be crossing many times from now on.

Chapter 23

Hundreds of ebullient, youthful voices, combined with the clatter and stomping of twice as many feet and the rattle of almost as many locker doors signalled the end of another school day. A veritable torrent of students were all pouring through the school corridors to burst into the open air through the many exits before flowing, like a river in flood, towards the squadron of yellow school buses lined up to take them home. Josh rounded a corner and almost walked straight into his friends.

"Well, hi, stranger," said a startled Chris, the smile on his face cancelling the sarcasm in his voice, "Where have you been all afternoon?"

"Yeah," added John, "We thought you'd left the planet. What did old McGregor want with you for so long?"

Josh hesitated momentarily. If they only knew, he thought to himself. "He's got me lined up for some additional tuition and skill development," he replied, trying hard to sound both nonchalant and slightly disapproving.

"Oh yeah? So are you gonna be the class swot now?" Chris asked, with very real concern in his voice. Though whether the concern was for Josh's well-being or how this news might affect his friends was difficult to tell.

"No way!" Josh exclaimed, eager to quash any such suggestion. "I'm keen to see what's on offer, but there's no way I'm gonna become a nerd," he added somewhat more soberly.

John grinned. "Hmm, we'll be the judges of that, won't we, Chris? Anyway you missed a whole bunch of homework assignments while you were hobnobbing with the elite. It wouldn't be fair of us to hold you back by not passing them on to you, would it Chris?"

Chris fell in immediately, enjoying the conspiracy, "Absolutely. First day back and three assignments to do. Don't you just love school?"

Josh's two friends were just warming to their theme when the tall and gangly frame of Ryan Samuels hove into view. As he walked past the group he acknowledged Josh, "Hi, Josh. Have a good summer?"

Unable to keep the slight note of surprise out of his voice Josh responded, "Yeah, thanks, Ryan. What about you?"

Continuing his stroll past, Ryan replied sarcastically, "Great, but glad to be back at the 'seat of learning' of course." He paused for a moment. "I hear you're joining the *gifted and talented* classes?" he asked without waiting for, nor apparently expecting, a reply since he continued, "Great. See you there," and continued to walk on.

John's face betrayed his puzzlement as he quizzed Josh, "I thought you said he'd ignored you this morning. Doesn't seem like he wants to ignore you anymore."

"No. I guess not," pondered Josh, assuming that he had just spoken with the real Ryan Samuels. He was still watching Ryan walk down the corridor when the older student reached a door which he opened before stepping back to allow Mr Jacks to walk through first. In the course of doing this he stretched his arm across the upper part of the door.

Josh noticed that Mr Jacks seemed to let his gaze linger over Ryan's now very exposed hand. He walked on a couple more steps before stopping, turning around and returning back through the doorway following Ryan.

Josh turned back to his friends and, with a sense of urgency in his voice, said, "I'll catch up with you guys later, I've just got to do something," before rushing after Mr Jacks.

Chris looked at John, slightly dumbfounded. "Obviously got something urgently *nerdy* to do!" They both laughed at their insightful humour and left the school in the opposite direction.

As Josh crashed through the doors, following Ryan and Mr Jacks, he was just in time to see his friend holding his hand and Mr Jacks patting him on the shoulder as they headed to the medical room a little further down the corridor. Josh watched, puzzled, as they entered the room and then was even more puzzled to see Mr Jacks come back out of the room on his own and walk straight out of the nearest external doorway.

Chapter 24

Mr Jacks made the short walk across to the black van in just a couple of minutes. As before, the side door slid open and Kimberley Walsh stepped out, took the tissue from the teacher and returned to the vehicle sliding the door shut behind her. The whole exchange was completed in less than ten seconds.

As he retraced his steps to the school Mr Jacks took his cell phone out of his pocket and made a call. "That sample is from the same kid as this morning. I need you to compare the results."

He hung-up abruptly, returned the phone to his pocket and re-entered the school as if nothing unusual had taken place.

Inside the van Brad finished a cell phone call, and addressed the other two agents, "Hmm. Agent Summers may be on to something. We need to compare these results to subject 31's."

Both he and Kimberley Walsh watched intently as Agent Fredericks snipped a tiny piece off the bloody tissue and added it to a test tube followed by a measured amount of one of the numerous chemicals from his kit. Not for the first time, Brad wondered why someone as obviously academic as Fredericks should choose to join the agency rather than earn a fortune as a research chemist. His approach, as always, was measured and highly complex. Logical and thoroughly thought through. The evidence never lied and he was prepared to accept whatever it told him, regardless of whether it was what he expected to discover. He placed the test tube into a machine, pushed some buttons and sat back as a variety of tiny, coloured lights began to flash intermittently on the front of the machine. Now it just required a little patience.

This was the part that Brad found the most frustrating. He could appreciate the forensic approach even if he, personally, would rather be interrogating a human suspect. At least they could be intimidated or persuaded by various means to reveal what they knew. Brad wasn't a dinosaur. He understood the need for this precise, analytical approach. But just as Fredericks was totally at home with his elaborate chemistry set, Brad was more at home chasing something down in the field. Running a suspect to ground and feeling the adrenaline pumping in a kill or be killed chase. Patience wasn't really his strong suit.

The machine beeped and brought Brad back out of his reverie. Fredericks hunched over the readout and looked up with a mixture of triumph and resignation on his face. "Well, it's the same blood group and it's Rhesus positive," he declared matter-of-factly, "So there's a match there -" his voice suddenly trailed off and he stopped speaking altogether as he stared hard at something in the results.

Brad felt his hopes race. Could this be something they could move on?

"Hold on, what's that?" Fredericks was saying, almost to himself. "Strange. That doesn't look right," he continued tantalisingly. He immediately checked his previous notes in case even his meticulous methods had overlooked something. No chance. "No, it's not there!" he declared.

Brad pounced on this piece of news, “So there’s an inconsistency?”

“I’ll have to re-run the tests on both samples before I can be sure,” Fredericks said, appearing to be totally oblivious to Brad’s eager excitement, “But it certainly looks as though the samples are from two different people.” He made it sound as if he was simply discussing an academic interpretation rather than the breakthrough it might be and, not for the first time in their partnership, Brad wanted to grab him by the shoulders and shake him into reality. But then again, mused Brad, they’d never get anywhere with this stake-out if he did that!

Chapter 25

In what seemed like a re-run of the previous morning, in fact of all previous mornings at Littrow High School and probably all schools across the world, numerous students were once again arriving via the same mode of transport as yesterday, talking to the same friends as yesterday and following the throng into the school grounds in the same way as yesterday. Josh was entering the building with his usual accomplices, Chris and John, and all three were, once again, deeply engrossed in their computer tablets.

Chris was feeling pleased with himself as he bragged to Josh, "I'm catching you up. I got up to 9,400 points last night."

This was short-lived, however, when Josh replied, without even bothering to look up, "Not bad. I raised mine to 12,460."

"Hmph!" muttered a crestfallen Chris before seeking some sense of satisfaction by comparing his score with John. "What about you, John?"

"8,300, but with all lives left," John replied with a smile. "Steady and sure, that's me. Not fast and furious like you two."

"That won't get you any prizes!" Josh suggested emphatically, before noticing a familiar face further along the corridor. “Hey, there’s Samuels. Do you remember what happened last night as we were leaving?”

“I remember you were chatting to him and dashed off after him saying something about catching up with us later,” volunteered Chris.

“Which you never did,” added John indignantly.

Josh acknowledged his friend’s point, “Yeah, sorry about that. I did mean to, but when I got home I had loads to do. But the reason I chased after him was because I saw Mr Jacks deliberately bump into him.”

“So?” Chris’ voice betrayed his puzzlement that Josh should think this behaviour strange.

Josh, likewise, was a little frustrated at Chris’ obtuseness. “For the second time that day!”

John genuinely was puzzled, “What do you mean, the second time? People bump into each other all the time at school.”

Josh figured he’d have to explain the whole thing if he was to get anywhere with his friends, “Yes, but this seemed deliberate – as if he was trying to hurt him.” He looked at their faces for any indication that they were beginning to understand his concern. “I saw him take Samuels to the medical room afterwards, so it was more than a casual bump.”

Chris decided to resort to sarcasm, “Whoa. Child abuse. Here? Excellent! We’ll make the media!”

But Josh didn’t rise to the bait. “Then he went out -,” he paused suddenly, realising that his suspicions must sound both far-fetched and a little unnecessary. He decided to curtail the conversation. “Well, he went out of the door.” Now that didn’t sound at all lame, he grimaced to himself.

John pounced on the opportunity that Josh had presented to them. “Oh my goodness. Don’t tell me he was going home? At the end of the day? Imagine that!” and both he and Chris laughed at Josh’s expense.

"Yeah, okay, okay. Maybe I am imagining it," Josh admitted, searching for something to change the subject. "Look I've got to go and see Principal McGregor again about these *gifted and talented* lessons. I'll see you both in math class."

Chris rolled his eyes, "Of course. We wouldn't want to stand in the way of a gifted *and talented* star!"

Josh laughed the long-suffering, humourless laugh of someone getting used to being the butt of the joke and walked off down the corridor.

Chapter 26

Josh found himself once again standing in front of Principal McGregor's desk. The nerves and apprehension that he'd experienced the previous day before were now a distant memory. Of course he wasn't here on school business so perhaps that accounted for it. Instead of feeling concern over previous misdemeanours, he was now excited over potential adventures as he waited for the principal's grey head to look up.

"Well, Josh, you did very well yesterday," the principal began, still putting the finishing touches to the work on his desk. "Are you happy to continue with training and testing?"

Are you kidding? Josh wanted to say, but replied with a slightly more respectful, "Absolutely, sir."

The principal smiled inwardly at the student's enthusiasm. Secretly, he was as pleased as Josh, and probably just as excited. From what he had gleaned so far, Josh was already proving to be a natural. "Great. Well, let's get things under way I'll need to get your duplicate standing by for memory copying again. We don't want a repeat of the Samuels episode, do we?"

"No sir," agreed Josh. He hesitated a moment then continued, "Sir, I'm not sure if I need to tell you this, but…"

Again, he seemed to be weighing something up in his mind.

"Yes?" queried the principal, his curiosity aroused.

Reassured by the principal's warm tone, Josh continued, "Well, yesterday I saw the new science teacher, Mr Jacks, bump into Ryan Samuels twice."

"And?" urged the principal gently.

"Well neither time looked like an accident." Josh hoped he wasn't overstepping the mark and straying into complaints against teachers' territory.

"How do you mean?" asked the principal, his attention now focussed solely on Josh.

The student weighed up the best way to explain what he had seen. "The first time, he seemed to scratch Ryan's hand with something he was carrying. He apologised and Ryan seemed OK about it. The second time, he scratched his hand again and took him to the medical room."

Josh began to feel that perhaps he had after all blown the whole thing out of all proportion when the principal replied, "Well, they could have been accidents. He certainly seems to have done the right thing after both incidents."

Deciding to go for broke, Josh played his full hand. "I guess so sir, but he left the school building immediately after the second accident and took something to someone waiting outside in a van."

Now he really did have the principal's attention. His voice became much more serious and he asked pointedly, "Did he do this after the first incident?"

"I don't know, sir. I didn't see," admitted Josh, wishing that he could supply this obviously important piece of information.

The principal seemed unfazed by his lack of evidence and pursued another line of questioning. "What time did these collisions take place?"

"I'm not exactly sure sir," replied Josh, again feeling a little lame, before adding hopefully, "But I know the first one was in the morning before lessons began and the second was at the end of school."

The principal sat back and ran his hand over his mouth and chin as he weighed up the story, "Hmm. So the first was probably his duplicate and the second the real person."

"Probably, sir," agreed Josh, keen to grasp any theory that would make his observations worthwhile. "Certainly the first time wasn't long before Samuels ignored me, but the second time he seemed his usual self."

The principal reached a decision. "Right, I'll look into it." He stood and gestured to the teleport doorway, "In the meantime, we'd better get you up to Space Corps."

Josh smiled with a sense of satisfaction that he had made the right decision in telling the principal as the two of them walked towards the portal.

Chapter 27

The sun reflected off the numerous large windows in the modern grey office block. A typically faceless building in a fairly spacious commercial district, there was nothing to distinguish this particular edifice from any of the other neat and well-kept offices lining one side of the street. Opposite, across the other side of the three-lane highway, was empty land. Clearly someone, somewhere, would have plans to develop it further as the economy prospered and demand for office space increased, but for now the dozen or so buildings of similar size and shape suited these particular occupants perfectly. Relative anonymity in a fairly quiet area on the outskirts of town.

None of the buildings carried much in the way of brazen branding. The majority probably housed accountants, lawyers and companies involved in the technology industry. All possessed sizeable car parks at the front and most were neatly occupied by a myriad of makes and colours of automobile. All, that is, except for this one. The preponderance of large black 4x4s was about the only clue to the occupants of this particular building, but only the well-informed or super-observant would notice and make the connection.

Inside a fairly typical, spacious conference room Brad McCoy, Kimberley Walsh and Ethan Fredericks were seated around a large glass conference table with their chief, Bob Henderson, and one of his assistants.

"There's definitely something going on with those students," Brad was explaining, "but we're not exactly sure what."

He winced as he detected the doubt in his boss' reply. Bob Henderson was a twenty year veteran of the service and had seen a variety of action in those years. He liked results and he liked facts. Theories and feelings didn't cut much ice with him. Tall and slender with closely-cropped hair, his glasses were about the only concession to age that he was prepared to make. "Okay. You want to explain that a little?"

Kimberley Walsh felt it prudent to try and salvage the situation. "We received two blood samples yesterday from the same student, but the results of the analyses were different."

"In what way?" Henderson still wasn't convinced.

Brad decided he might as well bring in the third member of his team, "Well, let Fredericks explain it. It's more his specialism."

Agent Fredericks didn't seem at all fazed by these type of inquisitions. The scientist in him was always keen to simply let the facts speak for themselves. And being a scientist, he'd long since given up any claim to machismo in the testosterone-rich environment of the service. He was more than happy to let his knowledge win the day. "The first sample that we received turned out to be regular blood – group O, Rhesus positive. Nothing particularly remarkable about it. But there was something that I couldn't quite put my finger on that didn't seem right." Unlike Brad, he didn't feel this type of admission to be a sign of weakness.

Kimberley Walsh joined in enthusiastically, "Yes I remember you saying something about haemoglobins, but I thought you'd dismissed it?"

"Well I pretty much did," continued Fredericks, warming to his theme. "You see, the levels of haemoglobins and haematocrits decrease with age. Now you wouldn't expect to see much of a reduction at age 15 and, to be honest, normal analysis results wouldn't get into too much detail. However, the equipment we use can be very precise and it just didn't show any measurable reduction at all – even at the minutest levels.

Even Brad now began to join in. "You said it was like the blood was 'too new'."

Looking vaguely apologetic for such a basic explanation Fredericks continued, "Well that was the only way I could think to describe it. Almost like somebody had taken a 15-year old body and filled it with brand-new blood fresh off of a production line! Of course such an idea is preposterous, so I just dismissed it as the kid being lucky and having good quality blood."

Now even Henderson was showing interest. "So what changed your mind?"

"The second sample," was the matter-of-fact reply.

Brad began to elaborate. "Agent Summers, our man inside the school, got suspicious and sent us a second blood sample from the same subject."

Fredericks continued to explain. "Yeah, and this time the haemoglobin levels were more in keeping with what I'd have expected. So, not only was the blood sample more 'normal' than the first sample, it had also aged 15 years over the course of about five hours!"

Brad now delivered the coup de grace. "And the real clincher was the reason why Summers sent the second sample. He noticed that the kid he had obtained the sample from in the morning no longer had the cut on his hand that he'd given him to get the sample in the first place."

Henderson's assistant who had, up until now kept a poker face as he sized up the field agents and their story, exclaimed, "What, you mean it had healed completely?"

"Or never been there in the first place," countered Brad.

Henderson sat forward in his chair and joined his hands on the table, "So what you're saying is that either the kid has amazingly advanced recuperative properties -"

"That are paradoxically linked to a rapidly ageing blood supply!" interrupted Brad.

"Or they're not the same people," finished Henderson ignoring the interruption.

Henderson's assistant asked the necessary, but unwanted spoiler, "Could Summers have made a mistake? Twins perhaps?"

But Brad was ready for this cheap shot, "No way. The subject has been under observation for a few weeks now and his background check reveals no siblings at all."

Now firmly focussed on what he had just been told, Henderson asked, "So if they're not the same people, one of them must be some sort of imposter."

"Or stand-in?" volunteered Agent Walsh.

Henderson regarded her with his steely gaze, "Either way, I don't like it." He pursed his lips as he chewed-over the evidence then reached a decision, "Right, I need a more detailed analysis of the blood samples."

This time it was Agent Fredericks who was ready with a response, "Already under way, sir." Brad allowed himself a wry smile. His team knew their stuff.

Henderson acknowledged this information with a barely susceptible nod of his head, "And more checks on the kid – family origins, lifestyle, social networks, school environment ..."

The assistant elaborated on the theme: “And perhaps some analysis of some of the other students as well?”

“Yeah, might as well,” Henderson agreed. “But don’t do anything to arouse suspicion.”

Brad’s tone was supremely confident, “OK, sir, we’re on it.” And he ushered his team out of the room before their moment of glory might fade.

As they closed the door Henderson looked at his assistant. “I don’t like this. It all seems so vague, but there’s definitely something not right.”

The assistant nodded sagely, “Certainly seems that way. So let’s wait and see what Agent McCoy and his team uncover for us.”

Henderson breathed deeply and lounged back in his chair, “I guess so, but I’d feel a lot more comfortable if we knew more about the source of our tip-off!”

Chapter 28

Josh felt right at home sitting in front of what looked like a typical gaming console and was totally absorbed by what he was doing. Not for the first time, Kirk Stevens, the head of Space Corps, felt respect for the scientists who had come up with the idea of designing the housings for the alien technology to mimic something so familiar to the very people who would be using it. It made the transition from games to reality so much smoother and faster.

Kirk had been on board the Space Corps project almost since the beginning. A veteran of NASA's space program and ex-military, he seemed an obvious candidate to approach when the space station had been constructed. He exuded authority yet understood the need for a light-touch approach to running the operation. After all, it was basically a giant scientific research project, not a military operation. In his mid-fifties and still as fit and agile as he had been in his mid-twenties, Kirk walked with purpose yet carried his six foot, muscular frame lithely as he approached his deputy.

Francesca Green, or Frankie as she was known to everyone, was monitoring Josh's progress. She wore her habitual look of deep concentration that bordered on a frown as she followed his every move. Her precise and analytical approach perfectly complemented Kirk's more practical and, sometimes unorthodox, style.

Much younger than her boss, thirty-eight-year-old Frankie was a native of Italy and had been recruited when she resigned from the European Space Agency over what she perceived as a lack of imagination in its direction. Educated to the highest levels at both European and American universities, she spoke four languages, all fluently and without a trace of any accent.

"Well how's he doing?" Kirk's question interrupted her concentration. Not for the first time in their professional relationship she hadn't heard him approaching. As always she was secretly impressed with his ability to move without detection. An obvious side-effect of his military past, she assumed.

"Quite impressive," she responded approvingly. "This is his first attempt at the drones but he's picking it up very quickly. The kid's a natural."

"Let's hope so," grinned Kirk. "The principals are only supposed to send us the best pupils." He looked around the room at the numerous consoles. "Even so, we still have more than enough equipment for the personnel we've got," he continued, indicating the many empty consoles. "It's just as well that all of this work is experimental rather than operational. We'd run out of manpower real quick if this ever got serious."

Frankie smiled, "That's one of the beauties of it – all the fun of experimenting and learning without the pressure to produce results."

"Don't you believe it!" Kirk responded with mock admonition. "One of these days the government is going to want to know exactly what we're doing up here and, more importantly, precisely what we've learned. From then it's just a matter of time before they start demanding to know what else we think we can do with all this stuff." His many years of working for government agencies in the past had left him with a healthily jaundiced outlook towards their motives.

"Well until then, let's just carry on training the recruits that we do have and seeing just how far we can push the envelope, shall we?" Frankie suggested with a smile, her tanned face lighting up and her deep brown eyes sparkling as she did so.

Josh's console suddenly beeped to signal the end of the exercise and he sank further back in the reclined chair as he allowed his body to relax.

Frankie moved around to stand in front of him, "Well, Josh, another impressive score. You really do seem to be taking to this very quickly," she informed him.

He was clearly delighted that everything was going so well and tried not to sound immodest when he replied, "Thanks, but it's nothing that new. It's pretty much the same as the PC games that we play at home."

"Except that these aren't games," Kirk was quick to point out.

Josh looked at the stranger. Yet another new face he'd need to get to know. "I'm not sure I follow. I thought this was some kind of flight simulator."

Frankie made the introductions quickly. "Josh, this is Kirk Stevens. He's in overall command of this Space Station."

Josh nodded respectfully, realising that he had been right, this was definitely a face he'd need to get to know.

Kirk continued his explanation, "What you've been operating, Josh, isn't exactly a simulator." He turned to Frankie, "Frankie, why don't you show young Josh what the games look like this far up?"

Frankie shrugged. "OK." She pressed some buttons on Josh's console and some additional viewing screens sprang to life above Josh's. But these revealed some futuristic-looking space fighters, docked with the space station. "What you've been doing is actually flying one of these unmanned spaceships," Frankie informed a somewhat startled Josh.

"We call them Cobras, without wishing to get all dramatic or military about it," Kirk continued. "They're defence drones – unmanned ships with a weapons capability – so we gave them a catchy name. It makes it easier to remember than a bunch of design serial numbers."

"The console you have been using is directly linked to the cockpit and readouts of one of the ships," Frankie explained. "When your simulator was showing you flying, that's precisely what you were doing."

Kirk smiled at a sudden idea. "Wanna see it for real?"

Josh could scarcely believe it. A real spaceship, was he kidding? He nodded enthusiastically, "You bet!"

Kirk looked at Frankie. "Re-run training sequence Alpha 2-40 and keep the exterior monitors on."

Frankie pushed some more buttons and one of the training ships lit up in readiness. "OK, Josh, you're in control again," she informed the student. "Try and concentrate on your screen just like you did earlier. Don't let yourself be distracted by these side monitors yet."

Josh eased back on the miniature joy stick set into his hand-held control panel and the Cobra moved away from its docking port. Trying hard to ensure that he concentrated on his control screen only, Josh slowly navigated the fighter away from the docking area before accelerating away and banking steeply.

"OK, now you're far enough away to risk taking your eyes off the controls," suggested Kirk. "Glance up at the monitors now and pull some sort of manoeuvre."

Josh completed the turn and glanced up at the monitors as he put the fighter into a barrel-roll before looping the loop. He watched with incredulity as his manoeuvres were all played out for real right in front of him. "Wow, way to go! I had no idea that I was actually doing this stuff. It's so cool!"

The exhilaration in his voice was making Frankie nervous. "But don't forget you still need to watch where you're actually going," she reminded him. "Bring it in now and dock again before we deal with any more excitement." She reached across and shut down the exterior monitor screens.

Josh sounded disappointed but replied, "OK, sure thing," before quickly and deftly docking the ship once more and releasing the controls. "But the controls all seem so realistic," he exclaimed. Realising what he had just said he added, "In a 'gaming' sort of way."

Kirk laughed, "I think I know what you mean. They were designed that way to make it easier for you guys to make the transition from one to the other."

"The original design specs that we found were somewhat similar to these controls," Frankie added, "So it only took a bit of adapting and we were there."

"Cool!" exclaimed Josh, all the time thinking, if only I was allowed to tell the guys at school.

Frankie indicated for Josh to walk with her and Kirk as they left the room. Passing through a doorway they entered what looked to Josh like some sort of control or monitoring room. A number of adults were seated at control panels and monitors, giving the impression of an updated version of the 'mission control' rooms that he'd seen on documentaries.

As they entered, one of the adult operators looked up and addressed Kirk. "Sir, you might want to take a look at this."

Kirk walked over to the console. "Why, what is it?"

"We're really not sure," the operator replied, "but one thing that is certain is that it's heading this way and there's more than one of them!"

Chapter 29

Samantha took a deep breath as she contemplated the large wall-mounted computer monitor in front of her. Her fingers were poised over her computer keyboard, yet she still felt it prudent to check one last time before placing the call. "OK, so you guys are certain this is what our equipment is telling us?" she asked Jacob and Callum.

"Yep. And we've checked it a gazillion times," Jacob reassured her.

"There's no alternative solution that can be put forward," Callum gently suggested, understanding why she would want to be absolutely sure.

Samantha agreed, "I realise that, but it's always good to check one last time before you risk making yourself sound like a complete idiot." She sighed, shrugged her shoulders and, sitting up straighter in her chair, clicked her computer to begin the call.

The image of NASA's emblem appeared on the screen as they awaited a response. After only a brief delay it changed to the face of Herbert Kennedy sitting at his desk in his office. "Well, Ms Mitchell, what do you have for me? Can I sleep easy tonight or is an asteroid going to land on my roof?" he asked with just the slightest hint of humour in his voice.

Samantha attempted a half smile then, shrugging her shoulders, gave up any pretence at levity, "I wish I could reassure you completely, sir. The answer to your question is, strictly speaking, 'Yes'. You can sleep soundly because an asteroid isn't going to land on your house," she paused before adding, "Tonight!" She hesitated further, trying to find the right mood and balance to continue.

Kennedy was now frowning and spoke slowly, "Go on," he requested, or was it more of an instruction?

Samantha cleared her throat. "The object appears to be breaking up, sir, as it gets closer to Earth," she began steadily, slowly picking up speed. "However, we think that this is simply a matter of it becoming more identifiable as a collection of smaller objects as it approaches. We now estimate there to be about 20 of them in the original mass, but it is still out by Jupiter so there could be more."

Kennedy remained calm and unexcited as he asked, "So what are they? Meteors? Asteroids?"

"Well, sir, they could be," Samantha answered. "They are certainly displaying all the characteristics of a cluster of rocks and they do seem to be affected by the gravitational pull of other objects such as the planets which they have passed."

She realised that her attempt to downplay their concerns hadn't worked when her boss asked, "Why do I detect a 'but' coming along?"

OK, she decided, time to stop pussy-footing around. She changed her approach and adopted a scientist's tone. "The problem is twofold: their speed and their size. Firstly, they seem to be travelling at a constant speed which is much faster than asteroids normally travel that far out from the sun and, secondly, they are all the same size and mass."

At this last revelation, Kennedy moved forward a little towards his camera. "The same size? Well, that's odd. You wouldn't expect rocks to all be a neat and tidy selection."

"Quite so, sir," Samantha agreed. "Of course, we need to continue our monitoring, but it is our opinion at this time that those objects might, in fact, be manufactured, rather than naturally occurring."

Kennedy raised his eyebrows as he relaxed back into his chair, "Well that's certainly interesting." His eyebrows came back down, "I assume that by 'manufactured' you mean spaceships of some sort?"

Jacob had been bursting to get involved in the discussion all along and now he just couldn't help himself as he blurted out, "Possibly, sir, but we just don't have enough data right now to be able to confirm one way or the other."

Samantha threw him a look and regained control of the conversation, "They're simply too far away to be certain, sir."

"Hmm," Kennedy pondered. "But they're definitely headed for Earth?"

"That certainly seems to be their trajectory at the moment, sir, yes," Samantha concurred.

Kennedy had already made a decision. "Well, I don't think it's worth worrying anyone else about this yet, until we know a bit more about what we're shouting our mouths off about. When do you think you'll be able to confirm your theories?"

Samantha felt a wave of relief. The hardest part was over. "At the rate they're approaching it'll be about another 24 hours, sir, before they come into the range of our high-gain antennae," she replied.

Now it was Callum's turn to interfere. He'd been weighing up this suggestion throughout the entire conversation, "We could ask the Russians or Europeans to see if they've got any new telescopes online that we're not yet aware of."

But Kennedy's reply made him wish he'd listened to Samantha's instruction not to speak unless spoken to. "I hardly think panicking the rest of the world over something that we're not even sure about ourselves would be the best course of action at this point." Samantha looked ruefully at Callum in the same way that a mother might regard a precocious child.

Kennedy continued, "No, I think we keep this under our hats until we know for sure. After all, look at how much courage it took for you to suggest it to me. Imagine what a laughing stock it'll make of this country if we can't prove it immediately." His expression hardened with his resolve as he added, "You're certainly right about one thing, Ms Mitchell, *you will continue monitoring!* Report your findings direct to me, and only to me. Is that clear?"

Samantha knew there was no negotiating on this, "Yes, sir. Crystal!"

"Good," said Kennedy, speeding up their parting. "Then I won't keep you from your work any longer. Let me know the minute you know anything definite." He reached forward and disconnected the call.

Jacob tried to lighten the mood and, at the same time, deflect any reprimands that might be heading his or Callum's way, "Well, that went well!"

Samantha totally ignored his sarcasm and she appeared not to have even heard him. She finished thinking something through and arrived at her own decision, "Let's get Sanjeev on a secure line."

Callum was shocked, "India? I thought Kennedy made it clear that no-one else was to know anything about this."

"You prefer that we flounder about on our own in the dark just long enough for it to be too late to do anything about whatever those objects are?" Samantha hit back.

It wasn't that Callum disapproved of her taking the initiative, it was just that he didn't expect it. It wasn't her usual style. Clearly she was more concerned about this discovery that she had been letting on.

Jacob was already thinking it through, "Sanjeev's people have got access to a particularly powerful array that they use to investigate deep space anomalies. Perhaps if they were to 'coincidentally' run a quick scan over the relevant section of the sky," he mused.

"Who knows what they might detect?" added Callum, falling in with the conspiracy.

"Precisely!" asserted Samantha. "Now where's that line?"

Jacob was already out of his chair heading for his computer terminal, "On it, boss!" he confirmed. Suddenly the excitement was getting very real.

Chapter 30

Chris arrived at the cafeteria table holding his lunch tray in both hands but carefully cradling his computer tablet under his arm. It was clear to any observer which he valued the most, yet he still managed to walk from the servery to the table without spilling anything, the result of plenty of practice. John and Josh were already seated at the table and had begun eating their lunch. Again, to any casual observer it certainly looked as though the student eating and talking with John was his friend. And that's precisely the result that the scientists at Space Corps set out to achieve with all the duplicates.

Not only did he look like Josh, but he walked and talked like him and, to add even more realism, he was also able to eat and drink like any normal human being. Neither John nor Chris were aware that the person in such close proximity to them was anything other than their close friend.

Of course, ensuring that the replicas always behaved with all the same nuances as their subjects often proved somewhat trickier to master and this first encounter was no different from many others that had taken place over the years, in selected schools across the planet.

Chris set his tray down on the table and immediately began to vent his frustration at the education system. "I can't believe that math assignment that we just got set this morning. It's gonna seriously interfere with my social life."

"And what social life would that be, Chris?" said a female voice as Kelly also joined the table. "I had no idea you were the man about town," she added in gentle mockery.

"You'd be surprised what I get up to," Chris replied feebly trying to defend himself.

"Yeah, like spending every waking hour trying to beat Josh's high score," laughed John.

Kelly's frustration and lack of understanding were genuine, "What is it with you guys and those stupid computer games? What's wrong with real life – not exciting enough for you?" she asked.

Josh's duplicate decided now was the right time to enter the conversation and suggested a little stiffly, "They are real life!"

Of course they didn't realise that he actually meant it, yet John still felt the need to clarify things. "He means they depict real life, but through a different means."

"What? Real life through flying spaceships and killing as many aliens as you can?" Kelly asked incredulously.

The duplicate replied matter-of-factly, "Pretty much."

"Yeah, right," was Kelly's somewhat sombre response as she began picking at the salad that she had bought for lunch. After crunching through a couple of pieces of bell pepper she paused and looked meaningfully at Chris, "So is that *all* your social life consists of, Chris?" she asked coyly. "No time for anything else?"

John feigned surprise. "What else is there?"

"Try hanging out with people," was Kelly's immediate put-down.

John looked at Josh's duplicate with a suitably chastised expression on his face. "We hang out," he fired back, trying to sound convincing.

"Yeah, with other gamers," Kelly shot back. She was on a roll and it was clear that she had the better of them. "Let's face it, there's not much conversation."

They had to admit she was right and Josh's duplicate conceded, "She has a point there."

"Music, sport, books, girls," Kelly was continuing.

Perhaps it was time, after all, to try and defend themselves and the duplicate tried, "You're a girl. We hang out with you sometimes."

Joining in the rebuttal John added, "Yeah. Why would we need other girls?"

Kelly looked meaningfully at Chris, "Well, Chris, do you need other girls?"

If Chris didn't get the message John certainly did, "Woah, Chris, is that an invitation?" he asked his friend.

Chris tried to settle things down, "Come on, Kelly, you're like us. One of the guys."

"Well, not quite like us, Chris. There are some differences," laughed John.

Now it was the duplicate's turn to play ally, but he wasn't quite as good at it as John. "Yeah, she's not as single-minded or focussed on the game," he offered.

John grimaced, "Not quite what I had in mind."

He let the rest of his sentence trail off as Josh's duplicate changed the direction of the conversation totally. "She's also able to pay more attention in class."

Now John just shrugged, "Again, not what I was thinking of."

Chris picked-up on the duplicate's last submission, "Hold on a minute. What do you mean 'able to pay attention in class'? What about you this morning in physics?" he countered.

Picking up the theme, Kelly asked, with perhaps a small hint of admiration, "Yeah, Josh. Where did that come from?"

"Huh? I'm not following. What did I do?" the duplicate asked with genuine puzzlement.

"That business about astronomical units," Chris answered. "How did you know what they were?" he almost sneered.

John joined in, "More to the point, how did you know what the value was for each planet?" he asked genuinely baffled.

Josh's duplicate completely missed their point, "It's just the distance to the sun," he replied blithely.

"Hmm. I'd vaguely heard of them before, but you knew the value for each planet in the solar system!" Kelly pointed out incredulously. "I'm not sure if that proves my point about you guys needing to get out more or John's point about paying attention in class."

Chris couldn't resist a jibe, "Well he is a *gifted and talented* student, remember."

Josh's duplicate laughed hollowly, "Ha, ha. Here we go again."

Kelly tried to defuse the situation, "Well, I thought it was impressive." She looked at Chris coyly. "Shame you can't all impress me with your knowledge. I guess I'll have to look for other things."

"But you're one of the guys, Kelly," responded John sarcastically.

"Yeah, one of the guys," she agreed ruefully. "Well, I can't sit here being 'one of the guys' all lunchtime: eating, playing computer games and farting like real men. I've got some stuff to see to. I'll catch up with you later." She looked deliberately at Chris. "Bye, Chris," she cooed before standing and walking out.

John picked up on this, "Am I detecting an interest there?"

“Huh? Maybe. I dunno,” replied Chris, uncertain whether to be pleased or embarrassed by the attention.

“Well it certainly seemed that way to me,” pressed John. “What did you think, Josh?”

The duplicate was a little confused, “Huh?”

“About there being some ‘interest’ going on between Kelly and Chris,” John explained long-sufferingly.

Josh’s duplicate decided that agreement was probably in order, “Oh, yeah. Certainly looked like it to me.”

“Yeah, right,” begrudged Chris, before deciding that perhaps it wouldn’t be such a bad thing after all. “Still, who knows, if she’s lucky ...” He left the sentiment unfinished as he powered up his tablet, “In the meantime, though, let’s see if we can get these scores up.”

As all three of them prepared to resume their gaming John returned one last time to the fun of gently baiting Josh. “I’m still trying to get over Josh’s sudden enthusiasm for knowledge. Do you think it’s catching?”

The duplicate looked blank, somewhat unsure how to respond, but Chris experienced no such uncertainty. “Hope not!”

Chapter 31

Mario Silvester, deputy administrator of the United States Antarctic Program, was sitting back in his chair trying to absorb the report that he was receiving from the Antarctic base. The 45 year old scratched his head through his black curly hair, then stroked his moustache as Alex Roughedge filled him in from thousands of miles and two continents away.

"Well, sir, you are not going to believe what our guys have found," Alex was saying. The excitement in his voice was almost palpable across the airwaves.

Mario looked at the image of his subordinate on the computer screen and appeared almost bored as he replied, "I guess you're going to tell me anyway."

If the tedium in Mario's response had got through, Alex didn't let it either show in his mannerisms or affect what he had to say. "Oh yes, but all in good time. Two members of our advance team – James Rock and Luke Richards – have been exploring a rarely visited area called Marie Byrd Land, about 500 miles west of the South Pole itself."

"So what is so special about this area?" Mario almost had to stifle a yawn.

"Before today, only that it is one of the upland areas, about two and a half to six and a half thousand feet above sea level," answered Alex. He continued with the mixed history and geology lesson, "Discovered in 1929 but not mapped or surveyed until 1935. Being so close to the actual pole means that it's very cold all year round. The thickness of the ice is about 4,000 feet on average." Then came the bombshell, "So when Rock and Richards arrived there yesterday morning and discovered that all the ice had gone, we were somewhat alarmed!"

Suddenly he had Mario's undivided attention. "What do you mean, all of the ice had gone? Gone where?" he almost barked.

Alex smiled almost as if he was enjoying startling his boss, "That's the point, sir, we don't know. It had simply melted – although the temperature when the guys got there was still below freezing."

"Had there been any recent temperature surges that would explain this?" Mario asked, resuming a business-like and scientific approach to the matter.

"Not particularly," Alex shrugged. "And the fact that it is inland and not sitting on the ocean itself means that it couldn't have simply fallen into the sea." He thought he'd add that last bit just in case the office-bound Administrator and his assistants needed help in their warm, cosy offices to appreciate the local topography.

"So where did it go?" Mario asked point-blank.

Alex wasn't entirely certain whether Mario actually expected him to be able to give a definitive answer. "We're still unsure. However, while they were exploring the bare rock faces they came across something much more mysterious." Again a slight pause for effect, "Sealed caves!"

"What?" Mario exclaimed leaning so far towards his computer screen that Alex thought there was every possibility he would actually head-butt it.

Alex elaborated calmly, "Caves that were deliberately sealed shut in the rocks that had been beneath the ice. And, get this, they weren't sealed with other rocks." Time for the third jolt he thought, "They'd been sealed with precisely engineered doors made out of some sort of metal!"

Mario's tone assumed a blend somewhere between a lawyer cross-examining a doubtful witness and a teacher addressing a juvenile miscreant, "You mean to tell me that thousands of feet underneath permanent ice sheets, someone has been installing metallic doors to seal off caves?"

Alex decided to adopt a slightly obtuse response, "Well, not quite, sir. From the style and engineering that we've so far discovered it doesn't look as though these were done recently."

"What? Well how can that be?" asked Mario, appearing to get slightly frustrated. "They couldn't have been sealed before the ice formed – that was millions of years ago."

Continuing to be obtuse Alex responded, "Between two and five million years ago, if we allow for the various melting periods."

"Either way, human beings hadn't evolved then, so the doors have to have been installed much more recently," countered Mario, once more the calculating scientist.

Now it was Alex's turn to address a child. "Sir, to have tunnelled and installed these types of doors would have been impossible to do without detection and I'm no engineer, but I'm certainly not aware of the technology required to manufacture them even now, let alone in the past."

Enough of these games. Mario decided to cut straight to the chase, "So, what? You're saying they weren't made on Earth?" he asked somewhat incredulously.

"It's at least a possibility sir," Alex replied, almost seeming oblivious to the impact of what he was saying.

Mario chuckled a little, "Oh come on, Alex. You're going to need more evidence than a bunch of strange doors," he teased.

"I realise that, sir, which is why I think you should take a look at these images." Now for the *piece de resistance* thought Alex, "When Rock and Richards managed to gain entrance into the cave things got even weirder."

"In what way?" asked Mario, clearly intrigued. There had surely been enough surprises in this conversation already.

"They found this, sir," replied Alex with just the slightest of flourishes in his voice as he tapped his keyboard. The picture on Mario's computer changed to the image of a vast hangar-like cave containing a number of spaceships of varying sizes, all apparently stored as if awaiting re-use.

Mario was clearly stunned, "Wow. I see what you mean now," he almost whistled. "There's clearly no way that they were made recently and hidden down there."

As if to reinforce the point, Alex added, "And I doubt if our prehistoric ancestors were stockpiling them either."

Mario chuckled at Alex's attempt at humour. "OK. Well, we've got to get a grip on this before it leaks out," he said, taking charge of the situation for the first time since the Skype conversation began. "I presume your end is all locked down?" he asked meaningfully.

"Absolutely watertight, sir," replied Alex confirming that they were both on the same hymn sheet now.

"Good. Now I'm going to have to involve some other agencies. NASA for one and the military for another, much as I don't want to," Mario continued, mentally reviewing his next course of action.

"You know what the problem will be once the military get involved don't you?" asked Alex, almost rhetorically. The last thing any of the scientists wanted was a major military takeover.

Mario pondered his options, "Hmm. I'll alert the State Department first. Since Antarctica is international territory we'll need their involvement before we can start sending any military presence down there anyway. In the meantime, make sure you keep everything under wraps. What is the situation at the site?"

Alex reassured him as best he could, "I've still only got Rock and Richards out there at the moment. A nasty storm blew up and has isolated them. They're still in radio contact and seem to be doing OK. I was going to send a relief team as soon as the weather allows."

"OK, understood and approved," Mario responded, the last bit just to emphasise that he was in overall command. "Just make sure that the only people to know anything about this are essential personnel," he warned.

"Absolutely," Alex agreed. "Perhaps you could let me know how you get on with the State Department?"

"I sure will," Mario reassured him and then terminated the link.

He sat pondering the information for a few minutes, stroking his moustache all the time. Then, apparently having reached a decision, he accessed another messaging program on his computer and spoke very matter-of-factly. "They've found the caves."

Instantly a deep voice replied from the computer speaker. "Understood. You know what to do."

Chapter 32

Lunch over, Josh's friends and his duplicate were collecting their things from their lockers. As always the din of numerous metal doors being slammed into metal frames created a wall of noise, almost as if a demonic percussionist was determined to produce the very antithesis of music.

Against this background of aural assault Josh's duplicate asked, "OK, what's next? Geography?"

With the semester so new nobody thought it odd that *Josh* didn't remember. "Yes, but you don't have to sound so cheerful about it," suggested Chris.

John picked up his buddy's beef, "That's twice today, Josh. First volunteering information this morning in physics and now displaying enthusiasm for geography. You're like a new man!"

At that very moment Mr Jacks walked around the corner and, unwittingly diverting a potentially awkward conversation between the friends, addressed who he took to be Josh. "Ah, Josh, I've been hoping I'd bump into you. May I have a word?"

"Of course, sir," the duplicate replied quite naturally. He turned to his friends. "Guys, I'll catch you up."

Chris smiled back blandly, "We don't doubt it!" he said with not a little sarcasm. Thinking themselves highly amusing he and John walked off laughing. Mr Jacks gave a puzzled look.

"Oh don't mind them, sir," explained the duplicate. "They're just having a laugh at my expense." Then, smiling himself, he added, "I think maybe they feel threatened."

Mr Jacks was momentarily unsure how to react, "Oh?"

"Oh, not in any physical sense," the duplicate quickly reassured him. "Just my brains, if you see what I mean."

"Not really," Mr Jacks replied truthfully and swiftly changed the subject, "Anyway, I wanted to speak to you about Ryan Samuels in 10th grade. You know him, I believe?" he asked.

The duplicate's memory banks kicked in with the necessary answer, "Yes, sir, I know him," and he added for good measure, "But I've only just got to know him."

"I see," ventured Mr Jacks a little timorously. "Would you know him well enough to know if he seemed to be behaving strangely?" he continued.

Josh's duplicate replied honestly and without any hesitation, "I doubt it. We only started being friendly at the end of the last semester."

Mr Jacks seemed slightly disappointed, "OK," then tried a different approach. Lowering his voice slightly he continued very seriously, "Now I want you to keep this to yourself. It may be nothing, but I'm a little concerned about him. Obviously I've only just joined the school so I don't know him very well at all, but he's crossed my path a few times and his behaviour seems a little erratic."

The duplicate's programming was working overtime, but remained super-efficient. "Have you mentioned it to the principal, sir? Or perhaps his parents? What about his closer friends?"

"Woah, steady boy. Let's not start running away with ourselves," protested Mr Jacks, raising both hands slightly in a calming gesture. Clearly he didn't like the direction the conversation was now taking. "I'm not sure if there is anything wrong here," he admitted, "So I thought I'd try approaching his friend first. I guess I'd overestimated the friendship between the two of you." He paused for a moment before continuing, "but when he was taken ill yesterday I noticed you followed us to the medical room. I'd assumed that was because you were good friends."

"Not particularly, sir," replied the duplicate, as he finished selecting books from his locker.

Clearly Mr Jacks felt he'd completely misread the situation. "OK. Sorry to have bothered you with this."

The duplicate turned to acknowledge the apparent end of the conversation and, as he did so, caught his finger on the thin edge of the metal casing. He instinctively pulled it away sharply, thereby exacerbating the problem, "Ow!" he muttered in surprise and looked down to see blood oozing from a small cut. Just like a human would do, he immediately put his finger in his mouth and sucked at the cut.

Mr Jacks instinctively pulled a tissue out of his pocket and offered it to the duplicate, "Here, use this," he suggested.

'Josh' took the tissue gratefully and wrapped it tightly around his injured digit for a few seconds before removing it to examine the tiny cut. "I'm alright. It's just a nick," he explained, happy to see that the blood was only slowly seeping out now. "Well, I'd better be getting over to my geography class sir if there's nothing further." He dropped the tissue into a waste bin as he spoke.

"Of course," replied Mr Jacks, "Thanks for your time." He watched absent-mindedly as the duplicate walked off. Then suddenly he appeared to get an idea. He walked over to the waste bin and, pausing briefly, reached in to retrieve the tissue.

Chapter 33

In the main control room at Space Corps, Jim Scott, one of the duty operators, was discussing their recent discovery with Kirk. “So what have you found out?” Kirk asked as they huddled over Scott’s computer monitor.

“Well, sir, we’ve been tracking these anomalies in the area of Jupiter for a few days now,” the operator explained. “At first they were reading like a bunch of asteroids, or even comet debris, but further analysis has shown them to be much too rigid in their movement to be simply natural phenomena. As they get closer to us we’re able to see that there are many more objects than we previously suspected.”

“Well, how fast are they travelling?” the commander asked.

“That’s the odd thing,” Scott replied. “They’re travelling way faster than anything we’ve ever tracked before. The typical speed of asteroids and comets that far out from the sun is somewhere in the region of 500 miles per second, but these things are travelling in excess of 2,000 miles per second!”

Kirk was suddenly very impressed, “Wow, that’s fast!”

"Yeah," agreed the operator, "But the really weird bit is that they appear to be slowing down as they get nearer to the sun, rather than speeding up."

"Well that doesn't make sense," mused Kirk before adding, "If they're natural objects!"

"Precisely!" Scott said emphatically. "Their speed a few days ago was certainly greater than it is at the moment and, if we project the rate of deceleration backwards, they could have been travelling at twice their current speed only two weeks ago."

"So based on their current deceleration rate, how long before they cross Earth's solar orbit?" Kirk asked.

Scott shrugged slightly, "About two days."

"And how close will they pass?" Kirk's mind was already making rapid calculations and identifying potential scenarios.

Scott tilted his head momentarily to one side in that habit that people have when they're not really certain about something, "Difficult to tell at this stage. It's too early to tell what sort of line of trajectory they're coming in at, but we'll certainly be in the same orbital sector."

Kirk was hoping to dismiss one of the scenarios he'd imagined. "Will the Earth's regular observatories have spotted them yet?"

But his subordinate's response didn't help. "I suspect so, but they'll be a little behind us in their calculations." He paused for a moment and then added as a throw-away line, "Unless they've got access to some new gear that we don't know about."

Chapter 34

The nondescript black van was once again parked across the street from Littrow High School. Inside Agent Fredericks had just finished his analysis.

“So what do you reckon?” asked Agent Walsh, eager to know his findings.

“Same as the other day,” he replied somewhat ruefully. “Brand new blood, but a different group this time. Must be from a different subject,” he continued, managing to regain his detached scientific composure.

Brad immediately took command and began issuing orders. This thing had gone on long enough and he was now determined to go on the attack, “OK. I want this new subject monitored 24 hours a day. I want to know everything there is to know about him, right down to the smallest detail. What makes him so special? What’s his family story? Has he anything in common with the other kid? Has he got a girlfriend? What are his hobbies? In short I need to know him better than his own parents know him. Better than he knows himself.” He paused for effect. “And get another blood sample from him to see if it suddenly ages like the last kid,” he added emphatically.

Kimberley Walsh recognised the tone in his voice and knew that nothing was up for debate, "Yes, sir, we're on it!" she confirmed.

Chapter 35

Another day at school was drawing to a close as the 9th graders came tumbling out of their last lesson. Hurriedly gathering up their belongings the whole class piled out of the classroom as if the bell was a starting pistol at the beginning of a sprint race. As usual, although Josh's friends were in the thick of the melee, they didn't seem to feel the need to lead the charge and were happy to let the sports jocks get out first. Carefully, but nonchalantly, judging their place in the throng they headed for the corridor.

"Well, at least no more outbursts of knowledge in that class, Einstein," John humorously ribbed Josh's duplicate, still totally unaware that he was addressing what was essentially a machine.

Chris joined in, "I guess too much knowledge can be tiring. Those earlier moments of genius must have left you worn out."

Once again it was Kelly who came to 'Josh's' defence, "Oh come on guys. Can't Josh show the occasional hint of intelligence?" she asked exasperatedly, before deftly changing to humour. "After all it is only occasional!"

All four of them laughed, including the duplicate. "Hey, what can I say? I guess you must be right, but just wait until tomorrow. I'll be raring to go again!" he said.

"Yeah, right," grumbled Chris. Suddenly serious he added, "Only don't go doing it too often, Josh – nobody likes a smart ass."

Kelly picked up on something else in Chris' voice, "Woah. Are you feeling threatened?"

"No way," he replied, perhaps a little too defensively. "It's just that I don't want Josh taking his mind off the really important things in life."

John backed his friend up, "Absolutely. Nothing must stand in the way of the game!"

Now it was Kelly's turn to be sarcastic, "Oh yes, the game. How could I have forgotten?" But she then surprised them all, "You know I've started to improve my own standings. Maybe you could teach me some tricks, Chris?"

A little surprised by the revelation, Chris was a little uncertain how to play this. He decided caution would be the best policy and replied slowly, "Sure, if you want me to."

"Hey, I thought I said *nothing* must stand in the way," John objected indignantly.

"I've no idea what you're insinuating," Kelly responded coquettishly. "I just want to be able to compete with you guys."

"So why don't you ask Josh to help you? He's the best," asked John, challenging her selection.

Chris decided that he needed to defend his own reputation, "Not for much longer. When I last logged on his lead was shortening."

By now they were nearing their lockers. "What? Don't tell me you're losing your touch, Josh?" exclaimed John. "Perhaps you are spending too much time concentrating on school work after all."

"So Chris would be the best person to teach me," Kelly confirmed triumphantly.

"Absolutely," confirmed Chris. "Call round tonight and we'll get started."

As they passed the administration offices Josh's duplicate appeared slightly distracted, "Look, guys, I've got something I need to do. You go and catch the bus. I'll walk."

This surprised them all. "Huh? Well that's a first," declared John.

"Yeah, you never walk anywhere," agreed Chris. "This *gifted and talented* stuff is really getting to you."

With his mind still apparently on something else the duplicate simply replied, "Maybe. I'll see you all tomorrow." He smiled at his friends briefly and then walked off in the direction of the offices.

The remaining three continued to walk towards the school exit, each casting just a brief glance back at the direction Josh had gone. "Come on then, if we don't hurry up we'll be walking as well," chided Kelly, picking up the pace. Like most of the students, she was only too aware that the bus wouldn't wait for long.

They all sped up, heading for the school buses and it was John who suddenly blurted out what they all were perhaps thinking. "Do you think Josh is alright? I mean he certainly seemed a bit different today."

Even Kelly was forced to agree slightly, "He does seem to have gotten a bit more serious since the *gifted and talented* stuff was announced."

Chris also agreed, but with less tact. "He's always had a stiff side lurking below the surface. He covers it up well because he's such a good gamer, but maybe that's why he's so good at games."

John concurred, "Yeah, the logical, studious type. Analysing the best strategies."

Kelly returned to John's initial question, "I know what you mean. It was almost like he was hiding something today. He didn't quite seem to be himself."

John simply shrugged. "Maybe he's just not well?"

"Could be," Chris agreed adding, "But if so, then there's never been a better time to overtake his score." He looked deliberately at Kelly, a mischievous grin forming on his face, "You stick with me, Kelly, and I'll show you how we beat the champion." All three friends laughed as they reached the bus with only minutes to spare.

Meanwhile, back in the school no-one was around to see Josh's duplicate enter one of the janitor's store rooms. Of course if they had seen it they might well have wondered why he was going in there and, possibly, have even challenged him. After all it was off limits to students.

It wasn't a particularly big room and the casual observer might also have wondered after a while why he hadn't come back out. Of course, if their curiosity had then driven them to open the door themselves, they would have been somewhat dumbfounded to find that the duplicate wasn't inside after all. But then they probably wouldn't notice the discreet button that resembled a light switch hidden at the back of one of the shelves either!

Chapter 36

As James and Luke explored the massive cave hangar, they continued to shout their findings, and their theories, across to each other. Their voices echoing in the hollow, cavernous interior only served to emphasise the bizarre situation in which they found themselves. Outside the cave, they knew the temperature to be below freezing and that a katabatic wind was gusting at about 30 miles per hour driving snow horizontally across the plain. However, inside the hangar, although it was far from idyllic, there was, of course, a complete absence of wind and snow and the temperature was above freezing. In fact they couldn't be absolutely certain that the temperature wasn't actually rising slowly.

"OK, I've counted 30 of these things. What about you?" called James, indicating the strange craft that occupied the interior. There were a large variety of styles. Some were short and squat, others long and sleek. Some were large enough for about a dozen men, some looked like single-seaters.

"Same here," Luke hollered back from the other side, his voice echoing off the walls and ceiling high up above them. "So there's at least 60 and probably more like 100 when they're all accounted for," he added, before adopting a quieter, more serious tone, "I guess we don't really need to call them 'things' either."

"No you're right," agreed James almost reluctantly. He looked around once more at the variety of models, yet they all seemed to belong to one type of vehicle. "It looks pretty obvious that they're some sort of airplane. I guess I was just trying to delay the inevitable," he admitted.

"Yeah, airplanes," Luke concurred slightly reluctantly. He paused briefly before raising his voice in objection, "Or spaceships!"

"Hey we don't know that," countered James, a little alarmed at such a radical suggestion.

"True," Luke admitted. "But consider the facts," he paused to allow James time to do just that. "Over 100 of these things stored and hidden down here, millions of years ago before the ice formed on top of the caves. How did they even get made, let alone how did they get here? I'm guessing that it's a pretty safe bet that they weren't made on Earth. In which case they must be some kind of spaceship," he concluded triumphantly, but in a matter-of-fact way.

"OK, so let's assume you're right," conceded James. "That raises a whole stack of other questions. Who built them? Who put them here? Why and when did they put them here? And why are they still here?"

"Maybe whoever put them here no longer needs them, or is no longer around to need them."

James looked at Luke quizzically. "Well, you did say they'd have had to be put here millions of years ago. Who's to say the owners aren't now extinct?" suggested Luke.

"Maybe. Or maybe they've been waiting for the ice to melt so they can get to them," countered James.

Luke was walking amongst the ships, occasionally reaching out to touch them and even running his gloved hand along the surface of one or two. "But why leave them here all mothballed in the first place? I mean the ice would have been forming over time, not instantly. So it's not as if they were suddenly caught out," he said.

"We've no way of knowing, of course. But maybe they were left here in some sort of storage," James paused to try and gauge Luke's reaction. "You know, a kind of 'sleeper' base that could be reactivated in the future."

"Hey, it could be anything," conceded Luke. "All we know is that we've got a hangar full of spaceships that have probably been buried here for two million years." He stared admiringly and not a little awestruck at the craft.

While he had been attempting to damp down what he considered to be his partner's excitable imagination James had continued examining his side of the cave and had now found another doorway. He walked through and called back to Luke, "No, that's not all we've got. Check this out."

Luke walked briskly across to where James now was and joined him in what they took to be some sort of control centre. "OK, so I guess this proves we're not just looking at some sort of inter-stellar storage facility," he suggested deadpan.

James stated the obvious, "This looks like some kind of control room." He paused to formulate his idea further, "Far too elaborate, I would have thought, just to oversee the storage of all those ships."

"And it looks like this place has even more to it than at first meets the eye," added Luke indicating a number of other passageways leading off the room.

James put his hands on his hips and declared, "It's gonna take a lot more than the two of us to check it all out."

"Yeah. When do you reckon the back-up team will get here?" wondered Luke. He'd had enough surprises for one day and would be quite happy for a relief to take over.

"They're gonna have to wait until that storm dies down before they can get anyone out here. But I bet the second it does they'll fill every available helicopter and head right out here with everything they've got," James suggested.

"Unless of course they mean to keep it a secret," countered Luke, adding, "In which case Alex'll only send a small team and probably lead it himself."

"Well let's just hope the storm dies down soon, before anything else happens," James responded. He had just verbalised what both men were thinking when, as if on cue, some of the control centre equipment suddenly sprang to life. Lights started to flicker, displays began to glow and even sounds began to emanate from some of the equipment. The two men looked at each other in stunned silence for a moment.

Luke was the first to speak. "Do me a favour," he pleaded. "Just keep any other thoughts to yourself. Because if you don't there's gonna be little green men running around down here before we know what's happening!"

Chapter 37

Callum nodded approvingly at what the man on his computer screen was saying to him. A young, tousle-haired Indian was looking at him with an eager, yet business-like, look on his face. "That's correct. That data fits in with ours. What about speed?" asked Callum.

"Well, whatever they are they appear to be decelerating," Sanjeev informed him.

Callum was a little surprised to hear this. "Are you sure? Our data indicated that they were travelling at a hell of a speed, but we didn't detect any slowing down."

Sanjeev nodded, "At that distance it's barely noticeable, but unless they've been grabbed by Jupiter's orbit, which doesn't seem likely, then something is causing a fraction of a second's delay in our reception of the data if we were to assume that the speed was constant."

"So if you factor in a speed reduction it addresses that anomaly?" Callum speculated.

"Exactly!" Sanjeev confirmed with an earnest smile on his lips.

"Is there any way of measuring the rate of deceleration?" Callum asked. He was sure he already knew the answer but needed to hear it confirmed.

Sanjeev did just that, "I'm afraid not. We're lucky to be detecting it at all."

"Fair enough," Callum conceded, "But that still leaves the puzzle of how or why they're actually slowing."

Sanjeev agreed with his western colleague. "Absolutely." Now that the dry facts were out of the way, he became quite animated as they moved into speculation. "Clearly they should be accelerating as they get closer to the sun. Maybe it's some sort of anomaly caused by the gravitational pull of Jupiter's moons." He thought for a moment then dismissed his idea without too much reluctance, "But I doubt it."

Callum needed to get these results to Samantha fast so decided not to get too deeply involved in theorising at this point, "OK. Well let me know if anything else turns up. We'll obviously continue monitoring it from here." He was about to sign off when he thought he'd better remind Sanjeev of the confidentiality of their discussion. "Oh, and Sanjeev, don't forget this is just between ourselves. We've gone out on a limb to bring you in on this, just keep it quiet. OK?"

The Indian nodded knowingly, "Of course. We're happy to help and, I must admit, a little intrigued by what this could be. I'll keep in touch." He hit the escape key on his computer and the image of Callum disappeared. He paused briefly and then turned to look back over his shoulder. "Well, it's certainly a mystery, but I wonder why they're so concerned?" he spoke towards the shadow concealed behind him.

Rashid Khan stood up and moved around to face Sanjeev. "Maybe there's more to this than meets the eye." He stroked his goatee and added, "Thank you for sharing it with me. I'll pass it on."

Sanjeev acknowledged the gratitude. "Always pleased to help my old colleagues at Space Corps."

Chapter 38

A bleary-eyed Josh walked into the kitchen for breakfast. His mother, father and younger sister, Megan, were already sitting at the large pine table consuming various items of food. The sun shone brightly through the large window and cast sunbeams across the assorted boxes of cereals, plates of toast and various condiments that were haphazardly arranged on the table. It was for precisely this reason that his parents had decided many years ago to locate the furniture in that particular corner of the room facing the doorway through which he now entered. "Morning, all," he said with a wide yawn.

"About time, sleepy head," his mother responded. "I began wondering whether you were going to make it to school today?" In her early 40s, his mother was typical of so many mothers of her generation. Average height, slim and neatly coiffed she had happily given up her career 16 years ago to have Josh and then his younger sister. For the last five years or so she had successfully juggled a part-time office job with running a home, of which she was quietly proud.

Her attempt at mild, early morning humour elicited a long-suffering laugh from Josh, "Ha, ha. Can't a guy get some sleep anymore?"

“Of course,” his mother granted, before adding, “But eleven hours? That’s very unlike you.”

His sister now saw fit to wade in in that way that siblings do when they feel an opportunity to score a few cheap points. “Yeah, you didn’t even spend any time on that game last night.”

Josh’s father barely looked up to register his surprise, “Well, that’s a first!” Slightly older than Josh’s mother, he rarely got involved in the day-to-day issues of the household. Not that he wasn’t interested, it was just that he spent so much of his time working that he happily abdicated any family organisational tasks to his wife. An arrangement that suited everyone comfortably since he would be hard pressed to identify any school holidays and, in all reality, even school start and finishing times were probably a mystery to him.

“Hey, sorry if I was tired,” Josh responded sarcastically.

“Maybe you’re working too hard,” his mother suggested helpfully, as she added some milk to her coffee.

“Now that *would* be a first,” his father added emphatically. This time he did look up and he was so pleased with his humorous contribution that he almost choked on his toast. Megan felt guilty laughing at her dad’s joke while he was still coughing, but he signalled that he was fine and gulped down some more coffee to prove it.

Josh’s response to all this good-natured abuse was to affect mock superiority as he replied, “Well they do expect more from us *gifted and talented* students.”

Seizing on the opportunity, his mother restored a little order to the conversation, “Yes, Principal McGregor did say in his letter that you’d be required to do additional lessons and spend longer at school.” She looked at Josh with slight concern in her eyes, “But are you coping with it alright?”

“Yeah, it’s no big deal,” Josh shrugged. “Just takes a bit of getting used to,” he added, smiling inwardly at the understatement.

“What kinds of things are they teaching you?” asked his father with genuine interest.

Josh hesitated briefly before attempting to deflect the question, “Oh, this and that.”

“Like what?” his mother insisted, never for one moment suspecting the revelations that this innocent question would reveal if Josh answered truthfully.

Josh continued his strategy of deflection. “Mom, you wouldn’t believe me if I told you.”

She feigned hurt as she responded sarcastically, “Or understand, I’ll bet.”

Thinking that he may have got away with it Josh muttered quietly, “Probably.”

But his mother had merely adopted that universal motherly tactic of changing her approach, “Well what about your friends? What do they think about it?” she asked innocently.

Josh felt more able to handle this avenue of questioning, “I dunno really,” he replied truthfully. “I’m not sure they even think about it. Apart from to have a laugh at my expense.”

Given the grilling that he was getting, good-natured though it was, Josh should have been relieved to hear his sister change the subject. “Oh, that reminds me, Chris called you last night at about nine o’clock.” But his heart sank when she added, “But I told him you were in bed.”

“Oh great,” he replied. “I’m never gonna hear the last of that. In bed by 9pm!”

“Well, you were in bed,” protested Megan.

“Yeah I know,” Josh sighed before asking, “Did he say what he wanted?”

"Something about that stupid game that you and he are always playing," Megan replied disinterestedly. "I think he said that Kelly was helping him."

Josh was clearly surprised, "Kelly helping him? More like Kelly trying to learn from him."

"Who's Kelly?" their mother asked innocently. She wasn't particularly interested but thought that she'd ask just to help defuse the slight tension between her offspring.

"Just a girl from school," Josh replied, adding for good measure, "I don't think you know her."

The realisation suddenly hit Megan and she blurted out with girlish enthusiasm at potential gossip, "Kelly? Kelly Malcolm? Are she and Chris an item?"

"How should I know?" Josh answered with corresponding boyish moodiness. "She's just a girl in our class who started hanging around with us a bit."

Megan persevered, "So now we know why." She thought for a moment and then threw in a barb, "But what does she see in you nerds? She's a bit of a babe."

"Well, maybe there's hope for you too son!" added their father, again quite pleased with his humour. He was on form today! Josh's mother and sister joined in his laughter.

"Ha, ha everyone," Josh responded. "Now if you've finished trying to second guess our lives, I need to get to school and try to repair any reputation that I might have left."

Even that appeal for some sort of filial sympathy was turned against him as Megan threw back, "Some hope, you're a nerd!" The two of them immediately began a friendly fight across the table as Josh grabbed some of her toast, got up from the table and left the room, laughing at his breakfast-thieving prowess.

Chapter 39

The various operatives sitting at the numerous computer screens throughout Space Corps' control centre couldn't help but try to listen in on the huddled conversation taking place around Jim Scott's terminal. They were all aware that something unusual was taking shape and that no-one really knew what it was, so their natural curiosity was making them all intrigued. Kirk Stevens had given them all a situation report when the news first broke and they were all totally dedicated to their particular responsibilities, yet they all knew that Jim had been tasked with sourcing more information from Earth. Now that he had received an update they were all eager to learn what Kirk and Frankie would make of it.

The three people poring over the data weren't particularly speaking in hushed tones, yet the gravity of their discussion seemed to be lowering the volume just enough to make the others wonder about the content. They all knew that Kirk would tell them everything pertinent when he was ready, but for now they'd try and formulate their own private theories as much as their duties would allow.

"We've fed the data from India that Principal Khan got hold of into our system and it certainly makes for some interesting results," Frankie was saying.

"Yes, I guess that perhaps some of the Earth's agencies have some technology that we're not aware of after all," Kirk responded with a pointed, but good-natured, jibe at Jim Scott.

The operative grimaced and acknowledged the light-hearted rebuke, "Yes, sir." He continued, "Using their additional findings," but couldn't resist a little defensive brickbat of his own, "And our generally more advanced equipment, we've now got a much better idea of what exactly is heading this way."

"It's definitely slowing and the rate of deceleration seems to indicate Earth as its destination," Frankie informed Kirk.

"Hmm, but we still don't know what it is, do we?" asked the commander very seriously. These sort of situations always brought out the military training in the man, a characteristic that Frankie found helpful and reassuring.

"No," she answered simply. There was no point in embellishing the response. The simple facts were that they did not know what the objects were, and trying to guess at this point would be precisely that – just guessing. Frankie knew that Kirk liked facts, not guesses.

"Is there any update of the number of objects involved?" the commander asked.

This time it was Jim Scott who supplied the answer, "Not much, sir. We still estimate there to be in excess of twenty, but it's still too far away for a precise answer."

"What about time? Do we have an expected time of arrival?" Kirk asked his two subordinates. He was beginning to wish someone would guess after all. At least they'd give the impression of knowing something.

"Again not precise," said Frankie. Kirk's hopes were almost completely dashed until she added, "but it should be some time tomorrow." At last something to actually pin some action to.

Kirk decided that was enough data interpretation. Time now to change their approach, "OK. Well, I think it's fair to assume that these objects are not naturally occurring, which raises a number of crucial questions that need addressing immediately." He began to rattle off the priorities as he saw them, "One – who, or what, are we dealing with? Two – Are they friendly? Three – What do they want? And four – Are we in a position to stop them if we need to?" Before anyone could begin to start hypothesising again he continued, "I want all the resources at our disposal brought to bear on these questions and I want answers as fast as possible. We may only have a few hours left to prevent a disaster."

"What about the usual space agencies? They must also be making plans?" asked Frankie trying to suggest that there might be others who could shoulder some of the responsibility in addition to Space Corps.

"I'm aware of that," Kirk assured her. "For the time being I think it best if our existence remains secret for as long as possible. If this all proves to be nothing I don't want to have blown our cover for nothing, but if things get nasty then we'll have to reconsider." He paused to add weight to his words. "I'm guessing that those who are aware of our existence will want to avoid unnecessary publicity if at all possible. So until told otherwise I want everyone trying to come up with answers and everything that we have to remain top secret!"

Both subordinates nodded their understanding and Jim Scott began accessing more of their specialist equipment via his console in the hopes of uncovering more information. Frankie left the control room and returned to her office, ostensibly to access more data. On reaching her desk she activated a communication program on her computer and typed a brief and to-the-point message which read, “We need to talk.”

Chapter 40

As the school bus trundled down the road it was, as every day, full of students of all ages engaging in numerous conversations at varying levels of volume. Josh and his friends were sitting near the back and, for such an early part of the day, were surprisingly animated. It was Chris who finally put an end to Josh's suspense and raised the elephant in the room when he asked, "So, why the early bedtime last night?"

"Nine o'clock? I had no idea you were such a diligent student," added Kelly.

Clearly word had already got around since John also chimed in, "Yeah, I don't think I've been to bed that early since I was ten years old!"

"Hey, can't a guy get tired?" Josh asked lamely, trying to get the embarrassing topic over and done with.

But Chris wasn't going to let him get away with it quite so easily, "Ahh, is all the *gifted and talented* work wearing you out?" he teased.

Josh decided to just hunker down until they were bored with it, "I dunno. Maybe it is."

"So why bother with it?" asked John. "I bet you never even got any gaming done last night, did you?"

Fair point thought Josh, as he decided to try humour to deflect their interest, “Well at least it’ll give you a chance to catch up!”

“Maybe we don’t need a chance. Maybe we’re just getting better,” retorted Chris, a touch indignantly.

“Perhaps,” conceded Josh. “But I’ll give you a chance anyway,” his tone getting slightly brittle.

John leant forward in his seat, “Well that’s mighty big of you,” he almost sneered at Josh.

Kelly felt it was time to lower the tension, “Hey, guys, calm down. It’s only a game anyway.”

But this backfired on her as Chris shot her a disapproving look, “Only a game?” he almost shouted.

Josh seized on the distraction, “Yes, only a game,” he snarled. He’d had enough of their sniping recently and now, perhaps, he needed to tell them some home truths. “Some day we’re all gonna have to recognise that fact. It’s called growing up!”

Just as the conversation was about to get wildly out of control, a car suddenly rushed out of a side street right in front of the bus. The bus driver was forced to swerve wildly and, at the same time almost stand on the brakes, to avoid a near-certain collision.

The students were thrown savagely around their seats and bags flew about like crazily misdirected missiles as the vehicle shuddered across the carriageway, narrowly avoiding parked cars. Josh was thrown forward by the sudden breaking and was brought to a painful halt as his nose impacted on the metal rail on the back of the seat in front. He heard a slight crack and his nose instantly became the source of a red and sticky deluge as blood poured out of his nostrils. He instinctively rummaged in his pockets with one hand for a tissue or handkerchief while the other hand was pinching his nostrils together in a vain attempt to stem the bleeding.

The bus finally screeched to a halt and the screaming and shouting was momentarily replaced by complete silence as the bus occupants realised that they had stopped. Within seconds the silence was broken by more than sixty young voices all jabbering wildly at the person closest to them. Josh's friends looked horrified at the state he was in. His shirt and jacket were drenched with blood and his face was smeared in varying shades of red and brown. They all began searching their own pockets and bags for tissues with which to help him.

No-one else on the bus seemed injured as they gradually began gathering up their scattered belongings. "Hey kids, is anyone hurt?" hollered the driver, standing up at the front.

Kelly cut through the collective mumblings. "Josh has a nosebleed." She looked at her friend earnestly, "Josh, are you OK? Is it broken?"

By now Josh had had enough time to take stock. He finished wiping his face as best he could and dabbed his eyes where the impact had made them water. "No, I don't think so. I didn't hit it that hard," he reassured her.

The driver nodded and asked the collective occupants once again, "What about the rest of you?" Everyone seemed to start speaking together, but the general consensus was that everybody else was OK. "In that case I'll continue on to school," the driver informed them before shaking his head and continuing, "I think we can put that down to a lucky escape."

Very few of the students seemed to be paying any attention to him anymore and he returned to his seat. Checking his mirrors, he pulled the bus back out into the traffic flow and resumed the journey to school. As things settled down he pulled his cell phone from his jacket breast pocket and hit a speed dial key. When he heard someone answer he simply said, "Meet the school bus when it arrives. I may have something for you," and hung up.

Josh continued cleaning his face and nose, which had now almost stopped bleeding. "How is it now? You feeling alright?" asked a concerned Chris, their earlier disagreement completely forgotten.

"Yeah, what the hell was that all about?" whistled John. "We're lucky no-one was badly hurt."

It was Kelly who unwittingly reminded them of their argument. "At least it stopped you guys arguing."

"Yeah, we're all gonna have to grow up or something," recalled Chris, "Right Josh?"

"Yeah, something like that, Chris," Josh replied ruefully, clearly distracted. "One day."

John decided that it wasn't worth resuming the fight, "Well maybe not today eh? We've just turned up at school and there aren't *any* grown-ups here."

"Apart from the teachers," Kelly corrected him.

John raised his eyes, "That's what I meant!" The tension finally broken they all laughed and, following everyone else, got off the bus.

Once everyone had cleared the vehicle Mr Jacks, who had been waiting to meet it, got on and spoke to the driver who pointed to where Josh was sitting. Pausing at each seat to check everything was in order he reached Josh's seat. Looking it up and down, he pulled a tissue from his pocket and wiped up some of the blood.

Chapter 41

The black sedan pulled up gently and quietly at the heliport and the driver got out to open the rear door. A man dressed in a business suit and with curly hair and a moustache got out and walked swiftly to a waiting helicopter. Once he was on board it took off.

Inside the passenger compartment Mario sat facing another man. "A wise choice of transport. Very difficult to follow or eavesdrop on," he applauded.

"In my line of work a crucial consideration," was the brief response from the other man.

"I'm glad you could respond to my message so quickly," Mario ventured.

"The circumstances suggested urgency. So tell me what you know," his companion demanded. It was clear that there wasn't going to be any small talk on this flight.

Mario expected nothing else and began, "The report I have is that all of the ice in the Marie Byrd area of the South Pole has completely melted. It must have done so very quickly because it hasn't been picked up by the monthly satellite passes yet."

"Well that should please the environmental lobby – more proof of global warming," the other man chuckled humourlessly.

"Hmm, but we're keeping the lid very tightly on this at the moment," warned Mario dryly.

"Can't say I blame you," his gruff companion responded. "You don't want every scaremonger and tree hugger getting hold of this. Four billion tons of ice disappearing in less than a month will play right into their hands."

"Damn right it will," Mario concurred. "But that's nothing compared to what else they found."

"Yes, the caves," the other man acknowledged succinctly.

"Strange how they should suddenly be revealed now," Mario pondered.

The other man cut to the chase, "Have your men discovered anything else?"

"Yes," Mario confirmed above the noise of the helicopter rotors. "The contents of the caves. So far about 100 machines that appear to be spacecraft, or at least some sort of means of flight."

"Well that's to be expected, I guess," mused the other.

"The question is, are the owners coming to claim them?" Mario proposed.

"After so long?" queried the man.

"Well there has to be a reason for them suddenly being revealed, and in such a dramatic yet isolated way," suggested Mario.

"You could be right," agreed the man. "Does anyone else know anything about this?"

Mario noticed that the helicopter had turned and seemed to be returning to the heliport. "No, sir," he replied, continuing, "You were the first person I contacted."

"Sensible. Keep it locked down tight," his companion urged, almost as an instruction. "Nothing about this must get out until we know exactly what we're dealing with."

"What are you going to do about it?" asked Mario.

“I think we’ll send a team down there to investigate and make sure protocols are in place,” was the reply. “We may not need them there for long.”

Mario could feel that the helicopter was now definitely descending. “Are the plans progressing as intended?” he asked, eager to know the answer.

“The fleet is on its way,” confirmed the man.

“How long before they arrive?” Mario asked.

The other man shot him a cold look. “You should know better than to ask that!” he rebuked him as the helicopter landed.

Mario attempted to reassure him, “Sorry. I’m just keen for them to get here.”

“Suffice to say the timetable is progressing as intended,” was the curt reply.

It was clear that the meeting was over and Mario exited from the helicopter to return to the waiting car.

Chapter 42

Kirk Stevens was in a hurry and his body language emphasised this as he strode into the Space Corps control and headed straight for Jim Scott. "Well, what have you got for me? Do we have my answers?" His tone wasn't totally demanding, but it was clear that time was running out.

"Not exactly, sir," Scott replied. He knew that his answer wouldn't be acceptable and was ready with additional information, "It does look as though there won't be many more ships than the original estimate of twenty. But more important is a second signal that we've detected."

"Second signal?" asked a slightly bewildered Kirk.

Scott smiled inwardly. Success! He'd managed to deflect his commander's attention away from the original issue and onto something new. This would buy him more time to get Kirk a proper answer. "Yes. In focussing so much on these signals we'd been neglecting the regular sweeps of the rest of the solar system," he explained. "I thought I'd just run a routine one before getting back to the main task and discovered something very unusual in the Canis sector. It's almost the same signal as the one we're monitoring, but it's coming from a different direction."

"You've checked the equipment?" Kirk asked, already expecting an affirmative answer. His people knew their jobs.

Scott didn't disappoint, "Yes, sir. Twice!"

"So you're saying there are two separate, but very similar signals, both headed for Earth and from different directions?" Kirk asked, just to be sure he correctly understood what he was being told.

Scott shrugged, "It looks that way, sir."

Kirk didn't seem too pleased with these additional facts, "Great! So if these are fleets of alien spaceships we've got two headed our way." He looked up at the main viewer screen and mused out loud for anyone, but no-one in particular, to hear, "Let's just hope they're both friendly," before smiling ruefully and adding, "To us and each other!"

Chapter 43

Herbert Kennedy had instructed his secretary that he wasn't to be disturbed and then activated a Skype link on his computer. It had been answered almost immediately and he was now deep in conversation. "As I understand it, my people have detected an anomaly somewhere near Jupiter, but we're keeping this totally under wraps." He paused to emphasise the confidentiality of their discussion. "They're currently trying to ascertain what it is," he continued. "All they know is that it is fragmenting slightly, but that could be due to Jupiter's gravity."

"And the destination?" the other person asked nonchalantly, as if it wasn't particularly of interest to them.

"Well at the moment they're uncertain, but it's not going to take much longer before they work it out," Kennedy replied ignoring the other's ambivalence.

"What about speed?"

Perhaps the other person was interested after all, thought Kennedy. "There's a suspicion that the objects are slowing down, but no proof yet," he reported.

"I doubt if it will take much longer to work that out either," came the reply.

Kennedy wasn't completely sure whether the other person genuinely thought that, or was simply mocking his previous assertion. He decided to emphasise its reality for good measure, "I've ordered my people to work on that, but not to involve anyone else."

The other person nodded gravely. "This has got to be kept as quiet as possible. The fewer people that know about it the better."

Kennedy was adamant, "I totally agree. The only person my team have told is me and I suggested that we wait until we know more before alerting anyone else."

The other person paused for a moment, then voiced his concern. "We need to keep this from the military as long as possible. Once they find out it'll make things extremely difficult."

Kennedy ignored the sentiment and appeared to change the subject, "What about Antarctica? Has that progressed as intended?"

The other nodded his head a few times as he replied, "The ice is melted and contact established. As far as I know, it has gone undetected." Then, without any pleasantries he terminated the link.

Kennedy wasn't offended by the abrupt end of their conversation. It often happened and he accepted that it was just how the other one was. He slowly turned his chair so that he was looking out over Washington and just gazed at the view, allowing his thoughts to wander. In a short time everything would come together as it was meant to. It was reassuring too, to think that no-one knew anything about any of it.

Chapter 44

Josh and his friends walked through the doors out into the warm sunlight at the end of another day at Littrow High. Using that inherent human ability to negotiate familiar crowds without actually bothering to pay attention they carried on chatting as they deftly negotiated various obstacles and numerous other students on their way to the buses.

"What a day, huh?" Josh asked, not really expecting any particular agreement from anyone.

"Well it could only get better after that bus crash this morning," suggested John as he struggled to fit a text book into his shoulder bag. He couldn't help but wonder what the purpose of these weighty and well-thumbed tomes was in this age of intranets and learning portals. But some teachers still seemed to value them, although whether because of the information they contained or just to make the students carry them around, he wasn't too sure.

"Yeah, but no harm done," Josh replied, watching his friend's struggles with mild amusement.

"Apart from your nose," Kelly reminded him as she bent down to pick up a pen that John had managed to drop. "How does it feel now?"

Josh shrugged it off, “It’s OK. Just a bit sore. I’ll be fine after I get some rest.”

Chris couldn’t resist picking-up on this, “In bed by nine o’clock again huh?” he laughed.

Josh decided to go along with the humour, “Maybe. I’ll see how I feel when I get home.”

John was looking relieved now that he’d finished tussling with his bag. “Well don’t forget to add a few thousand to your score, otherwise Chris will be overtaking you,” he suggested as he took his pen back from Kelly.

“Chris and Kelly!” she corrected indignantly.

“Oh yeah, I forgot. The ‘deadly duo’,” John responded with heavy sarcasm.

Chris was equally indignant, but for a different reason, “Hey, just remember I got this far on my own,” he told Kelly.

“Yeah, and you’ll stay that far if you remain on your own,” John threw back, laughing at his friend’s expense.

Kelly decided to defend her boyfriend, “Not if Josh keeps going to bed without playing.”

All three of them laughed and Josh affected a hurt tone. “Hey why all this sudden interest in my bedtime? I’ve not stopped playing.” He smiled at his own attempted humour as he added, “Let’s just say I’m giving some of you a chance to close the gap.”

But Chris’ short temper was, once again, beginning to get the better of him. “That’s real big of you,” he replied pointedly, before continuing, “Well, don’t do me any special favours. I don’t need your charity.”

Kelly misread the situation slightly and continued in a lighter vein, “Yes, you do, Chris. Josh has never been beaten yet.”

“But that was before he became the class swot and started spending all his time concentrating on his *gifted and talented* nonsense.” It was now becoming less like friendly banter as Chris began to let things get to him.

John felt uneasy at his friend's implied criticism. "Hey, steady on, Chris. It might be nonsense to us but it obviously isn't to Josh. Right?"

Josh tried to shrug off any intended slight, but it was clear from his reply that it had needled him a little. "It really isn't that big a deal. If you've got a problem with me doing it then I'm sorry, but there's not a lot I can do about that, is there?"

"I dunno. Is there?" asked Chris in a slightly menacing tone.

Kelly decided to intervene again, "What do you mean, Chris? Josh is right."

"Is he? So he got chosen to do this extra work. Yippee doo dah," Chris almost spat back. It was as if a dam had burst and Chris' inner feelings about Josh's new activities were tumbling out. "He doesn't have to be so superior about it, does he?"

Now it was John's turn to get serious as he once again attempted to defend his friend, "Hey, Chris, I think you're out of order. Josh isn't being superior."

"No? He keeps leaving us, his buddies, because he suddenly remembers he has to do something," Chris began, his voice getting louder. "He's become all keen to discuss lessons and work topics. And he can't be bothered to compete in the longest-running session of the game that we've ever had." He paused for breath as he got into his stride before continuing, "A session that he started and was, until a few days ago, dedicated to winning." By now his teeth were bared and his eyes bulging slightly as he leaned in towards Josh and virtually spat out, "In my book that's either a superiority complex developing or a denial of our friendship itself!"

Kelly seemed a bit shocked on seeing this side of her boyfriend's character. "I think perhaps you're reading too much into this, Chris," she suggested softly.

But Chris' blood was up and he wasn't about to concede, even to Kelly. "Well I don't. It's only been a few days but already I can see a difference in Josh and our friendship."

Finally Josh himself managed to get a word in, "Well, I'm sorry you feel that way, Chris," he said honestly, "but there's not a lot I can do about it."

"No?" questioned Chris. "How about telling us what goes on in those extra lessons?"

"I can't do that," Josh replied matter-of-factly.

"Why? Wouldn't our little minds be able to comprehend it?" argued Chris, allowing all his frustrations to boil to the surface now that he'd managed to draw Josh into the argument.

Josh decided to fight fire with fire, "Maybe!" he said, daring Chris to challenge him further. But when no response came he continued, "I dunno. All I know is I can't tell you. I also know, that as far as I'm concerned, our friendship hasn't changed. I'm just the same as I've always been. I'm sorry if you don't see it. But that's the truth." He could feel himself started to get angry and decided that a change of company would probably be a wise move. "Now if you'll excuse me, I've got work to do," and turned around to retrace his steps back into the school.

"Don't let us stop you," Chris called after him. "After all, the future of the planet might depend on it!" he muttered to himself.

John felt the situation diffuse slightly and asked exasperatedly, "What was that all about?"

Kelly also rounded on Chris. "Yeah, Chris, you need to chill out. Josh isn't doing anything wrong. In fact this smacks just a little of jealousy if you ask me."

Chris had retreated into a moody sulk. "I didn't ask you," he threw back at his girlfriend.

John, ever the diplomat, decided that enough was enough. "Come on. I think it'd be best if we just went home," he suggested and they all headed for the bus.

Only a few moments later Josh came back out of the school. Realising that his friends had all left, he started to make for the buses but a black 4x4 screeched to halt in front of him. Before he had time to react two government agents jumped out, grabbed him, and bundled him into the vehicle. In a squeal of tyres and the smoke of burning rubber the van sped off away from the school and quickly disappeared into the distance.

Chapter 45

Jacob rushed into Samantha's office at Kitt's Peak in a highly agitated state of excitement. She always kept the door open, but if she hadn't she doubted he'd have knocked, he was in that much of a hurry. "Sam, you'd better see this!" he blurted out.

Puzzled, and perhaps a little exasperated at the possibility of something else new she asked, in an almost accusatory tone, "What now?"

Now that he had got her attention Jacob's sense of urgency subsided a little, but he still wasn't making much sense, "Better check out the latest data. Come and look at the screens," he urged her emphatically.

Samantha pulled herself to her feet wearily and walked with Jacob through to the main observatory control room. 'Walked' being something of an understatement, since her subordinate was almost running in his haste to show her whatever was causing him so much excitement.

"Great. What, have they all multiplied again, or picked up speed or something?" Samantha asked him, speaking almost in gasps as they rushed along.

“No,” replied Jacob cagily and then added, “Well, not in the way you’re thinking.” At this Samantha’s curiosity peaked and she almost raced Jacob to the monitors.

“The array focussed on Sector 4b has just detected this,” Callum said with a flourish as he indicated the monitor in front of him. The star field they were looking at was instantly recognisable to Samantha, but there was a cluster of bright objects within it that she wasn’t familiar with.

“4b?” she asked incredulously, “But that’s a completely different area. Are you sure?”

Callum’s reply was laced with a long-suffering and resigned tone, “I’ve double-checked it.”

Jacob explained their findings, “It seems to be something similar to the other objects we’ve been observing, but coming from a different direction.”

“Oh, great!” Samantha was obviously not terribly impressed with this latest development. “So now we’ve got aliens coming at us from all over. What is this, a convention? I’m guessing that we don’t know if they’re the same things?”

Callum answered, almost defensively, “There’s no way of telling. Twenty years ago we wouldn’t even have been able to see them yet.”

“But they are close enough for us to determine that they’re slowing down just like the others,” Jacob volunteered helpfully, before adding, “and there’s a similar number.”

“And they’re headed for Earth?” asked Samantha, feeling that she already knew the answer.

Callum shrugged, “As near as dammit. We can’t be sure yet, but it’d be an awfully strange coincidence if they were just passing through.”

Samantha looked at her two subordinates and realised that her reaction was critical to their morale. She didn’t want to dissuade them from reporting anything else but she needed to vent her own opinion somehow. She chose irony. “So we go for billions of years without any alien visits, or even proof that they exist, and suddenly we’re on everyone’s travel plans?”

Her efforts seemed to have worked as Jacob, once more like an eager puppy, asked, “So what do you want to do?”

She figured she might as well try one more attempt at humour, “What do I *want* to do? Go and lie down and pretend this isn’t happening.” Again it achieved the intended effect as both men smiled knowingly. She continued, “But what I have to do is to inform the administration.”

“Kennedy’s gonna love this!” suggested Callum, injecting his own brand of sarcasm into the conversation.

Samantha shrugged, “Who knows? Perhaps he’ll enjoy the excitement.” She turned to retrace her steps back to the privacy of her office, feeling that this conversation was perhaps best held in private. As she left she reiterated her earlier instruction: “In the meantime, you guys carry on monitoring and get me as much information as you can.”

Chapter 46

Josh sat in a chair on one side of a large table in a nondescript room that was devoid of any windows or non-functional furniture. The only other objects it contained were two other chairs on the opposite side of the table which were currently occupied by Bob Henderson and Brad McCoy. The walls were a plain unadorned white and the grey door, seemingly matching the colour of the floor tiles, successfully completed the effect of isolation.

The student was still trying to get over the shock of the way he had been brought here. First of all bundled unceremoniously into an unmarked black vehicle, then ignored for the length of the relatively short journey despite his constant demands to be told what was going on, then finally escorted down a number of long, white corridors and instructed to wait in this room.

His initial fears had slowly given way to attempts by his mind to make sense of it. He had whiled away the wait for the two agents to join him by running a number of scenarios through his head. No matter which way he approached it, he almost always returned to Space Corps as the reason why this must have happened.

What else could it be? He pondered to himself. Nothing like this had ever happened to him before in his relatively short life and, as far as he was aware, nothing else of significance had changed recently. But he couldn't understand why he appeared to be in trouble. Principal McGregor had told him that Space Corps was a secret but not that it was illegal. He couldn't, and didn't want to, believe that the principal had misled him, any more than he wanted to accept that he would abandon him.

But what if it was illegal? He wondered. Was ignorance a defence? And what if this whole thing had nothing to do with Space Corps? Mistaken identity perhaps? He figured he'd try to avoid revealing anything for as long as he could. This could be his first real test as a member of Space Corps and he didn't want to let them down without some sort of fight.

"Now Josh, we don't want to frighten you, but we're a bit concerned over some things that have been going on at your school and we'd like to ask you some questions that might help clear things up," Agent Henderson said in a calm, soothing and re-assuring voice. "Is that OK with you?"

Josh felt his spirits rise slightly. Perhaps this wasn't anything to do with Space Corps after all. "Sure, I guess so," he replied trying to give the impression that he wanted to co-operate, before adding, "But shouldn't I have an adult here with me? My parents or a lawyer or someone?"

Henderson smiled and chuckled slightly, again helping to reassure Josh, "You're absolutely right, Josh, and we've informed your parents that you're here. We're just waiting for them to arrive."

"The issues that we're investigating are pretty urgent, Josh, that's why we picked you up at school rather than visiting your house," Brad informed him, again seemingly in an attempt to reassure him that everything was in order and that he had nothing to fear.

Henderson continued, "That's why we'd like to get started, if that's OK with you." He paused waiting for a reaction and added, "Do you want us to get you a lawyer? You've not been arrested for anything, but if it'll make you feel better?"

Josh decided that they were being perfectly reasonable and that he'd go along with it, hoping that he wasn't misreading the situation, "No, I guess not. If my parents are on their way it'll be fine."

Agent Henderson smiled and leaned forward in an attentive way, gently joining his hands on the table. "OK. So now, Josh, have you noticed anything strange going on at your school in the last few semesters?"

Josh paused to think, "Not particularly," he responded.

Henderson laughed, "Nothing more than the usual school weirdness, right?" Josh laughed along with him. So far this wasn't as bad as he'd feared.

"How about the students?" Brad asked, leaning back in his chair and locking his hands behind his head. "Have you noticed any odd behaviour?"

This time Josh didn't need to pause. "Not that I remember."

Brad pursued the question a little. "No-one behaving a little strange?"

"No, sir," Josh replied quite naturally.

Henderson's face became slightest more earnest as he pushed Josh a little more, "Now think carefully, Josh. We're happy to hear of anything out of the ordinary. It may only seem routine to you - you know, students seeming different in some way."

Josh hoped that his own face hadn't betrayed any of his true reaction as he now began to wonder if he had been right after all. Were they talking about Ryan Samuels? How could they know? He took a moment to consider his answer, hoping that the two agents would mistake his hesitation as him trying to recall anything that might help them.

Josh shook his head, "No. It's just like school's always been." He decided to elaborate in the hopes that they'd think he was trying to be helpful. "People are friends, then they have a fight, then they're friends again."

This time Brad's voice seemed a little impatient: "So you're saying that you've not noticed anything at all in recent months that you've thought a bit odd?"

Josh suddenly had an idea, "Well, there was one thing," he volunteered.

Brad sat up eagerly, "What was it?"

Josh paused before continuing, "Well, we've got this new teacher, Mr Jacks, and I may have seen him hurt a student on purpose."

Clearly this wasn't the answer that Brad was hoping for and he responded a little abruptly, "What, like hit him or something?"

Josh tried to remain factual and unresponsive to Brad's reaction, "No, sir. It was nothing like that."

"Then what?" Brad asked dismissively.

"I saw him help a student who had cut himself and then I thought I saw him deliberately cut the same student a little later," Josh explained.

Agent Henderson seemed a little more concerned than Brad and asked, "Cut? In what way, Josh?"

Relieved that one of them seemed to be interested, Josh continued, "Well it was nothing dramatic, but he seemed to deliberately scratch him."

"What did he do then?" Henderson asked.

"He helped him into the medical room," Josh replied, realising that it sounded nowhere near as suspicious as it had seemed when he had actually witnessed it.

Clearly Brad thought the same, "So he did what you'd expect a teacher to do?" he asked dismissively.

Josh was forced to admit, "I guess so."

Brad forced home his opinion. “So it wasn’t a big deal?”

Josh began to feel a bit stupid for thinking that they’d be interested in this piece of information. “Not really,” he replied adding defiantly, “But it did seem deliberate when he scratched him.” Brad was clearly unimpressed and Josh continued defensively, “Well, you said to tell you anything unusual.”

Agent Henderson seemed to come to the rescue of Josh’s self-esteem as he suggested, “You’re absolutely right, Josh. We’ll look into it, but I’m not sure if it has any bearing on our case.” He looked across at Brad and then back to Josh. “Look, I’ll tell you what we’re gonna do. We’re gonna take a short break now and then resume our chat in a little while. Would you like a soda or something?

“No, I’m fine,” he replied, feeling his spirits lift a little at Henderson’s tone. “Do you know when my parents are gonna arrive?” he asked.

“Soon, Josh, soon,” Henderson re-assured him. “We’ll bring them right in when they get here.” Turning to the other agent he asked, “Agent McCoy, can you spare me a few minutes?”

Brad nodded and both men got up and walked out of the room, leaving Josh to his own thoughts. Once outside Brad suggested in a conspiratorial tone, “I think he knows more than he’s letting on.”

“Of course he does,” Henderson replied with certainty. “He’s a smart kid. He clocked our Agent Summers’ activities after all. And he knows that he should have an adult here with him. That’s why we have to tread very carefully.”

Brad looked at the other man quizzically, “Yeah. What about his parents?”

Henderson’s tone was no longer that of the ‘good cop’ that he’d been using with Josh. He was simply the cold, calculating, efficient agent, “We’ll let them know he’s here when we need to. In the meantime, let's give him a little quality time on his own to consider his situation. It's amazing what facts some solitary thinking can loosen up."

Brad nodded slowly, but approvingly, "Yeah, OK. We'll let him start worrying some and see if that helps his memory."

Chapter 47

The storm had abated about an hour ago and the Antarctic plain in Marie Byrd Land was ominously quiet. The wind had been so strong that precious little snow had actually settled on the rocky surface. Most of it had been driven against the rocky mountainsides that ringed the area like a vast crater. Occasionally a light wind would moan through the numerous crevasses that punctured the surrounding mountain ranges like spokes in a wheel, and when it did blow it brought with it a wind-chill factor that caused a sharp temperature dip from the current ambient minus five.

When the wind wasn't blowing then the air seemed strangely still and so crisp it seemed that it might actually crack if something were to move through it. As if to prove this, the serenity was gradually fractured by the low, rhythmic, staccato heartbeat of helicopter engines, increasing in volume as three black transport helicopters approached the cave entrances.

As soon as the great lumbering machines touched down a swarm of something like thirty military-looking men, all dressed in polar gear and armed with machine pistols slung over their shoulders, began rapidly spilling out. They carried a mountain of equipment and quickly, with an appearance of well-practised purpose, started searching for the cave entrance.

Inside the hangar James Rock was sitting on the floor leaning against the wall, while his buddy Luke was moving around amongst the consoles.

Unusually for the upbeat, efficient and driven James, he seemed slightly despondent as he asked his friend and colleague, “So do you reckon the storm’s died down yet?”

Luke shrugged with an air of resignation, “There’s no way of telling down here. I guess we’ll have to go up and see for ourselves.” The two men agreed and began to ready themselves to go outside. But as they were walking through the various control desks a console suddenly burst into life, revealing itself to be some sort of observation terminal. The image on its screen was that of the helicopters outside.

“I thought we’d agreed not to touch anything?” James barked accusingly at Luke.

Looking as surprised as James, but with an added dose of defensiveness, Luke complained, “I didn’t touch anything.” He studied the screen for a moment and continued, “I’m guessing our presence has activated some automated settings.”

Walking over to the console James seemed to agree, “Hmm. It looks like the plain outside. Alex must have sent the relief team.”

For the first time in what seemed like ages, Luke was able to find something positive to say. “Well, at least the storm’s over.” He picked up his backpack and resumed his walk to the exit. “Let’s go and let them in.”

Outside, the military men were continuing to unload their gear from the helicopters when James and Luke strode cheerfully out of the entrance to one of the caves. They called out to the newcomers and attracted their attention. Some of them waved back and a small group trotted over to meet them.

"Boy, are we glad to see you," exclaimed James, relief evident all over his face and in his voice.

Luke was no less ebullient and added, "Yeah, you've no idea what it's like being cooped up here alone with him." They all laughed and Luke continued excitedly, "Wait 'til you see what we've found in there."

The leader of the new arrivals casually removed his snow mask to reply and James was immediately puzzled. "Wait a minute. Who are you? You're not from Base Camp."

The stranger's voice was friendly and non-threatening as he replied, "Quite right. I'm Captain Thomas Xavier and these are my men." His shiny, dark brown face seemed to emphasise the whiteness of his teeth as he smiled a large and friendly smile. "We've been sent down here by Washington. Your little report caused quite a stir!"

"I'm not surprised," offered Luke, quickly adjusting to the presence of the soldiers. "You sure got here quickly."

Captain Xavier finished removing his headgear and explained, "We're part of the South Atlantic fleet. It only took a few hours' detour to get us here."

James also now relaxed, happy with the captain's explanation, "Well it's good to see you anyway, even if you're not who we expected to see. I'm James Rock and this is Luke Richards, part of the US Antarctic Survey team." He held out his hand and Captain Xavier grasped it firmly before moving on to shake hands with Luke.

The Captain indicated the helicopters behind him, "We'll just unload our gear and then perhaps you can show us what you've found." As he finished speaking they all became aware of the sound of more helicopters approaching and turned to look in the direction of the noise.

Three red Base Camp helicopters were just appearing over the mountain ridge and inside the cockpit of the leading one the pilot turned to Alex Roughedge pointing to the party on the canyon floor, "There they are, Alex. Looks like they've got visitors."

Alex was both surprised and shocked to see the newcomers. Mario had told him to keep things quiet so who the hell had James and Luke been talking to during the storm? "What? Who the hell are they?" he shouted over the sound of the engines.

Down in the canyon, the sudden unexpected airborne approach changed everything. Captain Xavier swiftly unshouldered his machine pistol and levelled it at James and Luke. "I'm sorry gentlemen. I'm gonna have to ask you for that tour a little sooner than expected."

He hollered to his men, "Forget the rest of the stuff. Bring what you can and head for the cave." Then, ensuring that he kept his eyes on James and Luke, he spoke into his radio. "Pilots, get those helos out of here. Head to the holding point and await my signal."

The engines of the black helicopters whined into life and the rotors slowly began to turn. Within moments they had disappeared into an indistinguishable vortex of downdraft and the three aircraft, despite their considerable size, swiftly sprang into the air like demented jack-in-the-boxes. The remaining military men lugged their equipment towards Captain Xavier who gestured with his gun for James and Luke to return to the cave.

"What the hell are you doing?" James yelled indignantly above the noise of the departing helicopters. "This is a legitimate government operation. You've no right to do this."

But as the small group scurried, some reluctantly, into the cave Captain Xavier's tone was cold and matter-of-fact. "Let's just say that the interests of the government just changed."

Chapter 48

Principal McGregor's tone of voice and subtle suggestion of concern were having the desired effect as the telephone conversation developed. Sitting behind his desk with the telephone in one hand and his head resting on his other, elbow on desk, he was the classic image of earnest concentration.

As soon as his secretary alerted him to the fact that Josh's mother was on the telephone he had been focussed on nothing else. For the parents of one of his *gifted and talented* students to want to talk to him could only mean one thing – trouble! He'd never yet had anyone become suspicious, but there was always a first time, and he didn't want it to be this call.

Once he'd ascertained that Josh hadn't yet arrived home he decided that bluffing was the best course of action. It would give him time to try and sort things out, but he was well aware of the high stakes involved and what failure would mean.

Fortunately it seemed that, for the time being, he would be getting away with it. Force of character and parental trust in the education system should never be discounted, he thought to himself as he continued in a soothing and understanding tone, "Yes, Mrs Travis, I'm sorry that you were worried but Josh is doing a little extra-curricular physics here this evening for a few hours. I'm surprised that he didn't tell you."

As Mrs Travis confirmed that she knew nothing of the late finish he suggested, "I'll make sure that we e-mail you with future arrangements to avoid a repeat episode."

If he thought that would be the end of it he was mistaken. Clearly Mrs Travis wasn't someone who could just be fobbed off. Neither was she one of the many parents who displayed an ambivalence towards their child's education. Mind you, many of the *gifted and talented* students' parents exhibited an above-average interest in the progress of their children.

He listened carefully while she asked about Josh's progress before reassuring her, "Yes, he's doing fine with his studies." He paused momentarily and smiled inwardly as he added quite truthfully, "In fact I think it's fair to say that he's doing better than any of us expected." If only she knew how true that was, he thought to himself.

Finally he could relax. She'd bought it. They were now just exchanging pleasantries as she asked him to make sure that Josh told her about these extra lessons in the future. "Yes I'll be sure to tell him," the principal confirmed, before adding, "And may I say, Mrs Travis, that your concern does you credit." Nice touch, he thought to himself, perhaps a little conceitedly. Parents love to be praised! "My pleasure. Good day to you." He hung up and stared into the distance pondering his next move. He decided his gut reaction was correct and activated a Skype link on his computer. He needed to speak to Space Corps urgently. He rarely used the secure link, but time was of the essence and it was a lot faster than teleporting up there.

Kirk Stevens appeared on the screen looking very concerned. Something must be wrong for Jonathan

McGregor to be Skyping him. The principal quickly confirmed his theory, "Hi, Kirk. We may have a problem."

Kirk tried to lighten whatever the problem was, "Like what? You mean two unidentified fleets approaching the planet aren't concern enough?"

The principal quickly dismissed that approach, "Josh Travis has gone missing!"

"What? How can he have gone missing?" Kirk asked incredulously, all attempts at humour forgotten. "He was up here only two hours ago. Didn't he make it back?"

"Oh he made it back OK, but I've just had his mother on the phone telling me that he's not come home, and that he's not answering his cell phone."

Kirk experienced a brief moment of relief, "So? He's 16 years old. 16 year olds have a tendency to detour on their way home. Has she tried his friends' houses?"

But the principal quashed that reaction as well, "Apparently that's not like him and, according to her, there's been a little 'unrest' between him and his friends recently."

"What, the usual 'green streak' against being *gifted and talented*?" Kirk felt that this time, perhaps, he'd managed to get it right.

"I think so," confirmed the principal, before continuing, "Anyway, apparently tonight is his sister's birthday supper and it certainly wouldn't be like him to miss it."

Kirk was now wondering exactly what McGregor had in mind. "So do you have any ideas about where he is?"

"Not really," the principal admitted. "But I do remember him telling me something strange about one of our new members of staff. He seemed to think that this new guy could have been taking blood samples of our students and their replicas."

Kirk didn't like the sound of that. "Interesting. Have you checked it out?"

McGregor nodded reassuringly, "I looked into the teacher's resume and verified his previous appointments. Everything checked out. I've had him under CCTV surveillance ever since and nothing seems out of order. But Josh did seem convinced that something wasn't right."

Now it was Kirk's turn to be suspicious. "It could be that someone's on to us and trying to investigate the replicas." He thought for a moment, "I've never had the blood analysed other than to ensure it's the right type. I guess we should look into that just in case." He returned to the matter in hand. "In the meantime, what do you want to do about Josh?"

The Principal looked pointedly at the computer screen as he weighed up his idea, then said, "Well, I'd suggest that we get his replica back down here as fast as we can and send him to Josh's house for the night. That'll give us a little more time to see if we can find the real one. Just make sure that the replica is brought up to speed."

Kirk knew that such a strategy was fraught with risks, but couldn't really think of an alternative. "It shouldn't be a problem," he agreed reluctantly before adding, "But there may be a few gaps in his short-term memory. We'll just have to hope no-one notices."

The principal agreed. "It's a chance we'll have to take. In the meantime I'll see if I can find some way to track down the real one." He thought for a moment, "I think I'll start by talking to our new science teacher."

"So what did you tell his mother?" Kirk asked out of interest.

"That he was doing a little extra-curricular work that he must have forgotten to tell her about, and that he'd be home in a couple of hours," came the reply.

Kirk nodded. It was a good response in the circumstances and he was impressed by the principal's quick thinking, “Well, that buys us time, but it’s a risky gamble.”

The Principal agreed, “Well, if we use the replica then we’ll have about 24 hours before we have to report him missing.” He paused before adding what both of them knew to be true: “And start to fear for the whole future of Space Corps!”

Chapter 49

The interior of the office was as grand as the title of its occupant suggested it should be. Intimidating, but in an aloof, historic style. Huge old paintings of long-dead heroes, many in military uniform, adorned the walls, and smaller, more recent framed photographs of important people were arranged on hand-carved antique cabinets. Tasteful armchairs and soft furnishings were arranged around a central low table while the secretary of defense was seated behind a magnificent colonial-era desk.

Herbert Kennedy was being shown into the room by an aide and the secretary had no hesitation in standing to greet him. He was shorter than he appeared on the television and a little overweight. His balding head and brown, horn-rimmed spectacles gave him something of the air of a banker rather than someone very close to the nuclear triggers. But those who knew him were well-aware of the intellect, both political and diplomatic, that lurked inside his head "Herb. How are you?" he asked with genuine interest. It wasn't that often that he got to see his old friend nowadays.

Always careful to observe protocol, Herbert Kennedy remained formal for the initial greeting as he shook the proffered hand, "Mr Secretary. I'm well thank you and I hope the same can be said of you?"

The secretary was keen to breakdown the fussiness as quickly as possible and indicated this to Kennedy by his jovial reply. "Hey, nothing a few long years out of office wouldn't cure!" Both men laughed lightly. "Well, sit down," he continued. "Tell me, what's so important that it couldn't wait?" He chuckled and added, almost conspiratorially, "I've had to bump another couple of meetings this morning to fit you in, so it had better be good."

Both men sat in armchairs around the low table and Kennedy began to get straight to the point. Old friends or not, he was well aware of the Secretary's heavy schedule and he didn't want to either add to that burden or trivialise the subject of his own visit with small-talk. "I'll cut to the chase, Mr Secretary, and I'm afraid it's not going to do anything to help with that need to relax and unwind."

The secretary had known Herbert Kennedy for long enough to recognise his current demeanour and replied in a serious tone, "Go on."

"A few days ago my team at the Kitts Peak Deep Space Observatory detected an unusual object heading into our solar system seemingly on course for Earth," Kennedy began. He was speaking quickly but clearly, keen to explain everything simply and without fuss. "As it got closer," he continued, leaning forward to add gravitas to the subject, "They were able to determine that it was actually a cluster of about twenty similar-sized objects. What was even more puzzling was the fact that they didn't seem to be affected by the gravitational pull of other objects and that they are actually decelerating as they get closer to the sun!"

The secretary of defense was following everything very carefully and proved it by asking, "I'm no astronomer, Herb, but aren't they supposed to get faster?"

Kennedy nodded ruefully, "Yes, sir. That's what's been causing us concern."

"So what do you think they are?" asked the secretary. If he knew Herb, the administrator would not have come here without at least having a theory, even if he didn't yet have hard evidence to present.

Kennedy didn't disappoint: "The only logical explanation that my people can come up with is that they must be manufactured objects of some kind, with their own power source."

The secretary raised his arms in mock indignation, "Damn it, Herb, why can't you scientists use plain English? You mean spaceships of some kind?"

"Yes sir," Kennedy replied without a moment's hesitation, "Which is why I've come direct to you." From the level and tone of his voice you'd have thought he'd just delivered a weather report or other such daily triviality. That was one of Kennedy's strong points. He rarely got over-excited, especially when something was as serious as this.

The secretary didn't dwell on Kennedy's answer, but moved swiftly on to the next logical question: "Are they still headed for Earth?"

Again Kennedy remained purely factual, "Yes, sir and still decelerating."

The secretary pulled a face and asked, "So you think this could be the 'little green men' that Hollywood's been waiting on for years?" Despite his choice of words, it was a serious question and Kennedy knew that.

"I don't want to sound alarmist, but it does certainly seem likely," he replied. "Of course if they are headed here, we don't know if they intend to land or just observe us."

The secretary rubbed his chin. "Hmm, either way we need to be prepared for the worst, just in case." He paused, smiled briefly at his own thoughts, and admitted,

"Of course if they have the technology to build spaceships, I doubt there's much that we can do to defend against them if it becomes necessary."

"Let's hope it doesn't," agreed Kennedy before adding gravely, "Especially since there's another cluster of similar objects approaching from a different direction!"

This time the secretary actually laughed, but there was no humour in his voice, "Great, Herb! Save the best for last, huh? How far away are these ones?"

"About the same as the others. There's a similar number of objects as well."

The secretary paused to think all of this information through. He sat back and stared directly into Kennedy's face. "Do we think they're connected?"

"There's no way of telling." Kennedy realised the reply wasn't very helpful, but he wasn't about to start guessing. "At the moment they're millions of miles apart," he continued before conceding, "But it's a very strange coincidence if there's no connection at all."

The secretary nodded. He'd heard all he needed to hear and he also knew that Kennedy had told him everything that he knew, "OK, Herb I'll inform the president. You'd better get back to your office and keep me informed at all times."

"Of course, Mr Secretary," Kennedy acknowledged, reverting to his earlier formality.

"Oh and Herb, no second-guessing," the secretary added as they stood up and shook hands, "I want just pure facts, OK?"

Kennedy nodded seriously, "Understood, sir."

Chapter 50

Josh looked up as the door to the interrogation room re-opened after what had seemed to him a very long wait. He half expected to see his parents ushered in by Agent Henderson, but tried hard not to let his disappointment show when the agent was only accompanied by Agent McCoy and a woman.

Henderson's tone was just as friendly and reassuring as before, "Hi, Josh. Sorry to have kept you waiting so long. We've just heard from your parents that they're stuck in some really bad traffic because of an accident down town, but they'll get here just as soon as they can." He turned to indicate his female companion. "In the meantime I want you to meet Agent Walsh. She's a specialist in dealing with cases involving minors."

The woman stepped towards the table and smiled pleasantly. Josh thought that she had a sweet, good-natured smile as she handed him a drink in a cardboard cup, "Hello, Josh. It's nice to meet you. I thought you might like a soda."

He was grateful both for what he took to be a kindly gesture and because he was beginning to feel thirsty, "Thank you." He looked at Agent Henderson as he sucked eagerly on the drinking straw. “I thought you said I hadn’t done anything wrong.”

“And *you* haven’t,” the agent replied with the emphasis firmly planted on the word ‘you’.

“So what do you mean, ‘cases involving minors’?” Josh asked, a little uncertain of how things might be developing.

His concern wasn’t fully alleviated when Agent Henderson seemed to hesitate and stumble through his reply, “You see, Josh, it’s not you particularly that we’re interested in. It’s more the school authorities.” He paused and seemed to gather his thoughts before continuing more confidently, “We’ve had reports that the school might be abusing students. Your story about Mr Jacks only serves to reinforce these suspicions. Tell me, do you know this student?” He handed Josh a picture of Ryan Samuels.

“Yes,” Josh replied quite honestly, taking another sip of soda. “That’s Ryan Samuels. He’s the kid that Mr Jacks scratched.” There didn’t seem to be any point in denying that he knew him.

“Yes, we know,” Henderson responded. “He’s also come up before in our investigation.”

Now Josh was intrigued, “Why? What’s he done?” He was beginning to wonder if his earlier fears about Space Corps being the reason behind his detention might not be too far wide of the mark after all.

For the first time since they had met, Henderson seemed to take the tried and tested official approach to questioning that Josh had seen in countless movies and television shows. “We’re not at liberty to tell you that, I’m afraid, Josh, but we’re hoping that you might be able to clear up one or two matters for us that will allow us to eliminate him from our list of suspects,” he said without any hint of cliché.

Brad took over the questioning and the edge that Josh had previously detected in his voice now seemed a little sharper, "How well do you know him?"

Again Josh answered truthfully: "Not that well, we only became friends at the end of the last semester."

"So why did you become friends?" Brad was fishing and Josh could sense it, but he wasn't sure how to respond.

He opted for nonchalance and sucked on the drinking straw, almost deliberately slowly. "I dunno. We just started talking, I guess."

But Brad kept pushing, "Do you share any lessons with him?"

Again Josh stuck to the truth. "No, he's in a different grade to me."

Then Henderson joined in again with a more perceptive question, "What about extra-curricular activities – clubs, sports, and so on?"

Josh tried not to appear worried or evasive. "We both belong to the gaming club," he volunteered.

"The what?" Henderson asked, seemingly bewildered.

Josh had been asked the same question by adults a number of times in the past. He replied a little long-sufferingly, "It's a club for those of us interested in serious computer gaming."

"What? Like the school nerds and geeks?" Brad almost sneered the question at Josh.

Josh was pleased that his drinking cup was almost empty so that the slurping noise induced by his sucking served almost as an implied rebuke to Brad's attitude. "Some people think so," he replied.

Agent Henderson, however, seemed more interested than his colleague. "Are there many members?" he asked.

Josh shrugged, "I dunno. About thirty I guess."

To Josh's surprise Brad seemed to be a little more amiable. "So is that why you and Samuels became friends?" he asked quite innocently. Surely my little stunt with the drinking straw couldn't have been that effective, thought the student.

Josh tried to match the agent's casual pleasantness. "I guess so."

For a moment, Josh thought that Agent Henderson was changing the subject when he asked, "What about special lessons or tuition? Do you have any of this together?" But he then realised that the question was still leading in the same direction. He was beginning to feel a little tired and started to worry that he might let his guard down.

"Not yet," he answered trying hard to stifle, or at least disguise, a yawn.

Perhaps Agent McCoy had sensed Josh's tiredness and thought he'd increase the pressure. Whatever the reason, the hardness crept back into his voice. "What do you mean, 'not yet'? If you're in different grades would you ever expect to?" he asked quite forcefully.

The thought that he might have lost control of the situation suddenly overwhelmed Josh. His mind was beginning to feel fuzzy and his thought process a little dull. Had he said too much already? "I suppose you're right," he conceded. Perhaps he'd try going along with them, "I guess I just meant that you never know what the future might bring."

Josh was relieved to find that this tactic might have worked when Agent Walsh suddenly spoke for the first time since handing Josh the soda. Her voice seemed sympathetic as she mimicked his tactic of agreement. "I know what you mean, Josh." She looked at the other two agents and Josh thought that perhaps he detected concern in her voice as she suggested, "It seems to me that we've probably exhausted this line of questioning." He really was feeling very weary and was relieved to hear her say, "If you don't really know young Samuels then there's little you can do to help us help him." But his relief turned to a sudden chill running down his back when she completely changed tack and asked, "What about Principal McGregor. Is he OK?"

What could they possibly have against the principal? He was, to most people, a fair and dedicated teacher who'd been at the school for many years before Josh had got there. Surely they couldn't really suspect him of any wrongdoing? Josh was now very concerned that his initial fears would prove to be correct. This had to be to do with Space Corps! He hesitated before replying very guardedly, "Yes. We don't see him much, but he's a decent guy. Fair, I guess."

"So you don't have contact with him?" Once again, it was Brad who got straight to the point. Josh would have to be very careful not to get caught lying this time, after all they probably realise that it was the principal who approved the *gifted and talented* students.

He thought momentarily and replied, "I see him a few times a week."

Then the sucker punch hit him! "What about the *gifted and talented* students? You're one of these, aren't you?" asked Henderson, still smiling. But this time Josh thought the smile was more from a sense of impending victory than from friendliness.

Added to this sense of imminent disaster, Josh was finding it increasingly difficult to concentrate and even a struggle to keep his eyes open. He resorted to a monosyllabic answer in an attempt to buy himself time to think. "Yes," he answered nervously.

"Does Principal McGregor have anything to do with that group?" the agent persisted, gently pushing home his point.

Josh had had time to think a little and, still slightly ill at ease, replied, "He asked me if I'd like to join it."

"Why did he choose you?" Brad asked, almost spitefully.

Josh wasn't too sure whether Agent McCoy's tone was just because he didn't seem to like him, or whether it was deliberately designed to illicit a response. "He told me that I'd done better than average in my tests," he answered truthfully, but carefully.

"Is Ryan Samuels a *gifted and talented* student as well?" Brad asked. The question was seemingly innocent enough, but Josh felt that the agent already knew the answer.

Josh yawned long and hard, "I'm not sure," and was again relieved to hear Agent Walsh join in.

Her intervention seemed to Josh like the bell at the end of a round must feel to a boxer who is on the ropes. Pure relief. "OK, guys. I think Josh has helped us enough for now. He looks to me as though he could do with a rest." She paused to let her words sink in and then suggested, "Let's give him some peace and quiet until his parents get here."

Without any protest the two men got to their feet and all three left the room. Josh yawned once again and put his head on his arms on the table. He felt defeated and deflated, yet all he wanted to do was sleep. Perhaps he'd wake up refreshed and ready for more mental sparring. Somehow he doubted it, but he couldn't fight the sleepiness any longer and he quickly drifted into unconsciousness.

Moments later Agent Walsh re-entered the room, carrying a surgical dish from which she removed a small hypodermic syringe. She proceeded to take a blood sample from Josh's arm and then, collecting the empty soda cup, she left the room.

Chapter 51

The noise in the Space Corps control room was incessant. A warning siren was whooping on and off, people were shouting and rushing to their various work stations and numerous warning lights were flashing.

Kirk Stevens burst through the door at a run and crossed to the centre raised command dais. All around him operators were frantically tapping command instructions into their consoles, all seemingly determined to locate the cause of the commotion.

Kirk looked across to where Frankie was working feverishly with one of the senior members of staff, "What is it? What's happened?" he asked.

Frankie looked up, begrudging the distraction from the task at hand, but Kirk needed to know the answer and she realised that. "We're not sure yet, but the outer sensor posts have all suddenly gone offline," she informed him.

"Malfunction?" he shot back at her.

Frankie had stolen a momentary glance back at the screen she and the other operator were working on and Scott came to her assistance. "Unsure, sir. They shouldn't all go offline at once," he explained. Or was he protesting rather than explaining? Kirk couldn't be completely sure.

"How far out are they?" Kirk asked him. Space Corps possessed a number of such sensors positioned throughout the inner solar system.

"These ones are beyond Mars," Scott replied.

Frankie looked up, apparently having completed the checks she was performing. "They're hidden amongst the asteroid belt," she added to Scott's answer.

Kirk paused for a moment. He suddenly became aware that many of the operators in the room were now either looking directly at him, or perhaps just stealing sideways glances in his direction. Either way it was clear that everyone was now waiting for his instructions. He wasn't aware of any previous occasions when they'd faced a malfunction of this magnitude and the imaginations of his staff were probably working overtime. He had to act decisively and with authority to reassure any of the jittery ones and quickly to satisfy the self-assured ones. He spoke calmly and deliberately, "So if they're hidden, it should be a simple malfunction." He looked straight at Scott and asked, "Where is the nearest alien fleet?"

"About 160 million miles out," came the instant reply. Well done Scott, keeping on top of the situation, Kirk thought to himself. That's what he needed right now. Everyone doing what they were supposed to do.

But Scott's answer had also served to confirm Kirk's concern. "In other words, approaching the asteroid belt! In what sector?" he asked.

Again an instant reply, "Sector 52," followed up by more confirmation, "The same sector as those sensor posts."

"Have we sent visual confirmation probes?" Kirk asked, expecting another efficient response.

He was surprised therefore when Frankie intervened, "Not yet. I was about to do so."

His inner surprise elicited the addition of a slight sharpness to his tone as he instructed his assistant, "Then do it. We need to see first-hand what has happened to them."

Frankie looked down to the operator seated beside her. "Get Cadet Samuels on it fast. Ensure that he's briefed to stay as undetectable as possible." The operator looked up momentarily and nodded.

Kirk waited until Frankie had given the instruction and then indicated the door. "Let's go," he half invited, half ordered her. The two of them walked out of the control room and headed down the corridor towards Kirk's office.

As they walked they continued their conversation and Kirk voiced his concern, "I'm surprised that you hadn't gotten around to sending the probes. You're normally so ahead of the game."

Frankie knew that she had not only let the commander down, but also potentially embarrassed both him and herself by her tardiness in delaying launching the probe, "I'm sorry, Kirk," she admitted before explaining, "I guess I was just so startled by it all. It's not like we're used to this type of scenario."

They reached Kirk's office and both entered the room. "Yeah, OK. I know what you mean," Kirk acquiesced, feeling reluctant to pursue the matter. "Things certainly seem to be hotting up right now, both here and on Earth," he said, offering Frankie a degree of consolation.

His assistant looked surprised. "Oh? Like how?" she asked cautiously.

"It seems that Josh Travis has gone missing," Kirk informed her.

Frankie looked shocked. "How?" she asked.

Kirk thought the question a bit redundant. "How the hell do I know?" he retorted.

Realising how dumb her question must have sounded, Frankie regrouped, "Sorry. What I meant was, in what circumstances? Is it our problem?"

Kirk sat down at his desk and looked up at his assistant. "If you mean is the fact that someone who knows all about our operation cannot be accounted for then, yes, I guess it is our problem," he explained, before elaborating. "If you mean, does his disappearance have anything to do with that knowledge? the answer is we don't know. But with all the sudden strangeness going on up here I'm not prepared to take any chances."

"So what are we gonna do?" asked Frankie, still recovering from the news.

"We need to send his replica down to Earth immediately," Kirk told her.

Frankie's facial expression, that had been returning to normal after the earlier shock, suddenly reverted to alarm once again. "But he won't have had a memory exchange update," she protested.

"I know," acknowledged Kirk seemingly distracted by his own thoughts. He looked up at Frankie again and continued, "It's risky, but it might buy us the time we need. See to it now please."

There didn't seem to be any doubt in Kirk's determination and, knowing better than to argue in such circumstances, Frankie left the room to carry out his instructions.

Chapter 52

Ryan Samuels relaxed back into his recliner and checked the controls one last time. He'd flown hundreds of simulations and tested many new scenarios in the year or so that he'd been a member of Space Corps, but none of them carried anywhere near the weight of responsibility of the mission he was about to embark upon. For starters, none of his previous operations had been anything other than training flights. Even though they had involved the flying of real spacecraft, they had all had a theoretical purpose. If they failed it simply proved that either Ryan required more training or that the simulation needed tweaking. But this time it was for real. Ryan was very much aware that almost everyone on the space station was relying on his prowess as a pilot to find out why the sensors had gone offline. If he failed to complete this mission there would be real repercussions for so many people. With that thought in mind he took a deep breath and slowly pushed the toggle on the control pad that activated the probe's thrusters.

Outside in the cold vacuum of space, a Cobra spaceship that had been inertly orbiting Mars suddenly received the instruction from Ryan. The exhaust ports in the tail immediately began to glow blue as the plasma thrusters burst into life. With impressive agility the craft banked steeply and broke away from Mars' gravitational pull, heading out into space towards the asteroid belt.

Once clear of Mars, Ryan instructed the ship to go to maximum power and, with the equivalent thrust of at least two dozen Saturn V rockets, it shot away from the red planet, hurtling through space towards the collection of rocks and debris that make up the asteroid belt.

In no more than fifteen minutes it had covered the 70,000 miles or so to the nearest band of the belt. On Ryan's screen he could see the ominous shapes of the obstacles looming large in front of the Cobra. He had little option but to fly through the asteroid field and its maelstrom of hazards. He focussed as sharply as he had ever done and plunged in. Almost immediately he had to dive hard and then bank sharp right to avoid becoming a bug on the windshield of a flying rock. Boulders the size of countries were hurtling past, sometimes even crashing into each other and ricocheting wildly onto a different course. It was as much as he could do to see the dangers in time and he was quietly grateful for the automatic collision avoidance system that the ship possessed. But he knew that would only protect him from the asteroids that the computers could detect and instantly plot a course to avoid. In this environment there were many more that would remain undetected.

Finally he could see the field thinning out in front of him as he approached the first of the Kirkwood gaps - bands of relative calmness alternating between the bands of asteroids. As he was about to leave the turmoil of the tumbling rocks he homed in on the location of the sensor he was trying to locate. There! Right on the shoreline where the crashing tumult of tumbling rocks met the eerie stillness of the gap, he could see the metallic object following its sympathetic course, locked in to the surrounding asteroids. At first all looked normal, until

Ryan brought his space craft in over the top of the sensor. From this vantage point he could quite clearly see the smashed and scorched surface which had once housed the cameras and electronic equipment. Clearly this sensor was not merely malfunctioning.

But what had caused such physical damage? Had it simply been hit by one of the many rogue rocks flying around or had its location stabilisers failed, causing it to get too close to one of its marker asteroids? Moving on, he reached another sensor and found it damaged in the same way. Clearly there was more to this than simple system failures, unless the systems that had failed had been global to all the sensors. Somehow that seemed unlikely.

Then as Ryan was about to move on to a third set of co-ordinates that he had been given, he suddenly caught sight of something even more sinister in the upper corner of his view screen. He pushed his thumb hard against the small joystick to cause the Cobra to pull up sharply before diving behind another large asteroid. What he saw in that brief moment of exposition made his blood run cold and sent a shiver down his entire body. The object that had crossed his viewer and been seen by Commander Stevens with all the other duty personnel up in the control room was very clearly some other sort of spaceship! Much larger than Ryan's single-seat drone, it could well have been some sort of scout ship, but whatever it was it certainly didn't belong to Space Corps.

So the cause of the damage now seemed very obvious. Not a malfunction, not a collision but simply, and very sinisterly, sabotage! But who, or what, had been responsible for it and why had they done it? These were questions that Ryan was happy to leave to the adults in charge. His main concern right now was getting his ship back to Space Corps safely and without being detected, a task to which he immediately set about applying himself.

Chapter 53

The replica Josh opened the front door and entered the house. His duplicate memory knew the layout of the building and the furnishings that he saw all registered as familiar. As he closed the door nothing seemed unusual to him and he instantly recognised the female rushing to greet him.

Josh's mother threw her arms around the duplicate, not for one second suspecting that this automated replica was not even human, let alone her son. Why should she? He looked like Josh, he felt like Josh, he even smelled like Josh. "Josh! Where have you been? We've been worried sick!" she exclaimed, hugging him tight.

Josh's father then appeared at the door to the living room, concern etched all over his usually unemotional face. "Son, is everything alright? You usually tell us if you're going to be late home."

The replica regarded both of Josh's parents before replying with the same degree of inflection and emotion in his voice that Josh would have used. "I'm sorry you were worried. I just got carried away at school and forgot the time." His programming perfectly mimicked Josh's ambivalence in such a situation. There was nothing for his parents to suspect.

Josh's father looked relieved even if he didn't intend to. "I guess that *gifted and talented* programme must be starting to get results, eh?" he suggested, chuckling at the irony.

"So you'd rather be doing your extra lessons than getting home in time for my birthday supper?" Josh's sister wandered out of the family dining room and looked indignantly at her 'brother'.

The replica turned and looked at her with an impish smile on his face, just as the real Josh would have done, before replying sarcastically, "As if I'd do that to you."

"Bet you would if the stupid gaming club had a meeting," Megan retorted before disappearing back into the dining room.

Their mother intervened quickly to preserve what peace she could. "Now, now, let's not quarrel. Nothing's spoilt, there's still plenty of time to have supper. You go and freshen up, Josh, and I'll get the food on the table."

"And no sneaking a quick round of your game," Megan called out.

"I wouldn't dream of it," the duplicate responded, perhaps a little too literally, as he ascended the stairs to Josh's room. His memory knew that Josh normally went straight to his room when he got home to dump his bag and coat.

As her imposter sibling bounded up the stairs Megan sat down at the dining room table, muttering in response, "That's a first!"

Her mother immediately busied herself putting a variety of dishes containing food onto the table. "Now you just relax, Megan, and stop arguing," she instructed her daughter. "I'm sure Josh is sorry for being late and now that he's home we can all enjoy your birthday supper," she added trying to reassure her.

Within moments the duplicate Josh had returned to the room and the entire family were seated around the table.

As he helped himself to a spoonful of mashed potato, his father asked, "So what was it that you were doing at school so late, Josh, anyway?"

There was a momentary pause as the duplicate's programming attempted to fill in the missing part of his memory, "Ah, it was an extra math lesson."

"I thought Principal McGregor said it was physics," queried his mother innocently as she placed some meat on her plate.

Again a rapid piece of data processing elicited a response that the duplicate deemed appropriate. "Well it was a math problem in physics." His prime programming directive that he should be indistinguishable from Josh went to high alert for signs of suspicion in the humans.

Assistance came from an unexpected source as the real Josh's sister asked, "Mom, what would Principal McGregor know anyway? He's just the principal."

"Well it doesn't really matter anymore," Josh's father said. He loaded some chicken and sweetcorn on to his fork and he looked pointedly at the replica. "Just be sure to let us know in the future, Josh, if you're going to be late."

"Sure, Dad," the duplicate replied succinctly, glad that one slight hiccup had been overcome.

His father changed the subject abruptly, "So anyway, on to happier things." He picked up his glass of wine and looked at his daughter, "Happy birthday, Megan."

Her mother joined in, "Yes, happy birthday, dear."

The replica masquerading as her brother also responded, "Happy birthday," before attempting to make further conversation, "So, Megan, where are all your cards?"

If he had been capable of genuine emotional responses, he would have instantly wished that he hadn't decided to ask the question when Megan pulled a face and replied, "Doh, it's not my birthday until tomorrow, is it, Josh?"

Rapidly recovering, he simply agreed, "Of course." Again his processors attempted to fill in the memory gaps, "I just thought you might have had some from school friends."

His apparent sibling responded with subtle disdain, "Well, if I'm going to get any from them I'd expect them to give them to me tomorrow as well – you know, on my *birthday*." She emphasised the last word for effect.

Once again their mother employed that universal peace-keeping maternal tactic of attempting to deflect the conversation slightly, "Well I assume you remembered to get your sister a present, Josh?" She couldn't possibly have realised, however, that this time her diplomacy may have only made things worse, as another gap in the duplicate's memory loomed large.

"I believe so," the replica replied, instantly aware that that wasn't the appropriate response. Again his programming suggested that continuing the conversation might assist. "Would you like that now?" he asked his sister.

Megan replied exasperatedly, "No. Tomorrow will be fine. Just like we always do. What's gotten in to you tonight?" She looked at him with a puzzled expression on her face.

Josh's programming determined that apology would be the best tactic, "Sorry. I'm obviously not thinking straight."

At first it seemed that salvation was about to come once again from his sister as Megan dramatically changed the subject, but her new choice of new topic brought new confusion. "So, what about the bus crash this morning, eh, Josh?" she asked her 'brother'.

In a nanosecond the duplicate's sub-routines had determined that there was absolutely no reference to this subject matter in its memory. Automatic responses kicked in and the replica found himself saying, "Bus crash?"

Megan looked at him in total bewilderment, "Don't tell me you don't remember?"

Before he had a chance to respond, the impact of Megan's choice of topic had registered with both their mother and father, who both exclaimed incredulously, "Bus crash?" Their father following up with, "What bus crash?"

With the nonchalance of youth Megan explained completely matter-of-factly, "Oh, our bus almost crashed this morning," before looking to Josh for the confirmation that she had yet to receive. "Didn't it, Josh?"

Processors working overtime, the replica managed to offer a slightly confused agreement, "Uh huh."

Both adults were now in automatic parenting mode and their mother asked, with some bafflement, "How come you didn't mention this earlier?"

Megan shrugged, "I guess I just forgot."

Her father's face wore a stunned expression somewhere between open-mouthed incredulity and furrowed-brow anger, "Forgot? What do you mean, 'almost crashed'? Either it crashed or it didn't," he demanded to know.

Still completely missing the reason why her parents seemed so concerned, Megan began to elaborate with relish, "Well, some idiot pulled out right in front of us. Our driver did a great job of missing him. He slammed the brakes on so hard that everything flew all over the bus. There were books and bags everywhere."

It was left to her mother to try and get to the real meat of the story. "So was anyone hurt?"

Megan shrugged her shoulders as she stabbed some food with her fork. "Not really. I think Josh was the only one and he only had a nosebleed."

Her exasperation beginning to grow, their mother asked slowly and deliberately, "What happened exactly?"

All three people around the table now looked pointedly at Josh for some sort of clarification. The duplicate was clearly out of his depth and his automated programming determined that he needed to tread very carefully. It enhanced his visual and aural sensors to detect every possible reaction from the other three to what he was about to say. He'd need to adjust and counter-adjust rapidly as the conversation developed. In short, this machine was going to have to employ a particularly human trait and guess his way through it. "Well, I don't really remember too much. It all happened so quickly," he began.

Megan looked surprised, "You mean you don't remember anything? Your nose was bleeding all over the place."

A seemingly straightforward adjustment and explanation seemed appropriate, "I guess maybe someone must have bashed into me."

Megan immediately derailed the attempt. "The way I heard it, you cracked your face on the back of the seat in front."

No point in trying to correct, just push on, his programming told him. "Oh, well maybe that's what happened. I know it didn't really hurt much. Probably looked worse than it was."

His 'mother' intervened, peering at his face. "Let me have a look at it."

The replica knew what a typical teenage male human reaction to this suggestion would be. "No, don't worry about it, Mom. It's all fine now."

But mothers aren't that easily deflected in such circumstances. "Either way, I'd still like to take a look. After all, you might have concussion since you don't seem able to remember it." With that she leaned across the table, fussing away the duplicate's protestations, and placed her hands on his face. She manipulated his cheeks and delicately tweaked his nose, as she attempted to look up his nostrils.

The replica's programming was assimilating the experience in readiness for some sort of rapid response, but the technology involved in the manufacture of the machine had fortunately produced such a high standard of skin texture, colour and pliability that she was completely fooled. "Well, there doesn't seem to be anything obviously wrong," she pronounced as she relaxed back into her chair. "In fact there doesn't seem to be a mark on you," she added, but to the relief of the duplicate she didn't pursue the point.

"That's lucky. It must have been quite a bash," Megan remarked casually, before remembering some further detail. "Come to think of it, didn't you get blood on your shirt?" she asked, a little puzzled as to its total absence now.

Her duplicate 'brother' hesitated momentarily before arriving at a plausible explanation, "Ah, yes. But I washed it out as soon as we got into school."

"Did anyone report it all?" asked their father, concern still very evident in his voice.

Assuming that he was referring to the accident, rather than Josh's act of washing his shirt, Megan replied, "I think the bus driver did. I saw him make a phone call soon afterwards and Mr Jacks got on to the bus when we got to school."

This seemed to go some way to satisfying her father's concern, but he continued to probe just a little more. "Did he see you, Josh?"

The replica looked at his sister and attempting to affect some humour asked her rather endearingly, "Did he?"

Megan looked at him quizzically, slightly uncertain how to respond, "Why are you asking me?"

"Because you seem to know more about the whole thing than I do," he replied smiling. The sub-routines had determined that humour may help to defuse, and possibly even derail, the conversation.

Unsure whether her 'son' was trying to be funny, his 'mother' looked askance at him and asked, "Are you sure you haven't got a concussion?"

Megan supplied the information that the replica needed, and that his 'father' had requested, "I don't think he spoke to you."

The duplicate relaxed slightly and responded casually, "That's what I thought." He looked at his 'parents' and, gaining in confidence, informed them, "I just went straight into school on my own to clean myself up."

He might not be totally out of the woods yet though, as Megan elaborated, "I saw him get on the bus, though, and inspect the seats you had been sitting in."

Continuing his attempt to bottom out the subject, the duplicate acknowledged Megan's contribution. "Hmm," before suggesting, "Well, he must have thought it wasn't that serious, because he hasn't spoken to me about it at all."

Becoming more interested in finishing her dinner than prolonging the conversation, Megan appeared to concur. "He seemed more concerned with cleaning up the seat. I saw him wiping the blood up with a tissue."

Her father, however, had the bit firmly between his teeth, "This is too weird. I'm going to call the principal tomorrow and find out if he knows anything about it."

The replica tried to deflect any further involvement, "Don't worry, Dad, it's not important. No harm was done and I feel just fine."

Finally he also seemed to have some agreement from his 'mother'. "Well you certainly seem all right physically to me," she pronounced, now seemingly happy to continue eating her own dinner.

Megan busily mopped her plate with a piece of bread and suggested sarcastically, "Yeah. It's just mentally that he's damaged."

The replica knew exactly how to respond to the comment. "Thanks," he replied ironically. He looked around the table and entreated all of them, "Look, I'm absolutely fine, I promise. But I am a bit tired. Does anyone mind if I go to bed now?"

"What shall I say if anyone calls?" Megan asked innocently.

The replica's programming experienced something approaching deja-vu as, once again, a gap seemed to exist in its memory. "Huh?" he asked. This time he decided that a determined finality might just get him through. "Just say I've gone to bed," he instructed her, before asking, "What else?"

"Oh, so it's OK now to tell them that?" Megan retorted, slightly miffed.

Still unaware of what she was referring to, her 'brother' replied, "Sure. Why wouldn't it be?"

Megan had finished her dinner and pushing her plate away she looked across at the replica and explained, "'Cos the other day you got all mad at me for telling Chris that you went to bed early."

Recovering almost instantaneously from the potential gaffe, the duplicate replied, "Well, anyone but Chris, that is. Just tell him that I'm too busy earning points and increasing my lead to come to the phone."

Megan just shrugged, long-sufferingly. "Fine," was all she said.

The replica stood up and casually addressed the three of them. "Well, goodnight all." Then looking deliberately at Megan he added, "And happy birthday again, sis," before turning and starting to walk out of the room. He knew she would protest again and, with perfect timing as she was about to open her mouth, he called back over his shoulder, “I know. It’s not until tomorrow!”

Whether as a reaction to his humour or in defiant indignation, Megan muttered quietly to no-one in particular, “You didn’t go into school on your own to clean up. Chris and John went with you.”

Josh stopped momentarily, then continued walking as he replied with his back to her, “I know. But they don’t really count, do they?” and left the room.

Once he had gone, his ‘mother’ confided to her husband and daughter, “That’s very strange. Josh has always had such a good memory.”

His ‘father’ agreed, “And he’s usually so precise about these things.”

His ‘sister’ also seemed to concur and she muttered more to herself than either of her parents, “And you’d think he’d remember our birthday traditions.” Then with a sudden realisation she looked up to make a joke at her brother’s expense, “Hey, maybe *gifted and talented* isn’t all it’s cracked up to be after all.”

They all laughed lightly, but his ‘mother’ was still obviously concerned when she countered, “Or maybe he has got concussion.”

“Then a good night’s rest is what he needs,” suggested his ‘father’.

None of them, of course, had any reason to suspect that the person they thought was Josh had any other reason at all for his apparently strange behaviour. After all, why would they? And in this state of innocent ignorance her father turned to Megan and cheerfully asked, “Now, about that birthday. Fancy watching a movie?”

Chapter 54

Once again Callum found himself knocking on Samantha Mitchell's open office door and walking in to the glass and aluminium sanctuary. Samantha was busy reading and re-reading drafts of official statements that she had been preparing for Herbert Kennedy. "Hey, Sam, you wanted to know if there were any developments. Well, the first group has reached Mars," Callum blurted out, interrupting her thoughts and concentration.

His blonde boss looked up from the sheaf of papers that she was engrossed in. "OK, so from hereon in it's open season. Any major observatory on Earth will be able to see them," she stated ruefully.

Callum tried to offer some sort of consolation. "With luck it'll take them a little time to work out what they are, and even longer to see what's now going on."

Both he and Samantha knew there was some truth in what he had just said, but they also knew that it wouldn't slow the others down for long. "Which is what?" she asked as she got up and once more walked through to the main observatory.

As they reached Jacob's terminal, the younger astronomer started to explain, "It's a very faint signal that far out, but it looks as if some smaller objects have broken off and are headed our way."

"Kind of like an advance guard," Callum offered.

"Or a scouting party," Samantha countered. "What about the main objects?"

Jacob indicated them on his screen. "They seem to be falling into some kind of orbit around Mars," he explained.

Once more Callum interjected, "Setting up a base camp."

Samantha looked at him quizzically, frustration etched on her face. "Callum, do your analogies always have to have a military overtone to them?" she asked.

"Why not?" Callum shrugged. It seemed perfectly in order to him.

"Well for one thing," his superior began, as if lecturing a miscreant schoolboy, "We've as yet absolutely no proof of any hostile intentions and, for another, as scientists we're supposed to simply present the facts, not stylise them."

As usual Callum got a slight thrill from Samantha's reprimand. He knew it was said and meant gently and he enjoyed teasing her. "Yeah I guess you're right, but it's hard not to think of all the sci-fi movies isn't it?" he asked.

Samantha decided to let him know that it wasn't only males, geeks and nerds who knew about that stuff. Thirty-something blonde career girls might also occasionally enjoy it. "Not all of them ended in disaster," she pointed out. "If I recall some aliens came to help – what about *The Day the Earth Stood Still*?"

Surprised by her knowledge, Callum quickly shot back, "Original or remake?"

Hesitating to interrupt their banter, Jacob drew their attention to his screen, "Err, guys. You better just hope that these ones have only watched the benign movies, 'cos they're getting mighty close."

Samantha returned her attention to the matter in hand, "Huh?"

"In the time it's taken for you two to debate the finer points of our presentation style," Jacob explained, "The smaller objects have pretty much covered the distance from Mars to the moon."

Callum was incredulous. "But that's about 43 million miles." He paused before asking for verification. "In five minutes?"

Samantha raised her eyebrows and lowered the corners of her mouth as she commented, "Fast little critters, aren't they?" Shrugging, she hypothesised, "It makes sense though if you think about it. Ships' launches here on Earth are usually a heck of a lot faster than the actual mother ships."

"Yeah," Jacob agreed before protesting, "but only over short distances."

Samantha smiled, "When you consider the distance these objects have covered, 43 million miles must be like a walk in the park. Anyway, what are they doing now?"

"They look to be heading for either a landing or an orbit far down in the southern hemisphere," Jacob explained as he interpreted the data coming through rapidly to his screen.

"How far down?" Callum asked.

"It's difficult to tell," his colleague replied, "But it looks to be way below the tip of Africa."

Callum looked slightly puzzled and even concerned, "There's not much solid ground below there on which to land." He thought for a moment before musing, "Australia, New Zealand perhaps"

"Or Peru?" suggested Jacob. Both of his colleagues looked at him quizzically, forcing him to explain his thinking, "What? You guys never heard of the Nazca lines? You know, those massive strange pictures in the desert that can only be seen from the air."

"We know what the Nazca lines are, Jacob," Samantha acknowledged, before admitting, "I guess neither of us had made the connection." Then she added a contribution of her own, "There's also the Antarctic."

"What? But it's full of snow and ice," objected Callum.

"It's also one of the largest land masses on the planet!" countered Samantha.

Jacob nodded, "And virtually empty. Hardly any humans around."

Callum found himself beginning to agree. "Perfect for setting up an advance camp or bridgehead." He caught Samantha's disapproving look, "Sorry."

"Well, wherever they're headed they'll soon be off our scopes," Jacob reminded them. "The curvature of the Earth means we won't have a direct line of sight for our antennae."

"Good point," Samantha conceded. She appeared to consider her next action briefly before instructing Jacob, "Get back to Sanjeev. He should be able to get a signal."

Jacob began to open up the Skype link with relish, "What's the betting he's already getting it?"

Chapter 55

To anyone watching the school bus everything was exactly the same as the previous day, and probably most days before that. No-one would have been aware that the young student sitting with Chris, John and Kelly was not really Josh Travis. Certainly his friends weren't aware of the fact.

Even their conversation began to seem like a re-run of previous days, as Chris began to gently goad Josh once more about his increased workload and dedication. "So another late session at school yesterday, huh, Josh?" he asked, knowing the answer.

The replica's memory also knew the answer, "Apparently so."

"Were you very late home?" Kelly asked, seemingly concerned. "Megan was asking where you were. Something about her birthday supper."

The duplicate replied, weary with the topic, "Yeah, I know. She won't let me forget."

John joined in, hoping that his friend hadn't committed a social faux pas. "Tell me you didn't forget it was your sister's birthday."

"Of course not," the replica replied indignantly. "I just got delayed at school, that's all."

Kelly continued the friends' checklist, "And you did remember to get her a present, right?"

"Yeah," duplicate Josh answered, before adding a little sheepishly, "But I can't remember where I hid it."

Chris' shorter fuse was now beginning to burn brightly again, "Dammit, Josh, this just isn't like you. What the hell are those *gifted and talented* lessons doing to you? I bet you even forgot the game last night as well."

The duplicate was able to reply with a certain degree of smugness, "Actually, I increased my score by 2,340"

John was instantly impressed, "No shit?"

Chris also seemed to be reassured that his friend hadn't completely lost his way. But the reminder was, of course, detrimental to Chris' own effort. "Great. Just as I thought I was closing on you."

Kelly sat back in her seat disapprovingly. "You guys are something else," she complained, exasperation evident in her voice. "Josh forgets, or just plain ignores, his sister's birthday supper, then forgets where he hid her present but, alleluia, he did manage to play a session of that stupid game, so everything's alright!" She folded her arms indignantly, "Where's your sense of priorities?"

Chris suddenly remembered to side with his girlfriend. "You know, Kelly has a point. Come on Josh, shape-up!"

"What did Megan say when you couldn't find her present this morning?" asked John, eager to know if there had been a fight.

"Not much," replied the duplicate. "I think I managed to buy some time by telling her it couldn't be delivered until today. She'll have it tonight," he added confidently. At least it sounded confident but, of course, the duplicate knew that it would take either a memory update or the real Josh to have been found for the confidence to prove accurately placed. Neither of which seemed likely at this moment.

Kelly reacted to the confidence, "That's assuming you remember where you hid it!"

Chris suddenly starting laughing, enjoying his friend's potential discomfort. "Let's hope you don't forget what it actually is," he chuckled, not realising how close to the truth he was.

John indicated Megan sitting with her friends nearer the front of the bus, "Well, she seems happy enough, anyway."

As the conversation grew to a close, Chris stole a glance at Kelly before leaning in towards the duplicate Josh. "2,340? Pretty good going!" he muttered conspiratorially.

The bus pulled to a stop at the school and everyone piled off. Pausing to extricate his rucksack from where it had become wedged between two seats, Chris became separated from his friends and was the last person to exit the vehicle. Of course none of them had bothered to wait for him and he could see them at least 30 yards ahead of him making their way into the school grounds. He slung his bag over one shoulder and was about to commence a brisk walk to catch them up when he was confronted by an official looking man in a dark suit. Agent Fredericks flashed his I.D. and asked, "Chris Harris? I'm Agent Fredericks. May I have a word with you, please?"

Chris was somewhat startled and automatically agreed, "Sure. What is it?"

"It's about your friend, Josh Travis," the agent informed him. "Have you noticed anything strange about him lately?"

"Well he does seem to have begun to get forgetful, but I guess he's just working too hard," Chris replied both innocently and humorously.

Intrigued, Agent Fredericks asked, "Really? How forgetful?"

“Well he doesn’t always get around to playing the game that we’re all involved in,” explained Chris, wondering what all of this was about.

“What game is that, if you don’t mind me asking?” enquired Fredericks.

“Oh it’s nothing really,” Chris explained, instantly wishing that, perhaps, he’d just kept his mouth shut. Here he was about to admit that he was a nerd! “Just a computer game called *Last Line of Defense* We play against each other.” He hesitated, then decided what the hell he’d told him now, might as well finish what he had to say, “Josh is way out in front, but he doesn’t seem so dedicated to winning as he was only a few weeks ago.” Having answered the question Chris was now curious to know what all of this was about. “Say, why are you asking?”

Fredericks explained very matter-of-factly, “We’re investigating his disappearance last night and trying to build up a profile to help us find him.”

Chris couldn’t believe what he had just heard. “Disappearance?” he asked incredulously.

Assuming that, perhaps, word hadn’t filtered through to all of Josh’s friends, Agent Fredericks began to explain, “Yes. Oh, I’m sorry, I thought you’d know, being a friend of his.”

“But Josh hasn’t disappeared,” Chris protested, “He was on the bus with us just now.”

Fredericks looked alarmed. “What?” he exclaimed.

Chris continued, unaware of the impact of what he’d just said, “Yeah. Look he’s over there. Let me get him for you.” He turned away from the agent and called to his friend’s duplicate. Turning back he was stunned to find that Fredericks was nowhere to be seen!

Chapter 56

The floor of the control room was surprisingly not particularly cold or damp, especially considering that it was in a cave in Antarctica. Luke Richards didn't know if there was any particular reason for this – perhaps it was heated, he wondered to himself – but he did know that, like any uncarpeted floor, it was hard and uncomfortable. Both he and James Rock had had plenty of time to become acquainted with it since they'd been sat on it, with their hands handcuffed behind their backs, for many hours. Positioned in an out-of-the-way corner where they could be observed by their captors they had simply been left to watch as the armed men busily set up a vast array of military-looking equipment. Neither of them had been able to piece together much of what this was all about, but it was clear that efforts were being made to prevent any unauthorised people from gaining access to the caves.

The tall, and imposing figure of Captain Xavier, if that was his real name, was clearly used to giving orders and his men to carrying them out. Whatever else may have been a masquerade outside, the fact that they were all trained soldiers didn't seem to be in any doubt. But since they all wore plain white snow gear over seemingly black uniforms devoid of any national markings meant that their identity, and the identity of whoever sent them, remained a mystery.

They did, however, communicate in English with North American accents, and Xavier's deep, rich tones, that wouldn't have been out of place in a gospel singer, were now being addressed towards a shorter, stocky and bushy-haired white man wearing the rank insignia of lieutenant. "Jablowsky, did you manage to get those outer sensors in place before we had to rush in here?" he enquired with a firmness that said he expected a positive answer.

The younger, junior officer squared himself to his commander and replied factually, "Most of them, sir, but there's still a sizeable gap to one side that we'll have to be careful of."

Xavier nodded briefly and squinted slightly at the man, "But a frontal assault?"

Jablowsky gave a self-satisfied smile, "If there's a frontal assault we'll know about it as soon as they get within 500 yards of the cave entrance."

Another nod, this time decisive. "OK." He turned swiftly to call across towards a small group of men busily adjusting some equipment. "O'Reilly?"

A muscular-looking colour sergeant rushed across from the group, "Yes, sir?"

The captain instructed him, "O'Reilly, I want you to take a team of ten and start searching through this complex for another exit and see if you can't circle around behind those scientists out there."

Rock and Richards could hear these interchanges quite clearly in the echoing cave and the soldiers didn't seem to be bothered about keeping their voices down. James Rock smiled slightly to himself as he heard O'Reilly repeat his previous response, "Yes, sir." Man of few words, he thought, but as he watched the sergeant leave with ten armed men his expression betrayed his concern. He knew that their friends outside the cave would not be armed. After all, they were scientists.

Again Xavier summoned another man, this time another sergeant, "Murtoch? I need a full squad topside in defensive positions, armed heavily," he explained to the huge black soldier who had answered his summons. "We don't know how long we've got to hold this position, but I don't want to take any chances." He looked over at their captives and, perhaps specifically for their sakes he added menacingly, "Any of those scientists decide to play the hero, you let 'em have it, understand?"

Murtoch followed his commander's gaze, glancing at the two men, before replying, "Yes, sir." He nodded towards a group of resting soldiers and hollered, "OK, ladies, you heard the man. Let's go," before slinging a large machine gun over his shoulder and leading them out of the control room.

As they departed, Xavier walked across to a more studious and intense-looking bespectacled lieutenant. "OK, Jackson, we've been here for about two hours now. Have you managed to decipher this stuff yet?"

The officer was busily studying yet another of the many control consoles. "Not really, sir. All of the equipment seems to be locked down so I'm not getting any access to programs or software."

"Do you have any idea what it's actually for?" the captain asked.

"Nothing beyond the obvious assumption that it is some sort of giant mission control centre for all those aircraft in the hangar," Jackson replied, wiping his forehead. "But exactly what they're for and how they got here is still a mystery."

His commander nodded towards their captive scientists, "And I don't suppose these gentlemen know anything of use?"

Shifting uncomfortably, James responded, "Who, us? Look, buddy, we're simply scientists. We didn't know this stuff existed before we got here a few days ago, so we're certainly not gonna know what it's for or how it works."

Grateful for the excuse to speak after so long, Luke joined in. "Yeah, as far as we know we're the first to discover it. Which makes me wonder how you knew to come here since we sure as hell didn't call you."

Xavier remained impassive, "Let's just say we have friends in high places, shall we?"

Their fledgling conversation didn't, however, get the opportunity to blossom. A number of the consoles suddenly burst into life interrupting any opportunity that James and Luke might have had to entreat with the soldier. A variety of symbols began being displayed on the monitors and it was obvious that certain equipment was clearly showing major signs of operating.

The captain looked at the lieutenant, "OK, Jackson, tell me you did that, or at least that you know what it means."

Jackson who had been frantically trying to understand the development held his hands up in frustration, "Negative, sir - on both counts."

At the same time, Xavier's radio crackled into life and Sergeant Murtoch's voice could be heard emanating from it, "Murtoch to Captain Xavier. Murtoch to Captain Xavier, are you reading me, over?"

Xavier pulled it from its shoulder mounting towards his face and responded, "Go ahead, Murtoch, I read you."

The sergeant seemed slightly uneasy as he reported, "Sir, there's something very weird going on up here."

The exasperation in his commander's voice wasn't at all disguised. "Like what, sergeant?"

"I don't really know how to explain it, sir," Murtoch replied, before suggesting, "I think you'd better come up and see for yourself."

Clearly that wasn't what the captain wanted to hear, but he realised it must be serious for his presence to have been requested. "I'm on my way. Out," he responded curtly. He looked at Jackson again. "Keep trying to figure this out," then addressed the remaining soldiers in the control room: "The rest of you watch these two." He began to run towards the hangar and added, "They move and I want to know about it."

Chapter 57

Principal McGregor was sitting behind his desk listening intently to what Chris and Josh's duplicate had to say. Things seemed to be getting much worse and he was beginning to wonder if he'd manage to keep the lid on the whole operation for much longer. At the moment Chris seemed to be happy to accept that it was simply a case of mistaken identity on the part of the agent, but the principal needed to be sure. He leaned forward and asked very deliberately, "So what exactly did this government agent say to you, Chris?"

The student seemed to be a little uneasy, and the principal wasn't entirely certain whether it was because of his recently unsettling experience or because he was in unfamiliar and potentially intimidating surroundings. "Well, he seemed to think that Josh had gone missing," he informed him hesitantly, before elaborating, "He wanted to know if I'd noticed anything odd about him lately."

Trying to appear relaxed, the principal asked with a little trepidation, "And what did you tell him?"

Chris replied blithely, "Only that he seemed a little forgetful and that he wasn't as devoted to the game as usual."

“Ah yes, ‘the game’,” the principal retorted with a degree of relief. “It’s what keeps you gentlemen,” he paused, searching for the right word. “Motivated, right?” The student grinned, but the principal needed to be sure that that was all he’d said. “Did you tell him anything else?”

Chris had become eager to give the principal the whole story and resumed his tale with enthusiasm, “When he told me that Josh had disappeared, I told him he was wrong and pointed to him over the crowd.” A frown then appeared on his face, “When I turned back the agent had gone.”

Satisfied that, perhaps, Chris hadn’t become suspicious, the principal now turned his attention to the main matter of the missing Josh. “Hmm. Did he say which government agency he was from?” he asked.

Chris simply shook his head, “No.”

“Pity,” the principal sighed.

The student detected the disappointment in the principal’s voice and he beamed his big toothy grin. “But he showed me his badge,” he announced, suddenly feeling very pleased with himself. “It was the Department of Espionage, Counter Espionage and Prevention of Terrorism.”

The Principal looked momentarily startled, but it was difficult to determine whether that was because of Chris’, perhaps unexpected, efficiency at remembering the information or because of the actual information itself. “DECEPT. That’s interesting,” he mused.

Josh’s duplicate spoke up for the first time since they’d entered the office, “I’ve never heard of that one, sir. Who are they?”

The principal waved one hand in the air dismissively. “Oh, it’s part of the Department of Homeland Security,” he explained. “I think it’s a fairly small outfit connected to the CIA as well. Probably a kind of liaison department between the two branches." He paused to collect his thoughts. "I wonder where their local offices are? Probably share with Homeland Security," he mused.

"So what interest would he have in Josh and a supposed disappearance?" Chris asked, suddenly showing interest in the actual detail. "Wouldn't that just be the police?"

The principal thought for a moment. It might be that he'd need to change tactics after all. He tried deflecting the issue once more, "I'm afraid I don't really know the answer to that, Chris."

But the student persisted, "And anyway, why would he think that Josh had disappeared when he clearly hasn't?"

The principal made up his mind. "Because he has!" he said very matter-of-factly.

Chris was momentarily stunned and wasn't sure he followed. "Huh?"

The principal tried to explain things carefully and delicately. Who knew how Chris would react? He couldn't afford to have any more crises on his hands. "Chris, I hesitate to drag you into this," he began delicately. "But since you're already slightly involved it probably won't cause too much damage and could, in fact, help us all. Especially Josh," he explained, deliberately emphasising the last two words.

Chris looked at the duplicate standing next to him and protested, "But, sir, I don't understand. Josh is standing right here."

The principal searched for the right words, before continuing, "So it would appear, but I'm afraid things aren't all they seem. Josh isn't, in fact, Josh at all." Mentally he was crossing his fingers, and even his toes, that Chris would be able to handle this news without rushing out of the office screaming for the police.

But, unexpectedly, the student threw him a metaphorical lifeline. “You mean he’s a double?” he asked innocently.

Not sure he could believe his luck, the principal seized the opportunity, “Yes, I guess that’s what we should call him.” He leaned forward in his chair and indicated for Chris and the duplicate to sit down opposite him before continuing in a conspiratorial tone. “You see, the real Josh has been working on a highly secret project for the government as part of his *gifted and talented* course,” he said, feeling almost justified in stretching the truth somewhat. “Unfortunately, because it is so secret, it would appear that some other arms of the government have become suspicious.”

The duplicate tried to lighten the mood and further deflect any suspicions that Chris might have. “Talk about the left hand not knowing what the right hand is doing!”

Pleased at the intervention, the principal exclaimed, “Exactly, Josh!” Reverting to his semi-hushed, serious tones he continued, “So last night when we discovered that the real Josh had gone missing, we had to substitute his double while we tried to work out what had happened to him.”

Please don’t ask where the double came from, was all the principal could think as Chris opened his mouth to speak, but he needn’t have worried. “Which is why you didn’t know about your sister’s birthday,” was the student’s comment. Oh the joy of youthful innocence thought McGregor!

The duplicate smiled, “It was kind of hard trying to keep it up I have to admit.”

The principal was keen to keep the conversation moving in this preferred direction, “But now, thanks to you, Chris, I think we know where to find the real Josh.”

The duplicate was surprised, “You do?”

Chris was also somewhat unsure, “How?”

The principal sat back once more in his chair, relaxing slightly and enjoying his moment of adult know-how, "Well, as far as I am aware, we are the only people who know that Josh has gone missing and none of us has told the authorities yet."

"So how did that agent know about it then?" asked Chris looking confused.

McGregor leaned forward to emphasise his point, "Well, the only way that I can think of is that his agency is responsible for the disappearance in the first place."

The duplicate looked so human as the reality dawned on him, "Oh, I see."

The principal was on a roll. "I'm guessing that they've got him in custody at their local office," he suggested, continuing, "I doubt if they'll be wanting to frighten him so they're probably just using regular interview rooms in regular law-enforcement type premises."

"But where will they be?" asked the replica a little confused.

Once more the principal sat back, a little look of triumph appearing on his face, "The Department of Homeland Security has an office just out of town."

"So how will you be able to find out if he's there?" asked Chris, a little eagerly. He had to admit he'd been impressed by the way this middle-aged teacher had worked all of this out and was excited to find out how it would end.

"I have a few methods I can try," explained the principal a little secretively, before playing what he hoped might be a trump card, "But I'd like you to help us, Chris, if you don't mind."

The student jumped at the chance, "Sure, if it means I get my real gaming opponent back."

Chapter 58

The cold, dry Antarctic air almost took Captain Xavier's breath away as he stepped out of the cave. How people could choose to live and work in such a godforsaken place was a mystery to him. But he didn't allow himself time to linger on such philosophies. He had a job to do and that entailed concentrating on the here and now. And whether he liked it or not he was here, now. He looked up at the sky. Even that was weird down here, he thought. And what was that noise? He regarded the sergeant approaching him and shouted, "OK, sergeant, what's the problem?"

Murtoch was also struggling with the climate, but he'd been up here and outside for longer than his commander. He indicated the sky. Obviously Xavier wasn't the only one to have noticed the strange, other-worldly, purple glow. "This, sir," he replied emphatically. "It started just a couple of minutes ago."

The captain looked up again and slowly turned for confirmation that the effect was everywhere. As he did so he asked, "Any idea what's causing it?"

Murtoch shook his head and gave the reply that Xavier was expecting, "None at all, sir." He indicated the

Base Camp's landed helicopters. "The scientists are all still camped over there by their helicopters."

Xavier nodded, understanding the implication. "I'm guessing they're playing a waiting game until help arrives. So do you think this noise is anything to do with them?"

"Could be, but there's no way of telling unless we get over there," replied the sergeant, swinging his arms around a little to try and stay warm.

Xavier smiled a slightly sadistic grin but shook his head, "Too risky. My orders are to avoid confrontation unless it becomes unavoidable. The less evidence of our having been here the better." Then he reached for his radio and spoke into it, "Jackson, do you copy, over?"

The Lieutenant's voice crackled back at him, "Jackson here, sir."

"Jackson, send up one of those scientists with an armed escort," Xavier ordered.

Murtoch smiled as he realised what his commander perhaps had in mind. Jackson replied, "On their way, sir."

Xavier released the radio and noticed the sergeant smiling, "It's their Antarctic, we'll let them explain it. Maybe it's a natural phenomenon." He looked around again and tilted his head slightly trying to avoid the high-pitched noise that he'd been hearing ever since he came out of the cave. "Did the noise start at the same time as the sky changed colour?" he asked, wondering if he was actually shouting above it.

Murtoch nodded, "Yes, sir, it certainly seemed so. One minute the sky was clear and that cold blue colour. Next thing it suddenly went purple and the noise started." He glanced behind Xavier, distracted by the two soldiers coming out of the cave bringing James Rock, as requested, at gunpoint.

Xavier turned to follow Murtoch's gaze and immediately spoke to Rock. "OK, professor, what do you make of this? Have you ever seen it before?" he asked indicating the sky.

James started to nod sarcastically, "Oh sure, the sky regularly goes an eerie purple down here."

His humour, however didn't find much favour with his captor, who regarded him suspiciously, before continuing coldly, "Don't try and get funny with me, Rock. I don't have the time to indulge in silly mind games." He walked over to him and standing less than two feet in front of him asked very slowly and deliberately, "So, have you ever seen this type of thing before?"

James Rock decided that discretion was the better part of valour and answered simply, "No."

"What about this noise," Xavier persisted. "Ever heard it before?"

Again the scientist kept it simple, "No."

Xavier seemed to believe him and asked, "Any ideas what it might be?"

Again James remained monosyllabic, "No." He stared into the distance, shrugged his shoulders and continued, "But it might have something to do with that."

The captain turned to follow his gaze and could see snow on the distant mountains starting to slide down the slopes in enormous chunks. Even from this distance it was clear that the snow and ice were rapidly melting. On the lower slopes torrents of melt-water were already cascading to the valley floor. He frowned and spun round to face Rock once more, "What the hell can be causing that?"

James smiled slightly and shrugged, "Nothing that I'm aware of, except of course, for weird sounds and strange colours in the sky."

Chapter 59

In the Space Corps' main control room, Kirk, Frankie and Jim Scott were studying his console. It was obvious from their body language that they were trying to make sense of something. Hushed tones and frequent pointing at the screen all served to reinforce the impression. Scott was explaining, "So you see, those small ships descended to the southern hemisphere and assumed a fairly rapid orbit above Antarctica."

Frankie raised her eyebrows, "Interesting. What's down there of any interest? Just snow and a handful of scientists from around the world."

"Precisely," Kirk nodded sagely. "Ideal conditions to perhaps establish some sort of base undetected."

"Yeah, but it's a hell of a way to any centres of population if you want to make contact," Frankie countered, adding, "or worse."

"Maybe they don't want to make contact," Kirk suggested.

Frankie was genuinely surprised, "Why come all this way and not intend to make contact?"

Kirk shrugged, "Who knows? That's the problem. We know virtually nothing about these objects so we're making all these guesses. Even the assumption that they are 'manned' craft is making a guess. After all, ours aren't!"

"True," agreed Frankie. "But someone or something must ultimately be controlling them," she persisted, "So why the Antarctic?"

"Your guess is as good as mine," Kirk sighed. He paused and then suggested something that he thought might help explain their actions, "I seem to recall that the Antarctic is rich in minerals."

But Frankie wasn't buying it. "What, a long-range mining operation?" she scoffed.

Kirk looked slightly hurt and defended himself with a smile on his face. "It's at least a possibility."

Jim Scott had been busily interpreting some data on another screen and offered Kirk's theory some support. "You may have something there, sir. Our sensors indicate a localised increase in air temperature below their orbit."

Kirk didn't seem to grasp the impact immediately, "Huh?"

Scott explained, "Whatever those ships are doing is melting the ice on the ground."

Kirk looked at Frankie, "Still think mining is such a daft idea?"

"Maybe they just want a warmer place to build a secret base," Frankie suggested lamely, knowing that Kirk's theory was much more sound than she had originally thought.

Kirk was studying Scott's screen intently, "Well, it's not going to remain too much of a secret once millions of tons of ice melts and drops into the ocean," he responded without looking up.

Frankie smiled at her next thought, "The environmentalists will have a field day and global warming theories will get another shot in the arm."

Kirk looked away from the screen and faced his two crew members. "Well I think we've played an observational role for long enough now," he announced solemnly. "It's about time we started to ask our visitors to let us know their intentions."

One of the other younger female operators looked up, her face a mirror of calm. "Sir, the second inbound fleet has just passed Mars and looks to be heading for a lunar orbit," she announced without any panic.

Kirk was pleased that the team were holding it together. Goodness knows what they were thinking inwardly, but their outward demeanour was one of cool professionalism. Everyone busying themselves with their duties, yet they must be concerned about how things would develop. Seeing him, Frankie and Scott huddled together probably wasn't helping, but there wasn't much he could do about that. This was all uncharted territory. No-one knew how this thing was going to play out and he was trying to steer a steady course through what could become treacherous waters. "Hmm. Closer to the target. Less distance to travel to and from the base," he mused, almost to himself, before increasing the volume and looking at Frankie, "Or to transport the minerals that they mine."

Frankie retorted, "At this rate they'll be joining their friends in about ten minutes."

Kirk decided that it was time for action. They'd deliberated for long enough. Since the visitors had either not noticed their presence or had simply decided not to bother making contact he was going to have to force the issue somehow. He needed to know what they were up to. "OK. Get all available simulator pilots to their stations immediately and stand by to launch. Make sure all ships are fully armed but the order to engage must only come from me. Understand?"

Frankie seemed pleased. "Absolutely." She looked across at one of the other operators, "Get all pilots to their stations now," before turning back to Kirk. "You realise that if we launch that many ships and fly them that close to Earth there's a very strong possibility that they'll be detected?" she asked. "A lot of awkward questions could follow."

Kirk was very much aware of that likely scenario. "Yes, I know. But I don't see that we've really got much choice. We're the only ones with anything like the equipment to intervene." He had clearly already thought through his next move as, without any hesitation, he called across to the communication operator, "Johnson, get me the administrator of NASA on the scrambled frequency and patch the call through to my office."

As he began to walk towards the control room door he was pleased to notice that most of the operators were looking satisfied. It seemed that his decisiveness had certainly met with their approval. At least they were now doing something, rather than simply being spectators. More to himself than to anyone in particular he mused, "Why couldn't these guys have just called in advance to let us know they'd be in the neighbourhood?"

Chapter 60

A chilling breeze was starting to blow up outside the caves in the Antarctic. For those in the Base Camp party huddled around the landed helicopters it was nothing more than a slight irritant. They'd all been based down here in the South Pole for long enough to treat this type of weather as normal, even pleasant compared to some of the real weather that they got. Nevertheless, they weren't too proud to avail themselves of whatever shelter the helicopters could provide. To Alex, who was in the middle of a long-distance conversation to Mario Silvester on a radio telephone, it was more the occasional sound of the breeze than any chill factor that was most annoying. That and the fact that whilst having the conversation he was unable to move about as his team members might to keep warm. "Yes, sir, our men are still being held captive in the cave," he was saying in his deep, North American, treacly-thick accent.

He paused while he was asked the next question. "Well, we assume that they are since we've not had any word from them since we saw them being taken in there," he replied. Again another pause, "No, we haven't attempted a rescue – just stayed in position like you instructed us," he reassured his boss, before adding, "But I sure would like to try *something.*"

From the look on his face it was clear that he wasn't receiving permission, "Yes sir I do appreciate that they are armed and we're not, but how long do you think it will be before the help you're sending arrives?" The response to that question didn't seem to be any more helpful since it elicited a dejected, "OK. I see."

The members of his team close enough to where he was standing could tell that he was getting frustrated by the direction the conversation was taking. "That noise?" Alex confirmed the question before answering, "We've no idea what that is. At first I thought it had something to do with our visitors, but then we noticed that the sky had gone purple as well." He nodded in agreement, "Yeah, very strange. Must be some kind of freak weather event and we're right in the middle of it."

This time the pause was longer than before. Clearly he was receiving instructions. "OK. We'll wait here until that help arrives." Another briefer pause and then, "Yes, of course. I'll keep you posted." He flicked the switch and disconnected the call.

"Why didn't you tell him about the snow melting?" Olivia Green asked him innocently. The young meteorologist seemed aghast that such an obvious piece of information had been omitted.

"I don't know," Alex replied wearily. "Maybe I'm just getting tired of reporting things to Mario that I don't understand and that he can't fix. What's the situation now?" he asked, walking past the helicopter to get a better view. The entire top half of the mountain range across the valley was now bare stone and the melt-water had formed large lakes in the distance. "This is very weird," he said to no-one in particular.

Alex pointed towards the caves, "Do we know yet if it's anything that they're doing?"

"Not as far as we can tell," answered Olivia, adding, "But who knows?"

Lewis Wood asked a little disbelievingly, "Do you really think there's some sort of weapon been invented that can cause that sort of rapid temperature rise from that distance?"

Alex regarded the bearded geologist before replying with a wry smile, "Well, short of a hydrogen bomb, no I don't. And they clearly haven't set one of those off."

As all three of them grinned at his gallows humour a fourth member of the team came running around from the other side of the helicopter. Steve Roger's blond, shaggy hair was blowing wildly due to a combination of his running and the strengthening breeze. He was pointing up to the sky and asked frantically, "What about those?"

The other three scientists followed his arm to the sky and saw six sleek aircraft swooping down from an immense height before heading for the melt-water lakes. Silver in colour and with no discernible markings, the craft were almost dart-like in shape, consisting of a flat delta wing bisected by a vertical delta wing that extended above and below the fuselage. They looked almost as if a giant had taken an impossibly large arrow head and spliced another on to it at ninety degrees.

"Now that's more like it," nodded Alex, feeling slightly more on top of the situation.

"Who the hell are they?" asked Olivia.

Alex started to reply, but began to doubt his own confidence even as he spoke, "Well, I'm hoping it's the rescue party that Mario is sending. But I sure as hell don't recognise the aircraft type."

"Are we sure they are aircraft?" asked Lewis simply.

"Well, what else flies?" Alex retorted.

Steve also seemed somewhat doubtful about the correct categorisation of the machines. "They do seem to have come straight down," he pointed out.

"What, from space?" asked Alex incredulously.

Olivia seemed to agree with her boss that the unspoken suggestion being made by the other two was somewhat far-fetched. "Surely not," she countered.

"You ever seen a purple sky or snow and ice melt that quickly before?" Lewis asked provocatively.

"No," Olivia answered truthfully.

"Well, maybe that's the explanation," suggested Lewis blithely.

The aircraft suddenly seemed to halt their landing, as if the pilots had just noticed the helicopter party. They hovered momentarily before suddenly heading straight across the ice to fly low and fast over the helicopters and caves.

Steve whistled, "I, certainly, have never seen any *airplane* do that before."

"OK, so if they're not aircraft, whose spaceships are they?" asked Alex, equally in awe of what he'd just seen. "As far as I know the shuttle's no longer in service. And they couldn't handle like that either."

"Maybe they're the replacement vehicles being tested?" volunteered Olivia.

"Huh?" Lewis asked in disbelief at what he perceived as her apparent naivety.

"Well, they'd expect the Antarctic to be fairly empty," offered Olivia trying to win over the apparent hostility to her theory. "Good for secrecy," she elaborated.

"What about the sky, the noise and the melting ice?" Steve asked. "You're not gonna tell me that NASA is testing new space shuttles that produce those side effects."

Alex agreed. "Steve is right," he conceded, before asserting, "So if they're not from NASA, it's a safe bet they're not from Earth."

Olivia threw her arms up in disgust, "Oh great, so now we're not only dealing with kidnap and armed maniacs, but we're also in our very own sci-fi movie!"

A second woman came running over to Alex from another of the grounded helicopters, accompanied by three more male scientists. In her mid-forties, Julie Shaw was one of the top glacier specialists in the entire South Pole. “Alex, did you see that? What were those things?”

Steve answered before Alex could respond, a slight note of alarm in his voice, “Who knows? But they’re coming back.”

The spaceships flew past the helicopters once more at terrific speed for such a low-level run and landed almost vertically about the same distance from them as they were from the cave. Their grounded position created, in effect, the third point of a triangle formed with the helicopters and the cave.

Chapter 61

Further along the valley, on the slope of the mountainous ridge just outside the entrance to the caves, the military detachment had also been observing the arrival of the spaceships. Like the scientists they, too, had been loathed to accept the true nature of the flying machines, but with the same eventual resignation that their potential adversaries had also experienced, they finally bowed to the logic of the situation and accepted them for what they were.

Of course, being soldiers, they tended to take a slightly different approach to that of the scientists. They weren't prepared to sit it out and wait to see what might happen. "OK, sergeant, I don't know who the hell those guys are, but they definitely aren't on our side," Captain Xavier declared for all his men to hear. He continued issuing orders. "Tell your men to remain hidden and wait for my signal."

Sergeant Murtoch made a number of hand signals to his men, who had already assumed camouflaged positions all around their redoubt. Nobody moved and all had their eyes firmly trained on the new arrivals. Both Murtoch and the captain knew that they couldn't keep up this high state of readiness for too long. Staying hidden and alert wasn't too much of a problem, but in this cold climate and the steadily-intensifying wind, remaining motionless would not be very advisable.

Suddenly they all saw doors slide open in the undersides of the spaceships and steps extend down to the ground. They waited with an intense combination of curiosity, fear and excitement to see what would descend the steps. Nobody, whether it be the soldiers or the scientists away to the left in their encampment, was oblivious to the fact that they were about to make history as the first humans to see an extra-terrestrial!

After the briefest of waits, booted feet began to appear at the top of the steps of the ships and small groups of bipeds started to come into few. Some of the witnesses to this historic moment felt a little disappointed that the visitors appeared to be quite humanoid and a few wondered if they were, indeed, aliens or simply some sort of NASA test pilot. Their apparel didn't do much to dispel this latter suspicion since they were wearing what looked very much like a cross between a flying suit and a space suit. On their heads were helmets very similar to those worn by astronauts. The face plates were totally opaque, preventing any aspect of the real appearance of the wearers from being seen.

The visitors began to slowly fan out beneath each of the ships as they reached the bottom of the steps. Some groups began to move purposefully towards the cave, while some slowly advanced towards the helicopters. Amongst the scientists, Alex couldn't help but stand in awe as this tentative scene developed in front of him. It was almost like the delicate interplay between a human and a wild animal that he or she is trying to coax into trusting them. If any of the military group imagined the same analogy they clearly weren't going to wait to see if the wild animal wanted to be tamed. As soon as the visitors were within range of the cave Captain Xavier gave the order, "Fire!"

Immediately the crisp air became full of sharp cracks as a dozen machine carbines began to open fire on the seemingly inoffensive aliens. Three of them were felled immediately and the rest scattered for cover. But if they looked harmless, they soon proved otherwise. From the sides of their spacesuits they all produced firearms that had hitherto been concealed. Clearly they were trained to use them and within moments were returning fire. But whereas their attackers were using the traditional bullets to attempt to harm them, the aliens were using some kind of concentrated energy beam to return the compliment.

As both sides began to get the range and location of their targets, the skirmish began to escalate towards a minor battle, with deadly fire pouring out from both groups towards the other.

Chapter 62

Bob Henderson leaned forward in his chair with an intensity that only served to underline the disbelief in his voice. “Are you absolutely sure?” he asked Agent Fredericks who was standing the other side of the desk in Henderson’s office.

“Yes sir. One hundred per cent,” he confirmed, very much aware that what he was telling his boss was certainly not what he had been expecting to hear.

Brad McCoy was sitting in one of the guest chairs and almost scoffed at Fredericks, “What? You’re saying that Travis was at the school while he was also in our custody?”

Fredericks wasn’t about to begin a whole new career in pandering to preconceptions. He’d always said it as he saw it, and now was not the time to change. “All I know is that when I started questioning Chris Harris he was very surprised when I mentioned Travis’ disappearance and claimed to have just been on the school bus with him.” He paused momentarily, perhaps, Brad wondered, for effect before concluding, “He even pointed him out across the other kids that had just gotten off the bus.”

Brad had known and worked together with Fredericks for a number of years and knew that there was no point in trying to dispute what he had just reported. Instead it would be better to look for further explanations. "But that's impossible, unless they're using doubles," he protested. He thought for a moment and continued, "In which case this must be an even more sophisticated operation than we imagined."

Bob Henderson responded gravely, "I'm not entirely sure what *we* imagined, Agent McCoy. As far as I know we received a tip-off that foreign agents might be using student moles as a cover. Quite what we expected to find I don't think I'd ever decided." Leaning even further across his desk, he stared pointedly at Brad and asked, "Do you know more than the rest of us?"

Brad chose to ignore the implication that he might be hiding something, "No, sir." He thought for a moment and then ventured, "I guess I'd just begun to build a sort of theory in my head."

Henderson sat back and a slightly world-weary look descended across his face. "Perhaps you'd like to share that theory with the rest of us?" he prompted Brad.

The other agent looked slightly uneasy, but also seemed keen to share his ideas. "Well, sir I couldn't stop wondering how an unfriendly foreign country could be using young students unless they were originally from those countries," he began. "Clearly the one or two individuals that had been suggested to us were our own nationals, born and bred here." As he expounded his theory he started to gain confidence. "Background checks confirmed nothing unusual so there had to be some other factor at work here, such as indoctrination."

It was Fredericks who voiced the first objection. "How would they have managed that on students who are only in their mid-teens? Typically, the subject for indoctrination has to be exposed to the ideology for a number of years. Surely kids that close to parental control wouldn't fit the profile?"

But Brad was only just beginning. He agreed with his colleague, "That's what I thought, so there has to be something more sinister in play. I noticed that the subjects were all addicted to computer games and wondered whether it might be some sort of subliminal messaging, but dismissed that on the basis that they weren't all playing the same games. And how come half the country's not affected?" The other agents all grinned at the simplicity of the humour.

Henderson was intrigued by where this was going. "So what's left?" he asked.

"Drug-induced compliance?" Brad half suggested, but the tone in his voice made it sound almost like a question.

Henderson wasn't completely sure that he understood either what Brad meant or that Brad was clear about the implications of what he'd just said. "What? That would constitute a major threat, and a serious concern for the Government."

Brad nodded. "That's why we went to all the bother of placing an undercover agent among the school staff and took the risk of obtaining blood samples from subjects," he explained.

"And they showed us what, exactly?" his boss asked, pressing the unspoken point that the results were inconclusive.

"We're not entirely sure," Fredericks intervened. He'd been considering Brad's suggestion and offered, "But the fact that the samples we've taken from the same subjects show different results at different times could be due to the effects of drugs."

"That's what I was thinking, although the specific drugs involved have yet to be identified," Brad concurred. He was really warming to his theme now and his facial expression had changed to one of excitement mixed with self-satisfaction. "But now your experience at the school this morning opens up an entirely new possibility."

Henderson was ahead of him, “Doubles?”

Brad slammed his hand down on the desk in a gesture that said he’d hit the jackpot. “Sure. If they’re using body doubles then there’s no reason for the samples to match.”

Henderson regarded him not so much with a look of admiration, but a look of suspicion. “So you’re suggesting that there are two people for each subject – an agent and a patsy?”

Brad was confident that his theory checked out. “Sure. It would make sense of our findings.”

A brief silence fell over the room as Brad finished revealing his thoughts and the other two agents attempted to assimilate what they had heard. Agent Fredericks rubbed his chin and was about to say something when there was a knock on the door and Kimberley Walsh entered, “Sorry to interrupt, gentlemen, but I thought you might be interested to know the results of the blood sample that we took from our suspect.” Unaware of the timeliness of this information she continued, “It’s normal. The haemoglobin and haematocrit levels are just what you’d expect.” She was puzzled by the looks of disappointment on the faces of her colleagues. “What?”

Henderson chose not to respond to Kimberley’s question directly, but instead looked at Brad. “So, Brad, if your theory is correct we’ve got the wrong guy.”

“Not necessarily,” Brad replied, determined not to let this set-back trash his idea so quickly. “Surely they’d need some sort of co-operation with the patsy to ensure that they don’t both pop up in the same place at the same time?” he ventured.

His boss nodded, prepared to concede the point, “Yeah, I guess that makes sense, but we’re gonna need a lot more than these outrageous theories to allow us to hold this young lad for much longer.”

As if on cue the intercom on Henderson's desk buzzed and his female secretary's voice filtered through, "Mr Henderson. I've got the District Attorney on line one."

Henderson looked a little surprised and acknowledged, "OK, Miss Nixon, I'll take it." The other agents all made to leave but he indicated for them to stay. He picked up the phone and pressed the relevant button to make the connection, "Mr Montana, to what do I owe this pleasure?" He paused while the DA spoke at the other end and then replied, "Yes, we have him in our custody, but no charges have been brought." His face began to darken as his mood became more serious. "More for his own protection and to eliminate him from our enquiries," he said, obviously in response to a question. By now he was starting to frown and glower towards the colleagues in his room. "Sir, with respect, I think you'll find this is a federal matter." Clearly the conversation was not going well!

The other agents began to experience that unsettling discomfort that accompanies the witnessing of someone in authority being countermanded, as Henderson seemed to listen for longer this time before responding, "Is that so?" Again he listened. His eyebrows suddenly raised in surprise and he asked, "Really?" before continuing in a resigned tone, "Then I guess he must have friends in high places." But he couldn't resist adding, "Makes our suspicions even more worrying."

It was clear to everyone that, whatever the disagreement had been about, Henderson had lost. Perhaps not on a knock-out, but he'd lost all the same even if it was only on points. "No. No matter," he said, trying not to sound too bothered. "We were actually just discussing how we have no further questions for him." He paused once more to listen before acquiescing, "No problem. Happy to oblige." A weary smile crossed his lips and he tried hard to inject some sincerity into his voice as he added, "And give my regards to Mrs Montana." He replaced the handset before looking at the phone and muttering, "Asshole!"

None of the other agents wanted to speak first and it was left for Henderson to look them all squarely in the face and explain, "Well, ladies and gentlemen, it appears that maybe there's more to this than meets the eye. Just as we're about to release young Travis we get *told* to release him by the DA."

"I guess the Harris kid must have reported his conversation with you, Fredericks," Brad suggested, hoping to soothe any dented egos.

"Yeah. But how'd it get to the DA so soon?" protested Fredericks.

Brad ignored the question. "Anyway, we have federal jurisdiction," he argued to Henderson. "The DA's sticking his neck out on this one."

His boss relaxed right back into his seat and calmly explained, "Oh, it goes much higher than the DA. He was told to let him go on the grounds of wrongful arrest by the state attorney general who, in turn, had received a call from the federal attorney general's office!"

The other three agents looked as surprised as Henderson had a moment ago, when he received the news on the telephone. "Wow! This kid must know some people!" whistled a stunned Agent Walsh.

Henderson was thinking things through. "OK. We clearly don't have much choice in the matter, but I'm certainly not gonna just wave goodbye to a perfectly good lead." he looked at Walsh, "Where's the kid now?"

"He's in a holding cell downstairs sleeping off the effects of the tranquilliser we gave him," she replied calmly, as if drugging under-age suspects was quite normal and routine.

"OK, wake him up and give him some sob story." Henderson instructed her, continuing, "Apologise and return him to his school as soon as possible."

"His school? Not his home?" the female agent asked.

"Yes, his school," Henderson confirmed the order. "That's another oddity about this case. As far as we're aware, his parents haven't even made a missing persons call to the local police yet."

It was clear from the expressions on their faces that the other three all agreed with him. "We'll have him back there in half an hour," Walsh confirmed.

"But, Miss Walsh, I don't want to lose him. Make sure he's tagged," Henderson instructed her.

Walsh seemed mildly offended that he'd even have to remind her, "Of course, sir."

Henderson changed tack and looked at Brad. "Well, Brad, this case gets weirder by the minute. I'd sure as hell be interested to know how your tip-off got wind of this."

"So would I sir," Brad agreed. "But it was anonymous, so there's no way of telling," he added ruefully.

It was clear that the meeting was over and Henderson confirmed it, "OK, guys. Let's get back to work. Keep a close eye on Travis and be alert for any type of double-switch."

Eager to get things moving again the three agents all left his office.

Chapter 63

As they left their boss' office, Agents Fredericks and Walsh went in one direction to release Josh, while Agent McCoy headed in the opposite towards their situation room.

As soon as he knew he was out of earshot he pulled his cell phone from his pocket and speed-dialled. Within a few rings it was answered. "Hello? Yes, it's me. I'm gonna need more information if we're gonna make this case stick," Brad informed the person at the other end. "The kid's just been released on the direct intervention of the federal attorney general's office!"

He listened for a moment before responding, "Yeah, that's what I thought. Anyway, if you've got anything else now's the time."

He continued down the corridor listening, then terminated the conversation with, "OK, but don't take too long." Pressing the disconnect button, he entered the situation room on his own.

Elsewhere someone else was also hanging-up after the conversation. They replaced the handset on the desk phone and paused to consider the latest development. As was his habit when thinking things through, Mario Silvester stroked his moustache.

Chapter 64

The sky was moody and sombre behind Herbert Kennedy as he sat at his desk, receiving the latest update from Kitt's Peak. Heavy with dark, rolling storm clouds, punctuated every so often with patches of light. It was through these gateways to calmness that glimpses of orange sunlight, infused with a red glow, could be seen above the buildings of Washington DC. "So after we calculated that the objects had assumed an orbit above Antarctica, we managed to get some satellites realigned to see what they were up to," Samantha Mitchell was informing her boss.

"And?" Kennedy asked, seeming perhaps more interested than he had previously been in her reports.

"Well at first it didn't seem as if it was anything in particular," Samantha began, quickly adding, "But one of the satellites we are using also carries weather instruments for monitoring temperatures, studying the ozone layer and that sort of thing. It has detected that since the objects have arrived there has been a fifteen degree increase in air temperature at ground level."

At first she feared that she had, perhaps, misinterpreted the agency head's level of interest after all as he replied, "And the effects of this?" as if he was simply absorbing the facts.

The frustration began to show in her voice. Didn't anyone else grasp the significance? "Well, I'm no meteorologist sir, but I'd assume that if that keeps up it's going to start melting the snow and ice."

Kennedy shrugged, "Makes sense. Anything else?"

She smiled and began with relish, "Oh, yes. It looks as if six of the objects have entered the Earth's atmosphere and have probably landed at a part of Antarctica called Marie Byrd Land." Surely he had to be interested in that.

Again a spark of interest, "Really?" But it faded almost immediately into a routine reaction, "OK, I'll relay this to the Polar Exploration Agency. See if they know anything about it."

Oh no, thought Samantha, you're not getting off that lightly. "That's not all," she volunteered, waiting long enough to see some sort of reaction on his face. When she thought she detected a flicker of curiosity she continued. "We've now detected a second batch of objects, also heading for a similar orbit." Gotcha! She thought.

Kennedy genuinely did look surprised and suddenly seemed to take an interest. He sat forward in his chair and squared his body slightly before asking, "Really? How many?"

Samantha was trying hard not let her sense of triumph show on her face and fought to keep her voice calm and business-like. "About the same number. We estimate them to be of similar size and expect them to assume orbit in about one hour's time."

"What do you make of them?" Kennedy pushed.

"Difficult to say sir," the astronomer admitted blithely. "But we assume these objects are from the same point of origin as the others and here for the same reason."

Kennedy sat back in his chair, but retained the same alert body language as he lowered his voice slightly to speak very deliberately and gently. “Miss Mitchell, from what you’re telling me about these ‘objects’, assuming precise orbits, raising temperatures and now appearing to and, I think we can pretty much assume that they are indeed some kind of spaceships don’t you? We probably don’t need to keep up the scientific pretence that they may simply be inanimate objects.”

Samantha almost breathed a sigh of relief. She’d always preferred straight talking and knew that Herbert Kennedy respected it outside of purely scientific reports. “I quite agree, sir and I’m delighted to hear you say so. In which case, I guess we need to ascertain whether this is simply a friendly visit or an invasion.”

“You’re absolutely right,” Kennedy agreed. A reaction that did generate a smile from his young female colleague thousands of miles away, sitting at her computer. “I’ve already informed the Defense Department,” he continued, “And they’ve despatched a team to investigate. I’m guessing they should be there within the next couple of hours.” He paused for a moment and looked beyond the computer monitor as if searching for inspiration. “I’m more intrigued, however, by the second batch of ships. Why did they arrive separately?” he was almost thinking out loud “Did they approach from the same sector of space?”

“Negative, sir,” Samantha replied. “These ones came from sector 4b. In effect they joined up at right angles with the first batch in the region of Mars.”

Kennedy frowned and adopted a more serious tone, “And your assumption that they are from the same point of origin is based upon what exactly?”

Samantha wasn’t sure whether she was being reprimanded, but decided to simply stick to their theory, “Nothing sir, apart from the fact that it would be one hell of a coincidence if we finally get visitors from other worlds and two different species choose to arrive at the same time."

Kennedy grinned, much to Samantha's relief, but she detected a note of caution in his voice. "I can see where you're coming from, but despite what I said earlier, we mustn't forget that we're scientists and there is no evidence as yet to support your theory. Sure it could be a rendezvous, but it could also be an interception. Have you considered that possibility as well?"

"No, sir, I haven't," she replied a little sheepishly. Damn, he was good, she thought. She'd seen this many times over the years when he'd managed to see yet another possibility in debates and analysis.

Surprisingly Kennedy didn't seem too bothered that it had fallen to him to promulgate this alternative theory. "Well, don't let it worry you, but don't ignore it either," he responded almost cheerfully. Perhaps he liked playing trump cards, Samantha thought.

"Of course, sir," she reassured him.

"Right, I'm off to fill NASA in properly," Kennedy announced briskly. "They'll be champing at the bit to get a piece of the action and their technology will be needed, I'm sure. You keep monitoring and report any changes at all to me as soon as they happen."

Recognising his change of tone to be signifying the end of the conversation, Samantha simply repeated, "Of course."

Leaning forward, Kennedy hit the key to terminate the call and watched Samantha's face disappear from the screen. Almost immediately, he selected another contact and commenced another call. A face partially hidden in shadow appeared on the screen and asked simply, "Yes?"

"Are you aware of another fleet coming in from Sector 4b?" Kennedy asked.

"We have detected it," the voice replied matter-of-factly.

"Will it be a problem?" Kennedy wondered.

"Efforts will be made to neutralise it," was the answer before the call was terminated at the other end.

Kennedy turned in his chair and regarded the brooding morning sky, wondering perhaps if it was a portent of things to come.

Chapter 65

A black 4x4 pulled-up gently outside Littrow High School and Agent Kimberley Walsh got out of the passenger side. She casually looked around the vicinity as she slowly walked to the back door. There was no-one around that she could see. School had started and, judging by their absence outside, she assumed all of the students must be in class. Nevertheless, she couldn't assume that they'd go unobserved. After all the school did have windows! Plenty of windows, she thought as she renewed her acquaintance with the building she'd spent so long observing over recent weeks. For this reason she made a great show of opening the back door gently and helping Josh to get out in a very gracious way. "There you go Josh, back where you started," she told him reassuringly. "I'm sorry you were away so long," she continued, doing her best to sound concerned, "But after you were taken ill last night we thought it best not to disturb you once the doctor had confirmed it was nothing serious. Your parents seemed happy with the arrangement."

Josh really didn't know what he thought. Part of him wanted to believe her. To believe that this had all been a terrible mistake and that the agency was only too keen to forget all about it. But part of him was still suspicious about everything that had happened. The last thing he wanted to do now, however, was antagonise her in anyway, in case, even at this late stage, she changed her mind about letting him go. When he was this close to freedom he was happy to play along. “That’s OK, Agent Walsh, don’t worry about it,” he reassured her. “Maybe the school’ll let me go home for the day if I’m lucky,” he added with a smile.

Agent Walsh returned his smile and reached back into the car to retrieve his jacket. As she did so, she slipped a tiny tracing transmitter underneath the collar. “Here, don’t forget your jacket,” she said, offering his coat to him.

“Oh, thanks,” Josh said as he took the item of clothing from her. He tried to look his most apologetic as he continued, “Sorry I couldn’t help any more with your enquiries.”

“No problem,” Agent Walsh replied as she climbed back into the passenger seat. She smiled one last time at Josh and assured him, “We’ve got plenty to be looking into.” With that parting statement she shut the door and the car slowly pulled away leaving Josh to wonder whether he should be concerned about what she’d just said.

Concerned or not Josh was delighted to be standing outside school once more, an experience he wasn’t sure he’d ever expected to encounter. Space Corps was certainly changing his perceptions of things! He took a long, deep breath, savouring his liberty, before slinging his coat over his shoulder and ambling towards the school entrance.

Chapter 66

Of course, Josh headed straight for the principal's office where he was now sitting, together with his duplicate, across the desk from Jonathan McGregor. The principal was sitting up straight with his hands joined on the desk in front of him. "OK, so it seems pretty obvious that they're on to something or someone," he was saying.

"Yeah, but how?" the real Josh asked.

"That's something I think we'll have to work out with Commander Stevens up at Space Corps," the principal replied, as if it was a secondary consideration. He leaned forward a little more concentrating on Josh's face as he moved on to what was, perhaps, his primary concern. "In the meantime, what did they want to know?" he asked.

Josh tried to remember everything they had asked him. Most of the detail he could recall, but it was hard to get across the sense of intrigue that he'd experienced. "They just said that they had some concerns about Ryan Samuels but they wouldn't tell me what the problem was. They also asked about you, sir."

The principal pulled a face and sat back in his chair. "Hmm. I'd say they were fishing." he pronounced before continuing, "It sounds as if they've been given some sort of tip-off but don't really know what they're looking for.

My concern is that you were there for a very long time without any adults or lawyers present."

"Yes, sir, I thought that too," Josh responded enthusiastically. He was delighted that he'd obviously been correct to feel that it was wrong. "But I think I must have passed out because they said I'd been taken ill and that they had a doctor check me out then left me to rest in one of their cells while I slept it off," he explained. "They said they'd informed my parents," he added, although he wasn't sure whether that was to reassure the principal or himself.

His face displayed his sense of betrayal when the principal responded, "Well I think it's a fairly safe bet that they didn't do that."

"Why?" Josh asked in genuine puzzlement. He hadn't realised how much he was desperate to believe that the agency had acted lawfully.

The principal explained, "Because we sent your duplicate home last night to try and give us some time to work out what had happened to you."

"What?" Josh asked in disbelief. "So they were never even aware that I was there?"

The Principal shook his head and tried to reply as gently as possible, "I'm afraid not Josh."

The student wasn't sure whether he felt angry, betrayed or frightened, and if it was betrayed, then by whom. "So why has all this happened. I'm guessing it has something to do with Space Corps. Is what we're doing here illegal?"

The principal realised that Josh's allegiance and trust had been seriously put to the test. How he explained things now could be a crucial factor in whether or not Josh remained in Space Corps. He leaned forward in a fatherly way and used the most soothing, straightforward tones he could muster. "No, Josh. Just highly secret and there are always people wanting to get in on a secret, whatever the secret is. I'm guessing that someone has gotten wind that we're involved in something special and is trying to use the law enforcement agencies to investigate it for them." He paused trying to gauge from Josh's face whether he'd done enough. "The question is, after your little experience last night, are you willing to carry on with your training?"

He was delighted when Josh didn't hesitate for a nanosecond before replying, "Yes, sir, you bet!"

The principal breathed a, hopefully undetected, sigh of relief. "Well that's good news, Josh. From what I'm hearing from Space Corps, they could do with all the good pilots they can get at the moment." He decided to let the resilience of youth complete Josh's rehabilitation for him. "You get up there right away and report for duty."

Clearly working with students for so many years had taught him the correct way of dealing with the kind of setback that Josh had just experienced. "Yes, sir," Josh responded enthusiastically before heading for the door to the portal.

"Josh, one last thing," the principal added, getting up out of his chair and walking towards him. "If they were suspicious about you before they're gonna be even more suspicious now that we used the attorney general's office to get you released. They're not gonna want to let you go that easily." He held out his hand, "Let me see your jacket."

Josh handed his jacket over to the principal, who began examining its various seams until he reached the collar, where he felt a lump. "Just as I thought," he nodded. "This is probably some sort of location beacon." He turned back to indicate the duplicate Josh who had been sitting silently throughout the whole conversation. "Why don't you swap jackets with Josh here and we'll see if we can't throw them off the scent."

The two Joshes swapped jackets with each other and the real one entered the portal corridor to resume his training in space while his duplicate remained with the principal, to concoct a little confusion for the agency and whoever they were working for.

Chapter 67

The icy wind had picked up a little and occasional gusts helped to deflect the sounds of the fire fight now in full swing further down the valley from the scientists' encampment. But they didn't need to be able to hear the incessant crack of the semi-automatic weapons to know it was still going on. The incandescent red beams of light that flashed brightly from the cluster of aliens towards the entrenched soldiers on the hillside were proof enough that weapons were being discharged. The fact that the scientists rarely saw any movement on either side seemed to indicate that both warring factions were pinned down in their positions.

Despite its distance from them, the scientists all felt safer clustered around the small amount of cover afforded by their bright red helicopters. Steve Rogers was shouting above the wind, "What the hell is going on? And who the hell are those guys?"

Alex Roughedge responded a little more calmly, "Who the hell are any of them? I don't recall inviting anyone to our little isolated wilderness."

It was Olivia Green who pointed out the obvious, "Well, sooner or later one or the other of them is gonna realise that we're unarmed over here."

Lewis Wood scurried back to the group from a little foraging mission of his own. He'd been rummaging around in the supplies routinely carried in the helicopters and now proudly displayed his finds. "That is apart from a couple of hunter's rifles and three flare pistols." When the other scientists all looked at him in disbelief he defended himself, "What? We might as well be prepared." To further plead his case he indicated the aliens and the soldiers on the hillside, "None of those guys seem to be boy scouts."

They were distracted from a potential debate about the merits of defending themselves against well-trained professionals with such limited resources, by the sudden awareness of the sound of many helicopters approaching from behind them. The entire party turned to scan the sky and could see about twelve large troop-carrying military helicopters approaching. As they started to land near the scientists Alex and his colleagues began to fear the worst. They were no longer protected by distance from the combatants, now that these reinforcements had arrived.

Large numbers of soldiers began to disembark at full alert and quickly assumed what, even to the untrained eye, looked suspiciously like a perimeter around their own helicopters and those of the scientists. But whether it was to protect them or capture them Alex couldn't be sure, until an officer wearing the insignia of the United States of America approached the little group. Accompanied by a small retinue of other soldiers wearing the same uniform, the officer assumed the same crouched posture as the scientists and saluted Alex. Removing his snow goggles and the scarf from across his face he identified himself, "Major Tom Landis, US Marines. Are you from the Polar Exploration Base?"

Alex found it very difficult to keep the smile on his face from bubbling over into a hug of greeting. "Yes. I'm

Alex Roughedge, Chief Scientist. We sure are glad to see you."

"What's the situation here?" asked Landis. "We were told to secure this area against possible aerial attack, but it looks as if they started without us."

Alex indicated the spacecraft occupying the valley floor ahead of them. "Those six craft landed not long ago, right after the sky changed colour and the ice on those mountain ranges started to melt."

The major quickly glanced at the spacecraft before allowing his gaze to linger on the distant mountain ranges. "How far is the ice affected?" he asked.

"I've no way of knowing from here," Alex replied, explaining, "We don't carry the right sort of equipment." He nodded in the direction of the marines' helicopters, "Didn't you detect anything as you flew in?"

Landis shook his head, "No. All our radar and electronic imaging equipment went down about ten minutes from here. That's why we came in ready for a fight." He looked across again at the spacecraft and the aliens sheltering amongst them, "OK, I'm gonna deploy my men to take out those hostiles. We'll try encircling them before mounting an attack." He nodded towards the soldiers on the hillside, "Are they your guys over there, keeping them pinned down?"

Alex was a little surprised by the unexpected question and smiled ruefully, "No, we've no idea who they are. They were already here when we got here and they high-tailed it into the caves when they saw us approaching." The major looked surprised by this unexpected detail and even more surprised as Alex filled him in further. "They seem to be well-armed and had arrived in military-type helicopters. They've been holding two of my scientists in those caves for about twelve hours now. We got the distinct impression that we were not invited to approach and have just been waiting here for help to arrive."

Landis indicated that he'd taken it all in and made a swift decision, "OK. Well, I guess we'll argue with them later, but at the moment we seem to be sharing the same enemies which makes us allies – at least for the time being." He turned to one of the other marines gathered around him and singled out a youthful-looking captain. "Matt, I want four squads to flank around those bluffs and rocks either side so that they can attack from the other side. Get the men over here fanned out and ready for an encircling operation." The captain rushed off and, gathering a large group of marines around him, set off away from the helicopters towards the middle of the valley. They moved cautiously, but determinedly, from one cluster of rocky outcrops to another as they began an encircling movement towards the aliens.

As the wind dropped momentarily, the staccato gunfire from the battle could be made out and both Major Landis and Alex watched the action for a moment. Seemingly noticing the light beams for the first time, Landis asked Alex, "Those sure as hell are unusual weapons. Do you have any idea where those guys are from?"

Alex shook his head, "I've no idea, Major." Then, indicating the spacecraft, posed a question of his own, "But have you ever seen aircraft like those before?"

Landis answered factually, "No, sir."

"Well I'm certainly not an expert," admitted Alex. "But I think it only fair to tell you that I suspect you might be about to go into battle with extra-terrestrials."

"What?" the Major asked incredulously. "Aliens?"

Alex nodded and grinned ruefully, "Yes, sir, little green men."

Trained to expect the unexpected, the major tried to take this latest development in his stride, "Well, that'll certainly be a first." He glanced at his shoulder harness as his personal radio crackled into life.

The young captain's voice emanated from the radio, "We're in position, major."

"OK, Matt," Landis replied. He continued, speaking slowly and very deliberately, "Be aware that the enemy may be extra-terrestrials. Be alert for advanced weaponry."

There was an understandable pause from the other end before the captain replied, "Understood, major."

The major explained, "I'm gonna start our advance from this side to create a diversion. I want you to be ready to attack on my signal."

This time there was no delay as the reply came through, "Roger that."

Turning to a lieutenant in the cluster still with him, Landis explained, "OK, lieutenant, I want covering fire at 500 yards." The younger officer scrambled over to the perimeter that the marines had established and within moments a steady stream of gunfire was being poured towards the alien group.

Of course this had the effect of drawing down alien laser fire on the location of the scientists, who hunkered down as best they could amongst the rocks and helicopters. Although the aliens were now having to divide their fire between the twin targets of the soldiers at the cave and the marines at the helicopters, there was still enough fire power coming their way that Alex began to wonder whether the arrival of their 'saviours' had actually made things worse. After about five minutes of trading machine gun and mortar fire with weaponry that seemed to belong in a science fiction movie and neither side noticeably making an impact on the other, everyone's attention was distracted once again to the sky as another batch of spacecraft descended at rapid speed. These were different to the first batch, more rounded and slightly larger, but nevertheless distinguishable as spacecraft when compared to known human technology. When they began to strafe the alien redoubt the original aliens seemed to activate some kind of energy shield around their position and the brightly coloured laser beams raining down from above ricocheted off with dazzling explosions of light.

Major Landis was the first to react. “What the hell? Who are these guys?” he asked no-one in particular.

Alex, who as the only resident of the area was almost a surrogate host of this somewhat surreal meeting of cultures, felt compelled to answer. “No idea, but they certainly don’t seem to like those guys.” He noticed that the new ships bore very different marking to the originals. “More aliens?” he suggested with a shrug.

“I guess so,” Landis agreed, “but it’s all so crazy.”

Some of the new batch of spacecraft landed reasonably close to the originals and disgorged a number of alien soldiers, who started to attack the others on land while the aerial strafing continued. Just as things seemed to be about as intense as they could get, a new batch of the first alien spacecraft arrived and engaged the newcomers in aerial combat.

“This has got to be the weirdest fire fight I’ve ever been involved in,” Major Landis confided in Alex. “No-one knows who the hell we’re fighting or who we’re fighting with.”

Alex nodded. “Yeah, but everyone seems agreed that those guys down there are the target,” he suggested, indicating the beleaguered aliens sheltering behind their energy field. The field itself was beginning to glow an ominous orange colour. None of the humans watching knew whether that was normal. By now there was traditional gunfire pouring into the shield from three positions around the valley, and the bright red laser fire directed at it from the newly-arrived aliens and their spacecraft. Laser beams were also being directed out of it towards the newcomers and the three groups of humans. Of course, with its intensity diluted by the necessity of targeting so many positions, it certainly seemed to Alex that they were enduring a much less deadly amount of firepower than when it first began. Indeed, the aliens seem to have determined that the other aliens posed more of a threat to them than all of the humans combined and were focussing most of their effort to repelling the extra-terrestrial attack. Above all of this, of course, two groups of alien spacecraft were performing dazzling, but deadly, aerobatics as they fought to destroy each other. Whatever the outcome, Alex was pretty certain that life in the South Pole was never going to be the same again!

Chapter 68

As Josh made his way down the corridors of Space Corps he was struck by how much the ambience had changed since his last visit. Whereas before the corridors were fairly empty they now seemed full of people. On his previous visits, the people he did encounter in the corridors seemed serene and went about their business calmly, in an unhurried manner. Now the many people he saw were all dashing about, rushing from one place to another in a purposeful hurry. Josh felt that he had left an early morning village and returned to a city in rush hour. Whatever it was that Principal McGregor had been alluding to when he told Josh that Space Corps needed everyone it could get must sure be important, Josh thought to himself as he dodged yet another totally focussed female crew member steaming down the corridor.

When he reached the control centre he figured he'd find out what all the fuss was about, but he'd have to wait just a little longer as he was almost flattened against the wall by an outward bound crew member bursting through the door. Recomposing himself he entered what he half expected to be a cauldron at boiling point, and was again surprised by what he found. Instead of the trading room atmosphere he was preparing himself for, he was momentarily taken aback by the calm, almost library-like surroundings he encountered. But if it was library-like then the library in question would be at Yale or Harvard, only days before the final exams, such was the intensity of the duty crew members. All of the work stations were occupied, and everyone was 100% focussed on the job at hand. Moving purposefully, but trying not to disturb anyone, Josh made his way to the central raised command dais where Kirk Stevens was busy talking to Frankie. He looked around as Josh approached. "Hey, Josh, glad to have you back. You OK?" he asked with genuine sincerity.

"Yes, sir," Josh replied enthusiastically. The last thing he wanted at this point was to be denied further action because of concerns over his well-being. He hesitated almost imperceptibly before continuing, "Principal McGregor told me to report to you. Said something about you needing every pilot."

Kirk smiled, "We sure do, kid."

It was left to Frankie to be the voice of reason or moderation as, with a little concern in her voice, she pointed out "But Josh is still undergoing training. He's not yet finished all the simulations."

Kirk nodded his agreement, "True," before winking at Josh as he turned to face her, "But didn't you tell me he was a natural and that his scores were very high?"

"Yes," Frankie replied, emotionless.

"Well, in the circumstances I guess we'll just have to put your opinion to the test," Kirk informed her, with a little humour in his voice.

Josh was eager to know what all this was actually about. "So what's happening, sir?"

Kirk regarded him for a moment before explaining, "All we know is that we have two alien fleets amassing in the area of Mars. Both have despatched small scout-type ships to Earth. The first ones to arrive immediately started attacking the planet by melting huge areas of ice at the South Pole. The second group have only recently arrived and began attacking the first group. We're just getting organised to help the second group."

Josh was understandably surprised. Aliens? Here? He'd only just gotten involved in this whole Space Corps thing and suddenly he was about to fight real-life aliens. "Do they know we exist yet?" he asked, wanting to make some meaningful contribution to the conversation beyond simply saying, "Wow!"

"We're not sure," answered Frankie. "When they first approached Mars the second group destroyed our outer sensors. but we don't know if they knew they were connected to us or simply assumed they were just part of Earth's observation programme."

"But why would they want to destroy Earth's sensors or defences if they're friendly?" asked Josh with genuine curiosity in his voice.

"We're not sure they are friendly," Kirk replied flatly. "But we do know they're attacking the first bunch, who are actively attacking our planet at the moment."

Frankie seemed slightly impatient with what she regarded as Josh's impudence at asking so many questions. "Maybe they wanted to try and keep the whole thing private?" But she didn't seem prepared for the look of astonishment that she received in response from both Josh and Kirk. "You know, tidy it all up, eliminate the threat to us and move on in the hopes we wouldn't notice too much," she tried to explain.

"What?" Kirk asked incredulously. "You're suggesting some sort of police action?"

May as well keep going, thought Frankie. You're in too deep with this theory now to just give it up. "Why not?" she asked. "It makes sense."

Kirk considered it for a brief moment and then simply shrugged. "Maybe. Someone else'll have to sort this mess out when they can, but in the meantime all we know is that one group is attacking our planet and the other group is attacking them. I guess we stand by to assist the one that seems to be wanting to help us." He turned back to Josh who was waiting silently for the rest of his orders. "OK Josh, report to the flight deck and get reacquainted with how things work. You'll find all the other students that we can muster already settling in."

"The controls have been reprogrammed to identify the two different groups of aliens," Frankie added helpfully, continuing with a smile, "So it should help to avoid shooting down the wrong ones."

Josh nodded and immediately left the control room. Adrenalin was coursing through his veins and he couldn't wait to get stuck in to the task he'd been assigned. Kirk watched him go then looked at Frankie again. "You know I still have a nagging feeling about all this."

"In what way?" Frankie asked him innocently.

"Well, to simply join in someone else's fight without knowing the facts. Suppose we just make matters worse?"

"Kirk!" Frankie exclaimed before remonstrating with her commander. "All we know for sure is that one group is attacking Earth and the other isn't. What more do we need to know?" The frustration in her voice was not difficult to detect.

Kirk rubbed his chin thoughtfully. It was fine for Frankie to see things in terms of cause and effect, but he had to weigh up the more long-term risks of making the wrong decision. He'd never shied away from making decisions in the past and he wasn't about to do so now, but he just wished he had more information to base it on. "I don't know, but I'd be happier if at least one of them had had the decency to contact Earth first."

Frankie tried to help him out. "Well, our friends at NASA confirmed that there'd been no contact and they keep ignoring our own signals. What else can we do?" she asked.

"Not a lot, I guess," Kirk reluctantly agreed. "I just hope that by joining in we don't tip the balance towards a group who are even more of a threat?" He thought for a moment before adding a real poser. "Just suppose they're actually fighting over who should have the right to conquer our planet?"

Frankie decided that they didn't have time for the luxury of debating that particular point. "Well, if we don't act soon there won't be a planet to conquer – it'll all be under water."

Kirk conceded her point and replied, "OK. Give the order to attack."

Chapter 69

Less than 200,000 miles from Earth, closer even than the moon, someone else's war was being played out. For reasons that were still entirely unclear to any humans who knew of the conflict, two warring alien fleets had journeyed many light years from their home worlds to stage a spectacular showdown almost within sight of the inhabitants of this seemingly insignificant blue planet. Scores of small scout ships were buzzing about in incredibly close proximity, given the limitless void of space, performing an intricate dance of death where the slightest wrong step meant oblivion. The dart-like ships of the first group seemed evenly matched with the more rotund, stubby craft of the second group, leaving the deciding factor of who lived and died down to the skill of the pilot. No sooner would one side lose a ship than one of the other side's would disappear in a fiery riposte.

Into this maelstrom the drones from Space Corps descended, like extra grains of rice being poured into a pan of already boiling cereal. The numerous tiny craft twisted and roiled together, bursting to the surface only to descend once more into the depths of the chaos. The new arrivals scored a couple of quick victories, but also lost a few of their own ships. Clearly this was very different to the simulations that the human pilots were used to!

On the flight deck at Space Corps' orbiting headquarters the young students were frantically controlling their drones while Frankie walked amongst them. She mirrored the action of one of the students as both instinctively turned their heads away from the sudden bright eruption on his screen and shielded their eyes. Yet another drone destroyed! "Damn! They're good!" exclaimed the crestfallen student.

"Of course they are, Charlie, they're fighting for their lives. All you've got to lose is a drone," responded Frankie, putting her hand on his shoulder to reassure him. "Hook yourself up to another and re-join the fight."

Further round the circular flight deck Josh punched the air. "Yeah, way to go! That's three!" Returning his attention to the battle he muttered ruefully, "But we don't seem to be even making a dent in their numbers. They're all over the place."

As he was speaking Kirk Stevens entered the flight deck. Compared with the intense quiet of the control room, this area seemed more like the starting line at a major sports event. A frisson of excitement permeated the recycled air and the tension was palpable. Like a humid summer's evening it was punctuated every so often by the lightning crack of another student exclamation, both victorious and defeated. "How many ships have we lost now?" he asked Frankie.

Frankie knew without checking the monitor. "Nine so far," she replied.

"And kills?"

This time she did consult a terminal. "Seven."

Kirk's face showed his displeasure and worry. "That's not too impressive is it?"

Frankie shrugged despondently, "There's simply too many of them."

"But you'd think our arrival would've tipped the balance," Kirk suggested.

Ryan Samuels was just approaching the fight with another fresh 'droid and took the opportunity to contribute his opinion. "But that's just it, sir, they don't seem to want to fight us. They're much more interested in the other aliens." He quickly returned all of his attention to his screen as he had to swerve sharply to avoid incoming laser fire. "Whoa, that was close!"

Kirk raised his eyebrows and agreed, "That's what I thought." He stood in the centre of the flight deck, observing the proceedings from the vantage point of standing behind all of the students, watching their screens. After a few minutes of scrutinising exactly what was going on in the battle he reached a decision. "OK, disengage. Retreat to assembly marker Alpha 2 and hold position."

Frankie looked at him startled, "What? Are you sure?"

"No" he replied honestly. "But I'm not exactly seeing a blood-lust amongst our enemies. Let's just hold fire for a while and see how things develop."

"But it might then be too late to do anything about the outcome," protested Frankie.

Kirk studied his assistant's face carefully. "I'm still not convinced that we should be interfering at this stage," he admitted.

"But they're attacking Earth." Frankie's tone was getting perilously close to argumentative.

Kirk thought that perhaps it was time to remind her who was in charge. "Withdraw, Frankie! I'll let you know when I want another opinion." There was a steely authority in his voice that didn't invite debate.

Frankie begrudgingly addressed the students, "All drones withdraw and hold at Alpha 2." She paused for a moment before adding, "But be ready to get straight back in there at any time." She shot a defiant look at Kirk and walked out of the room.

Chapter 70

Frankie stormed into her quarters and headed straight for her desk. Sitting down heavily she activated her computer. She paused for a moment seemingly weighing up something in her mind, before clicking on a Skype address.

The call was answered almost immediately. There was no exchanging of formalities or even a cursory greeting. Frankie just got straight to the point. "I'm getting a little concerned. Stevens seems to be losing the enthusiasm to fight."

A male voice responded, "Why? What's the problem?"

"He's not convinced that the aliens are our enemies," Frankie explained.

The voice was a little puzzled. "Why not? They're attacking the Earth."

"He thinks we might be jumping to conclusions."

The voice sounded incredulous. "Jumping to conclusions? Just how bright do you have to be?"

Frankie continued her explanation, "He's noticed that the aliens don't appear to be fighting back against us – only against the other aliens."

The voice wasn't convinced. "Yeah. And who's to say they won't turn their attention to us once they've finished off the other aliens?"

"That's what I've been trying to tell him, but he seems to be relying on some sort of 'gut instinct'." Frankie's exasperation was starting to show.

"Well, that's a hell of a way to fight a war," came the dismissive response.

"I agree," confirmed Frankie. "But suppose the others start to side with him?" she asked, adding, "After all, he is right!"

The voice reacted sharply to this opinion, "Enough!" There was a pause before he said in tones that made it sound like a direct order, "Keep applying pressure to get him to change his mind voluntarily, but if he won't budge you might have to take over."

Frankie looked concerned at this new development. "Let's hope it won't have to come to that. It'll be difficult to do so without blowing my cover."

"Just keep me posted and stand by," the voice instructed her.

On Earth, the owner of the voice gently stroked his moustache as he leant forward and terminated the connection!

Chapter 71

The secretary of defense's office seemed somewhat crowded despite its spacious appointment. Five men were sitting on the easy chairs grouped around the antique coffee table and a sombre air of concern pervaded the room. Three of the men were regular visitors and wore uniforms representing the marines, the air force and the navy. Herbert Kennedy was the only civilian amongst the guests and it was to him that the secretary of defense turned first. "OK, Herb. In your opinion, what exactly is going on down there?"

Kennedy adjusted himself in his seat and began a brief report, "Well, Mr Secretary, it sure is a mess. We seem to have two different groups of aliens and two different military units as well."

The secretary nodded ruefully. "So I believe." He looked at the generals, "Can someone explain how that happened?"

The general wearing the dark green uniform with black buttons and insignia of the US Marines responded. "As far as we can ascertain, sir, the second unit is not US military."

"Are you saying they belong to another country?" the secretary asked.

“It’s certainly a possibility sir,” came the honest and simple reply.

The secretary was understandably bothered by this information. “But how would they know about the situation? We’ve kept it under tight security.”

“Yes, sir,” the general agreed. “But the polar exploration community is multi-national, isn’t it? Perhaps someone got wind of what the US team had discovered and decided to make a call home.”

“But how would they have got there without us detecting them?” Kennedy wondered.

This time it was the blue-uniformed general from the air force who responded. “Well, the latest pass by one of our security satellites has revealed a small support vessel about ten miles off shore,” he told them. “It could be theirs.”

“Are you able to identify it yet?” asked the secretary.

The general shook his head. “Negative, Mr Secretary. In fact, it doesn’t appear to conform to any of the expected ship types known to be used by the relevant foreign military and we are so far unable to detect any national markings.”

Now that they had veered into nautical matters the admiral joined in. “There’s also the matter of distance and timing,” he suggested. “The US, Russian and Chinese navies are the only ones big enough to have a permanent presence in those waters and we’ve checked with our contacts. It’s certainly not one of theirs. Which means it’s either had to come from a country close to Antarctica or it was way ahead of us in finding out about the invasion.”

The secretary picked up on his reference to proximity. “I like to think that Argentina and Chile aren’t involved, but I’m not sure I like the idea of a rogue organisation being aware of this highly sensitive situation in enough time to be able to beat us down there.” He looked at Kennedy. “What do you think, Herb?”

"Well, Mr Secretary, I'm with you," he assured him, before continuing, "But I really don't see what other alternatives we have. Somehow a small military force got down to the target area quite some time before our own marines and even before the aliens arrived, it would seem."

"Well, friend or foe, we do know that they at least managed to engage the aliens and perform a holding action until our boys arrived," the marine general reported.

"But do we know that the aliens had harmful intentions?" asked Kennedy, feeling that, as the space specialist in the room, he ought to at least make some representation on behalf of the visitors.

But the general wasn't buying any pacifist intent. "Well there's quite a fire fight going on down there at the moment," he retorted, his voice heavy with sarcasm.

"I'm well aware of that, general," Kennedy replied, "But since it wasn't our men who made the first contact we don't really know what their original intentions were."

The air force general decided to change tack slightly. "According to the Polar Agency, they do seem to have been responsible for melting all the ice," he pointed out.

Once again Kennedy could see two sides. "Yes, but why? How do we know they are hostile?"

The admiral looked a little surprised by the question. "Melting millions of tons of ice and all the environmental damage that can cause hardly seems friendly," he suggested.

The marine general decided it wouldn't hurt to remind the civilians of another aspect of the situation. "Let's not forget that they are currently engaged in a fire fight with US Marines."

Kennedy knew that he was running the risk of incurring the general's disapproval, but felt it necessary to point out, "Yes, possibly to defend themselves! They may not have started the fight, after all."

Aware of the mounting tension amongst his advisers, the secretary of defense moved to nip it in the bud. "Gentlemen, we need to come up with a plan to get us out of this mess, not start making recriminations about what caused it." He turned again to Kennedy, "Herb, you seem to have different views from the military."

Kennedy sighed and sought to offer his opinion. "Mr Secretary, I'm simply suggesting that since we weren't in control of the situation when it started, we might be missing some crucial facts."

"Such as?" the Secretary asked.

Kennedy was secretly hoping that he wouldn't be asked that question. All he really had to go on were his own impressions, unlike the military who had hard facts to back up their interpretation of events. "I don't really know," he admitted, but before the generals could pounce he explained, "But the Polar Agency did report that those other troops had taken some of their members hostage and their actions do suggest that they were seeking to gain control of the caves and their contents." He paused to draw breath and was relieved to see the military leaders paying attention. "That, in itself, suggests that they certainly aren't particularly friendly to us. They may have started the battle to further muddy the waters."

It was clear that he still had quite a way to go before they'd shift their opinions. "What about the reports that other aliens also seem to be attacking the ones who melted the ice? Doesn't that suggest something to you?" asked the air force general.

"Only that they already had enemies," Kennedy replied. "So now they're fighting two forces – us and other aliens. I doubt they would have planned such a strategy," he suggested, continuing with a, perhaps impertinent, question: "Would you?"

"You may have a point, Herb," the secretary agreed. "But at the moment we need some decisive action. It's a real mess down there, with our marines fighting alongside some kind of rogue soldiers who may, or may not, be on our side against a bunch of aliens who may, or may not, be our enemies, who are also being attacked by another bunch of aliens who may, or may not be, our allies."

Given the complexities of the situation, Kennedy found it difficult not to sound ironic, or even humorous. "Nicely summarised, Mr Secretary." He looked at the marine general and asked, "What would happen if our marines disengaged?"

"What?" came the incredulous response. "You mean surrender?"

Kennedy held his hands up, palms towards the general in a gesture designed to reassure him. "No. Just stopped fighting. Maybe just for a while," - he paused momentarily - "To see what the aliens do."

The secretary sat back and gently sucked in his cheeks as he considered the idea. The corners of his mouth turned downwards as he ruminated, "Interesting proposal, Herb." He looked squarely at the general. "What do you think, general?"

The marine realised that he needed to tread carefully with this one. He didn't want to appear too hawkish when it was clear the secretary of defense seemed interested in the idea, but neither could he countenance anything that would leave his men open to danger. "Well, sir, it could put them in a really dangerous position," he began cautiously. "They'd need to secure a defensive perimeter," he glanced over at Kennedy and then back at the secretary with slightly narrowed eyes, "And reserve the right to fight back."

Now it was the politician's turn to reassure the military. "Of course. No-one's suggesting they throw down their weapons," he declared categorically. "Let's be clear on this – they're not surrendering, just disengaging."

Kennedy jumped in while he could see things moving slightly his way. "Absolutely. And if I'm right, they won't need to re-engage." He looked purposefully at the three military men sitting around him, "In fact, they might be able to withdraw."

But perhaps he'd misread the situation, he thought, when the secretary cut in. "Woah. Now hold on, Herb, let's not get carried away," he cautioned. "If we withdraw, we'll be leaving those caves and their contents to either a bunch of warring aliens of a group of renegade humans who, for all we know, are terrorists. They certainly don't seem to be legitimate representatives of any acknowledged authority."

Once again the air force general seemed to try a different approach to the discussions. "What about NASA, Mr Secretary? Don't they have anything to offer on the situation? After all, isn't this what they've always been waiting for? Contact with beings from other worlds." Kennedy wasn't sure whether the look he got from the general was accusatory or smug, or perhaps even both.

"That's a good point, general," the secretary responded before looking at Kennedy. "Herb, what's the story?" he asked.

"Well, Mr Secretary," Kennedy began, wondering whether he was actually being asked to defend himself and his organisation. "As you know, NASA detected the first fleet four days ago and were tracking them all the way in. When the second fleet arrived there was no way to determine if they were from the same point of origin or not," he admitted openly before adding, "The likelihood of two different species of alien both deciding to visit Earth at the same time, without there ever having been any known previous extra-terrestrial incursions to this planet, seemed extremely remote. Consequently it was assumed that they were both part of the same fleet and from the same place." He looked across the table to see the reaction to his next point, "Of course, some of that may still be true."

"But they're fighting each other!" the air force general objected.

Before Kennedy could point out the obvious, the secretary did it for him, "Yes, but we fight amongst ourselves, don't we?"

Kennedy spotted the chance to offer an olive branch, "I'll admit that it might be unlikely. We always tend to assume that a species that can travel through space will come from a unified home world. But none of us has actually seen any of these aliens yet. It is possible that they are from a warring planet that is continuing its fight in space."

He was delighted when the admiral appeared to respond in kind. "OK. I guess that's possible. But what, if anything, can NASA do to help? After all it gets huge budgets each year." He leant forward meaningfully, "Do you have any kind of defence contingency?"

Kennedy shook his head. If the admiral was hoping that the situation would lead to an unexpected revelation that NASA had secretly been developing science fiction weapons he was going to be disappointed. "Our remit is exploration and discovery, admiral, not fighting," he reminded the sailor. "We do have some probes and drone satellites that may be able to gather intelligence or even be equipped with rudimentary lasers, but we've nothing to compare with their technology."

"So we're a sitting duck!" declared the marine general emphatically.

Kennedy felt that now was perhaps the time to reveal his agency's latest discovery. "Not quite, general. Our sensors have detected a third player in this." He paused to let the effect of what he'd just said sink in. All four other people in the room looked either surprised or uncomprehending. He tried to explain further, “There seems to be another group of spacecraft engaged in combat out near the orbit of Mars. It’s too far away for us to know exactly what’s going on, but as far as we can tell they’re engaging the first group of aliens in some sort of battle.”

The air force general seemed to be the first to grasp what Kennedy was saying, “How do you know they’re not just the same things that are fighting at the pole?”

Kennedy shrugged, “The signal is totally different and they originated from a different part of space.”

The secretary of defense was frowning. How long had Herb had this information, he wondered, and when precisely was he thinking of telling him? “Where exactly?” he asked slowly and deliberately.

“Well we’re not entirely sure,” Kennedy admitted, before dropping the bombshell, “But they seemed to come from our own orbit – albeit a very high orbit.”

Chapter 72

The cold wind continued to bite, despite the numerous layers of protective clothing and Alex Roughedge was glad that he didn't also have to fight and operate complex weapons in these conditions. But if the US Marines fighting around him had any such qualms they kept them well hidden. It also occurred to him how incongruous they looked, clothed from head to foot in white Arctic gear yet fighting amongst barren grey rocks in the valley that was bizarrely devoid of any snow. In fact the more he thought about anything to do with this situation, the more he realised that almost everything about it was bizarre, not just the weather!

The battle had been raging now for about an hour yet precious little headway seemed to have been made by any of the combatant groups. He himself seemed to have spent most of the time sheltering in a rocky hollow with various members of his team, while the others were dispersed to similar features that offered some sort of protection from the laser fire.

Major Landis and his headquarters party were grouped not far from Alex, sheltered by a rocky outcrop that formed part of the base of the valley side. Not for the first time during the past hour, Alex glanced over to the marines. He wasn't entirely sure what he was hoping, or even expecting, to see and he could only barely make out what was being said, but perhaps it just gave him some sort of reassurance, seeing them still there.

For his part, Major Landis was trying to make his own sense of the situation. His men were correctly dispersed for an encircling manoeuvre yet the fearsome weaponry they were facing was making it extremely difficult to get any closer to their alien enemies. He consoled himself with the knowledge that at least his men were able to contain the extra-terrestrials. He was in the middle of telling a lieutenant to move one of the squads to a different location that appeared to offer a wider field of fire when the radio operator hurried over to him. "Sir, I've got the Pentagon for you," he informed him as he offered him the radio phone.

Landis took the proffered handset and spoke into it, "Sir? Yes, this is Major Landis."

The radio operator watched his commander listening to the person at the other end and then responding. "Well, sir, we haven't taken any casualties yet, but we've not made any headway either. It's like something out of a sci-fi movie – they're using laser-type weapons and have even got some kind of force field down there."

In the secretary of defense's office the occupants were having the same experience as the radio operator half a world away as they watched, and tried to listen in to, the marine general's side of the conversation. "Do the aliens on the ground seem particularly hostile to you?" he asked into his radio telephone.

Unlike the radio operator, the others in the office had the advantage of the general's speaker and were able to hear Major Landis respond in a somewhat confused tone, "Well, sir, we are involved in a fire fight with them."

"Yes, I'm well aware of that, major," the general replied. "But what about the other antagonists? There are four of you in this fight, don't forget. Who do you think represents the biggest threat?"

"The first aliens do seem to be concentrating mainly on defending themselves," Landis explained, continuing, "But I guess I'd do the same if I was being attacked by three groups of hostiles at the same time. Of the others I'm not really sure, but the second group of aliens did arrive 'with all guns blazing'." He paused before appearing to change the subject slightly, "And I sure as hell would be interested to know who that group of soldiers is who seem to have such an interest in the caves. They're pretty well tooled up as well."

The general paused and looked at the others in the room before continuing very sombrely, "OK, major, I need you to pay very careful attention." He seemed to lower his voice slightly and speak more slowly. "I want you and your men to disengage from the fight. Stay in position, but cease firing. Is that clear?"

This time Landis' expression was way ahead of curious. Outright surprise would be a fair description. "Sir, you want us to stay in the combat zone but not to fight. Is that correct?"

The general remained calm and clear. "Affirmative, major, but be absolutely clear on this. You have my full permission to do whatever you deem necessary to defend yourselves if you are attacked. You are not surrendering," he paused for the right words. "Call it 'observing'."

The major seemed uneasy as he replied, "Understood, sir. Let's just hope the other combatants understand as well."

The general decided that he owed his commander on the ground at least some sort of explanation. "There's some doubt up here that the first group of aliens is actually hostile, and we want to test their reaction. For the record, major I'm not really sure what to expect. That's why you're free to fight back if provoked."

Landis was a career marine and highly trained. He'd follow orders but he also appreciated the brief explanation that the general had given. He knew that he had been under no obligation to do so, but it helped give him confidence in his orders. "Confirmed, general. We'll disengage now. Landis out."

Kennedy, who had been out of the room during the conversation, re-entered just as the major terminated the link. "Well, general, how'd they take it?"

"As you'd expect, with concern," he replied, his own voice only thinly disguising his own deep concerns. "But they're marines and they'll follow orders."

Trying to sound confident, Kennedy settled himself back into his chair. "I have a hunch that we'll be proven right."

At the bottom of the world, Major Landis contacted his exec on the radio. "Stewart here, sir," came the reply over the static.

The major took a deep breath. "Matt, I need you to disengage from the enemy. I say again, I need you to cease firing. Do you copy?"

Captain Stewart sounded incredulous as he replied, "Cease firing, sir?"

The major nodded. "Affirmative, Matt. I've just received orders from General Winstone that we are to disengage and observe."

Again the discipline of the service kicked in and the exec replied, "OK, sir, if that's what the general wants."

Within moments, the order had been passed to everyone and one quarter of the combatants in the battle suddenly fell silent as the US Marines ceased firing. Almost immediately, the aliens stopped firing at American positions. Major Landis assumed it was to allow themselves to concentrate solely on the other two remaining hostile groups, but was forced to rapidly re-think his appraisal when the aliens suddenly retreated back inside their ships which almost immediately took off, leaving the atmosphere at high speed.

Having taken advantage of the lull in the firing to scramble across to the major's position, Alex gave voice to his surprise. "Would you look at that? Why have they left when things just got easier for them?"

Landis shook his head. "I've no idea, but I think the general's little gamble just paid off." He rapidly surveyed their surroundings, which suddenly seemed a lot more favourable now that no-one was shooting at them, and looking in the direction of the cave entrance he suggested, "Now let's see if we can't set about freeing those scientists of yours."

Chapter 73

Chris, John and Josh's duplicate weren't so much walking to their lockers as gently strolling. History lessons never started on time and very few students bothered rushing to get there promptly. The teacher was an amiable and knowledgeable old traditionalist who, whilst very interesting, was easily distracted and frequently had to play catch-up from the previous lesson. Consequently everyone knew that they had probably double the usual five minutes allotted to changing rooms and even if they were a little late, profuse apologies were usually enough to avoid any demerits.

As they ambled along the conversation inevitably got around to their favourite subject. "OK, just one more lesson today then we're all set for the Gaming Club," John enthusiastically reminded them. "You know I've got a feeling that I'm gonna be making a dent in that lead of yours, Josh."

Chris smiled inwardly. It seemed unfair that John was the only one not in on Josh's little secret, but the principal had insisted that Chris keep his new-found knowledge to himself. Having seen how highly-connected Mr McGregor was when it came to forcing the release of Josh, he felt it probably prudent not to test his resolve in the matter. "You know you just might have something there, John," he responded before asking Josh's duplicate, "Say, what is your current score, Josh?"

Without pausing to think the replica replied, "16,571."

"Is that so?" he teased him. "You know, someday you really must let us in on your secret, if you get my drift?"

The replica looked at him slightly confused. "You know I can't do that, Chris."

Chris had to quickly disguise the fast-broadening smile that was creasing his face when John, responding sarcastically to who he thought was Josh, looked at Chris for support. "Well we certainly wouldn't want you to give us any breaks now, would we, Josh?"

Fortunately for Chris the duplicate seemed to recover some sort of composure. "Hey, guys, what can I say? Some of us just have what it takes," he replied, sounding convincingly like the real Josh.

Chris thought he'd just fool around one last time and asked, "Remind me, Josh, what does it take?"

But before the duplicate could react, all three of them were interrupted by Mr Jacks opening a door further down the corridor. He looked straight at who he presumed to be Josh and asked in that teacherly way that is really more of an instruction than a question, "Mr Travis, may I see you a moment, please?"

The replica was momentarily startled and replied, "Ah, yes, sir, of course."

Continuing to feel somewhat liberated by his recent discoveries, Chris leaned in towards the replica and whispered, "This ought to be good."

His attempts at humour elicited a slight frown from the duplicate, which Chris wasn't sure whether to interpret as disapproval or non-comprehension. "I'll catch up with you guys in a few minutes," the duplicate told the two humans as he entered Mr Jacks' classroom.

As the remaining two friends continued on their way John's frustration was becoming more overt. "So once again it's just you and me, Chris," he grumbled.

Chris now found himself in a total reversal of roles as, knowing what he now knew, he felt he should defend Josh. However, thinking that such a change of attitude might arouse suspicion, he decided that deflecting the criticism would be worth a try. "Hey, don't knock it. It'll give us the chance to hone our skills and knock Josh off his perch," he suggested, adding with a mischievous look on his face, "Then he'll regret neglecting his friends."

They climbed a short flight of stairs and reached a large concourse. With windows on all sides and architecturally positioned fixed seating it was a popular place for students to gather if they weren't in lessons and this afternoon was no exception. Among a number of students killing time was Chris' girlfriend, Kelly, who casually acknowledged their approach. "Hey, guys." She half-expected not to see Josh with them nowadays and sought confirmation. "Just the two of you?"

"Yeah. Captain Fantastic had to go and do something incredibly gifted and talented for a while. So it's just us lame brains left." The resentment in John's voice was growing at an alarming rate.

Chris decided that defending Josh might, after all, be the only tactic left. "Hey, come on. I think Josh is finding it hard as well."

Both of the others looked at Chris with surprise. "But you've been the one giving him the hardest time out of all of us," objected Kelly.

The regret was obvious in Chris' voice, even if the reason for it remained obscure. "Yeah, I know, but maybe we should cut him a little slack now." He was trying hard to inject just the right mix of reluctance and sincerity into his body language when he was suddenly distracted by something he saw through the windows on one side of the concourse. Below their position and back along the outside of the school buildings, he could see two men roughly escorting Josh's duplicate to a car while Mr Jacks walked with them!

"What the hell?" Chris exclaimed, before turning to his friends and hurriedly instructing them, "Go get the principal and meet me in Mr Jacks' room." Without waiting for an answer he ran back down the stairs and along the corridor to Mr Jacks' class and burst inside. The exterior door was swinging open and he rushed to it. As he ran outside he was just in time to see a black 4x4 speed off with the two men, Mr Jacks and Josh's duplicate inside.

Behind Chris the classroom door opened and Principal McGregor hurried in, followed by John and Kelly. "What happened?" he demanded of Chris.

Still shocked at what he had seen, but with adrenaline coursing through his veins, Chris replied, "I'm not sure sir. Mr Jacks asked Josh to see him just now and then I saw him and two other men taking Josh to a car. I rushed down here but the car was already pulling away."

"Shall we call the police, sir?" Kelly asked enthusiastically. She wasn't sure why, but all of this seemed incredibly exciting and very worrying all at the same time.

She was somewhat surprised when the principal appeared to hesitate before replying, "No, I don't think that will be necessary." He looked at Chris thoughtfully, "Chris, that government agent who spoke to you this morning, can you remember his name?"

"Fredericks, sir. I remember his name being on his badge," Chris replied without hesitation, a self-satisfied look briefly crossing his features.

"Good," the principal nodded. "I think perhaps we should give him a call." As he spoke he appeared to suddenly hit on an idea. "Probably best not to let him know that anyone else here is involved. Do you think you'd be able to make the call yourself?"

"Sure, sir," Chris replied, relishing the opportunity to play a part.

"Right, let's get to my office," the principal suggested. He looked at John and Kelly, who both wore expressions of bewilderment. "You two had better come along too."

Chapter 74

The discovery of these concealed caves seemed like a distant memory to James Rock and Luke Richards. In the few days that had passed since they'd stumbled into this underground storage complex they'd not only discovered a fleet of mothballed spaceships and a possible control centre, but they'd also been taken captive at gunpoint, catching only a fleeting glimpse of the rescue party sent to retrieve them; witnessed the landing of presumably more alien vessels; experienced totally unexplainable weather phenomena; seen the beginnings of, perhaps, Earth's first conflict with extra-terrestrials; and, most frustratingly of all, spent much of the last twelve hours tied up and sitting on the hard rock floor of the cave while all the action was taking place above them!

Their current location was a small room off the main control room where their captors presumably thought they'd be less of a potential nuisance. Clearly they still felt that they might be useful, perhaps even if only as bargaining chips, since neither man could think of any other reason why they were still alive.

A large window allowed them to see into the control room while also allowing the soldiers to keep an eye on them. In addition, two guards had been positioned on the other side of the door. Luke nodded his head in the direction of Captain Xavier and a number of other soldiers who had just returned to the control room. "I'm guessing whatever the panic was up there must now be over," he suggested.

James decided to see if wry humour might lighten their mood. "Either that or they just got bored!"

Luke didn't seem to notice. "Hmm," he replied distractedly. "But what was it all about?"

They both sat up and strained in an effort to see more as they noticed a small number of other figures enter with more soldiers. From their build and dress they could only have come from the aliens' spacecraft. "I suspect those guys must have something to do with it," James suggested.

Dressed in flight suits not too dissimilar to those worn by the first group of aliens, these ones seemed much taller and very muscular looking. Their torso seemed disproportionately long for their limbs by human standards and the way they moved suggested a greater degree of lateral flexibility. They were entirely encased in their pressure suits and their helmets contained opaque visors, but at a quick glance nothing seemed too extraordinary about their appearance – no tentacles or wings or multiple heads, thought Luke. "Woah. D'you reckon they've come to reclaim their spaceships?" he half-jokingly asked James.

"Could be, but I don't get it," James replied in a more serious and thoughtful tone.

"What?" Luke enquired, uncertain what James was referring to.

"Well, the last thing I saw was a purple sky and melting ice," James explained.

"And you said there was a weird sound," Luke reminded him.

"Sure," James agreed, before suggesting, "I guess all of that must have been to do with spaceships landing or something."

Luke shrugged and agreed. "Makes sense."

"So what was all the rushing around with guns and stuff?" James asked, his tone one of slight bewilderment. "It all looked as if there was one hell of a fight going on up there."

Now it was Luke's turn not to understand. "Maybe there was. So what's your point?"

"If there was a fight, how come they all seem so friendly now?" James asked, looking over to where the soldiers and the aliens were gathering.

Luke shrugged again and smiled. "Perhaps they've negotiated a truce, or maybe it never did actually come to a fight."

"Yeah, but doesn't it strike you as a bit odd?" James wondered aloud. "If those guys in the spacesuits are alien visitors, how come they're already so friendly with this bunch of mercenaries? You'd expect an official 'first contact' to be made with legitimate government representatives."

Luke wasn't entirely sure that any of this had any real relevance right now. "Maybe they don't understand. The fact that all this stuff is here in the first place indicates that they've been here before without any official greeting." Then suddenly hitting on a pertinent point he added, "And this is the Antarctic. It's an international territory. Who would do the official greeting anyway?"

James reluctantly accepted his friend's observation. "You may be right, but it still seems very odd to me. Almost as if those mercenaries were here deliberately to meet them."

Now Luke's exasperation began to bubble to the surface. Whether it was exasperation with his friend's meanderings or with their apparent helplessness he wasn't sure. All he knew was that he had to react against something. “How in the hell would they have known they were on their way?”

“I dunno,” James replied defensively. “But maybe the same way that they knew about these caves.”

Struggling to calm down, Luke ceded the point. “Hmm, I see where you’re coming from. OK, so what do we do about it?”

“There’s not much we can do while we’re tied up in here,” James admitted, struggling against the bonds behind his back. He wriggled his body and twisted his wrists against the ropes until the skin burned, but to no avail. Clearly, whoever had tied his hands together knew what they were doing and took pride in their work. Adding to the difficulty of trying to struggle free was the fact that they had to keep all movement to the minimum so as not to attract the attention of their captors, who could see them quite clearly through the glass.

He rotated his shoulders against the wall a few times in the hope that it might relax his arms enough to loosen the tension in the rope. When he thought he might be supple enough he once again tried to rotate his hands to allow his fingers to grip the knot, but after a few moments of growing increasingly red in the face he flopped back, defeated. The frustration clearly evident on his face suddenly turned to shocked disbelief as Luke calmly removed his untied hands from behind his own back and smiled mischievously. “You mean like this?” he asked in response to James’ assessment of their situation.

James’ surprise turned to delight and he had to stop himself from laughing out loud. “Hey, way to go! How’d you manage that?”

Luke grinned and nodded sideways towards their captors. “I think they were so busy dealing with aliens and dragging you outside that they didn’t tie me up quite as well as they thought.”

Not wanting to lose any time, James seized on the now, potentially favourable, situation. "OK. Help me out of these," he asked, and turned around slightly to show his ropes to Luke, who then began to swiftly untie them.

"So what's the plan?" he asked as the ropes finally fell away.

James rubbed his red and swollen wrists, trying to return the circulation to his hands. "I've no idea! I'm making this up as we go, but the main thing is to get as far away from those gun-toting maniacs as possible." He almost sneered the last sentence as he kept focussed firmly on the soldiers in the control room.

Luke looked doubtful. "Difficult when we're locked in here with only one way out."

"Are we sure about that?" James asked hopefully. "Look around. From this side you'd be hard-pressed to know where that door was." He nodded in the direction of where they had both entered the room and Luke understood his point. Instead of a traditional door, or even the discreet grooves that might be found surrounding a sliding door, there was just the barest hint of a hairline crack where the doorway was. It was almost as if the door itself had melded with the surrounding wall. "What if there are other ways out of here?" James suggested.

"But how will we open them?" Luke asked, suddenly aware that they were talking in even more hushed tones. The vague possibility of escape had intensified their need to remain inconspicuous.

"Let's find them first, then worry about that," replied James, and both men began to scrutinise their surroundings, staring hard at every inch of the opposite walls.

After a few moments Luke whispered, slightly dejectedly, "I don't see anything that looks like a door," but his voice trailed off as he noticed James focussing intensely on the opposite corner. “What?” he asked insistently.

James replied without taking his eyes off his area of focus, “I’m not sure. I can’t see any openings, but why would you put light sensors over there when you’ve come in over here?”

Luke followed his gaze and noticed what looked to be some sort of futuristic light switch embedded in the wall, close to the corner itself. “It’s a long shot, but I can see what you mean,” he admitted. “Those things on the wall look just like the ones by our door.”

“And if I’m right, then simply standing near it should open it,” replied James conspiratorially.

“What if it’s locked?” Luke objected. He indicated their captors. “They managed to somehow lock that one.”

James was becoming totally focussed on the task at hand. “It’s a chance we’re gonna have to take.” Looking at his friend for the first time since he’d spotted the potential exit, he explained in very serious tones, “I’m not too keen on hanging around here for much longer. Now that these guys all seem to be making friends we’re probably not as important to them as a bargaining chip anymore.”

Luke realised that James had a point and agreed, “OK, let’s give it a try. But we’ll need some kind of distraction to stop them noticing what we’re up to.”

As both scientists looked towards the cluster of soldiers one of the aliens, as if on cue, began to unlock its helmet and slowly remove it. As the seal was broken a small cloud of gas escaped from inside. The alien lifted the helmet tentatively as it acclimatised to the atmosphere and gradually the gas cloud cleared to reveal its head. Its basic layout was very similar to that of a human, but the skin was purple, like a fingertip after a rubber band had been wound around the digit for too long. The nose was completely absent and there were three diagonal slits on either cheek reminiscent of gills. But the most striking thing was a black, bulbous protuberance about the size of an eye in the middle of the forehead positioned just above the two eyes that occupied the expected area of the face. Possibly because of its position it looked like a third eye, yet it didn't share the same physical characteristics of the other two. Where they were alert and moving, this was deep and unfathomable. Above it the head was covered in a dark green coating that could have been hair. Understandably, all of the soldiers were completely absorbed in the revelation taking place in front of them.

"Just what we need," realised Luke. "Now, quickly. Move," he urged James, but was astounded when his colleague pulled his cell phone out of his pocket and started taking pictures of the aliens. "What are you doing? We've gotta get outta here," Luke protested.

"I reckon our friends outside might be interested to see some of this, don't you?" replied James, returning the cell phone to his pocket.

Luke raised his eyes in desperation. "Yeah, you're right, but if we don't get going now no-one's gonna see your holiday snaps!" and he shoved James towards the far corner.

Both men now crawled over to the hoped-for door and stood up in front of it. Nothing happened! The two scientists looked at each other and then back at the blank wall. Their assumption about there being a doorway here was obviously wrong! In desperation they began running their hands all over the wall, not really knowing what they were searching for, but they weren't yet ready to accept their mistake. Just as all hope was about to evaporate, James hit one of the small sensor panels and immediately a door slid open to reveal a dimly-lit system of dusty corridors.

"C'mon. Quickly," he urged Luke and both men rushed through the doorway before the door slid shut behind them. They stood, almost frozen to the spot, adrenalin flooding through their veins as the realisation of how lucky they had just been dawned on them both. The air was much cooler in this corridor, which was lit with the same dim luminescent panels as the entrance through which they had originally come.

Luke was the first to resume the business of escape. “Which way?” he wondered out loud.

James shrugged as he looked to his right and left, “Who knows?”

Luke pointed to the right. “This way,” before explaining his rationale. “It’s going away from that lot.” He indicated their captors and the aliens over his shoulder and through the wall behind them.

James seemed to agree with his thinking and they both set off at a gentle run down the corridor. When they reached another passageway joining theirs at right angles they turned down it, using nothing more than a survival instinct as guidance. The more twists and changes in direction they could make, the more they might be able to avoid recapture. After running for at least five minutes they both began to wonder if they were ever going to find any purpose to the passageways. They must have been put here for a reason, but the one they were now in seemed to be leading nowhere.

Just as they were both thinking of stopping to reconsider their strategy, they finally came across another door. This one wasn’t particularly concealed in the way that the others had been. It was discreet, but fairly discernible. The scientists stopped in front of it and, feeling more confident now, set about looking for the opening sensor. After a mere few seconds of examining the surrounding wall they found it and the door slid open to reveal a simple rocky tunnel. A blast of very cold air slapped them in the face and they both instinctively pulled their coats tightly across their bodies.

The tunnel was unlit and primitive, but they could see light at the far end. With barely a quick look at each other for agreement they plunged on, stumbling over the rocky surface. The door closed behind them, cutting off any assistance from the corridor's lights, but they pushed on towards the cold white light ahead. As it got nearer they began to pick out the rocky surface and increased speed until finally they burst out of the opening onto the hillside overlooking the snowless valley.

Instinctively, they quickly sought concealment amongst the rocks. They both sat back against a large boulder to catch their breath and gather their thoughts. Emboldened by the silence all around them they slowly peered out. Way down below them on the valley floor they could make out some landed spacecraft. Crawling across the rocks from one outcrop to another they gradually gained a better view until they could make out the red Base Camp helicopters and, to their surprise, the black helicopters of the US Marines. They'd emerged from the cave on the opposite side of the hill to the entrance. Now all they had to do was work out how to get across to their friends and safety.

Chapter 75

Chris took a deep breath and steadied his nerves as he waited for his phone call to be answered. He looked up at Principal McGregor and his friends John and Kelly standing around the desk, their faces a mixture of concern and enthusiasm as they all willed him on. With a jolt, he returned his attention to the job in hand as a voice at the end of the line answered. "Hi," Chris was desperate to sound relaxed. "May I talk to Agent Fredericks, please?"

The other three in the office held their breath when they heard him respond to the receptionist's answer. "I don't understand. He spoke to me this morning. I'm sure his badge was your agency."

Chris looked to his principal for help and McGregor indicated that he needed to explain the problem. Thinking quickly, Chris spoke once more to the receptionist, "Could you hold, please?" before covering the mouthpiece and speaking to the principal. "She says they don't have an Agent Fredericks."

McGregor was thinking on his feet. "She's probably just covering for him. I'm guessing this particular agency likes to stay fairly low-key. Tell her who you are and that you're calling about Josh."

Chris returned his attention to the phone. "Ma'am, can I ask you to check again, please? My name is Chris Harris and I'm phoning from Littrow High School about my friend Josh Travis. I'm sure the man who spoke to me was Agent Fredericks and he'd be interested in some information that I've got for him."

Everyone in the room waited tensely for a few seconds before a collective moment of relief when Chris said, "Thank you." He nodded at the others to indicate that he was getting somewhere and the tension in the room ratcheted up a notch as they all hung on his every word.

"Hello. Agent Fredericks?" Chris asked, verifying the identity of the person who the receptionist had informed him only moments before didn't exist. "This is Chris Harris. I'm Josh Travis' friend. You spoke to me this morning at our school." Chris paused for a moment then, steeling his nerve, changed the tone of his voice to one of indignant accusation. "I want to know what you've done to Josh? Where have you taken him?"

The others were desperate to know what Agent Fredericks was saying at the other end, but realised soon enough when Chris replied, "What do you mean? I saw two of your guys take him away in a car with Mr Jacks, one of our teachers."

They waited for that information to sink in at the other end, but were slightly puzzled when a confused look began to cross Chris' face. "Just now, about ten minutes ago," he told the agent.

Once more a brief pause and then Chris asked, the steel in his voice now more authentic than previously, "Well who else would want him?" He was clearly not getting very far and his frustration was fast turning to anger. "I'm one of his best friends yet I don't even know what he's supposed to have done, but suddenly he's top of everyone's 'wanted' list."

As he listened to the response he looked once again at Principal McGregor, who gave him a look of encouragement. Emboldened, he decided to try their pre-arranged bluff, "So, should I just call the police and register a missing persons report? Maybe they could help if I told them we suspected a kidnapping."

The smile that creased his face confirmed that it had worked. "If you think it's gonna help," he said, trying to keep the relief out of his voice. "OK, I'll tell the principal you're on your way."

He couldn't hang up quickly enough, and experienced a mixture of relief, exhaustion and euphoria as he flopped back in the chair. He'd come on strong to a government agency and won! "He claims they know nothing about it, but they're on their way over now," he informed the others, suddenly feeling drained of energy as the adrenalin rush left him.

The principal once more took charge of the situation, "OK, let's wait to see what they have to say for themselves."

Chapter 76

Huddled around a Base Camp helicopter inside the slight protection offered by a tarpaulin, Major Landis and some of his officers were grouped around a military-issue laptop. The major had just begun a Skype call with the secretary of defense's office and was giving the military chiefs the latest update. "No, sir, they've not been harmed. They just managed to sneak away during a distraction."

Luke Richards standing behind him leaned across to James Rock and muttered quietly, "Makes it sound so easy, doesn't he?"

"They've brought out some photos which I think you should see," the major continued. "I'm having them sent over to you now. I'm not entirely sure what they tell us, but I certainly have a hunch."

On the screen the group in the Antarctic could see all five occupants of the secretary's office, but it was the marine general who leant forward to speak first. "Gentlemen, my congratulations on your escape," he told James and Luke. "Time is very much against us, so I need to ask you some important questions right now. Did you get a sense of what they were actually trying to do?"

"Not really," James replied, wishing his answer didn't sound so lame. "There's a network of caves down there.

Some are natural, but many have clearly been carved out by machine. I'm guessing that we didn't see all of the complex or everything that's down there." He paused to make sure the Skype link had caught up before adding, "But I can tell you that there's a whole bunch of assorted aircraft or spacecraft in there."

"Did it seem as if they belonged to the aliens?" the general asked.

Again, James wished he could be more definite in his response. "Difficult to say. They spent most of the time that we were down there communicating with those guys who took us captive."

On the screen they could see the general look away as he studied something else, before returning his attention to them. "Yes the pictures have just come through," he confirmed then, referring to James' last comment, asked, "What did you make of that?"

James decided to call it as he saw it. "It looked like two teams in an operation meeting up."

"You mean like two military units establishing contact?" interjected Major Landis.

James turned his head sideways to face the major. "I guess so. It certainly seemed as if those soldiers or mercenaries, or whatever they are, had been expecting the aliens. Almost like they'd been holding the fort until their arrival."

The marine general looked thoughtful as he pondered the suggestion. "Hmm, or surrendering to the victors," he postulated.

"Well the mercenaries had their weapons and everything seemed very casual if they'd just been beaten in a fight," James countered.

The general suddenly appeared to dismiss the entire conversation as if he either had something more important to do, or had simply become bored with it. "OK, Mr Rock, thank you for your input. The pictures could be very useful." He appeared to be absorbed in thought as he added almost absent-mindedly, "No doubt Major Landis may have some more questions for you. Your help is appreciated."

It was clear that he had finished talking to James as he looked straight past him and turned his attention to the marine commander. "Major Landis, I want you to prepare for an attack on those caves in the event that we decide this evidence and Mr Rock's interpretation are actionable."

"Yes, sir," the major replied very simply, and the monitor returned to its default image of the US Marines badge, as Washington terminated the link.

Alex Roughedge, who was also in the group, tried to reassure James and Luke. "Well, I for one am glad to see you two out of there safely, even if Washington aren't exactly setting off the party poppers."

"Yeah, I thought he could have been a bit more enthusiastic about our pictures," grumbled Luke, conveniently forgetting that he had been none too enthusiastic about James stopping to actually take them. "Perhaps even shown some gratitude?" he added.

Major Landis almost felt compelled to justify his superior officer's attitude. "I'm sorry, sir, but the general is just being cautious."

"Why?" Alex exploded. He'd had enough of all this fighting and intrigue down here on his patch. The Antarctic was supposed to be a non-military territory, yet possibly the most important fight in the history of humanity might just be kicking off right here in his own backyard. "All hell is breaking loose down here. What does he need to be cautious about?" he asked forcibly.

The major was clearly not going to disagree with his superior officer and his tone emphasised that. But he did feel that some sort of explanation might help. "Well, for one thing, we still don't really know for sure who the good guys are?"

James was also fast running out of patience after all that he had seen and been through and he found himself taking exception to the major's point. "Well, major, I'm pretty sure that the guys who took us prisoner and then launched an unprovoked attack on a bunch of scientists, not to mention visitors from another planet, have got to be top contenders for 'bad guy'"

"Yeah, and if they're the bad guys then surely the aliens that they seem to be friends with must also be bad guys," reasoned Luke, whose impatience had long-since gotten the better of him in the diplomacy stakes.

"I guess the problem is knowing whether the aliens knew what their new friends were already up to," suggested the major.

"He means they don't know whether to trust your story or not," Alex said disparagingly to James and Luke.

"Like we'd make it up?" Luke asked in exasperation. "Haven't they seen the pictures we took?"

"Pictures can be faked or posed, I guess," James conceded, his natural calmness returning.

"Precisely," confirmed the major. "That's why I need the two of you to tell me everything that you can about those caves and what you saw inside. I may well have to lead my men in there and any help you can provide could well save lives."

"And make your stories more acceptable to the military," suggested Alex sarcastically.

Major Landis nodded and grinned slightly. "That as well!"

Chapter 77

The fight was being vividly relayed to the Space Corps Command Centre main display screen. Everyone in there not busy on their terminal was transfixed by what they could see. Numerous small spacecraft weaved in and out of each other, almost like they were trying to embroider some sort of gigantic quilt, where the bright laser fire was the thread. Every so often a ship would disappear in a momentary fireball that lasted less than a second. A flash in time to mark the end of a life. With their own fleet still in a holding position, the members of Space Corps felt almost like the audience at a movie. Disconnected from the dangers, but enthralled by the action. Yet they all knew that the danger could become only too real at any minute, should any of the aliens decide to turn their attention towards the space station.

"I still don't like the idea of us just sitting here watching them slug it out, hoping that the winner is the friendliest," Frankie complained to Kirk.

"I'm not too keen on it myself," the commander replied. "But I don't really see that we have a choice."

"My money's still on the second batch of guys to arrive. After all, they did start fighting the ones who were melting the ice," argued Frankie.

"I know, I know," agreed Kirk, the frustration growing in his voice. "We've been through all this and I'm not changing my decision. We hold our position and wait to see what happens." He pondered the battle on the screen before adding, "If nothing else, they'll at least be weakening each other for us. That has to be a good thing if we end up having to fight either one of them again."

"But suppose the bad guys win?" asked Frankie desperately. "We'll have lost our allies."

"Frankie, there are just too many unknown factors at the moment and too many aliens on either side," explained Kirk for what he felt must be the hundredth time. "We just don't have enough pilots to be wading in where we may be welcomed by either side."

Frankie seemed surprised by this latest suggestion. "Huh?"

Perhaps he was beginning to get through, thought Kirk, as he asked, "Well, has it occurred to you that neither side may actually be friendly towards us anyway?" He looked at Frankie for a response and when none came he continued, "I mean, one group arrive and immediately start melting ice caps. The other group arrive and start attacking them. You're assuming that that puts them on our side. But supposing they also want whatever it is that the first bunch want and are just fighting them for possession?"

Frankie had had enough time to regroup and compose a response this time. "Well, then, perhaps it won't hurt to join in on their side and maybe earn some sort of negotiating rights by helping them to win."

Kirk knew that her argument was flawed. He also knew that she realised it. "Or simply play right into their hands," he responded. "No, by forcing one or the other of them to win at a cost serves us better in the long run," he stated categorically.

Everyone's attention was immediately distracted by a sudden explosive flash on the screen, away from the main battle, quickly followed by two more.

"Sir, the aliens are destroying Earth's satellites," Jim Scott informed Kirk, looking up from his monitor.

"Which ones?" Kirk shot back.

Scott shook his head ruefully. "Unknown, sir."

"Which side is destroying them?" Kirk asked, walking over to Scott's position.

Scott played with the keys on his computer console and the image on the main view screen begin to increase in magnification. As Scott panned across the battle to the location of the explosions there was another flash of bright light, as yet another satellite was blasted into oblivion. As the brightness of the flash dulled a small squadron of squat, rounded spacecraft could be seen heading away from the explosion towards the distant pin-prick of light that represented another satellite.

Kirk spun around to face Frankie. "Still think they're on our side?" he asked accusingly before turning back to Scott and instructing him, "Get these images down to Earth fast for passing on to NASA. They need to know down there just what they're dealing with up here."

He returned his attention to Frankie, but this time the tone was more measured, if not quite free of any smugness. "Well, aren't you glad now that we hadn't been helping make things any easier for them?"

Satisfied that his strategy had been vindicated, Kirk walked towards the door as he told Scott, "I'll be in my office. Let me know of any other new developments as soon as they happen."

Frankie followed Kirk out of the control centre and, once the doors had closed behind them, Kirk stopped to implore her, "Frankie, I hope you're not gonna keep trying to convince me that they're the good guys?"

Kirk noticed two other crew members approaching and assumed that Frankie would wait until they were out of earshot before replying, but to his surprise, she carried right on. "No, Kirk, I'm not gonna bother wasting my breath. The time for convincing has passed." He was even more surprised when she suddenly pulled a gun from her pocket and pointed it right at him. He momentarily glanced at the other two crewmen, uncertain whether to seek their assistance. "Now I'm simply telling you!" Frankie stated menacingly.

"What? Have you gone outta your mind?" Kirk demanded.

"Maybe," Frankie replied. "But maybe I'm finally in my right mind," she suggested.

Kirk looked around, considering his chances of escape.

"Please, Kirk. We've known each other a long time." Now it was Frankie doing the imploring. "Don't make me have to use this."

Kirk realised that he had no other options. The other two crew members had stopped and were standing with Frankie, clearly in league with her. Any attempt at escape was blocked!

"Move," Frankie ordered.

"Where to?" Kirk asked simply.

"Your office. That's where you told Scott you'd be, so let's not disappoint," she replied matter-of-factly, before warning him, "but my people have disabled the comm links in there so you won't be able to call for help."

Chapter 78

The four agents were shown in to Principal McGregor's office by his secretary, who shut the door firmly behind her as she left. The four occupants of the office weren't quite sure whether the agents seemed surprised to see the three students waiting for them. If they were, their leader didn't let it faze him too much as he addressed the principal.

"Principal McGregor?" he asked routinely. As the only other adult in the room it was a pretty safe guess. "I'm Special Agent Henderson. These are Agents McCoy, Fredericks and Walsh." He flashed his badge perfunctorily before asking, "So what appears to have happened?"

"Well, Mr Henderson, that's an interesting question," the principal began. "Are you referring to earlier today when one of my students – Josh Travis – was returned to us from your custody, or are you referring to the fact that he's just been kidnapped again by your people?" He watched for a reaction and just as the agent was about to reply, continued, "Or perhaps you're referring to the potentially illegal questioning of young Chris Harris here, by your Agent Fredericks this morning on school grounds about the apparent disappearance of Josh when he was actually here all the time?"

This time he did wait long enough for Agent Henderson to respond. When he did his tone was abrupt and official. “Now look, Mr McGregor, I don’t care for those accusations.”

Jonathan McGregor was not about to let some official with attitude bamboozle him just because he had a badge. “And I don’t care for one of my students being held in custody without his parents knowing. Neither do I care for what is either deliberate subterfuge or blatant incompetence on the part of a government agency,” he demonstrated that he was just as capable of an official tone. “Either he was in your custody or he wasn’t, but your agent seemed to think he was when he wasn’t! Now he’s missing again!” He let the implied accusation sink in and added, “Where is he this time?”

Henderson neatly side-stepped the litany of accusations to concentrate of the last question. “I really have no idea,” he replied calmly.

“More incompetence?” asked the principal.

“No. The truth!” Henderson assured him. “I’ll admit that young Mr Travis was helping us with our investigations last night but, as you have acknowledged, we released him this morning. I think that perhaps the decision hadn’t reached Agent Fredericks when he had his little conversation with Mr Harris earlier today.”

The principal, of course, knew that the last part certainly wasn’t true, since the real Josh hadn’t returned until after Chris had been questioned by Agent Fredericks, but he decided to change tack anyway. “So what is this investigation about?”

The official tone and line returned. “I’m sorry, principal, but that’s classified.”

“And you don’t think we should know despite the fact that Josh has once more gone missing?” the principal asked. He decided to increase the tension, “Especially since you and your agency seem to be the ones responsible."

Agent Henderson remained calm, but it was clear his patience with this impertinent civilian was beginning to wear thin. "Sir, I can assure you quite categorically that this recent disappearance has nothing to do with us. But it may well have something to do with our investigation, so I can also assure you that we'll do everything in our power to track him down." He wasn't used to not being the one asking the questions and had had enough of this cross-examination. He decided now was the time to resume the norm. "Now, who actually witnessed the abduction?"

Chris spoke up, hesitantly. "Me, sir. Chris Harris."

Henderson's years of experience kicked in and he adopted a soothing tone with the teenager. "So you're Mr Harris. OK now, Chris, can you tell us exactly what you saw?"

Chris seemed delighted to be the centre of attention again and regaled him with the story. "Sure. Josh went into Mr Jacks' classroom and about five minutes later I saw them both leave the room by the outside door and get into a car. There were two other men with them and the car seemed to drive off in a hurry."

For the first time since they'd entered the office, Agent Walsh spoke up. "Chris, can I ask why Josh went into Mr Jacks' classroom?"

Chris shrugged. "He asked him to."

"I see," she acknowledged. "And were the two men in there at the time?"

"I don't know. I didn't go in with him," Chris replied.

Now it was Brad's turn to get involved. His more direct style of questioning was aimed at Principal McGregor. "Do you have CCTV footage that might show us the car?"

The principal handed Brad a DVD that had been sitting on his desk. "I thought you might ask for that. We've already checked for a license plate but it was covered up."

Brad nodded. "It could still be of use to us."

"Surely you know what car you sent down to do the job, don't you?" asked Chris a little malevolently. Clearly he hadn't yet decided that the agency was innocent of the abduction.

"Young man, as I've tried to reassure your principal here, we had nothing to do with this," Henderson replied. The soothing tone now absent from his voice.

Principal McGregor decided that it was make or break time. "OK, Agent Henderson, if you didn't, who did?" he asked directly.

"That's what we're gonna find out," the agent assured him.

"Well, would you at least mind telling us how you're going about that? Bearing in mind that these students here are actually friends of his and I'm the person who was ultimately responsible for his safety when he went missing?" the principal enquired in a business-like manner.

Agent Henderson looked around the room, locking eyes with everyone in there, before looking directly at Jonathan McGregor. "I understand how you're all feeling sir. Agent McCoy here has a potential lead."

Brad stepped forward and explained. "Our investigation has been based upon a highly-placed tip-off and the same person has been feeding us bits of information at timely moments." So far, so good. But now, Brad decided, it was time to stray off-script. "It's almost as if he has a particular angle in this whole investigation. He's been in regular contact with me and I've a feeling he might know something about this disappearance." Quite why he decided to let this piece of information slip he wasn't sure. Perhaps it had to do with his frustration at being given the run-around, or maybe it was because he was bored with this seemingly unending investigation. Or perhaps he didn't like the fact that it had now graduated to the kidnapping of juveniles, something that he might even be accidentally responsible for.

Whatever Brad's reasons, Henderson was clearly surprised. "What are you saying, Brad? That our informant could be involved in this?"

"Well it's at least a possibility, sir." Brad admitted. "After all, he's been very keen for us to find evidence at the school to support his claims. He knew we'd returned Josh to school – maybe he decided it was time to take matters into his own hands."

The principal leaned forward in his chair, aghast at what he was hearing. "You mean your informant was given details of the investigation? Is that usual?"

"In most cases, no," Henderson replied, trying not to betray his own surprise at Brad's revelation. He decided to improvise, "But when the informant is as important as this one it's not unknown for them to be kept in the loop."

The principal looked at the agent, not sure what to think. "OK. So what now?" he asked.

"I think it's time we reeled him in," Brad replied. It was now very clear to everyone in the room that Brad was taking this latest development personally. He didn't like being made a fool of, and was determined to get even. "Find out what he knows and what, if anything, his connection to this whole thing is."

Henderson seemed to be feeling something similar, but the personal affront he was feeling was to his agency rather than himself. "Hmm. Better still, why don't we go pay him a visit? After all, we do know where to find him, don't we?" He looked to Brad for confirmation.

"Who exactly are we talking about?" asked the principal.

"I'm sorry, principal, but that's classified," came Henderson's reply, officialdom safely restored.

Chapter 79

As the last of the generals returned to their seats, the secretary of defense looked around the group. “OK, gentlemen. I think we’ve all now had more than enough time to consult with our teams. It’s now about time that we made some hard decisions.” He looked carefully at each of the men before addressing the marine general. “General, would your men be capable of capturing the cave complex?”

“Difficult to say, Mr Secretary.” came the honest reply. “The two scientists who escaped said that they had only seen a small portion of the complex and suspected that there may be quite a bit more still undiscovered. If that’s the case, then we have no intelligence about what else might be down there.”

“Whatever it is it seems that our alien visitors are mighty keen to get their hands on it,” interjected the air force general.

“They might only be interested in the spaceships that were in the photos that the scientists took,” suggested the admiral, but whether his suggestion was more hopeful than helpful, nobody was quite sure.

The marine general objected. “But we still don’t know that they don’t actually belong to them.”

A note of frustration and impatience crept into the secretary's voice. "Gentlemen, we're starting to go round in circles again." He eyed them all with intensity. "You should know that I've spoken to the president and his main concern is, of course, the security of US interests which, in this case, also means the security of the planet. He's not about to allow uninvited and belligerent visitors to our planet to wage either their private little war or stage an unprovoked attack on our world." He let his words sink in before looking at the marine again. "So I ask again, general, can your team capture the caves?"

The general took a deep breath. "Truthfully, Mr Secretary, I really don't know. Major Landis has a crack team of marines down there and there are very few better trained at attacking concealed and well-defended positions. But the weaponry they'll be facing just adds a hugely unknown factor." He dropped his voice slightly and continued very seriously, "They'll definitely take major casualties." He knew that no politician wanted to be responsible for the futile loss of military lives.

The air force general came to his assistance. "And for what? Maybe we'd be better off keeping the aliens and those mercenaries bottled up in the caves until we can figure out a more effective way to neutralise them."

They were interrupted in their deliberating by a knock on the door. An aide entered with a message for the secretary of defense "Excuse me, sir, but there's a Miss Mitchell from Kitt Peak Observatory trying to contact Mr Kennedy. She says it's urgent."

Herbert Kennedy immediately opened his laptop as he acknowledged the message, "Thank you." He looked at the secretary of defense for approval, "If you don't mind?" The secretary of defense nodded for him to continue.

Kennedy had already activated the Skype link to the observatory and swiped it on to a large TV monitor on the wall of the office. Samantha Mitchell's pretty face filled the screen. "Yes Miss Mitchell. Kennedy here," he confirmed. "What have you got for us?"

"We've just been sent images from one of our associate observatories in India," she informed her boss. As she spoke, her face was replaced by images from space of the destroyed satellites. All of those in room sat forward, desperate to see the detail in full.

"They appear to show spacecraft attacking a number of Earth satellites." As the still images were replaced by video footage of the spacecraft actually carrying out the attacks, the air force general spoke up. "Those ships look like the ones flown by the aliens now inside the caves."

"OK, gentlemen. Does anyone still think they mean us no harm?" the Secretary of State pointedly asked them all. "In my book attacking our satellites is a deliberate attempt to reduce our intelligence gathering and therefore put us at a disadvantage."

The marine general agreed emphatically, "To weaken us."

"Exactly!" the secretary confirmed authoritatively. "General, order the attack on those caves now!" he instructed him without further debate.

Herbert Kennedy was finishing his Skype connection with Kitts Peak. "Thank you, Miss Mitchell. Those images have been most valuable. Please thank our Indian colleagues and," he paused for effect before slowly emphasising, "and let them know that we will be retaliating."

"Yes sir, I'll tell them," Samantha confirmed and terminated the link.

Kennedy closed his laptop and addressed the secretary of defense He wasn't too sure whether his tone was sombre or ironic. "Well, Mr Secretary, it's not every President who gets to go to war with a completely different species!"

Chapter 80

"Understood, Sir. Landis out." The marine major closed the Skype connection and stared across the plain, deep in thought.

"So you're going in?" asked Alex, forcing the officer to bring his thoughts abruptly back to the here and now.

Landis seemed to shake himself back to reality and turned to face the chief of the Antarctic Survey. "Yes sir. That's what the general ordered." He reached for his radio, any temptation to dwell on the enormity of their task now firmly behind him, and asked, "Matt, are the men all in position?"

The voice of his executive officer came back almost immediately. "Yes, sir, been waiting for some time now. Just give the order and we're in." Alex marvelled momentarily at the enthusiasm these brave men had for risking their lives.

"Mr Stewart, the order is given. Attack the caves!" the major responded sombrely, adding for clarification, "Prisoners could be useful, but our main concern is neutralising the enemy. Be alert for unfamiliar weaponry." Again the huge difficulties and unknown factors that the marines were about to encounter tumbled into Alex's thoughts. Not only were they going to be fighting in restricted surroundings against a well-dug-in enemy, but they would also be facing unfamiliar weapons and technology far in advance of anything they'd ever encountered before. Who knew what could happen?

Captain Stewart's voice returned over the radio. "Yes, sir. All squads commencing attack."

Outside the cave entrance, the captain gave a signal to two of his marines, who were concealed in forward positions. Like pre-coiled springs they instantly hurled two hand grenades through the opening into the outer cave, closely followed by some smoke grenades. The noise of all four hand grenades exploding in such quick succession in the enclosed space was deafening. No sooner had they all gone off than the crack of the smoke grenades was followed by thick, billowing white smoke pouring out of the entrance. Immediately the lead marines rushed through the opening, their guns firing in short bursts spraying from side to side. As soon as they could, they dived for cover behind the various misshapen protrusions of the rock walls in the cave.

Once the initial shock from the attack had passed, the defenders began to return fire. No sooner had the lead marines hit the dirt behind the first rocks than they found the air full of the crack of rapid fire weapons as bullets whistled down the tunnel towards them. Bits of rock and stone splintered off the sides of the tunnel adding to the deadly hail of projectiles filling the air.

As more marines moved up to join their comrades the fusillade of firepower being poured into the tunnel increased and the two sides began to dance a deadly duet, as if competing in some sort of lethal tennis match where every volley of fire had to be returned with even more determination.

With so little room for lateral manoeuvre the fight remained evenly matched for so long, yet slowly the marines' superior training and tactics began to tell and they gradually advanced, inch by inch towards the enemy.

Inside the control room, Sergeant Murtoch rushed to Captain Xavier with the news. "Sir, we're under attack," he gabbled breathlessly. "US Marines have penetrated the caves to some considerable depth."

Xavier's eyes narrowed and he demanded of the sergeant, "How did that happen?"

Unfazed by any implied accusation of failure, Murtoch replied, "It was in the area where the sensors weren't all positioned in time."

Moving swiftly away from wasting time with recriminations, the captain asked, "So what's the situation?"

"We're holding them," Murtoch reassured him, before adding a warning. "But only just."

The alien who seemed to be in charge and had been leading the inspection of the extra-terrestrial technology pushed a button on his chest plate and began to speak. The sergeant assumed that the six inch square device in the upper part of the alien's space suit must be some sort of translation device since clearly the sounds coming directly out of its mouth bore nothing in relation to the words he actually heard. "What has happened?" the somewhat stilted translator voice asked.

Captain Xavier answered directly, "The soldiers outside have started their attack. We were expecting it, but not this soon."

The alien's face barely changed as he simply informed them, "I will deploy my men."

"Better keep them near this equipment, general," Xavier advised him. "Let my men try to hold them off first." Of course the totally unfamiliar appearance of the visitor's face meant that the look he gave in response was completely lost on the captain.

In the tunnel, the fight was intensifying, but still the marines inched forward. As they approached a slight bend in the tunnel startlingly bright beams of energised light suddenly erupted from a side tunnel. Most of them exploded against the tunnel wall behind the marines, but a couple actually hit human flesh and two marines fell to the tunnel floor.

"Where did that come from?" yelled a clearly shocked sergeant as he instinctively dived for cover.

"Hell, sergeant, did you really expect to go up against aliens and not see lasers being used?" yelled Captain Stewart above the noise of the battle. He knew how absolutely critical it was that he reassure his men after such a game-changing development. The last thing he needed was a collapse of morale.

He was slightly relieved when the sergeant shouted back, "No, sir, but how are we supposed to fight back?" At least the NCO was still thinking about fighting!

"With the weapons that you've been trained to use," the officer replied keeping his voice even. "Just because they've got sci-fi guns doesn't mean we can't shoot back." Inwardly he wondered if that would be enough as he reached for his radio. "Captain Stewart to Major Landis. Do you copy?"

The commanding officer's voice crackled back, "Landis here. What's happening, Matt?"

"We've encountered stiff resistance but have made our way deep into the cave network," his executive officer informed him. "Now encountering laser fire."

"Copy that. We've got the same here in this sector," came the reply. "What's your casualty status?"

"We've lost two, with at least six injured," the captain informed his commander as the combination of bullets, shards of rock and now laser fire whistled all around him.

"OK. Similar here," Landis informed him. Returning to the real issue at hand he urged him, "Just keep piling on the pressure. As far as I know we're the only ones taking the fight to these invaders so we've got to make a difference."

"Roger that sir," Stewart confirmed before his attention was dramatically diverted as a marine, firing from just behind and to the side of him, managed to hit one of the aliens. The extra-terrestrial slumped forward and lay motionless, with a small trickle of green blood running from the bullet wound.

"Well at least we know our bullets are just as deadly to them as their lasers are to us," he said to no-one in particular. The sergeant looked across to him and gave a thumbs-up signal.

Chapter 81

Inside his quarters, Kirk sat at his desk with an armed guard watching over him. Outwardly he tried to appear calm and relaxed, but inwardly he was a raging turmoil of thoughts and counter-thoughts, ideas and emotions.

How could he have let things come to this? He kept going over and over recent developments, but no matter how he approached it he couldn't see how he might have suspected Frankie would turn on him like she had.

They'd been together for so long that he thought he knew what made her tick. She had always been so loyal and supportive both of him and of the aims of Space Corps. Yet here he was, a prisoner on his own space station, because of her. So who was she really working for and how long had she been doing so?

Just as worrying to him as that thought was the fact that she was about to launch an attack against the wrong side. All of the evidence pointed to the newest arrivals being more of an immediate threat, yet she was about to go to their aid in this mess of a battle.

Once more he felt his anger bubbling up, directed this time at himself. Not only had he allowed himself to be caught off-guard but now, because of that lapse of judgement, things were about to get a whole lot worse. And here he was powerless to do anything about it!

As he started yet another re-run of going over recent history, he thought he heard the noise of what sounded like a scuffle outside the door. Kirk looked up, jarring his thoughts back to the moment. The guard caught the sudden alertness on his face and cautioned him, “Stay where you are sir. I wouldn’t want to have to shoot you.”

Kirk gave a wry grin. “The feeling’s mutual, I can assure you.”

The noise outside had stopped almost as quickly as it had begun and the guard moved cautiously to the door. As he approached it, it gently slid open and he was relieved to see his partner-in-crime from outside look in. The tension in his body relaxed when he realised it had been a false alarm, but just as he was about to turn around, the guard from outside suddenly lunged towards him, shoved violently from behind. Both guards fell to the floor and looked up to see Freddie Han standing over them holding a gun. He deftly reached behind him and pushed the door close button, while at the same time kicking away the pistol that the interior guard had dropped in his fall.

“Freddie! Am I glad to see you,” exclaimed Kirk.

“I thought something must be up when Frankie ordered an attack on the aliens,” Freddie responded, a look of concern on his face.

Kirk’s shock was all too visible as he realised his worst fears were real. “Which ones?” he asked, already knowing the answer.

As the two men set about tying up the guards Freddie answered, “The ones she’s been routing for all the time.”

“The ones that destroyed Earth satellites,” Kirk muttered.

Freddie interpreted it as a question and confirmed, “That’s right.” As he pulled the belt tight that he was using to restrain the guard’s hands behind his back, he continued, “I knew you wanted to stay out of it until we had more information, so I thought I’d come and check with you. When I saw Johnson standing outside looking like he was guarding the room I got suspicious.” He stood back, tugging at the bonds to check their effectiveness. “And it looks like I was right.”

“You certainly were, Freddie,” Kirk confirmed ruefully. He had just finished immobilising the other guard and asked, “I’m guessing that Frankie is up in the command centre?”

Freddie nodded, “Yeah. She’s getting ready to commit our drones to an attack at any minute.”

Kirk was now thinking out loud. “OK. I need you to round up as many non-operational personnel as possible. Make sure they’re loyal. Arm them and bring them to the command centre in about ten minutes’ time.”

Freddie nodded, but looked concerned. “What about you? Are you going up there on your own?”

Kirk indicated the two trussed-up guards. “If I’m right, Frankie won’t have many more allies than these two. Perhaps one or two more, but that’s all.” He looked to Freddie for confirmation, “I’m guessing she’s giving the impression that she acting on my behalf?”

“Oh, yeah,” Freddie replied. “She’s not told anyone that she’s relieved you or anything.”

“Excellent.” Kirk snapped, suddenly the man of action once more. “That’ll make it more difficult for her to argue with me.” His decisiveness was reassuring to Freddie. “OK, quick as you can, but no more than ten minutes.”

He reached down and picked up the guard’s pistol before both he and Frankie rushed out of the door, pausing just long enough to lock it behind them.

Chapter 82

In the Space Corps Command Centre, Frankie continued to issue orders, oblivious to developments elsewhere within the space station. Calm and decisive there was no hint in her mannerisms of the mutiny she was attempting to stage.

"OK. Are all pilots now ready for attack?" she asked, as naturally as she might enquire whether someone wanted a cup of coffee.

"Yes ma'am," Scott replied, "All standing by." He turned to face her, with a look of concern on his face. "Are you sure that this is what Commander Stevens meant to do?"

"Absolutely." The reply was delivered without any guile or hint that it was a lie. Scott pulled a face and turned back to his console just as the control room door opened.

"Thank you, Frankie, I'll take it from here," said Kirk as he strode to the command dais.

This time Frankie wasn't quite so able to keep her real thoughts off of her face. She stood looking at Kirk, unsure quite how to react. Kirk took this lack of action to mean that he had been right. She didn't have many allies, otherwise she'd have stopped him in his tracks. "Status, Mr Scott?" he asked.

"Flight plans all downloaded into pilots' computers and drones all massed at holding point," came the reply.

"Thank you," Kirk acknowledged before turning around to face Frankie. "Well, Frankie, it looks like you've done a thorough job as usual," he complimented her, buying time.

This confused her even more. "Thank you, sir," she replied hesitantly, trying to work out what her recent captive was up to. "I thought you were overseeing the operation from your quarters."

Kirk had been surveying the room, trying to take stock of the various personnel in the command centre. "I was, but once I'd worked everything out I figured I ought to be up here."

"Are you sure?" ventured Frankie, trying to match his mind games with a counter attack of her own. She realised that he was as unsure of his position as she was of hers. "I think it might be a good idea if we're in separate locations in case we're attacked."

"Hmm. Good point," Kirk conceded, "But I'd rather be up here."

One or two personnel look slightly uneasy as the exchange began to get frosty. Kirk continued to study their faces and body language, trying to gauge who might be on Frankie's side. He looked across at Scott, trusting the gut instinct telling him that Scott had remained loyal. "Hold those drones in position and tell the pilots to stand by."

A young female operator, Louise Church, who hadn't been in Space Corps long, looked up from her communications console. "Sir, message coming in from Earth." Could he trust her? he wondered. "It's from Principal Khan at the Indian observatory."

Kirk felt a moment of relief. It had to be genuine. "Put him on screen, please," he instructed. For Rashid to be contacting him must mean that it was important. Perhaps important enough to reinforce his own position Kirk figured. Letting all of the command centre personnel see and hear the discussion could be to his advantage.

Rashid Khan's handsome, mature and, most importantly, trustworthy face appeared on the main viewing screen. "Hello, Rashid. What have you got for us?" asked Kirk, trying to remain as natural as possible. He felt himself tense just slightly as he awaited the response.

"Hello, Kirk," replied Rashid, always a stickler for manners. "We've just received word that the US secretary of defense has ordered an attack on the aliens who destroyed the satellites. Apparently they have evidence that has convinced them that these aliens are the biggest threat to Earth."

Kirk felt himself breathe a sigh of relief. Anyone siding with Frankie now would clearly be at odds with the official line, and everyone in the command centre would know it. "Thank you, Rashid, that's most interesting." Kirk smiled as he signed off, "And very helpful!"

As the viewing screen cleared, Kirk looked at Frankie. "Well, Frankie, looks like we'll need to change our plans after all."

But if he expected her to give up without a struggle, Kirk was wrong. She flashed a look across the room to a handful of operators stationed behind Kirk. Turning to follow her gaze, he saw three crew members start to move from their positions. The atmosphere within the control room suddenly intensified to a point where everyone's face wore a look of concern, puzzlement, uncertainty or just plain disbelief.

The time for trying to end this all quietly was clearly passed and Kirk turned back to face Frankie, removing the pistol from inside his clothing as did so. He pointed it first at Frankie and then returned his attention to her allies. After what seemed like minutes, but in reality was no more than two or three seconds, the control room doors suddenly opened and Freddie burst in, followed by a large group of various personnel. Each of them was carrying a pistol. Kirk indicated Frankie's henchmen and Freddie moved straight for them. Realising that they were clearly outnumbered and out-gunned, they meekly held their hands aloft in surrender.

Turning back to Frankie, Kirk's voice was now suddenly cold. "Frankie?" he queried, surprising himself at how little vengeance he felt. "I hope you're not gonna do something stupid. It's over. Whatever you and your followers were hoping to achieve is not gonna happen. If Earth has decided that those guys who took out the satellites are the bad guys then that's good enough for me."

He turned to Freddie, relief now slightly detectable in his voice. "Well done, Freddie. Your timing is, once again, impeccable." Suddenly he was very business-like and his tone assumed a cold detachment. "Please take Ms Green and her people to a secure location."

"This isn't over yet, Kirk," Frankie spat. She was either determined not to go quietly or genuinely felt that her fortunes would turn again.

Kirk retained his coldness, "Let's just wait and see, shall we, Frankie?" he told her as Freddie and his motley group of heroes escorted her and the others out.

Kirk turned his attention to the clearly shocked personnel still in the command centre. He didn't have the luxury of time to explain everything to them all individually. They were in a quasi-military situation and he knew just how to behave. Clear and decisive action was called for. "OK. Let's just settle down now, shall we?" He decided that a short, sharp pep-talk might also be in order, “We’ve got a job to do. A very important job and the future of our planet might just depend on it.”

He looked straight across at Scott. “Mr Scott, change those attack plans to target the other fleet and inform the pilots that they will be going into battle very soon.”

Chapter 83

The contents of the large store room had recently been increased by four unusual and incongruous additions. Around the walls were arranged neat metal shelving units containing numerous files and stationery items. A simple table, supporting a computer, was positioned in the centre of the room. In front of this table a chair contained the first of these foreign objects. Josh Travis' duplicate was blindfolded and tied into the chair. Across the room from him Mr Jacks was also blindfolded and tied into a chair. Unlike the duplicate, he was unconscious. Adding to the security of their bonds were the two other occupants of the room. The two men who had kidnapped the duplicate and Mr Jacks provided a menacing presence. One stood motionless at the door and the other sat poised at the computer as if awaiting imminent instructions.

The door opened and, after reassuring the guard, Mario Silvester entered. He barely waited for the door to close behind him before he began addressing Josh's duplicate. "OK, Josh. It's time to bring an end to all these lies and cover-ups. I think it's time you told the truth."

It was clear that he wasn't about to waste time with pleasantries or mind-game interrogation techniques. This man was in a hurry and he wanted answers fast. He ripped the blindfold from the face of the teenager and continued menacingly, "Who the hell are you?"

The duplicate blinked at the sudden invasion of bright light and tried to focus on his surroundings. He looked at Mario with a look of bewilderment on his face. "I'm Josh Travis."

Clearly Mario was in no mood for playing games. He knew something was amiss, and wasn't prepared to be fobbed off with rehearsed answers. "No, you're not. I don't know who you are but you are not Josh Travis." He paused to let his conviction sink in. "Oh yes, you look identical to him. You even act and behave the same way as him. But you are not him!"

The duplicate's programming required him to persist with the deception. "I'm sorry, sir, but I'm confused," he responded, adding an element of deference and courtesy for effect. "I am Josh Travis."

"Huh. *You're* confused?" Mario replied scathingly. "What about the rest of us?"

For a brief moment the duplicate's sub-routines interpreted the response as genuine puzzlement on the part of the inquisitor. "I really don't follow, sir. I am Josh."

Impressions that Mario might be being fooled were immediately dispelled as he violently slammed his fist down on the table, passing only inches from the duplicate's face. "No, you're not!" he almost screamed. "Separate blood tests have shown wild fluctuations in the haematocrits within your blood. Now either you are regularly getting a complete blood transfusion or the blood is from different people. So what is it?" he demanded to know. But without waiting for an answer he added his own theory, "According to our records you are suffering no health problems that would require blood transfusions, so that only leaves the two people option doesn't it?"

The duplicate's programming had had time to select an alternative set of tactics during Mario's rant and opted now to run them. "I guess so. But that assumes your tests are accurate," he said allowing his new-found belligerence to surface. "I don't remember having any blood tests."

"Of course you don't," Mario spat back, a little unsettled by this youngster's resilience. "We didn't actually invite you to participate. There is more than one way of obtaining a blood sample from someone - you don't have to use a syringe and a nurse." He paused to allow the implied menace to sink in. "Perhaps you remember accidentally cutting yourself or being involved in a bus crash?"

Despite being a machine, the surprised realisation of what he'd just been told registered on the duplicate's face in exactly the same way as it would have done on the real Josh. He frantically searched for an adequate response. "But surely that's illegal?" he offered feebly.

Mario waved his hand scornfully. "That doesn't matter. What matters is whether you are an imposter."

"What do you mean, an imposter? How can I be?" asked the duplicate, rediscovering his fledgling belligerence. "And what right do you have to keep me here without a lawyer?"

Mario's disdain for both the question and, clearly, the notion of Habeas Corpus, showed in his body language as he shrugged and moved away from Josh, rubbing his moustache as he thought through his next approach. As he did so he cleared the duplicate's line of sight towards the far corner, revealing the slumped teacher. "What have you done to Mr Jacks?"

Mario spun back to the duplicate and slapped him hard across the face. "I'll ask the questions, boy. I don't need any rights to keep you here. Who's gonna come looking for you?" he asked sneeringly.

Reeling from the blow and shaking his head to clear it the duplicate stuck to his story that he was the real Josh. "My family, for one."

"Are you sure?" Mario countered, lowering his voice to add even more gravitas to his threat. "If you're an imposter, how do you know that the real Josh Travis isn't already sitting at home right now?"

"I doubt that," the duplicate replied flippantly, with just the right addition of confidence.

"Oh, do you? Is that because you know where he really is?" Mario threw back at him. He looked across to the kidnapper seated at the computer. "Have you made contact yet?"

"No, sir, this is really odd," the kidnapper replied without looking up. He was clearly intent on concentrating on his computer display as he added, "I'm not getting any response at all."

"That's unusual, she's normally so punctual," Mario responded, stroking his moustache again in thought.

For a brief moment the duplicate detected a sense of puzzlement both on Mario's face and in his voice. "What's wrong? Things not working out as you planned?" he asked his captor. "Maybe your theory's not so watertight either," the belligerence was growing now with every moment.

"Listen, kid, I'm gonna give you exactly 60 seconds to start coming up with answers. otherwise things are gonna start getting messy," Mario snarled at him. Clearly any patience that he had ever possessed was now totally exhausted.

"How can I tell you what I don't know?" the duplicate replied, playing dumb again.

"Well. perhaps Agent Summers, or Mr Jacks as you know him, might be able to help," Mario suggested as he changed tack completely, turning towards the other captive. "He was already on to you when we picked you both up."

The duplicate's face registered confusion. Clearly he knew nothing of this subterfuge and Mario noticed. "Oh yes. He and his agency have had you and your school under investigation for some time now."

Fortunately for Josh's duplicate, the suddenly-charged atmosphere within the room was somewhat diffused by the interruption of Mario's cell phone ringing. He yanked it out of his pocket, clearly frustrated that the moment was gone, and glanced at the display before answering curtly, "Yes?" He paused to listen to the caller and then replied, "I see. Tell them I'll be right out," before ending the call abruptly. He turned back to the duplicate, "Well, Mr Travis, it appears that Agent Summers' agency are here. Time for us to leave."

Loosening the ropes that were tying him to the chair, Mario dragged the student to his feet, and addressed the kidnapper still trying to obtain some sort of connection on the computer, "You come with us."

As they walked to the door, he looked at the other kidnapper and nodded his head towards Mr Jacks. "Keep a close watch on that one," he ordered him. Then drawing a gun from inside his jacket he and the other kidnapper half-pushed, half-dragged Josh's duplicate out of the room.

Chapter 84

As the door slammed shut behind the departing trio of Mario, Josh's duplicate and the kidnapper, Mr Jacks' body slumped forward and the chair toppled over on top of him.

Clearly no fool, the remaining kidnapper detailed to guard this prisoner pulled his gun from the concealed shoulder holster and stood watching for signs of movement. When, after at least a minute, none had been forthcoming, he cautiously advanced to the pile of chair and prostrate teacher. Circling warily, he slowly got closer, but no matter which angle he looked from he couldn't see any signs of consciousness, or even life.

He was beginning to think that maybe the captive was genuinely comatose beneath the item of furniture and apprehensively reached out with one hand to shake the chair, while keeping his gun trained directly at the centre of the pile of plastic, metal and flesh that represented Mr Jacks' position. He grasped the rim of the chair and just as he was about to try moving it he realised, a split-second too late, that the restraining ropes were lying loose on the floor beneath the upturned arm closest to him. A sixth sense tried desperately to warn him of the danger, but it was too late. With scythe-like precision Mr Jacks' leg swung out from his prone position and caught the side of the kidnapper's calf muscle, throwing him off balance. As if to prove how tense he had been, this jolt caused his finger to squeeze a fraction harder on the trigger of his pistol firing a round high up into the wall above. In that instant Mr Jacks hurled the chair up and towards the kidnapper, who had now recovered enough to be levelling his gun at his captive. But he had lost the advantage and the agent, now on his feet, brought an upper-cut punch, straight up with the momentum of his own bodily thrust, into the diaphragm of the kidnapper. As the man crumpled forward, gasping for air, Mr Jacks picked up the discarded chair and swung it neatly round to connect with the back of the head of his captor, sending him sprawling unconscious, and for all Mr Jacks cared dead, on to the floor in front of him.

Standing up straight and rubbing his wrists to try and speed up the return of blood circulation after the restrictions imposed by the ropes, Mr Jacks surveyed the scene. Spotting his discarded cell phone on the computer table in the middle of the room, he dashed to it and selected a speed dial number.

It was answered almost immediately. "It's me. They've taken Josh. Probably trying to get him away from here. I'm gonna try and follow." There were no lengthy acknowledgements or discussions. Clearly he was talking to a highly-trained and experienced person who knew what he meant and just what they had to do. As he moved towards the door he caught sight of something on the computer screen which made him stop and look. Absorbing the information, he opened the door cautiously and, having ascertained that there was no-one outside, left the room.

Chapter 85

Special Agent Henderson and Kimberley Walsh stood waiting patiently at the reception desk of the Polar Exploration Agency. Ultra-modern, it was three or four stories high and made almost entirely of steel and glass. The actual reception area was an atrium soaring right to the top of the building, with the floors above forming sparkling balconies throughout the ascent, rimmed with numerous exotic green plants tumbling down into the void.

Agent Walsh had her back to the reception desk and the attractive young lady staffing it as she gazed almost absent-mindedly through the full-length tinted windows at the car park outside. At least half of the cars in it were faceless black 4x4s just like the one they had arrived in. If you ever wanted to advertise the location of a government agency, she thought, this was probably the best way to do it!

Special Agent Henderson was just finishing a cell phone call. Agent Walsh turned back to him as she heard him terminate it. She guessed it had to have been important from the brevity of it. "That was Summers. He says they're trying to escape with Josh," he informed her.

As if on cue a black 4x4 suddenly sped into view from the side of the building and turned wildly into the car park making for the exit. Henderson immediately speed-dialled his phone. "Brad?" he checked perfunctorily before continuing, "They're trying to get away with Josh in a black 4x4. Probably the one that they used to kidnap him from the school. It's just barrelled through the car park at the front heading for the exit. Where are you?"

In yet another faceless, black 4x4 Brad and Fredericks were approaching the building from the main road. As Brad received Henderson's call they suddenly saw Mario's car speed out of the car park and cut across in front of their lane, about four cars ahead. It sped past them in the opposite direction and Brad immediately turned on their siren and concealed lights.

"That's them," he informed Fredericks. "Quick, follow them." Then, speaking into his cell phone he told Henderson, "We see them and are in pursuit."

Fredericks checked his mirrors and then spun the car around with much squealing of tyres and smoking of rubber. Within seconds the car had bounced to a stop, facing the opposite direction, and the driver floored the gas pedal as they began their pursuit of the suspect.

Clearly Mario had heard their sirens and, in his rear view mirror, seen Fredericks' little manoeuvre, as he increased his speed in an effort to get away before his pursuers could begin to gain ground. Weaving in and out of traffic, he was slowly increasing the gap between his vehicle and the agents as he forced his way recklessly onwards.

Agents McCoy and Fredericks had already made the calculation that the danger to civilians was great but the danger to the kidnap victim was even greater if they lost their quarry. With this in mind, Fredericks was chasing down the suspect utilising all of his training and concentration to stay in touch with the rogue driver.

As they sped along the highway at breakneck speed, Mario approached an innocent-enough looking right hand bend. It was a gentle curve that shouldn't give him any trouble, and as he cleared the initial traffic and zipped past cars in the inside lane he allowed himself the luxury of a split-second glance in his mirror. The agency car was still there but not gaining at all. He flipped his concentration back to the road in front and, to his horror, saw a twelve-wheel truck lumbering along in his lane overtaking some slower RVs. With no time to brake and nowhere to go, Mario had little choice but to swerve towards the grass median. Unfortunately for him, the speed the car was travelling and the angle at which the wheels hit the kerbside meant that he completely lost control of the vehicle. For a moment the entire car was airborne by a couple of inches and when it thumped back to earth the front offside wheel dug deep into the grass, causing the heavy vehicle to spin laterally across the median, colliding with the concrete upright running down the centre. This caused the car to ricochet up before it crashed down on to its side, skidding along until the soft roof suddenly made contact with the upright concrete pillar of a bridge support. The sickening thud and gut-wrenching sound of twisting and crunching metal could be heard even by the driver of the truck, who was still wrestling to bring his lumbering behemoth to a controlled stop after seeing the accident unfold around and ahead of him.

Fredericks brought their car to a screeching halt behind the mangled 4x4, as all of the traffic on both carriageways also came to a complete standstill. Both he and Agent McCoy jumped out and rushed over to the smoking wreck. Trying desperately to gain access to what was now nothing more than a crushed and twisted tin can, they eventually managed to force one of the rear doors open just enough to see inside.

All three occupants lay motionless. Josh's duplicate was bleeding profusely from a head wound and Brad reached in for a pulse. Moving his attention to the kidnapper, he also checked him for a pulse before performing the same action on Mario's inert body. He backed himself out of the wreck and, straightening up, looked at Fredericks before shaking his head. Sombrely, bearing a heavy weight of mixed defeat and, perhaps, guilt, he speed-dialled his boss.

As he waited for Henderson to answer he peered back into the mangled car and glanced down at Mario again just as the call was picked up. "Sir? It's McCoy," he began without any emotion. "There's been a crash." There was no easy way to say this, so best just to get it over and done with. "I'm afraid that none of them made it."

He listened to Henderson's response before answering his inevitable question, "Yes, sir, the kid as well." He knew the special agent in charge would not take this news well and he listened to the disappointment in his voice as he acknowledged Brad's information.

"I know," he confirmed when Henderson suggested that they'd now lost all their leads, before adding what he hoped might re-instate his boss' opinion of him. "Sir, there's something else. I think you ought to get over here. As fast as possible, before the police arrive."

Henderson knew Brad well enough to trust his instincts, but still felt compelled to question why his presence was required so urgently. "Let's just say I'm not sure it was the kid's blood that we should have been worrying about," replied Brad as he continued to stare at the green liquid trickling from Mario's wounds!

Chapter 86

Staring fixedly at the giant Polar Exploration Agency crest on the wall behind the receptionist, Henderson terminated the call. "There's been a crash," he informed Agent Walsh. "Brad says that they're all dead, including the kid."

Before Walsh could even process the information fully, let alone respond, Mr Jacks, or Agent Summers as they knew him, rushed out from one of the corridors. "Sir! Where the hell are we?" he asked, glad that at last he'd found some allies. "Have you got Josh?" he asked eagerly.

Henderson spun to face his agent. "Summers! At least we know where you are."

"What about Josh?" Agent Summers repeated. "Have you got him?"

He didn't really need a verbal answer to his question. Bob Henderson's face told him all that he needed to know, even before the special agent spoke. "I'm afraid there's been an accident." He paused before confirming, "Josh is dead."

"Dammit!" exclaimed Agent Summers. "I knew I should have acted sooner."

Kimberley Walsh knew only too well the dangers of guilt by association and moved to nip it in the bud. "There wasn't anything you could have done. It was a car crash," she informed him gently. "Brad's at the scene now."

"Which is where I need to be," Henderson remarked abruptly. "You two stay on here until a team arrives. I want this place closed up so tight even the oxygen has to ask for permission to leave, you got that? No-one comes in or goes out until we're through." It was clear that he meant business. This place was going to get a very thorough going-over. He turned towards the doors. "In the meantime I'd better see what Brad says is so urgent."

Chapter 87

Far away from the mayhem at the Polar Exploration Agency, there was a different kind of mayhem going on. Hundreds of thousands of miles above the Earth's surface three groups of combatants were locked in an explosive battle for supremacy. The first batch of aliens were continuing to slug it out with the second batch and the drones of Space Corps had now waded into the fray with a determination to do something to help. Quite who they were helping, and for what eventual purpose, they weren't entirely sure, but they were skilfully trying to tip the balance in favour of the first group. At least these ones hadn't yet turned on any aspect of the Earth's infrastructure.

But it wasn't easy. All of Space Corps' pilots were incredibly skilled at the computer games that so closely mimicked what they were now doing for real. Most of them had been training for many months with the drone space craft. Yet none of them had ever been in any type of combat before and no-one had ever envisaged that they might ever be involved in such activities as part of Space Corps. Their training had been purely a matter of mastering the manoeuvring and speed characteristics of the ships. Sure, firing lasers when you'd manoeuvred your ship didn't take too much extra skill, but ducking and diving to avoid other ships and incoming fire was a totally different ball game.

As yet another Space Corps drone exploded in a fiery display, its pilot turned his face away from the brightness suddenly invading his display screen and threw his arms up in frustration. Freddie watched the reaction as he had watched all of the others for the last half hour and walked through to the command centre where the fight was being watched on the main viewer.

"I don't know how we're gonna keep this up. They're just too many of them and they're much better than we are," he told Kirk, frustration evident in his voice.

"Hardly surprising," Kirk replied without taking his eyes off the screen as he witnessed the annihilation of yet another Space Corps drone. "They do this for a living. We're using students who've never been in a real combat situation before."

"Well if it comes to that, how many of the *adults* have ever been in combat before?" Freddie asked. "You're one of the only ones with any real military experience."

Kirk pursed his lips and stared at the view screen some more while answering Freddie's observation. "Nevertheless, we've got to keep going. Our involvement in the fight is a huge gamble but it does seem to be taking some of the pressure off the good guys."

Freddie shot Kirk a wry look. "Let's just hope that when all this is over, they still are the good guys."

"Hmmm," Kirk replied, seemingly distracted, before changing the subject. "OK, I want you to move Red Group to Sector 4. It might take some of the pressure off Yellow Group. Continue to hold Blue Group in reserve and reinforce Green Group where they need it. What else do we have in reserve?" Clearly Kirk was totally engaged in military mode.

Inwardly, this reassured Freddie. At least they had someone in charge who knew a little about tactics and combat. Nevertheless, his answer didn't necessarily serve to reassure anyone else. "Precious little. Gold and Silver Groups are about the only thing that we have left, but they're made up of the most inexperienced pilots." He hesitated a moment before delivering the really bad news, "We're also running out of drones to actually pilot."

"But we still have more ships than pilots, right?" asked Kirk, more by way of confirming his information rather than trying to appear optimistic. "And there's still those inactive ships as well," he added.

"Yeah, but that's the point," stressed Freddie. "They're inactive. We still haven't figured out how to get them working. We've only been trying for five months. It took five years to get the others serviceable."

Now it was time for Kirk to play the optimist card and he suggested blithely, "Well, let's just pray for a miracle, shall we? Because the way things are going, we're likely to need them in a couple of hours." He looked back at the viewing screen to see more of his fleet being destroyed. "In the meantime we need to get more pilots!"

"From where?" Freddie asked, incredulous at the suggestion.

Kirk turned to face him and suggested with deadly seriousness, "The schools! They only ever send us the best and most promising students, but they usually have quite a few who don't quite make the grade. I want you to ask the pilots for names of their gaming friends. Be quick, don't distract them for long, but get names! Then contact the schools and ask the principals to try and recruit them urgently."

Freddie wasn't too sure he approved of the plan and the sucking in of air as he spoke betrayed his doubts. "It's risky. They might not be as good as we'd like and it could well blow our cover on Earth."

"I know," Kirk replied earnestly. "But if we don't get those pilots there may well not be an Earth to worry about. We really don't have a choice as I see it."

Looking at it from that point of view, Freddie had to agree that there really wasn't much of an alternative. "OK, I'll get on it," he confirmed.

Kirk's attitude softened as he explained his reasoning, speaking as one friend to another, "Freddie, I want to use as many ships as we have and swamp the battle with good guys."

Chapter 88

Chris and John stood in front of Principal McGregor's desk, not quite sure of what they were hearing. The look of shock and uncertainty was common to both as the principal rounded off what he'd just been telling them. "So you see gentlemen, that's about the sum of it."

Chris was incredulous. "You mean Josh is up in space right now, fighting aliens?"

"Well, not exactly," the principal explained calmly. "Josh is up in space but he's using a drone spaceship to fight the aliens. It's kind of like your computer games, but for real."

"And this has been going on for how long, sir?" asked John, still unsure whether to believe what he had just heard.

The principal smiled, understanding his uncertainty. "This entire semester. He was recruited right after the summer vacation."

"So the Josh we've been hanging out with is really a robot?" Chris ventured hesitantly.

"We prefer to call them 'synthetic humans'," the principal corrected him. "Robot suggests some sort of metal, clunky machine. I think you'll agree that what we have is somewhat more refined."

"So that's been Josh all this time?" queried John, uncertainty running thick through his voice.

The principal sought to reassure him with a smile. "No, not all the time. Only when the real Josh has been needed in space. Your friend has probably been with you about seventy-five per cent of the time. And now he needs you to be with him to help him and the others in what is fast becoming a desperate struggle." He looked long and hard at each of them before asking, "So, will you go?"

"To space? To play computer games for real?" asked John. The incredulity in his voice wasn't so much directed any more at the potential reality of what he'd just been told, but rather at the need for the question itself. It was like someone had just offered him a free ride on a space shuttle and was checking whether he was scared of flying! "Are you kidding, sir?"

Chris thought he'd better clarify their response. "Of course we'll go, sir."

The principal stood up immediately and ushered them both towards what they had always assumed was a cupboard. "Right, then let's get going."

Chapter 89

The stillness of the crisp, cold air was suddenly shaken by the high-pitched whistle of many powerful engines as a number of large black shapes grew rapidly in size in the clear blue sky. The US Marines guarding the perimeter of the cave area found themselves watching as ten alien spacecraft of the squat, rounded variety descending on their position. Within minutes they had all landed and began disgorging their cargo of alien soldiers down the rapidly extended ramps. Clearly they had arrived ready for combat!

Readying themselves for the inevitable battle, the marines hunkered down in their positions, awaiting orders. The young, quietly confident lieutenant in charge watched through his binoculars, alert for any sign of an attack. He didn't have to wait long!

As soon as the leading group of aliens had got their bearings they began to loose volleys of laser fire in the general direction of the defenders. Although untargeted, it was clearly an act of war and the lieutenant had no hesitation in ordering his men to return fire. First blood went to the marines as three of the aliens were dropped within seconds of each other. Hardly surprising, since they were fully exposed, whilst the marines were well dug in.

For a moment it appeared too easy until, almost too late, the Lieutenant realised that the aliens at the front line were being sacrificed to allow others to spot the positions of his men. No sooner had the first ones been killed than accurate, sniper-like laser fire began to puncture the rocks around their positions.

Fortunately the marines were using a tactic of shoot and move, whereby they changed position after every few shots as a means of avoiding precisely what the aliens were attempting. Nevertheless it wasn't always successful and the two smouldering human corpses now lying not far from the lieutenant's concealed position were a grisly reminder of how exposed he and his men really were.

Another two aliens went down and the firepower directed at the marines intensified. Boy, what he wouldn't give right now for one of those defensive force fields he'd seen the other aliens use earlier, the lieutenant thought. He signalled to the two mortar teams at the outer edge of their position and the whistle of their deadly shells was immediately added to the growing noise across the polar plain.

The explosions seemed to shock the aliens momentarily and, using the distraction as cover, many of the marines adjusted their positions again. At the same time the sacrificial aliens all now sought cover amongst the rocks. At least it looked as though they were now going to settle down to something more akin to a conventional fire-fight, thought the lieutenant. But he soon realised how wrong that assumption was when a new type of alien weapon began raining down unseen explosives amongst his positions. Unlike the marines' mortars, these were almost silent in their approach, but just as deadly in their effect as sudden flashes of bright green energy bursts erupted across the hillside. Too late, the lieutenant realised that not only had the lead aliens been acting as fodder for target spotters, but they'd also been screening the setting-up of these artillery positions.

Fortunately the marines were also well-equipped and the officer instructed his detachment armed with Carl Gustafs to commence firing air burst rounds into the alien positions. As the time-delayed projectiles began exploding above the rocks on the plains, more aliens began to pay the ultimate price.

And so the battle went. One side seemingly gaining an advantage only for the other to neutralise it. But from the marines' point of view, any action that prevented the aliens from advancing was a tactical victory buying crucial time for their comrades deep inside the caves to accomplish their mission.

As laser fire and bullets ricocheted off the cave walls all around him, Major Landis was brought news of the situation outside by another young lieutenant. "Sir, Lieutenant Sanders reports alien spaceships landing outside the cave entrance and troops disembarking," he shouted above the din. "They're now engaged in a fire-fight with them."

Concern registered on Landis' face as he asked, "Can they hold them?"

"Sanders thinks they'll be OK for a while," the lieutenant reassured him, before adding the caveat, "Just as long as they don't send any more."

With most of his forces committed to this two-pronged all-out offensive Landis couldn't afford for the enemy to take the cave entrance. He and his men would be caught like rats in a trap. They'd be slaughtered if there was an attack from their rear. He reached for his radio. "Captain Stewart, come in. What's your status there?"

"About the same sir," the voice of his executive officer replied from the radio. Landis could hear the sound of intense weapons fire close to the radio as Captain Stewart continued, "I've lost another three men but we just don't appear to be making any headway. I'm certain we've killed at least another six aliens but there doesn't seem to be any way to get close enough to breach their defences."

Major Landis nodded and replied in heavily underlined tones. "Understood. Now listen carefully. The situation has changed." He paused to add gravitas to what he was saying. "Additional alien troops have just landed outside. Lieutenant Sanders thinks his men may be able to hold them for a while, but if he fails they'll come pouring into the tunnels right behind us. They'll be no escape route and we'll be slaughtered. We have to break through. Exploit any advantage you find, but cut through. I'm gonna regroup and try a frontal assault from here. I say again, it is crucial that we break through. Landis out." Cutting the message off before its recipient had time to respond was his way of emphasising the importance of what he'd just said. There was no room, or time, for debate! He also knew that his friend and exec would carry out his orders if at all possible.

Turning his attention back to the lieutenant he instructed him, "Move Alpha squad back to the rear and tell them to prepare to repel a possible counter attack. Replace them with Bravo squad and get Charlie and Dog to stand by to reinforce the attack. Tell the squad leaders to report direct to me. I'm gonna lead us in myself."

Chapter 90

In the Space Corps Flight Deck, Chris and John were amongst the couple of dozen new recruits settling themselves at consoles. Try as hard as he might, John just couldn't get the smile off his face. He'd given up pinching himself yet he still would not have been surprised to suddenly wake up and discover that this had been nothing more than a dream.

Chris was just as enthralled by what had happened in the last hour, but seemed to be managing just a little better than his friend to disguise it. Yet he also felt a slight sense of trepidation. He wasn't really sure what was going on as far as the bigger picture was concerned but he knew he and John were being asked to help bolster the efforts of Space Corps' regular operators. Quite why they needed bolstering wasn't entirely clear, but it had crossed his mind that it might be down to the effects of attrition. Had young people been losing their lives? He'd been assured that they were only flying drones, but was that the full truth? In all honesty he really didn't care. Even the possibility of a violent end wouldn't have changed his eagerness to get involved. Were they kidding? Going to space, flying real spacecraft and fighting in a real battle with aliens. He'd have agreed to come even if they guaranteed at least minor injury!

All of the existing pilots were so focussed on their current activities that they barely even noticed the sudden influx of fresh blood. When they did suddenly become aware of a freshman taking a seat next to them they hardly dare take their eyes of their monitors long enough for the new faces to register with them. Josh's reaction would, no doubt, have been the same when Chris and John sat down next to him, but for the fact that he already knew them. The surprise on his face was almost instantly replaced by the joy of recognition, closely followed by a slightly sheepish expression. "Well, guys, I guess I owe you an explanation, or an apology. Or both," he suggested.

"Yeah, you probably do," agreed Chris with mock hurt which he found impossible to continue, "But this is so cool!" He looked at the various controls in front of him, "How do these things work?"

Josh returned his attention to his own monitor before replying, "Freddie'll explain everything in a moment, but it's really like playing an advanced round of *Alien Invasion.*" He deftly avoided an alien ship and spiralled down through the battle to get out of trouble.

John was staring almost open-mouthed at the manoeuvre that he had just seen Josh pull, but still managed to react to what he had said with a note of disdain. "But that was last year's game. Haven't they got anything a bit more challenging?"

"Believe me, this is quite a bit more difficult," replied Josh, struggling to shake off two aliens that were pursuing him. "For starters, that's a real drone you'll be flying and it can really be destroyed." He pulled up sharply, watching the aliens fly straight past before managing to level out and blast one of them from behind.

Chris' face showed his appreciation and admiration of what he had just witnessed. "Yeah, but we can really destroy the aliens, can't we?"

Almost as if to prove the point, the ship that Josh had been firing at exploded in front of them. "If you can catch 'em," Josh hissed triumphantly. Still watching his screen intensely, he explained, "They're pretty good and they're playing for real."

Freddie moved to the centre of the flight deck to address the newcomers. "Right, now you've all been shown the basics and, from what we hear from your principals, you're all dedicated gamers." He looked around at the new faces. All of them showed a mixture of excitement and trepidation.

"Just relax into the controls and think of it as the latest game release," he told them, trying to preserve their confidence despite what they could see happening on the other pilots' screens. "You'll find quite a bit of similarity with games you've already played, but remember we can't just re-boot and get your ships back if they're destroyed." While he didn't want to dampen their enthusiasm, he felt it necessary to temper their eagerness with a little cautionary warning. "Neither can we use cheats to get to a higher level. This is for real!"

He could see that some of what he was trying to impart was sinking in, but still felt it incumbent upon him to underline the real home truth of what they were about to get involved in. "It's also worth considering that if we don't help the good guys win, then the bad guys are likely to start attacking this space station when they've nothing to distract them."

Almost every new pilot was twitching at their control panels and straining to get in to the action. This was where they'd find out if Commander Stevens' gamble would pay-off. Freddie couldn't delay the inevitable any longer. The time for talking and demonstrating was over.

It was now up to the skills of the students. Let's just hope the principal's gauging of these kids' abilities is accurate, he thought as he let them loose. "So go get out there and destroy as many alien ships as you can!"

Feeling the sudden surge of power through the interactive control panel as his drone suddenly sprang free, Chris couldn't resist an exuberant, "Yee-hah!"

Still swerving and spinning in the thick of the battle, Josh found just enough time to roll his eyes and react, "Always so dramatic!"

Outside the space station, a sudden swarm of drones launched from numerous docking pods and exploded into space like a puff of dust. Almost immediately, the cloud broke up into its constituent parts as each of the various spacecraft came under the control of its new pilot and headed for the battle in its own individual way. Some headed arrow-like straight for the centre, others headed up or down to join the fray from alternative directions, while some took a slightly more cautious, circuitous route to come in from the other side. But all of them, without exception, headed confidently for the fight!

Back inside Space Corps, Freddie entered the command centre and answered Kirk's unspoken question as he approached. "OK, sir, that's everything we've got now engaging the enemy."

"Reserves?" Kirk asked, vaguely hopeful.

"Just Gold and Silver groups, with their much older ships," Freddie confirmed his concerns, adding almost as an afterthought, "Oh, and those new ships that won't fly."

"OK. So we're pretty much fully committed." Kirk's thoughtful and serious expression underlined the desperation of their situation. "Let's just hope we can overwhelm them."

Initially it looked as if his tactic of flooding the battle with more spacecraft was turning the tide. The sudden influx of Space Corps drones resulted in the destruction of a large number of enemy alien ships. Simple weight of numbers was paying off!

But once the moment of surprise had passed, the lack of experience in the new students began to show. The enemy aliens had clearly been overwhelmed temporarily, but their combat readiness soon restored the balance and gradually counterbalanced the weight of numbers. More and more of the drones piloted by the new students began to explode throughout the battle zone as the youngsters' greenness led them into dangerous manoeuvres and deadly dances with the hotshot alien ships.

Inside Space Corps, Kirk ran a hand through his hair and grimaced. His tight-lipped expression said it all. "Well, Freddie, it looks as if my gamble has failed," he said, shaking his head.

Partly out of loyalty and partly because he couldn't think of a better strategy, Freddie tried to reassure his boss. "Hey, it was a good attempt. But what are we supposed to do? I was kind of hoping that seeing us throw more ships into the fight might stimulate the good guys to make more effort."

Kirk shrugged. "Maybe they're running out of ships as well," he suggested, but was interrupted by Louise Church at another console.

"Sir, there's something odd going on with those new ships in the dock."

Fearing the worst, Kirk spun to face her, "How odd?"

"Well, they've all just powered up," she informed him, raising her hands in a gesture indicating that she neither had anything to do with it or even understood how it had happened.

"Huh? How come?" asked Freddie, just as surprised as the young operator. "I thought we couldn't make 'em do anything."

"That's the point, sir, *we* didn't make them do anything," she replied emphasising her complete noninvolvement in what had happened. “They just came on, all by themselves.”

“And what are they doing now?” Kirk asked cautiously.

“Nothing, sir,” the operator replied, checking the readouts on her console for any change in status. “It’s as if they’re waiting for instructions.”

“From whom?” asked Freddie.

Kirk raised an eyebrow, without daring to raise his hopes, as he suggested, “Whoever turned them on.”

“Well if it wasn’t us, who the hell was it?” Freddie demanded to know.

Church looked up from her console before informing Kirk, “Sir, they’re moving.”

“On screen,” Kirk ordered with a sense of urgency, tempered with a certain uneasiness.

The view on the giant screen changed from the battle to a section of the space station that had, until that moment, rarely featured on it. A large number of larger fighters, different in design to the regular drones, were pulling away from the space station and seemed to be also heading for the battle. They appeared slower at first than the drones, perhaps due to their size, but as they cleared the space station they took on a whole new menacing appearance.

They were much less streamlined than the drones, yet their bulkier, more angular appearance suggested greater power and resilience. As they moved into something akin to a battle formation, numerous holes could be seen opening along the length of the ships and across the arrowhead-like fronts. From some of these apertures small pods could be seen emerging. Given the circumstances of their sudden activation it was only natural to assume that all of these revelations were connected to some kind of advanced weaponry.

Everyone in the command centre seemed to be holding their breath as they watched the manoeuvres taking place. Since no-one seemed to know who had activated these ships, it was not at all beyond reason that they could be about to attack Space Corps itself. As they pulled away from the space station gaining speed at an alarming rate a small group peeled off and headed down towards the Earth.

"Where the hell are they going?" Kirk asked nobody in particular.

It was Scott who provided the answer. "They're heading for Antarctica, sir."

"Great!" was Kirk's rueful response. "So whose side are they on?"

Chapter 91

Inside the caves of Marie Byrd Land, the battle between the US Marines and the unknown soldiers with their alien allies was raging fiercely. After Major Landis' leading of the charge had re-galvanised his troops, the marines had started to make headway. It was still touch and go and a heavy slog but there was no denying the fact that the quality and superior training of his men was beginning to tell and slowly, very slowly, they had begun to push the enemy back further towards the actual hangar caves.

As yet another salvo of mixed lasers and conventional bullets raked across his position, the major paused behind some cover to receive a message in his headpiece. "Landis here, go ahead, lieutenant."

He strained hard to hear above the tremendous noise in the tunnel. "What? How many of them? Whose side are they on?"

Outside the cave entrance, Lieutenant Sanders and his men were continuing to deny the aliens an advance, but casualties had been mounting, when a totally different design of spaceship had suddenly descended from the heavens to presumably join in the battle. "There's about ten ships, sir. They're too far away to see whose side they're on, but they look different to the other ships that we've seen," he was informing his commanding officer.

He raised his binoculars and watched the new arrivals fly in low and fast. He held his breath as they approached, diving in low to hug the contours of the ground. At the last possible moment they opened fire with an ear-splitting salvo of intense weapons fire and began strafing the alien soldiers.

Letting out a shout of mixed joy and relief, the lieutenant and most of the other marines cheered at this apparent arrival of the cavalry, before resuming their own defensive fire-fight against the enemy infantry, who had now been thrown into complete disarray and confusion.

Chapter 92

In the Space Corps Command Centre, Kirk had ordered the view screen to focus once more on the battle, when it began to seem as if the space station was at least exempt from attack by the new ships.

After their initially slow departure, they had covered the distance from the space station to the battle faster than any of the other alien technology that the humans had so far witnessed, leading to an increase in concern as they approached the fight.

But once they joined the battle and began destroying the enemy alien ships, an almost palpable sense of relief radiated through the command centre.

"Well, sir, that's just what we needed!" an exuberant Freddie exclaimed looking at Kirk.

"Too right!" his commander agreed. Now that one of the alien groups had seemingly demonstrated a willingness to ally themselves with Space Corps he decided to go for broke. "OK, commit Gold and Silver Groups to the attack. We're not gonna get another chance like this."

Scott immediately relayed the order to the flight deck. "Gold Group, Silver Group, engage alien ships. I say again, engage alien ships."

On the flight deck there was almost a cheer from the students who had been tasked with piloting the reserve drones, as they were now finally allowed to join in what they still saw as the 'fun'.

As the two new waves of Space Corps ships descended on the battle it soon became clear that the enemy aliens were being forced back towards their mother ships. As their losses began to mount, more and more of them started to disengage and retreat, whole scale.

In the Space Corps Command Centre, Freddie asked, "Do we follow?"

Kirk thought for a moment. Their losses in terms of ships had been enormous. If victory was now in sight he'd prefer to preserve what he had left. "No. Disengage now. Form a holding pattern at the outer marker."

"Are you sure?" Freddie asked, for the first time questioning his commander's tactics. "We could finish this."

Kirk shook his head slowly. "They're retreating. I don't see the point of risking any more ships. Besides it might not hurt to show some clemency. If they're leaving we don't need to destroy them."

Freddie indicated the screen. "Better tell that to the new fighters."

Once more Louise Church turned to Kirk, with an almost apologetic look on her face. "We have no control over those ships, sir, and they're still attacking."

"So are the other aliens," Freddie added, noticing that there seemed to be no reduction of hostilities on their part.

On the view screen, which was now operating at maximum magnification, the enemy aliens could be seen rejoining their mother ships, but they were being continually harassed all the way by both the original aliens and the new Space Corps fighters. Gradually, the mother ships of the original aliens could be seen hoving into view and heading for the enemy alien ships.

As they closed in proximity, they began opening fire with yet another form of weaponry that seemed to produce what looked like intermittent streams of electricity between the enormous ships. Clearly it was more than just electricity. Some sort of plasma energy? wondered Kirk, as he watched the frequency and ferocity of the exchanges increase.

After a few minutes one of the enemy alien mother ships disappeared behind an enormous black cloud that seemed to momentarily hide the surrounding star field, before imploding and releasing a spectacularly bright explosion. One, by one, more of the enemy mother ships met the same fate, until only one remained. Perhaps that ship was just lucky or perhaps it had a more skilled commander or helmsman, but just as the original alien mother ships were starting to close in it appeared to momentarily expand in size before something resembling a multi-coloured hole opened up in front of it, through which it instantly disappeared. The watching humans assumed that that was what entering hyperspace must look like!

No sooner had it disappeared than the remains of the original alien fighter fleet returned to their own mother ships and the new Space Corps ships banked slowly around to retrace their route back to the space station.

"Well, I'll be damned," exclaimed Freddie. "Those aliens must have been controlling the new ships."

Kirk looked at him and raised one eyebrow quizzically, before replying sarcastically, but in good humour, "You think?"

Church confirmed, "Sir, the new ships are returning to their docking bays and shutting down."

"So the question is: How did they manage to take control and how did they even know the ships were here?" pondered Kirk.

“Don’t look at me!” Freddie smiled defensively. He stopped to consider a thought for a moment before venturing, “Someone had to have designed all of this stuff in the first place. You don’t think it was them, do you?”

Kirk raised both eyebrows this time and shrugged. “Who knows?” he thought, but there were more urgent considerations requiring his attention right now. “Get this information down to Earth as fast as you can,” he ordered Scott. “It may have some bearing on what’s going on in Antarctica at the moment.”

Chapter 93

Outside the caves in Antarctica the remains of the alien ships were just smouldering wrecks and the ground around them littered with the bodies of the would-be invaders as the Space Corps fighters screeched heavenward, returning to the space station that none of the marines even knew existed.

Lieutenant Sanders activated his radio, "Major? This is Sanders. The perimeter is secure and I'm sending two squads to assist you." He indicated to the NCO accompanying him who immediately set off with a group of marines.

Inside the caves, the US Marines were continuing to advance under fire. Major Landis' group had now managed to reach the main hangar and were now engaged in a furious fire-fight at what seemed to be the final redoubt of the enemy.

With more space now to spread out, the marines were taking full advantage of the situation and it wasn't long before most of the leaders of the rogue human soldiers were either dead or captured, and the leader of the aliens dead.

Finally backed into a corner with no possibility of escape, the remaining aliens were in a hopeless situation.

Major Landis signalled for his men to cease fire and an eerie silence suddenly enveloped everyone in the hangar. Calling to the aliens from his secure position, the major's voice shattered the new-found quiet. "I don't know if you can understand me, but fighting on is pointless." he paused, wondering how futile trying to communicate with these extra-terrestrials might actually be. "You're completely surrounded. Surrender your weapons."

Nothing happened. Everyone waited tensely for a moment, fully expecting the fighting to resume. Then, unexpectedly, there was some movement among the aliens as they all slowly stood up.

"Throw down your weapons!" Landis called to them.

But the next movement the aliens made was to collectively utter a guttural, staccato sound, almost like some sort of growling laughter, before they were all blown to oblivion by some sort of explosive device that left most of the marines who had been in close proximity requiring treatment for damage to their ears.

Outside the caves Lieutenant Sanders had just finished talking on his radio and was now updating Alex, James and Luke. "Yes sir, it seems that Major Landis has secured the caves and captured the remaining mercenary leaders. I guess they'll be useful for interrogation."

Out of the corner of his eye James thought he saw movement behind the rocks adjacent to the young officer and, trying not to be too obvious, quietly suggested, "Lieutenant, you might want to check out that rise over there."

Indicating to a small group of marines to follow him, the lieutenant suddenly sprinted over to the rise. They covered the ground in no more than four or five seconds but when they arrived they found a small cave opening, but no sign of anyone. After a perfunctory search of the area they decided that it was a false alarm, and were just starting to return to the others when Captain Xavier jumped out from behind an outcrop and grabbed Lieutenant Sanders from behind.

"Nobody move," the mercenary ordered, eyes wide with a determined rage. His voice took on a deep and menacing tone as he continued, "Now, lieutenant, let's walk nice and slowly to a helicopter."

Quite how far he thought his audacious escape attempt would get him the captain didn't really know, but he surely thought it would be further than the meagre two steps he managed to take before a rifle barrel was rammed into his head and a voice calmly said, "Now, now, captain. Where do you think you're gonna go?"

Taking advantage of the sudden reversal of fortunes, Lieutenant Sanders spun around and disarmed Xavier, before looking up to see a triumphant James Rock standing at the side of a boulder, holding a rifle and grinning from ear to ear!

Chapter 94

Having now had the chance to check in with their relevant departments the various military leaders, together with Herbert Kennedy, once more found themselves sitting on the antique soft furnishings in the secretary of defense's office.

"Well, gentlemen, it looks as if we backed the right horse after all," the secretary was saying. "What's the situation now, general?"

The marine general looked justifiably proud as he straightened up and replied. "Well, Mr Secretary, Major Landis reports that the caves are now secured. The aliens who weren't killed in the battle destroyed themselves rather than be captured. So all we've got are a bunch of dead bodies for the scientists to start examining. We do, however, have a number of mercenaries in captivity including their leader. They're being flown to a secure location to be interrogated."

The secretary nodded approvingly and congratulated him, "A job well done, general." Then turning his focus to the root of the problem he looked at Kennedy. "Herb, what's the story in space?"

The head of the Space Exploration Agency was still slightly puzzled by some elements of what had been happening and by the source of some of the information he had been receiving, but he decided that now was not the right time to voice these and so stuck simply to the facts that he knew to be correct. "It appears from our various observatories that only one group of alien vessels remain, sir. They belong to what we decided were the 'good guys'. So far they're remaining static and not making any contact."

"Regrouping for another attack?" postulated the admiral.

Kennedy paused to give the suggestion polite consideration, then replied, "No, I don't think so, admiral."

But the air force general wasn't quite as ready to give the same due consideration to Kennedy's response as the astronomer had accorded to the sailor. "And why not? They know we're defenceless."

Kennedy shrugged. He really couldn't be bothered to worry about coming across as too relaxed. "Call it a hunch, general, but if they were determined to invade they could have done that as soon as the other aliens had been defeated." He let that suggestion of an indisputable military tactic sink in before returning to just the facts. "Our observatories report that all of the smaller craft have returned to their mother ships and everything is quiet."

The secretary of defense declared his support for Kennedy's opinion. "I'm inclined to agree with Herb on this, gentlemen. After all, his people did get it right over who to back in the fight."

The military men all smarted from the thinly-disguised rebuke and the marine general came to the aid of his colleagues, "Understood, Mr Secretary, but it's still too early to consider the problem resolved." He let his statement sink in and then voiced his concerns, "We've helped one bunch of potential invaders to defeat the other bunch, now let's pray that we haven't simply cleared a path for them."

Kennedy wanted to let the generals know that he was more than capable of holding his own in this debate with, or without, the support of their boss. "I understand your concerns, general, but not only did we help the winning aliens, they also helped us. Your own men reported that they sent fighters to take out the bad alien counter attack down at the pole."

As if on cue, Kennedy's computer bleeped to indicate an incoming Skype request. He glanced down at the caller identification and then asked the secretary, "Mr Secretary, may I take this? It's from Kitt Peak and may be important."

The secretary nodded enthusiastically. "Of course, Herb. Put it on speakers."

Kennedy transferred the connection to the wall-mounted screen and the image of Samantha Mitchell appeared. "Miss Mitchell, what do you have for us? Something useful I hope."

Samantha took just a moment to register the other faces in the room and appeared untroubled by her unexpected audience as she informed them, "Our Indian colleagues have detected movement of the alien ships towards Earth, sir. But even more important is a message that we received, apparently from the alien fleet."

This was clearly an unexpected development and everyone in the room looked at the screen intently. "Go on," Kennedy instructed her slowly.

"It reads simply: 'Friends. Meet to confer,' and then it gives a bunch of numbers which we've taken to be map co-ordinates."

"Where are they?" Kennedy asked with a mixture of curiosity and caution in his voice.

Samantha was pleased both to have the information ready to supply and with the information itself. "They're at the South Pole, sir." After all of the recent activity down there, where else could it be? she thought to herself. It all now began to make sense. "It looks as if the aliens want to set up a meeting," she added to emphasise that there would need to be some sort of response.

"Did they say when?" Kennedy asked, his mind clearly trying to consider any number of potential development scenarios.

Samantha shook her head. "No, sir, but at the speed they're now moving it won't take more than a few hours for them to get there."

Well, the die was cast. There was no point in trying to duck the issue, reasoned Kennedy. Might as well embrace the situation and see what would come of it. "Excellent work, Miss Mitchell." He hesitated for a moment and thought he might as well at least get a little more clarification, even if no-one else in the room would understand it. "One last question. How trustworthy is this information?"

Samantha smiled an enigmatic smile before replying, "It comes from our most reliable source, sir. Relayed from an outpost via India. Mr Khan himself passed it on."

Kennedy nodded approvingly. "Thank you, Miss Mitchell." He disconnected the call. He looked at the secretary of defense, "Well, Mr Secretary, it's over to you now. What do you want to do?"

"You're happy this is genuine?" the secretary asked searchingly.

"As genuine as it'll ever be," Kennedy reassured him.

The secretary shrugged and slowly looked at each of the men in his office before agreeing. "OK. I'd better alert the president. He'll need to be ready to travel." He thought for a moment then added, "And I guess he'll want to inform other world leaders as well."

Chapter 95

As hundreds of students left Littrow High School at the end of yet another typical school day, four students amongst them headed for the school bus knowing that they had had anything but a typical school day.

"Hey, what a day!" Chris was saying, feeling that he would never come down from the high that he was currently experiencing.

John agreed. "Who'd have thought school could be so much fun?" he asked. His whole life had, in the past 12 hours, changed completely and irrevocably.

Even Kelly was experiencing the euphoria. "I can't believe what you guys have been up to." No matter whatever happened in the future they would always know that extra-terrestrial life exists!

"That's the problem," Chris asserted ruefully. "No-one will believe it!" To think that he had just helped save the world and no-one knew!

As usual, it fell for Josh to be the voice of reason. "That's just the point Chris. No-one is supposed to believe it, or even know about it." Perhaps because he'd gotten involved with Space Corps without there being an emergency, he seemed more able than his friends to take recent developments in his stride.

"Yeah, but not being able to tell anyone about it. I think I'll just go bust!" exclaimed John, wondering how he'd ever manage to stay silent about it.

"To think I destroyed three alien spaceships," boasted Chris, reliving the euphoria.

"Yeah. And I got four!" boasted John.

"Must have been a lucky shot!" Chris responded begrudgingly.

"What about you, Josh? How many did you get?" Kelly asked, feeling just as elated as the boys.

Josh just shrugged. "I'm not really sure," he replied and added hastily, "And anyway, I was involved for a lot longer than these two."

"Hey, don't try to be modest," admonished Chris. "You're a hero and so are we. We helped save this planet. It's unbelievable!" he said, in a not particularly quiet voice and with plenty of overt body language. A much younger student walked past, looking at them with a mixture of disbelief, puzzlement and confusion.

Josh noticed his attention and informed him, very matter-of-factly, "Computer gaming. *Last Line of Defense* You can join the Gaming Club when you reach the 10th grade."

The student gave him a weird look, as if to say *Like I'd want to?* and walked on.

Smiling at the reaction, Josh turned to his friends. "See? No-one will believe you even if you do try to tell them. They'll just think you're even weirder than you are." He paused to let his subtle and well-intended insult sink in before advising them, "Just stick with the gaming cover. It'll save what street cred you have left."

Kelly began laughing. "To even think that you gaming nerds have any street cred at all is weird." She quietly grabbed Chris' arm and cuddled up to him. "All the same," she added, "It's a shame you can't get any for what you really did."

"It's better this way, Kelly," Josh confirmed with confidence. "Tomorrow we'll get the synthetic humans for Chris and John and they can begin their training properly."

"Yeah, and a new one for you, Josh, as well!" Chris added.

"But how will I know whether it's the real Chris or not?" Kelly asked with concern.

Chris looked at Kelly conspiratorially and winked. "Oh believe me, you'll know," he assured her, laughing.

"Hmmm," John wondered, as he began laughing.

"What's with you?" Josh asked puzzled.

"Oh I'm just wondering how you're gonna explain some of your last synthetic human's behaviour to your family," John replied as Kelly and Chris also began laughing at the realisation of Josh's impending embarrassment.

Josh looked slightly alarmed. "Why? What did he do?"

"Oh, nothing so bad that you can't wriggle out of it," John reassured him.

"But Megan might want you to explain your behaviour at her birthday supper," Chris informed him, laughing even more.

"And have you actually got her a present?" Kelly asked, wiping the tears of laughter from her face.

"I'm sure that your mom and dad will understand," John informed him.

"Oh, great!" exclaimed Josh with resignation and turned around.

"Where're you going?" Chris asked him.

"Space Corps. I think it's probably safer up there!" he informed them.

The other three all grabbed him and turned him back in the direction of the bus, saying, "Oh no, you don't."

“Besides, you just said that they can’t think you’re any weirder than you are!” Kelly exclaimed and his three friends resumed their laughing at his expense.

Chapter 96

Marie Byrd Land at the South Pole had never been so populated as it suddenly was now. For countless millennia it had remained an isolated and undiscovered part of the most inhospitable continent on the planet. Perfect for a base for occasional alien visitors. Yet in the last 100 years its situation had changed dramatically. Discovered in 1929 by US Naval Commander and explorer Richard E. Byrd and named for his wife it was now regularly surveyed by the various Antarctic Survey Teams based at the South Pole. It was bound to happen that, sooner or later, humans would develop the technology to allow them to inhabit, even if only for temporary periods, this most inaccessible of land masses. The alien base would then begin to slowly reveal its secrets. The process had been accelerated purely by the chance that human awareness coincided with one of the periodic routine visits by the alien squatters.

So now, in a matter of days numerous heated pavilions had been erected in the snowless valley, every one of them surrounded by a plethora of support vehicles and buildings. Outside each of the pavilions flew the flag of the nation that it represented. All of the major industrial nations of the planet had a presence and each presence consisted of a large deputation of representatives, security personnel, maintenance technicians and communications specialists. The entire complex formed a giant horseshoe in front of the mountain range, where the ice was still melting and where a massive alien transport ship had landed. It, too, had a variety of outbuildings situated below its boarding ramp to accommodate diplomats from all sides.

On this most auspicious of occasions Marine 1 made a slow and gentle arrival at the US pavilion. As the president himself disembarked and began to greet other world leaders there was suddenly a very real sense of purpose. No longer would the people of the Earth be able to wonder and speculate about the existence of aliens. They now had incontrovertible proof! And how would that affect their view of themselves in the universe?

Would it serve to remove petty divisions or would it just exacerbate them as individual nations and interests vied for dominance in relationships with the aliens. Only time would tell! But in the meantime, now that the president had arrived all of the leaders present boarded a fleet of large all-terrain vehicles and headed out across the valley to meet, for the first time, the representatives of an alien race.

Chapter 97

Bob Henderson let his head flop backwards against the headrest of the easy-chair he was occupying in his office. He reached down to the low table in front of him and retrieved his mug of strong coffee, took a long, deep gulp of the warm liquid and slowly swirled it around the inside of his mouth before swallowing. He exhaled loudly and sat gazing across the room, past the other easy-chair and his desk to the darkening sky.

He sat motionless for a while, letting his thoughts distil gradually. He glanced down at the Manilla folder in his lap before, almost grudgingly, lifting it back up to a more comfortable reading height. He picked up his glasses from the table and replaced them on his head before resuming his review of the case notes.

Clearly this one had not been plain sailing. Nor had it gone necessarily according to plan. It certainly hadn't had the type of ending he'd have wanted in a case involving juveniles.

Yet no matter how many times he read and re-read the notes it was clear that his agency had acted properly and in good faith to investigate the information they had received. Not only that, but despite occasional outbursts of frustration, his team had all adhered precisely to the rules. He should feel vindicated and relieved that there would be no comeback.

But he was ill at ease and it wasn't because Agent McCoy had displayed some of his old maverick tendencies. He knew he possessed them and would be issuing yet another reprimand that would, once again, see Brad exercise a tighter control of himself for a while. Neither was it because the agency had found themselves on the back foot in the latter stages of the investigation and he, personally, had been on the receiving end of a potentially embarrassing accusation from a school principal. He'd been in this business for long enough now to have developed a very thick skin. Ruffling other people's feathers and having your own ruffled occasionally was part of the territory.

No, the more he thought about the outcome and reflected upon the final developments of the case, the more he knew they were playing their small part in some sort of cover-up. And he didn't like it!

He took another draught from his coffee cup and removed his glasses, once more returning his gaze to the window and the sky beyond. He brought his hand up to his chin and began absent-mindedly massaging it and his lower face, contorting his mouth into grotesque shapes as he pulled on his lip.

Finally he let out a long, resigned sigh. He'd squared his decision with himself! Mario Silvester's body had been secreted away by another government agency to an undisclosed location from where it would probably never depart. Green blood was now their problem, not his.

But the final detail that he saw within the file as he closed the cover had remained the property of his agency. Agent Summers' testimony of what he'd seen on the kidnapper's computer screen could not be explained away with any of the usual intelligence parlance. Clearly it must have had some relevance to the case, but just how broad was his remit?

He decided in that moment, as he enjoyed the calm and serenity of watching the night sky descend, that it wasn't that broad. They'd investigated the details they'd received and had concluded a resolution. He wasn't about to set off in a totally different direction purely on the strength of one spurious testimony, not matter how much he trusted and regarded the agent in question.

His face hardened and he pursed his lips as determination replaced his rumination and he leaned forward to place the file on the table. He reached for the stamp and pressed it down on the cover with finality, before straightening up and looking one last time at the file, now stamped with the words 'Case Closed'.

"But for how long?" he wondered, ruefully.

Chapter 98

Now that all the excitement had died down, Herbert Kennedy had managed to resume something approaching his normal routine. For the last few days he had been making every effort to create the impression that it was simply business as usual. Of course he had contacted Samantha Mitchell and her team at Kitts Peak Observatory to both congratulate them and inform them of the latest developments. He knew that they had gone out on a limb to get some of their information, and he knew that Samantha knew he knew. Yet neither had said anything, keeping up the pretence that everything had been above board.

The secretary of defense had contacted him once to keep him in the loop, but it had of necessity been a brief conversation. Clearly the politicians had more pressing things to do right now. That suited the head of space exploration perfectly and helped his efforts to re-establish the status quo. Constantly receiving communiqués from senior members of the government that weren't directly responsible for his department would have been a little difficult to simply shrug off.

Now, as the mid-morning sunshine was casting light-hearted shadows across his office wall he was back at his desk, engrossed in yet another video call on his computer. "Well it was a close-run thing," he said casually.

The voice of the other person replied, "Yes. It could all have gone so wrong."

Kennedy lounged back in his chair and without any hint of conceit observed, "It's a good thing that I was able to persuade them to trust the good guys."

"And even more fortunate that Space Corps had got so much of that old technology working again," the voice added. "Without their drones the battle could have had a very different outcome," he conceded.

"So what's happening now?" Kennedy asked almost lazily as he began to sit more upright. Clearly the person with whom he was conversing was involved with recent developments.

"The visitors have explained to Earth's leaders that they have only come to harvest the surplus water from the polar ice melts," the voice divulged knowledgeably. "They've done so on many occasions in the past when Earth has got a little closer to the sun and the planet's started heating up a little."

"I guess no-one knew they were here in the past," Kennedy interrupted with a rueful smile on his face.

"Absolutely," the voice concurred. "Although, of course, the inhabitants of South America did leave some clues with those Nazca drawings."

Kennedy smiled and nodded. "Yes, but they've always been dismissed as primitive superstitions." It just goes to show, he thought, how keen human beings had always been to explain away any mysteries.

"A good job, too," suggested the voice, before continuing with his situation report. "The visitors will re-activate their harvesting fleet in the same way that they re-activated their dormant fighters up at Space Corps during the battle. They can draw off the excess water for the next few decades."

Kennedy was enjoying the fact that everything, for once, seemed to be falling into place. "Well, it'll certainly help Earth to be rid of it." He chuckled to himself, "Although it's going to upset the global warming theorists!"

"Yes," the voice agreed. "The planet's warming up and cooling down is a cyclical thing but it's the first time in Earth's history that technology and communications have been sufficiently advanced to risk causing a panic."

"It's just a good job that the harvesters arrived when they did," Kennedy suggested.

"That's the whole point of having you and me around, isn't it?" asked the voice rhetorically.

Kennedy sat forward in his chair, pondering what the other person had just said. He scrutinised the familiar image on the screen in front of him. The moist, green, lumpy skin and large eyes located in protruding sockets at the top of the forehead reminded him vaguely of a frog or toad. The results of millennia spent evolving on a wet planet.

Not for the first time he wondered what the Earth's astronomers would now be making of the fact that it wasn't essential for a planet to have a rocky surface for intelligent life to develop. But then, he figured, that's the whole point of science and exploration – always changing the accepted rules as new discoveries are made.

Thinking of change brought him back to his interlocutor's last comment. "Yeah. But isn't it about time I got another posting?" he blithely suggested, before frowning and asking a more direct question that had been troubling him for some time now. "And by the way, why were the Selachons on your tail like that in the first place?"

The End